IT WAS POWER GIVEN A VOICE!

Rearing back its awesome spined and crested head, the icedrake roared—in challenge, maybe, or in scorn, and the sound that it made was beyond imagination, a cry of incalculable strength and majesty that made the air tingle and the earth shake.

From the terror stamped deep into the wizard Gemmel's features, it was obvious that the dragon's power was not his to command. Yet despite that, he screamed out the ancient spell words, willing the nightmare creature to turn its wrath against those who sought to slay him.

And the icedrake's jaws yawned wide, a frigid, blue-white cavern lined with ragged icicles, and it sent forth a smoky silver blast of unimaginable cold. It was a blast as silent as midwinter, no storm, no blizzard, no howling rush of wind; only the faint, brittle sounds of icy stillness which told of an end to warmth and life. . . .

DAW Titles by Peter Morwood

THE BOOK OF YEARS:

THE DRAGON LORD

PETER MORWOOD

DAW BOOKS, INC.
DONALD A. WOLLHEIM, PUBLISHER

1633 Broadway, New York, NY 10019

First DAW Printing, December 1987

1 2 3 4 5 6 7 8 9 0

PRINTED IN THE U.S.A.

To Anne McCaffrey, Dragon Lady,
For all you are and have been,
And all you were, unasked:
This book. And much love.

Late October—early November 1985

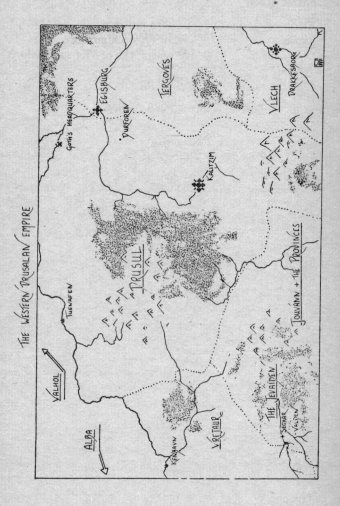

THE WESTERN TRUSALAN EMPIRE

FROM ALBA:

Aldric—*ilauem-arluth;* of Elthan province.
Rynert—*mathern-an arluth;* of Prytenon province.
Dewan—*eldheisart,* his bodyguard; late of Vreijaur province.

FROM THE DRUSALAN EMPIRE:

Ioen—nominal emperor; of Drusul province.
Marevna—his sister; of Drusal province.
Goth—*coerhanalth,* their guardian; of Tergoves province.
Bruda—*prokrator;* of Vlech province.
Voord—*hautheisart,* his deputy; of Vlech province.
Etzel—*woydach,* nominal military dictator; of Tergoves province.
Kathur—courtesan, of Jevaiden province.
Aiyyan—lorewoman and storymaker; of Jouvann province.

FROM OTHER PLACES:

Kyrin—late of Valhol.
Gemmel—*an-pestrior;* late of many lands.
Ymareth—of Techaur Island.

PREFACE

'. . . by the style and tytle of an Empyre, and as soche held Domination over all those landes for nygh an hundred yeares.

Men full wys in War and Politickes do make assured declaration that, by enbuilden of great Shipes and ye subtleties and Wickednesse of ye Necromancer Duergar Vathach (ysenden hither by ye War-Lorde Etzell to make mischief), this Empyre did desyre and make essay to take enseizen of this lande of ALBA.

Yet by HEAVENES intervention are all preserved from soche sore Distress, for in Spring-tyme of this yeare did Droek Emperor of Drusul go unto his Ancestores, and since that his first-born sonne is dead before him and ye Succession thus ymaden doubtfull, ye Empyre now is rent by great Confusion whereas its Lordes do stryve each against ye other to have power and Mastery—for they are men of no Honour and shew not that Respect which all retainers owe by Duty unto their Lordes and which obligation demandes from those same Lordes unto their vassals . . .

Now it was yknowen unto all what reasones were engiven that LORDE ALDRIC of ye clan TALVALIN did journey to this Empyre: being full of Sorrow. Yet there are men whose wordes are recognised as Truth in all thinges, who do Declare that this LORDE did but execute a very certain Strategem commanded unto him by RYNERT-KING, and that small Honour if at all was done him by soche a Taske . . .'

Ylver Vlethanek an-Caerdur
The Book of Years, Cerdor

PROLOGUE

Night and fog lay heavily on Tuenafen, and heaviest of all in the narrow streets of the port's Old Quarter. Nothing moved there save errant skeins of mist. Most of the houses were in darkness, their doorway lanterns shattered in the riots of the past few weeks. The few lamps which remained served only to emphasise the depth of shadows into which their light could not reach.

The horseman emerged from a silent swirl of fog that drew back like the curtain of an ill-lit stage: a black-clad man, astride a coal-black horse. Both were featureless silhouettes against the slow shift of grey, sable outlines lustrous with a sheen of condensed moisture.

The horse moved. Its hooves struck hollowly against damp-slick paving slabs, muted echoes slapping up and down the street between the blankly shuttered houses. Three paces only. Three heavy clanks of iron on stone; a blacksmith sound. Then silence once more as reins were twitched and the black horse stopped.

Its rider rose a little in his stirrups, turning warily from side to side. There was a tenseness in him, in the angle of his head and the set of his shoulders. For all his ominous appearance he seemed as nervous as a cat.

Somewhere close, a clock began to strike the hour and startled his horse into sudden, stamping movement. The sound of its shoes against the ground mingled with a crackle of invective as the rider's hands jerked back on shortened reins. Doubly betraying after those three unconsidered steps of half-a-hundred racing heartbeats past, the noises made by man and horse rang clearly in the muffled quiet.

All too clearly . . .

Boots clattered at his back and a voice was raised in the harsh imperatives of command. The rider's heels kicked home and his mount plunged forward, away from the wan fog-filtered unlight and into the dark maw of a nearby alley.

There was an impact; the sound of something falling heavily to the ground; a muttering of satisfaction.

Then nothing but the noiseless movement of the mist . . .

ONE

King's Gambit

The Hall of Kings in Cerdor was an awesome place, a vast
reverberant emptiness lined with pillars of stone to support
the carven magnificence of its vaulted ceiling. Autumn sunshine slanted down through windows of painted glass to
splash the tinctures of Alba's high-clan crests across a floor
of tessellated marble. Flames danced and flickered in nine
great hearths to drive chill from the air, but their heat could
not thaw the ice which edged the voice of Gemmel Errekren.

'Do you know what you have done?' he snarled. The old
enchanter was in such a passion as he seldom allowed to
possess him, and the energies summoned up by high emotion
swirled in lambent coils about his hands and the black,
dragon-patterned stave they held.

A lesser man might well have flinched from the rage of
such as Gemmel—and with good reason—but Rynert the
King remained at least outwardly unruffled, sitting straight-
backed and aloof in his great chair. 'I do what must be done,'
he said calmly, 'for the good of the state.'

Portentous yet indefinite, such a statement might have
sounded good in the ears of a Councillor, but it failed to
satisfy Gemmel. His teeth clenched so that cords of muscle
stood out on his face beneath its beard, and the pulsing nimbus
of his wrath grew more intensely visible.

'For the good of the state,' he echoed in a flat sneer. 'You
give my son to the Drusalans and then you say it is for the
good of the state . . . ?'

'Your foster-son, wizard. My vass—'

'*Enough!*' The Dragonwand in Gemmel's hands struck
once against the floor—a sharp, punctuative noise—and glowing shreds of power fluttered free like incandescent moths.

13

'Don't *ever* quibble with me . . . !' There was an unsteady shrillness in his musical old-young voice which had not been there before. 'Your "reason" is no reason at all, King, and well you know it. No excuse—for all it can excuse so much. . .'

Rynert shot a glance towards the only other occupant of the hall, hoping maybe for support—but Dewan ar Korentin's face was as stony as the wall at his back. There would be no approval from that source.

The king's gaze returned reluctantly to Gemmel. 'Explain,' he said.

'Must I?' The enchanter was openly scornful, but Rynert chose—as he had perforce chosen all along—to ignore the lack of courtesy.

'Yes. You must. I am . . . curious.'

'I wonder that you need be. Your . . . your reason has birthed too much misery down the years for any right mind to give or accept it without question. Save perhaps in matters of convenience . . .'

Gemmel's voice was lower now, introspective, as though he spoke mostly to himself, and there was a brooding shadow on his face which Rynert could see plainly even at ten paces distance.

'For it has created lies. Betrayals . . . And deaths. Oh, so many, many deaths! Both by the hand which holds a blade, Lord King—and by the hand which offers gold . . .' The enchanter's green eyes bored into Rynert's translucent hazel as though reading the secrets buried deep behind them in the hidden places of the king's mind, and Rynert dared not be first to break the contact for fear that by doing so he would betray himself.

'Yours is a reason I have heard before, *mathern-an arluth*— but the language was not Alban then . . .'

Only he could hear the whispered words; they were no more than a thread of sound, quiet as the metallic exhalation of a drawing sword, but they seemed to flay Gemmel with the lash of some reawakened shameful memory. Something other ears were not meant to overhear . . . but Rynert heard it.

'Once there was a village. Small. Ordinary. An Imperial village. And its people—small, ordinary people—had committed some infraction of the Empire's laws. They were being . . . chastised. I could have helped them. I did not. Instead I asked why the soldiers were doing what was being done; their

serjeant told me that it was for the good of the state and none
of my affair. And it was not. So I did nothing. Though it
would have cost me so very little of my power, even then.
But my son tried. And it cost his life.'

The enchanter hesitated, as a man will when he realises he
has said too much, and shook his head before staring again at
Rynert. 'I lost more than a son that day. More than your mind
can grasp, King. Much more. I lost the ability to go ho—
Everything. So do not use that excuse to me again. Ever.'

Rynert drew in a swift, ragged breath. He was not and
never had been a sturdy man, and now the heart within his
chest was jerking like the legs of a snared rabbit so that it
took all his small store of physical strength just to conceal the
fact. Anger, outrage and affronted dignity; all these and more
blended most incongruously with a pain that went deeper than
his own frail flesh. Gemmel's story troubled him, touching a
guilt which his own conscience had failed to rouse, and
reflected endlessly to and fro in his mind like a candle poised
between two mirrors; guilt begetting shame, begetting still
more guilt. . . .

'I am as you say, wizard. King.' The word snapped out, a
verbal whiplash laid across the white-bearded face before
him, righteous anger that a man could hide behind . . . 'I
must make such decisions whether I will or not. The way of
kingship is like a narrow path: it must be walked alone.'

Once more the studied, courtly phrases failed to impress.
Gemmel was no longer angry, merely saddened by his own
ancient griefs—and he was a man very conscious of his own
dignity, regardless of how he treated that of others. So he did
not follow his first impulse, which was to spit the sourness
from his mouth on to the stones at Rynert's feet. Instead he
gazed levelly at the slight, crook-shouldered king.

Then turned his back and stalked in silence from the hall.

Dewan ar Korentin broke that silence. Straightening from
the wall where he had leaned, and watched, and carefully
said nothing, he padded forward on soft-shod feet to where
Ykraith the Dragonwand had notched the marble floor. 'State-
craft,' he muttered, looking at the damage. 'Be careful,
Rynert. It could well be the death of you.' On Dewan's face
was an expression close to that on Gemmel's.

'Then what,' asked Rynert, not liking what he saw, 'is
your word on this?'

'You already know it. I warned you before about Aldric
Talvalin and my protest is on record. Again I warn you—and
again I wish it recorded. Do not play with him as you do with
the other diplomatic games-pieces you employ. He is different, he is . . . strange. And his notions of honour are
strange. Archaic, sometimes. Especially in the matter of duty
and obligation.'

'Qualms, old friend?' The smile which curved Rynert's
thin lips did not quite fit. 'I had not expected scruples from
you.'

Dewan's nostrils flared a little at that and he did not even
attempt to mirror the smile. 'Neither qualms nor scruples.
Simple caution. And simple decency. You commanded him
to perform what is a foul act for one of his rank—'

'A killing, foul . . . ? For that one? He merely does for me
what he has already done for himself! I remind you, Dewan,
that he is my vassal . . .'

'Vassal maybe, but he deserves better. Much better. I can
speak as an outsider here: and I say that deceit may have its
place, but that place is not in matters of Alban honour. It cuts
two ways, Rynert. He owes you duty—but you owe him
respect. And the situation seems just a little one-sided. May I
remind *you*—with first-hand authority—that he was not named
Deathbringer in idle jest. Perhaps . . . just perhaps, he will
understand why you betrayed him—' he raised one hand to
forestall Rynert's protest, 'for I assure you, that is how he
will see it.'

'For his own safety's sake . . . !'

'For reasons of state, you said. Well . . . Perhaps he'll
accept it. Or perhaps not. But if not, Rynert, then I wouldn't
wish to wear your collar. Not if you were king of all the
world. . . .'

Perhaps deliberately, Dewan ar Korentin's accented voice
no longer used the formal mode of the Alban language. There
were some at court who would have regarded his addressing
of the king in any other way as an insult, but Rynert was not
one of them. He understood.

'It no longer matters, even if it once did,' Rynert said
dismissively. 'The piece has moved; now I must watch how it
affects play.'

'Publicly. You must be seen to support your own decisions. But in private—as secretly as you sent Talvalin—could you not send me . . . ?'

'Dewan, you grow overwrought. Go away. Return when you feel calm again. And convey my compliments to your lady wife.'

Ar Korentin stiffened, bowing acknowledgement of his dismissal with a marionette's rigidity, then strode towards the great double doors with disapproval plain in the arrogant straightness of his back. Rynert's voice followed him up the hall.

'But until you come back—feeling calm, of course—please regard your time and business as your own affair . . .'

Dewan halted, stood quite still for perhaps two seconds and then turned to face the king. Rynert had that suppressed brightness around the eyes and mouth which accompanies the concealment of a smile. Dewan watched it fade and felt uneasy even as he snapped through the punctilious movements of an Imperial parade salute. Then he bowed from the waist, Alban-fashion, and took his leave, knowing deep inside that there was an ugly wrongness about this whole affair.

But able to fathom no more than that. Yet . . .

Gemmel was waiting for him. Indeed, Dewan would have been more surprised had the enchanter not been there. 'Wizard,' he said quietly.

'*Eldheisart* ar Korentin,' Gemmel retorted. If Dewan was taken aback to hear his old Imperial rank spoken aloud by such a man as this, he gave no indication of it. 'Now do you believe?' the enchanter continued. 'Was I so very wrong?'

'Not wrong—but not entirely right.'

'How so? I lost one son to the Empire many years ago—I will not stand by and lose another for the . . . for the good of the state!'

'We should walk,' said Dewan in a flat voice, his eyes indicating the sentries flanking the doorway of the Hall of Kings. None was obviously listening; in the presence of their captain they stood rigidly to attention and stared straight to their front. But they had ears even so . . .

Gemmel nodded once, minutely, and walked.

'Now hear me,' ar Korentin began again, once he judged them a safe distance away. 'Rynert has—'

'—Forefeited what little allegiance Aldric or I might have owed him!'

Dewan ar Korentin was a patient man and slow to anger, but his patience was rapidly wearing thin. Both hands came up to grip Gemmel's shoulders and if necessary shake him back to coherence, but something in the old man's expression suggested that anything approaching violence would be countered tenfold. He hesitated, hands in the air as he considered, then contented himself with a spread-armed shrug.

'Just once, wizard, try listening to someone besides yourself!' he snapped. Gemmel's teeth shut with a click, and his indrawn breath was an audible hiss; but Dewan pressed home his advantage in the relative silence. 'As I was saying,' the irony was if anything overdone, *'mathern-an* Rynert has granted me permission to go after Aldric. Into the Empire.'

Gemmel lifted an eyebrow. 'Tacit permission, of course. Nothing direct, and certainly nothing committed to paper . . . ?'

'Certainly not!' Dewan's sense of propriety was outraged by the suggestion. 'This is of the utmost delicacy.'

'So much so,' the enchanter's voice was flat and nasty, 'that your worthy lord might need to wash his hands of it at short notice. Mm?'

That possibility had not occurred to Dewan; but he had only to consider how Aldric had been—and was being—used, to realise that Gemmel was not making idle criticism. Yet he persisted: 'Will you come with me? After all, Talvalin is your—your son.'

'Foster-son,' Gemmel corrected absently. 'What you really mean is, will I come and help pull Rynert's political fat out of the Imperial fire before it flares into—Lord God, "incident" wouldn't begin to describe it.' The cold, clear emerald eyes transfixed Dewan like needles. 'No. I won't.'

The shock of that refusal could not be hidden, and ar Korentin floundered for several seconds before he managed to say anything remotely sensible. 'So what do I do—go alone . . . ?'

'Not necessarily. *You* could come with *me*.' With each emphasis the enchanter's long finger poked Dewan in the chest.

'What's the difference?'

'Between black and white. My way—you know and I

know. His way—who knows who knows . . . ?' Gemmel was plainly recovering what passed for his sense of humour.

'All right,' Dewan conceded. 'Where do we go?'

'First, to the coast. By *my* route.'

'And afterwards?'

Gemmel grinned a swift, vulpine grin which showed most of his teeth. 'Restore all the marks of rank to that Imperial armour of yours. No. More than all. Exaggerate it. Promote yourself. It may be more useful that way than you think. But as for afterwards . . .' The grin flickered again. 'Leave afterwards to me.'

'This place is supposed to be secure—so how did it get in?' Both the harsh voice and the man who used it were out of place in this room of graceful furnishings and delicately muted colours. He was burly, florid and middle-aged, with a spade-shaped iron-grey beard, and he was encased to the neck in vivid scarlet-lacquered armour which was brilliant with the precious-metal geometric shapes of lofty rank. A sharp reek of oily metal hung about him—cutting discordantly through the fragrance of incense smouldering in a burner by the door—and leather creaked whenever he moved, as he did now in leaning forward to smooth an already-flat sheet of paper with blunt fingers. It creaked again when he twisted to stare at a tall, lean figure outlined by sunlight at the window. 'I asked you a question.'

The other man turned. 'And I thought you were being rhetorical,' he replied mildly, seeming undisturbed by his companion's brusqueness—although because of the glare at his back and the deep cowl which covered his head, no expression could be read from his shadowed features. 'Set aside its delivery. Is it genuine?'

'Perhaps,' the armoured man conceded, turning the paper this way and that as if closer scrutiny might reveal some stamp of authenticity. 'The codes were correct and the seals unbroken when it was found?'

'They were.'

'Or so we must assume . . . But this translation,' he slapped at it with the back of one hand, 'is it accurate?'

'You wrote it. You translated it. You should know . . .'

'Most evasive.' The armoured man's chuckle was a dry sound, devoid of all humour. 'But that's only to be expected.' He set aside the enigmatic piece of paper and lifted the slim dossier to which it referred. Originally secured by wires, and by seals of both lead and wax, the folder's contents were plainly not meant for idle fingers to flick through.

As it was prised open once more, the man by the window left his place in the sun and walked lazily across the room. Each step was marked by the austere click of a long ash cane gripped easily in the fingertips of his left hand.

Flimsy sheets drifted across the table-top like the leaves of autumn; half-a-dozen pages in which—he knew—a man's life was laid open for inspection like something gutted on a surgeon's slab. 'Impressive, is it not?' he asked softly.

There was no reply at first; each document was set out, carefully spaced and minutely shifted. Then, inevitably, one in particular was singled out for closer scrutiny. It was a portrait—or more correctly a likeness, for it boasted little in the way of artistic excellence. But its accuracy was uncanny, almost inhuman, for surely no human hand could capture tones and textures and nuances of colour with such painstaking and subtle precision. It was as if the image in a mirror had been printed on paper.

'Impressive,' said the armoured man at last, 'is scarcely adequate.' He glanced up with a crooked smile, but as usual could discern no response to his comment even though by now he could see within the deep, dark hood.

There was only his own face, distorted and reflected back at him from the surface of a mask of polished metal . . .

The ash cane rattled slightly as it was laid down on the table; then gloved hands came up to throw back the cowl and burnished silver emerged from its concealment like a weapon being drawn. There was that same cold, impersonal menace; yet at the same time a very human satisfaction in the way the masked man purred, 'I had sketches made. And distributed wherever they might prove useful . . .'

'Such as?'

'Every west-coast seaport which runs the Elherran trade to Alba. I have agents in them all.'

'Of course . . .' The armoured man nodded once, as if he had expected nothing less. His eyes were inexorably drawn back to those of the portrait: dark eyes, grey-green and icy as the northern sea in winter. Looking at those eyes, he had no difficulty in believing what he had already skimmed from the dossier about this young man. 'Talvalin,' he mused. 'Aldric Talvalin. An Alban clan-lord. And you still think that Rynert sent this—betrayed one of his own?'

'I know he sent it.' Now voice and mask were one, for there was something remote and terrible in that short sentence; and as the metal-shrouded face moved slightly, light slid sparkling away as though flinching from any prolonged contact with its surface. 'I have known for two months now. And I have not found him yet.'

'But that still leaves him loose in my . . . our . . . jurisdiction.'

'Loose . . . ? I think not.'

'*What?*'

'He may seem . . . loose, if you prefer the word. Because we do not know his whereabouts. Yet. But he must leave us'—a quick gesture recovered the cane and stirred the papers on the table—'and we know where he will try. And then . . .' The leather-skinned fingers of his right hand spread wide, like a claw. The armoured man looked at it, then at the mirror-blank masked face beyond. 'Then we will have him and we will hold him. *Here!*'

The fingers closed.

TWO

Perfidious Alba

The beach edging Dunacre Bay was almost four miles long; it curved away below the Morhan Hills to the south-west, and out in a great shallow arc past the old fortress which gave the bay its name, off north and east towards the Ring Rocks and Sallyn Point. At low tide it was featureless and flat, admirable for walking and the exercise of horses; for then the surf-line—such as it was, except in stormy weather—lay seven hundred yards or more from the necklace of pebbles which divided sand from marram grass and bracken-covered dunes. The beach shelved leisurely out into the sea, and only those who knew this coast were aware of the sudden precipitous plunge as the sea-bed fell away into black depths which would grant access to ships of even the deepest draught.

Gemmel Errekren was one with such knowledge.

For all that, Dewan ar Korentin was not yet wholly convinced that the wizard knew what he was doing, no matter how well he claimed to know the vagaries of sea and shore. This very beach was an instance of his doubt. The tide was out, just at the turn; consequently there was a long, conspicuous walk before they reached the water and the safety of whatever vessel had been provided for their use. Hopefully the sentries on Dunacre's ramparts would think them fishermen, or crab-catchers, or gatherers of seaweed. Anything except what they were: two men creeping illegally out of Alba and even more illegally into the Drusalan Empire.

And maybe the sentries wouldn't see them at all, for though Dewan flattered himself that his eyesight was better than most, he was unable to penetrate the opalescent wall of mist and spray-spume which had rolled in from the sea just as their feet touched the sand . . . Again he glanced thoughtfully at Gemmel's back, as he had done more than once since the weather took its so-convenient turn for the worse; and again shrugged it aside as common sense took over . . .

In so far as any man could shrug under the burden which he carried.

Gemmel had insisted that they leave their horses stabled at the tavern and merely walk towards the shore, having hidden their baggage in that direction during the previous night. Unencumbered by the necessities of travel—he had elaborated, as he inevitably did—they would seem no more than two gentlemen taking their ease with a constitutional stroll along the beach.

They might have been unencumbered when they left the inn, thought Dewan wearily to himself, but they weren't bloody unencumbered now—though it was remarkable how Gemmel had contrived to foist all the truly heavy gear on to Dewan's broad shoulders whilst himself stalking elegantly along with no more than his staff and an oiled-leather satchel of books. If he was such a powerful sorcerer as young Aldric Talvalin had insisted, then why couldn't he just wave that magic Dragonwand of his and make the bundles float out by themselves . . . ?

Even as he thought it, Dewan knew his notion was little more than nonsense. He had seen very little sorcery—although even that was more than enough—but it had made him aware that the Art Magic was as exact as any science. Certainly too precise to lift the weight off *his* back . . . ! He grunted, swore to himself as the unbalanced stuff he carried slipped still further to one side and hitched at it so ferociously that it continued to slip . . . this time down the other side.

'Wizard! Where's the bloody boat, wizard?' Gemmel showed no sign of having heard him, which was hardly surprising; the wind from the sea pulled Dewan's words right off his lips, tugged them to meaningless syllables and noise, then tried to push the fragments back down his throat.

And that was another thing—how the hell could any fog remain so solidly in place when there was such a wind to disperse it? Any natural fog, at least . . .

It brought a recollection of the fog which had blanketed the battlefield of Radmur Plain: a fog created and locked in place by this same slender, scholarly old man.

As if sensing the trend of his companion's thoughts, Gemmel

hesitated and half-turned with the shadow of a smile still crooking one corner of his mouth. 'Oh yes, Commander, —and although Dewan's shout had been lost on the tumbling wind, the enchanter's soft voice carried clearly and without strain—'I caused this fog as well. But note: it's a mere disruption of sight, no more. So I can spare more energy to secure it. Much more . . .'

The explanation, if that was what it was, told Dewan ar Korentin little that he understood; only that he need have no worries about being exposed on an open beach half a mile from any shelter by some vagary of the weather. It didn't reassure him; for his concern was not now so much with the possibility of betrayal, but with its consequences.

Mist or no mist, he still felt like some small black bug crossing a vast expanse of floor, with the same choked-back anticipation of a lethal swat coming out of nowhere. With one difference: he knew exactly where the swat would come from.

Dunacre . . .

His rank and position as Captain of the King's Guard—his *late* rank, he reminded himself, for it was certain that he had left it behind along with everything else but his self-respect— had given him access to such military information as the disposition of Alba's coastal defences; and while Dunacre was far from the newest of the south-eastern fortresses, it was by no means the weakest or most poorly manned. There were at least three wings of heavy horse stationed there—that much he knew for a certainty, because one of them had recently been stiffened by a training troop seconded from his own personal command, the Bodyguard Cavalry. And they were good. Very, very good.

Far too good for comfort in fact, especially when he was anonymously and illegally walking along a shoreline that was tailor-made for the kind of shattering Imperial style charge he had taught the Bodyguard to execute. And in the name of the High Headsman at Cerdor, 'execute' was definitely the best word for it.

'As I said before,' and this time Dewan shaped the words on his mouth so that Gemmel, still looking at him, could at least read them, 'where's the boat? And how big is it?'

Gemmel grinned that toothy fox's grin of his, and enhanced it with a gesture of the Dragonwand which covered a

thirty-mile sweep of open ocean. 'Big enough,' he replied.
'And out there . . .'

It was not an answer with the sort of precision for which
Dewan had hoped, but he chose not to argue. As he trudged
after the old sorcerer, he was trying with little success to
forget the many things he knew about the coastal citadels,
uncomfortably aware of the truth in that old proverb about the
dangers of too much knowledge. They were all matters of
casual interest when read in the comfort of his quarters over a
glass of red and some honeyed fruit, but became of pressing
import here where their effectiveness was likely to be demon-
strated in the most unequivocal manner.

Things like the powerful long-glasses installed—at his own
suggestion!—to monitor the route of any potential invasion
force; things like the awesome projectile batteries whose
counterpoise petraries could launch flaming missiles which
would cinder and sink any Imperial battlefleet long before
shipboard catapults were close enough to make even ranging
shots worth-while . . .

As if to add weight to his apprehension, the ghostly outline
of a white painted tree-trunk loomed out of the fog. Tall as
the mast of a galion, it was identical to hundreds of others up
and down the eastern coast of Alba: fall-of-shot markers for
the shore batteries. Nor, guessed ar Korentin as he came
close enough to see the grouped gouges scarring the wood,
did it indicate extreme distance. He was entering the killing-
ground, the area where a practised crew might hope to ignite
their target with a single launch—and certainly to succeed in
no more than three if they wanted to avoid a punishment
detail. Once they were able to see what they were shooting
at . . .

Dewan quickened his pace in an effort to draw level with
Gemmel, who was striding out as though he was in very truth
walking for the good of his health. Which, if he knew what
Dewan knew, was an accurate enough assumption. Yet the
old man seemed unconcerned—so unconcerned that perhaps
he didn't know after all.

Dewan considered that possibility, then dismissed it as
unlikely. In his opinion, Gemmel might not know everything
even though he often seemed to do so. But without doubt, the
wizard invariably knew a damnsight too much.

He was drawing as much breath as the weight on his back would permit to tell Gemmel a few home truths about the beach where he was so idly strolling, when the sorcerer turned abruptly and held up his hand. 'Silence,' he commanded. 'Listen!'

Dewan could hear nothing at first but the hiss of wind and waves—and what was important about them? Then he heard something else and it was a sound made all the more immediate by nervous brooding:

The distant, dissonant clangour of alarm gongs.

Gemmel drove the Dragonwand butt-downwards into the sand with a spasm of irritation. Not anger, not fear; just irritation, such as a parent might feel at some child's act of pettiness. 'So,' he said.

'So . . . ?' echoed Dewan.

'So King Rynert has decided we are not to go our—my—own way after all. Despite all his assurances, of course.' There was a dreadful calm contentment in the way Gemmel spoke, the cold satisfaction of logic proved.

'You mean to say—' Dewan knew that it was crazy to begin a discussion or even talk unnecessarily until they were both clear of this mess, but the words came tumbling out anyway, '—that Rynert had the choice of yea-or-nay right up to where we are now?'

'His representative had.' Gemmel had already plucked the Dragonwand free and was walking rapidly towards the mist-wrapped sea, talking as he went. 'The thin-faced gentleman I hoped was still asleep in the tavern.'

Dewan could think of nothing sensible to say about that and kept his mouth shut.

'I decided not to point him out to you,' the wizard continued, 'because if you recognised him, you might do something regrettable, and if you didn't then you might do something unnecessary. I thought we might shake him for long enough to reach the boat, but he must have marked our absence and made directly for the fortress. Probably didn't like our destination—after all, from this coast there's only one place we could be going . . .'

'But Rynert knew about that!'

'But did he tell his man? No. I doubt it.' Gemmel's speech was growing staccato as his long legs raked over the ground, quick as a wading bird. He wasn't running, there was no need for anything so undignified just yet, even though Dewan had been for the past dozen strides. 'Credit him with that subtlety. He didn't give instructions—not exact instructions. General, yes. But not exact. So he isn't responsible. Regrettable mistake. Nervous troops. Suspected spies. Not identified until afterwards . . .'

'Afterwards?' repeated Dewan stupidly. And it was stupid; maybe it was the running, or the shock of what Gemmel was telling him, because later he felt sure that in normal circumstances he wouldn't have uttered a word. But this time he did. And was flayed for it.

Gemmel stopped in his tracks with anger livid on his high-cheekboned face. 'Compassion of God, must I draw diagrams?' That shrillness which Dewan had heard only once before was threading his voice again like poison in wine. 'I had almost four years to kill the habit of idiot questions in my son!' His lips writhed back from his teeth in an expression which might have been many things but most definitely was not a smile. 'My *foster*-son,' he corrected himself with ponderous irony. 'You had best learn it in the next four minutes, Dewan ar Korentin, if you want to survive the next four hours. Know this: you have crossed Rynert of Alba—so you are a dead man.'

'But I have served him faithfully for—'

'Years . . . ?' Gemmel sneered. 'And now you no longer serve him. Therefore you are no longer of use to him. So you are *dead!*'

That was a moment which Dewan knew would haunt his dreams, should he live long enough to have any—the moment when a sorcerer whose eyes blazed like phosphorescent emeralds told him in tones which defied doubt that he had been utterly betrayed. And betrayed, moreover, by the lord for whom he had shed blood, lost blood, suffered pain and gained his first-through-fiftieth grey hair. That he had been cast aside like a torn cloak; that he was to be smashed into oblivion by 'accident' and by the men he had trained himself, so that the embarrassment of a difference of opinion would be snuffed before it passed the bounds of simple gossip.

'If I live through this—' he began savagely.

'If any of us live through it, you'll have to take your turn after my foster-son.' Again there was a hard gleam of teeth in the foggy light. 'No. Call him my son. For he is. And more than I deserve to regain, even though I don't yet deserve to be called his father. Now run, Dewan ar Korentin. Run as if your life depended on it—for it does!'

They ran, a slop of wet and salty sand flying up around their booted legs at each footfall. Somehow the mass of gear across Dewan's back was lighter than it had been—still as bulky, still as awkward, but no longer the same crushing dead-weight. Gemmel's work? Or just adrenalin?

He neither knew nor cared—but he was thankful all the same.

The wizard's voice reached his ears again, piercing the sounds of wind and water, gasping breath and the thick wet splat of running feet; but this time the old man was not addressing him.

Gemmel was speaking to the fog!

Something—some *thing*—sighed over Dewan's shoulder and for one heart-stopping instant he thought that Dunacre's weapon batteries had opened up on them. Even shooting blind into the mist, those things were capable of setting the beach aflame from surf-line to shingle and in the process roasting any living creature on it. But whatever passed Dewan had nothing to do with human weapons. Or even with humanity at all . . .

The surge of energy which had passed him on the wings of a hot wind tore open a tunnel in the fog that was two men wide, one man high and ran straight as a spear-shaft out towards the sea. He could suddenly see parallel white bars of foam where waves curled in to break on the shores of Alba, and beyond them the small dark blot sliding swiftly closer which could only be the wizard's promised boat. Boat, not ship, was right.

Cockleshell was more right still.

Had he possessed more breath than that required for running, Dewan might have made some biting remarks about the vessel's size, speed and potential seaworthiness, not to mention passing comment on certain sorcerers who seemed to think that if something could float then that sufficed.

But all criticism was leached from his mind by the sound in the sky.

It was a huge rush of displaced air, as if something monstrous was falling from the clouds—and if Dewan's wild guess was correct, then that was no more than the truth. He

flung himself bodily at Gemmel and both men went headlong
onto the sand . . . and into a tidal pool already ankle-deep
with chill salt water.

'*What!*' There was outrage and real fury in Gemmel's
voice, so that if he had guessed wrongly Dewan didn't like to
consider the consequences of his hasty act; but before the
wizard could say more, everything was justified.

They felt the thump of impact through the ground beneath
them a split-second before the fog flared incandescent orange
and washed their backs with heat. The vast tearing roar of
detonation came a full two heartbeats later, flooding the air
with ravening noise and the naphtha stink of wildfire.
Greasy smoke boiled through the mist and the blast of fire
which gave it birth thinned the concealing vapour even as its
creator struggled to his feet.

Gemmel brushed uselessly at the mess of sodden sand
which caked his clothing, shrugged and extended one hand to
Dewan as the Vreijek hauled himself and his burden from the
mire. Their eyes met, and in the wizard's there was true
friendship for the first time that Dewan could remember.
'Thank you, Commander,' was all that he said. It was enough.

Dewan nodded once, then looked from side to side, spit-
ting to clear his mouth as he surveyed the beach. There was
more of it to see now than before the missile landed—too
much more. 'They must know this isn't a natural mist,' he
muttered, not so much talking to Gemmel as thinking out loud.
'The wind would tell them as much. And,' his gaze returned
to the sorcerer, 'I remember you told Rynert once how hard it
was to stabilise such a charm.' There was no accusation in his
voice. 'It's just the thing he would remember—and warn his
dogs accordingly.'

'Enough heat would burn off even a real fog,' said Gemmel
matter-of-factly. He was already jogging seaward again, moving more slowly now so that the noise of his own progress
didn't drown the sound of more incoming shots—or whatever
else the fortress commander might decide to fling at them.

Twice more they flattened against the beach, cuddling the
gritty wetness of the shingle as if it was the softest feather
quilt whilst the world around them was torn by fire. Gemmel's
cunningly constructed shroud of mist was all but usurped by
an acrid layer of black smoke which twisted in the wind and

made them choke on its bitter reek—scoring throat and eyes
and nostrils so that each lungful of air was an enemy.

Then there came another sound than that of airborne flame:
the high, sweet scream of a cavalry trumpet. Gemmel bared
his teeth and broke into a run again, aware that once more
safety lay in speed. But ar Korentin did not move.

An instant later the wizard jolted to a splashing halt,
shocked to a standstill as he heard a sword scrape from its
sheath. 'Dewan, no!' He was shouting the words even as he
turned. 'For God's sweet sake, *no!*'

Dewan's head jerked round and there was unconcealed
scorn on his moustached face. 'No? Then will they ride us
down without a fight?' The eyes in that face were cold and
flinty, an expression Gemmel had seen before. On Aldric's
face. In Aldric's eyes. The eyes of his son . . . that were not
the eyes of his son.

It was an expression that presaged violence.

'Don't kill!' The sorcerer's hand closed around Dewan's
thick wrist and forced his swordpoint down with an inexorable pressure that made the Vreijek's thick brows lift in
astonishment—forced it down until it grounded on the sand.
'Don't kill,' he repeated with a silky firmness brooking no
questions. 'They will be king's-men. Maybe *your* men. To
kill would be . . . unthinkable.'

'Then what will we—' Dewan hesitated, a wry smile twisting his tense mouth. 'What will *you* do?'

'All that I must. Now get to the boat if you can. Move!'

Dewan shrugged his least-laden shoulder and returned the
broadsword to its scabbard. 'Your game, then,' he conceded
reluctantly, backing towards the waves so that his eyes could
remain fixed on the place where the trumpet had sounded. A
place hidden by drifting smoke and the remnants of the mist.
A place right behind them. 'Play it your way if you must—
but remember that the blade is still here if you need it.'

Gemmel glanced at Dewan and shook his head. 'I hope
not,' he said, and walked swiftly onward with more words
trailing over his shoulder and down the wind to ar Korentin's
ears. 'With any luck, I won't even—'

'—but you will!' The interruption was harsh. 'Because our
luck has just run out . . . !'

They came out of the smoke at a parade walk: a column of

eight riders in skirmish harness. Eight—no more than a patrol. That was very like an insult, thought Dewan. Maces, swords, axes—but no spears. And no bows. So it was close work, then; someone wanted to be sure.

Over the whistle of wind in his ears he could hear the sound if not the sense of the red-plumed officer's commands as he waved his longsword overhead; it was a long-drawn, nasal singing such as cavalrymen use. And despite the threat, despite the menace, he felt something approaching a dark pleasure as the small formation swung from column to line of attack without the slightest ripple of excess movement. Perfect . . . He wondered if perhaps he had trained these men himself. Or some of them. Or none at all . . .

It was an idle thought, for what did it matter when they were about to try to kill him anyway?

And then they stopped. One horse snorted; another stamped, scraping at the sand with one forehoof as its head nodded up and down, up and down like a mechanical toy until the rider shortened his reins. There was silence now; all but the ever-present wind.

'Captain ar Korentin?' That was the officer again—a light, youthful voice contrasting sharply with his ominous appearance. A boy's voice. The entire troop was probably composed of such youngsters; men who had never trained under him, never served under him, never heard of him except as a name—and a foreigner's name at that—in distant Cerdor.

Very clever—and very wise, for if men of his own command had been ordered to take him Dewan knew that they would have disobeyed. Theirs was the old, old loyalty which King Rynert had so arrogantly flouted in his dealings first with Aldric Talvalin and now with Dewan himself; a loyalty based on the ancient Honour-Codes, born of obligations and duties between a lord and his retainers, and something which Dewan himself respected through nothing more than common courtesy.

'Captain ar Korentin, you must lay down your weapons!' The lad was trying hard to be officious, without much success. 'You must come with us!'

'I must do *nothing!*' Dewan's parade-ground bellow slapped out across the beach, and he had the small satisfaction of seeing two troopers jump in their saddles with startled jerks so pronounced that even at this distance they were visible.

'What I do is my own affair—and by the King's own leave!' That shook them even more. 'And what I do now is no affair of yours!'

'You shouldn't have said that,' muttered Gemmel at his back.

Dewan glared at the wizard, then at the soldiers, and clamped down on his anger far, far too late. Just because this officer was young didn't mean he was a fool as well. Such words out of his quarry's own mouth were a gift—and one which was put to immediate use.

'But it is, Captain; it is.' The voice seemed older now, harder and more sure of itself. 'You are trying to leave this country in a most suspicious manner—that *is* my concern!' His sword gestured and the troop moved forward a little, closing knee-to-knee before halting for what Dewan knew would be the last time. The officer rose in his stirrups. 'You-will-come-with-us-*now!*'

Gemmel laid a restraining hand on Dewan's shoulder and stepped in front of him to plant the Dragonwand upright in the sand. It was an action oddly reminiscent of the way in which an archer might drive home a palisade stake, and for the same reason—as a defence against cavalry. But Gemmel was no bowman and the reptilian spellstave was much more than sharpened wood.

'What of me?' the old man demanded, and though he did not shout Dewan knew from his own experience that the soldiers would hear him well enough. 'I am Gemmel Errekren,' the wizard said. A small fidgeting ran down the line of horsemen. 'Do I not warrant a threat or two?'

There was no response. Either the troopers had not been told about Gemmel and were at a loss—or else they knew as much of his reputation as any other man in Alba. And that was sufficient to make anyone fall silent.

'Hear me well, for I will say this only once.' A bleak serenity was lacing Gemmel's words as he closed the fingers of his left hand around the Dragonwand, just below the carven firedrake's head. Dewan felt a single pulse of power well out of the adamantine talisman, a pulse that clad his entire body in gooseflesh. There was a sonorous humming in the air and the sorcerer's hard voice sliced through it like a blade. 'You are all meddling with forces which you cannot comprehend. And you are meddling with me. And I am subject to the human failing of impatience. So be warned. *Leave me alone!'*

His clenched fingers snapped open like the talons of a hawk and unleashed a great dry crack of thunder which sent all eight horses bucking and plunging madly across the beach. Two of the riders were unseated and slammed against the wet, unyielding sand inside all the dragging weight of their armour. Only one got up again.

The remaining six wrenched their steeds back under control more by brute force than any skill; then, staring and confused as the animals they rode, they huddled into a poor copy of their original formation and sat quite still. The officer, one of the two fallen men, took an unsteady pace forward and tried to support himself with his sword—as best he could, for its unsheathed blade sank easily into the sand. His plumed helmet had been lost, and without it he was indeed the boy that Dewan had suspected—beardless rather than shaven, fair both of hair and of complexion. But now the fresh pink of his cheeks was darkened by a flush of rage and his voice held all the shrill spite of youth. 'Ride over them!' he screamed. 'Cut them down! Kill! Kill! *Kill . . . !'*

Whilst the soldiers hung back uneasily, Gemmel raked them with a dispassionate stare that ended disdainfully on the raving officer. Then he pulled the Dragonwand out of the beach as a man might draw a sword. 'Oh, thou fool,' he murmured. 'Watch, and learn, and be wise.'

Gripped in both the old enchanter's hands, the spellstave reared up to poise over his head like an executioner's blade. The wind from the sea died to a moan and thence to silence as if the world held its breath. And perhaps it did.

'Ykraith,' invited Gemmel softly in the stillness, *'abath arhan.'*

And the air went cold . . .

Dewan ar Korentin felt a shudder rack him as midwinter rigor bit with icy teeth at the exposed flesh of face and hand; he shuddered again—though not this time with the cold—as the remnants of fog turned pure white and tumbled with a tiny crystal tinkling to coat the beach with frost. Underfoot the sand crackled with the crisp noise of rimed grass on a freezing night, and puddles of sea-water snapped like sheets of glass beneath his weight. Breath hung like smoke on the

unmoving, bitter air, then sifted down like snow to join the
frozen fog.

'*Ykraith, devhar ecchud,*' said Gemmel; the words almost
visible in the milky exhalation from his bearded lips.

They were whipped into nothingness by a sourceless gale
which scoured the long beach clean of frost and piled the
million, million sparkling motes high above the sorcerer in a
vast inverted cone whose apex centred on the upraised
Dragonwand. It was a wind to cut the breath from a man's
lungs, a wind to flog clouds helplessly across the sky or raise
a ship-killing storm. It was a wind which all but tore Dewan
off his feet.

It was a wind which had been given birth by the jolt of
energy unleashed by the spellstave, a jolt which sent a solitary ripple scudding out across the surface of the sea far faster
than any arrow from a bow.

And yet it was a wind which scarcely ruffled Gemmel's
beard.

The island was an uninviting place. Except for one small inlet
and an even smaller beach, it rose sheer out of the ocean,
rimmed by ragged talons of rock that tore wounds of white
surf in the dark and swirling water. It did not encourage
visitors; and nothing had disturbed its brooding solitude for
months now, save the whisper—or the storm-driven shriek—of
wind through the mantle of vegetation that concealed whatever dwelt upon it from the gaze of casually prying eyes. Not
that there had been any such for a long time; no ship had even
come close. Until now.

She was a deep-sea patrol vessel of the Second Fleet and
she was hunting pirates in the disputed waters of the Thousand Islands group, south and west of Alba. The *Ethailen
Myl*, although that term was neither recognised by the Drusalan
Empire nor used on their charts. And pirates whose attacks,
directed singlemindedly against the Imperial convoys, suggested rather more than just a taste for the most profitable
victims afloat. It suggested that they might be more than
simply pirates after all.

For all her bulk, the warship came dipping delicately as a
swan around the headland and into the shelter of the island's
solitary cove. As her crew made ready to drop anchor and to
lower a boat for closer investigation—or just to replenish the

water-barrels—her commander up by the stern batteries was studying everything most intently through a long-glass. So intently that when the deck lifted beneath his feet, he did not look to see the cause.

A ripple crossed the flat surface of the bay; its movement, a wrinkle on the oily calm of the water, was that of a current, or a breeze, or something monstrous moving rapidly beneath the surface. But though it was none of these things—for the water was sheltered and still, because the wind was from the south, and there was plainly nothing in the deeps alongside— yet it was in very truth something monstrous. And it swept towards the island far, far faster than any arrow from a bow . . .

So fast, indeed, that few afterwards could attest to having seen its passage through the sea, though there were many who could swear to seeing all that followed. It struck the beach and crossed it with a hiss of disturbed sand and gravel which many heard aboard the warship, even above the sounds and distractions of shipboard activity; and that crisp rustling of unexpected noise where no noise should have been drew the eyes of those on deck who should have been about their own affairs.

So it was that many saw the trees wave madly with a movement that, for all it happened with great force and at blinding speed, exactly matched the passage of a harvest wind across a field of ripened wheat; saw the shiver of the trees sweep up and up until it was no more than a tremor crossing the scrubby grass on the island's solitary peak; and saw the unexplained disturbance sink into solid rock as a wave sinks into sand.

Then there was time for gossip, time for speculation, time for such a falling-off in normal duties that the captain himself stalked to the rail of his quarter-deck and barked his crew back to work. But there was no time for that work to resume. No time for anything at all—

—Before the island of Techaur blew up . . . !

It was a very little detonation, as such things were reckoned by those who survived them. Nothing like the blast—in living memory—which had flung a dozen small islands off the sea-bed near the coast of Valhol. But then the gods—or Heaven, or most appropriately the Father of Fires, depending on one's beliefs—had never really finished making Valhol . . .

This, though, was another matter altogether.

A shock-wave of concussion slapped out across the bay, bringing with it shattered trees, lumps of red-hot rock and a steaming spray of gravel from the beach. The warship reeled and lost part of her rigging, but because—for various reasons—she had not been secured at anchor, she was able to ride out both the blast and the vicious twelve-foot wall of water running in its wake.

The island had lost maybe a hundred feet of height; most of that hundred feet was either smacking into the sea and raising columns of white water like good practice from a shore battery, or was still rolling skywards amid the dome-topped mushroom cloud of smoke and dust which reared above the abruptly-truncated mountain.

But it was the fire which flared around the abbreviated peak which most disturbed the warship's captain and was most instrumental in his decision to put several clear miles of water between himself, his ship and this place. A decision to leave it to the pirates, or the Albans, or the Elherrans—or anybody mad enough to want it. Because whatever else it was, this fire was not that of a natural volcano; one of his crewmen, who had seen Valhol's *Hlavastjaar*—that great rip in the world aptly named Hell's Gullet—had come babbling to him about the wrong way that this mountain was burning.

As if, the captain had wondered privately, there ever was a right way for stone to blaze like tinder.

But he could see exactly what the sailor meant: there was no thick spewing of honey-viscid rock, nor—save for the first explosion—any spray of ash and cinders. There was only that single intermittent jet of flame, so hot and white that it approached a shade of blue and so bright that it hurt the eyes even at this distance. He was not so foolish as to use his long-glass, but even unaided vision could see how the narrow flame sliced at the remnant of the mountain like a knife in tender beef. No, the captain corrected himself, like nothing so crude; this cut like the blade of a skilled surgeon, shearing with such precision that there might almost have been a mind directing it.

That was what frightened him most of all. The captain was a brave man—he would not have been commanding this police mission otherwise—but he truly did not want to meet whatever possessed that mind, and controlled that white fire.

For just a moment it was as if the sun had descended from

the sky to poise in glory atop the ruined mountain of Techaur, and every man aboard the warship heard the sound which accompanied that glare of splendour. It was not the flat reverberation of another blast, nor was it the rumbling of falling rock.

It was a roar such as could only have been born in some colossal throat . . .

No orders were given by the captain or his under-officers; none were necessary. But someone flung the ship's helm hard over, heedless of the submerged reefs nearby, and with that strong southerly wind still tugging at her sails the patrol vessel reacted like a scalded cat, heeling about with foam creaming up from her long ram as she accelerated towards the open sea on no particular course except out and away from Techaur.

And from whatever being roared and flamed and dwelt there.

The plume of frost roiled and twisted as though imbued with some eerie life of its own, and a wan light glimmered deep within it so that each writhing contour was backed by a chasm of shadow; black rifts in reality where anything might lurk unseen. Strange shapes formed and faded in its turbulent depths, flitting in and out of the darkness like bats half-glimpsed at dusk.

There was no sound now from the soldiers; even their officer had ceased shouting. He—all of them—gaped wide-eyed at the fugitives they had been sent to capture or to kill. A simple mission that was simple no longer. There was not a man of the patrol who did not plainly wish himself elsewhere.

The crystals of fog constricted more closely together, forming the curves and angles of a geometry that had no place this side of madness. Even to look at it was to court vertigo and nausea. A harsh grin was etched into Gemmel's face as he used years of study to construct such nightmares as would make sleepers fear the night.

There was a thin, doleful note threading down the wind, a monotonous reedy piping like a dirge played on a solitary flute, and as if the whining melody had summoned them, things moved in the cloud. Amorphous obscenities squirmed slowly in a tangle of serpentine limbs, unclean creatures with a shocking suggestiveness in their grossly deformed outlines.

Dull yellow eyes glared down at King Rynert's troopers with
heartstopping malevolence and a perverse lust that went far
beyond mere hunger after flesh and blood.

A moment more of this, thought Dewan ar Korentin quea-
sily, and they must break. Or *I* will. His stomach was churning, sending sour bile burning up a throat that was already
clogged and overcrowded by the beating of his heart, and he
was so centred on his own misery that he did not see the
ripple of disturbed water streak up out of the southern ocean
and lift clear of the sea with a quick spume of spray that
whirled up to join the writhing horrors in the air.

And without warning—certainly without any bidding from
Gemmel—all movement ceased. The cloud hung monstrous
and immobile over its creator's head for just an instant before
contracting in a single spasm to a shape that was unmistakable. Reason and logic insisted that this too was an illusion
conjured out of frozen water—but neither reason nor logic
had a place here, not from the instant that ar Korentin glanced
sideways and saw the look on Gemmel's face change.

For a single beat he caught the remnants of the wizard's
grin, mixed with an air of confusion that was almost puzzlement. Then that had gone. And only the twist of naked fear
remained.

'Lady Mother Tesh . . . !' Dewan unconsciously blessed
himself at lips and heart. His soft exclamation had been no
oath, but a sincere prayer for protection in this moment when
all the defences of his scepticism had been shattered and the
very structure of his mind was reeling under a shock that left
him sick and giddy.

No matter now that he had seen something of this sort
before, even in the coolly unquestioning company of Aldric
Talvalin; still Dewan couldn't comprehend how something so
huge could remain airborne. Its flight, and indeed its very
presence here, made nonsense of everything he had ever been
told.

Not that anyone had deigned to tell him much about dragons . . .

Rearing back its awesome spined and crested head, the icedrake
roared—in challenge, maybe, or in scorn of the little scraps
of humankind who cowered beneath the shadow of its wings—
and the sound that it made was beyond imagination. Impossi-

bly bass, unbelievably piercing, it was a noise like the rending
of sheet steel and a music like the harmony of choirs, a cry of
incalculable strength and majesty that made the air tingle and
the earth shake.

It was power given a voice.

But from the terror stamped deep into Gemmel's features,
that power was not his to command.

Yet as the dragon's silvery head swung down and around
to regard him with great calm eyes that were the translucent
blue of glacier ice, the wizard flung both arms wide in a
greeting that was almost a salute. Gripped near its spike butt
by his right hand, Ykraith the Dragonwand swept an arc
through the cold, clear air and left a trail of pearly vapour in
its wake. The stuff hung like smoke for a moment before
sifting softly as snow onto the beach.

For a man so plainly frightened, Gemmel carried himself
well and his studied arrogance betrayed nothing; only Dewan
was close enough to read the truth in the sorcerer's dilated
eyes. A sweat of exertion which had filmed his skin was
frozen now into a cracked mask; each hair of his beard was as
stiff as wire and his skin was crusted and crumbling like the
time-fretted visage of an antique sculpture. If any vestige of
his grin remained, it was now no more than the rictus born of
hidden fear, and when he leaned on the Dragonwand it was
the action of an old, old man, with an ordinary walking-stick.
For Gemmel looked *ancient*.

And then he seemed to recover himself, straightening his
back with a heave as though throwing off some ponderous
weight. The semblance of extreme age faded and was gone as
if it had never been, and once more Gemmel Errekren assumed the aura of an enchanter at the peak of his powers.
Watching, Dewan wondered how much of that was real and
how much just another illusion.

The icedrake hung above them on barely moving wings,
gazing with huge patience at the small creatures whose efforts
had called it into being and waiting for their reasons. The few
seconds it had filled the sky seemed hour-long.

'Time stops,' said Gemmel hoarsely, 'as it stands still.'

The enigmatic words meant nothing to Dewan, creating no
answers but only questions. 'What will—?' he tried to ask,
but was hushed by a peremptory flick of the sorcerer's finger.

'Peace. Be silent. Be still.' As if knowing he would be

obeyed, Gemmel turned from the Vreijek and glanced towards the watching soldiers—fascinated like small birds before a snake. He raised Ykraith two-handed, the spell-stave's dragon tip pointing towards the leisurely hovering icedrake. Its chill, remote eyes blinked once and it seemed to listen as the wizard spoke again, this time in a language which was neither Alban nor any of the Imperial dialects even though it had audible affinities with them all. '*Sh'ma, trahanayr,*' he intoned. '*Y'shva pestreyhar—y'men vayh't r'hann arhlaeth . . .*'

It was a strange tongue, jarring and glottal, somehow incomplete and yet somehow familiar, and with it Dewan guessed that the sorcerer was trying to assert his mastery over the summoning. Yes, trying, for by the tremor in Gemmel's voice he was still far from certain of success. Staring up at the great, graceful being, ar Korentin wondered apprehensively what its response would be—and even, in a dark and secret corner of his mind, whether an adverse reaction would hurt.

The thing which punched wetly between the bones of his left forearm did not hurt. Not for the age-long second after it struck home. *Time stops . . .*

But then it felt like the icy anguish of a razor.

Dewan flinched as it hit, clapping one hand to the wound as if that would do any good. His blood felt very hot as it washed over spell-chilled skin, and though he had been wounded many, many times before he still felt sick. Yet there was more offended outrage than anything else in his mumbled protest to an uncaring world: 'But I was *sure* they didn't carry bows. . . .' Then he looked down, and saw the stub-shaft of the small steel dart, and knew he had been both right—and very stupid.

None of the troopers had had a bowcase amongst his gear. But they were Alban horse-soldiers and the paired *telekin* holstered either side of the high pommels were as much a part of military saddle-furniture as the double girths. It was a fact—one so obvious that only a foreigner, and one preoccupied with other matters at that, could be excused for the oversight. But Dewan's disgusted oath did not excuse himself, neither for forgetting about the Alban *telek* nor for failing to watch the youngster who commanded this patrol. Even before his shock-blurred gaze had focused on the missile's point of origin, he knew which of the men had shot at him. There was really only one candidate.

As if in confirmation, the young officer knelt on one knee and racked another dart from his spring-gun's magazine. The hard click-click of reloading carried clearly in the still, cold air. This time the weapon's stock was gripped in both his outstretched hands and he was squinting along it with one eye while the other squeezed shut in a demonic wink of aim. There was killing on his boy's face.

The *telek* steadied, unwavering now, and Dewan stared into its black bore for a time that seemed as long as the years of a man's life. Time enough to live—and time enough to die.

Time stops, he thought, and closed his eyes.

Preoccupied with his magic and with fighting his own fears, Gemmel had not seen the shooting. But he had heard that sound which is unlike any other—the meaty slap of sharpened metal piercing flesh. In that same long, long time which in real-time was less than half a second, he turned—registering another somehow significant double click even as he moved— and he *saw*.

Saw the levelled *telek* and the spurting wound, saw Dewan ar Korentin trying vainly to hold his own arm together, and saw not these things but another, older image. Not an injured companion, but a tableau which had haunted his most secret dreams for years. A sequence of inexorable events whose grim ending he was for ever helpless to avert. The inevitable conclusion which had taken away his son.

Gemmel saw, and knew, and ceased to care about himself. *'Trahan-ayr!'* he screamed, and above him the great white-armoured wedge that was the dragon's head moved fractionally, expectantly, its eyes slitting like a cat's. *'T'chu da sh'vakh! TAII-CHA!'*

And the power which terror said was not his to command obeyed him.

The icedrake's jaws yawned wide, a frigid blue-white cavern lined with ragged icicles, and it sent forth a smoky silver blast of unimaginable cold. A seagull rash enough to fly too close tumbled from the freezing air and shattered like a bird of blown glass when it struck the beach. Yet the dragon's blast was itself silent as midwinter. No storm, no blizzard, no howling rush of wind; only the faint brittle sounds of icy stillness which told of an end to warmth and life.

King Rynert's cavalry went down like wheat before a new-honed scythe, men and horses together in one heap. There was not even the clatter of their gear, for by the time they hit the ground all had been sheathed and muted by an inch thick crust of snow.

Nothing escaped—except the slender object which whirred like a wasp as it flicked clear of the settling blanket of frost . . .

Dewan uttered a small noise like a cough. His mouth opened to make the sound and remained open as one hand tried to touch his chest. Then he toppled backwards like a felled tree and did not move again.

Without any further word or sign from Gemmel, it was over. The sky above the wizard's head was abruptly empty once more and the slowly warming air was as clean and clear as polished crystal. The soldiers and their mounts lay where they had fallen, moving sluggishly like sleepers in the grip of dreams. Gemmel spared them barely a glance; his concern was all for Dewan.

The Vreijek sprawled face-upwards, his spine bent at an ugly angle by the bundle strapped to his back, his half-hooded eyes neither open nor truly shut. A ribbon of blood crawled from the corner of his mouth and dripped to the sand behind his head, and when Gemmel ripped open his tunic there was a mangled welt over his breastbone where the last *telek* dart had driven home. The wizard scooped it up and found the missile had been bloated three times as thick as normal by the layered ice which caked it, and its needle point was no more than a rounded stub of frosted metal.

But it had still hit Dewan like a hammer right above the heart, and there was a bluish tinge about the Vreijek's slack lips which Gemmel disliked most intensely. Ar Korentin was in the prime of his life, a strong, fit man—surely cumulative shock had not brought on . . .

Even as the thought formed, Gemmel was fumbling for a pulse with hands made clumsy by the cold which he himself had created, and when at last he found one he swore, viciously and with desperation; its fluttering was more a nervous tic than a pulse, too fast and totally irregular. Even as his fingers pressed down to confirm its presence the beat faltered, returned, faltered again once, twice . . .

And stopped.

No more blood dribbled from Dewan's mouth. The trickle of fluids from his torn arm ceased. He no longer breathed.

He no longer lived . . .

Gemmel's knuckles blanched as his grip tightened on the Dragonwand's adamantine surface; but he had learned during the past few terrible minutes that he could no longer trust the talisman to do his bidding. Its powers had passed beyond his control—and he suspected to his own great secret shame that he knew the reason why.

Ykraith dropped with an unheeded thud as his hand opened, and when it closed again it was to form a clenched fist which with carefully-judged force slammed squarely against Dewan's chest. Gemmel struck twice, then gripped his own wrist and began a rhythmic pressure with the heel of the free hand that was almost enough to break the bone beneath it. Almost, but not quite.

Push—push—push; fist, then pressure, then fist, then the firm steady pressure which tried to persuade Dewan's heart to beat again for itself. Again, and again—a hard task for two people, it was well-nigh impossible for one alone. Gemmel was panting now, breathless and sweaty with exertion and with the fear born of his own increasing despair.

Suddenly the bruised and battered rib-cage expanded with a convulsive jerk as Dewan's lungs wrenched in a whooping gasp of air. Gemmel felt the movement under his hands, and his fingertips sensed the drumming of a renewed heartbeat which pounded almost loudly enough to hear.

Ar Korentin began to breathe, and bleed, and live again.

The old enchanter, now feeling truly old, sat back on his heels and watched while his own heart-rate slowed and the sweat cooled on his trembling limbs. A little smile stretched his thin mouth thinner still as he realised that even without the Dragonwand, he had performed magic of a sort after all. Necromancy. Restoring the dead to life.

'I think,' he whispered to nobody at all, 'that makes us even.'

After a short while he straightened, easing the kinks out of his spine, and cast a wary glance towards the other bodies which littered the beach. No worries there; they would be a quarter-hour or more just remembering how to use their legs. He squatted and slid the Dragonwand into the back of his belt, silently reminding himself for perhaps the hundredth time to buy or make the spellstave some kind of shoulder-strap; then hunkered lower still and lifted ar Korentin from the ground.

There was no visible expenditure of effort now: only a smooth surge of strength that seemed somehow more than human. He cradled the big man's limp body in both arms as he might a child; as he had once carried his dead son; as he had once carried the young Alban warlord who was now his son. His own, most honourable son.

Gemmel laid Dewan gently athwart the stern of the boat; then he raised the sail, steadied the tiller and spoke the soft sibilants which summoned up an offshore breeze. And though he was tired, unutterably drained and wearied by fear and physical effort and mental strain, he did all in the same abstracted manner—automatically, without thought.

For his thoughts were elsewhere now. They were out *there:* across and beyond forty miles of grey water, a distance too far for even a suggestion of the Empire's coast to shadow the horizon. All his thoughts, his hopes, his fears both real and imagined. Out in that far place. With the son who was not his son.

And he wondered if his son was safe.

THREE

Fire in the Night

Outside was dark and cold; an autumn night already edged with the oncoming winter. A scimitar moon cut fitfully through weak places in the overlay of rain-swollen clouds.

Inside was almost as dark, but within the small anonymous tavern the night was distinctly warmer. Flame-lapped pine logs burned slowly in a hearth of black wrought-iron. Sparks glowed and spat; the blue, smoky air was scented with a sharp tang of resin; nimble shadows danced among the rafters. From one corner of the common-room came the protracted minor chords of a three-stringed rebec—each note nasal, penetrating, cruel as loss.

The few patrons sat uncomfortably around low tables, drinking from plain pottery cups and thus convinced that they behaved with the elegant austerity just now fashionable in the Drusalan Empire. Several looked back and the rest forward to days where a certain degree of luxurious excess was—or would again be—more socially acceptable. Their quiet conversation was overlaid with a falsely carefree tone which made the unease beneath it all the more apparent; and the source of that unease was not difficult to find.

He was dressed severely, all in black; and he sat alone with his thoughts and a redware cup of cheap corn spirit, bent over and staring into the amber liquid as if it contained the secrets of infinity rather than the oblivion which he had sought since sundown.

Uncertain of strangers at the best of times—and these were not such times—even a friendlier people than the sullen few who sipped and murmured well away from him would have been deterred by his appearance. He needed a shave, the pallor of his face throwing both a five-day beard and the bruise-dark shadows under each eye into sharp relief, and his shoulders were hunched almost to the point of deformity by a *coyac*, a sleeveless jerkin of dense black fur. It made him seem not entirely human.

The number of empty jugs strewn across his table told of how long and hard he had been drinking, and by rights he should have slumped onto the floor an hour ago. But he had not; the quick, economic movements which filled and refilled his cup were still improbably sure and precise, and his icy grey-green eyes remained unglazed. That, too, was not entirely human.

There was a sheathed longsword lying on the table amid the clutter, its hilt within easy reach and its unsubtle presence a blatant threat to peace. The innkeeper had wanted to take the weapon from him after the first two jugs had been drained far too quickly, but he had been warned off in a grotesque mixture of stilted high-mode Drusalan sweetened by gutter Jouvaine, both threaded with an accent that had nothing to do with either.

Silver—a great deal of silver—had changed hands immediately afterwards, as if the stranger repented of his hard words. He spent the Empire's florins as if they had no value, and now was left alone to drink himself into a stupor since this had plainly been his intention all along—except that the stupor seemed as far away as ever.

Aldric Talvalin poured more spirit into his cup and gulped down half of the raw liquor with the wrenching swallow of someone taking a medicinal draught. It burned, making his nostrils flare and his eyes squeeze shut. Tears jewelled their corners, tears which were not born of mere maudlin drunkenness. Maybe tonight, if he drank enough, there would be no dreams.

Dreams. Memories. And within the dreams and memories, nightmares. Fear and fire and candle-light. Again they came, rising through the haze of alcohol which was trying to fog his conscious mind. It was an ill thing to jolt awake in the dark stillness of deep night, soaked with sweat and strangling in the sheets with the echoes of your own cry of terror in your ears. But it was worse by far to be awake already and to be jolted stone-cold sober.

Aldric sat as he had sat before, trembling all over, while the drink which should by now have laid him gratefully senseless on the floor became no more than an acid heat in his gullet. And still the dreams returned to haunt him.

Blood, and flame, and shrieking. Things that were, but are not: things that are, but should never be. Huge wings in a starlit sky. A tall tower stark against iron clouds, and a swirl of snow. Sobbing . . . Blue smoke streaming upwards, the incisive reek of heated metal and the sweet, sweet scent of roses.

Aldric dreaded his dreams, for they seemed always to presage only evil and bitter experience had proven the truth of that foreboding. His ringed left hand reached out to a crumpled thing on the table near Widowmaker's lacquered scabbard. It shifted as his fingers touched it, making a small, sere crackle. Once more he could smell roses. He had plucked this blossom from between the withered talons of an ancient corpse three months ago, standing at the heart of a burial mound in the Deepwood of the Jevaiden plateau. Now the rose, too, was withered: dry and dead, its baleful brilliance had faded to a more natural hue and the once-unwholesome richness of its perfume was diluted by time to a fragrance which was almost pleasant . . .

Even though it was dead, the Alban thought as he cradled the desiccated flower in the palm of his hand. Or *because* it was dead?

As dead as Crisen Geruath.

As dead as his own honour.

Although he had already contrived to send a note to Rynert the King—a terse, enciphered message of success at Seghar, delivered by the master of an Elherran merchantman—the task he had been set was still incomplete. There remained the messages locked by sorcery within his skull: proofs, he had been told, to Lord General Goth and Prokrator Bruda of Alban support, and confidences which might sway those overlords whose fealty yet wavered between one side and the other. Except that his part in the deaths of two other overlords made any meeting with these powerful men merely an elaborate form of suicide. Aldric had few illusions about Imperial judicial process; in all likelihood he had already been sentenced for the 'murders' of Lord Geruath and his son. No matter now that had things gone otherwise it would have been Geruath himself whose introduction would have made any meeting easy.

Aldric had made his own decision after Seghar; the brutalities and the casual wickedness in that rotting heap of masonry had sickened him at last. He no longer cared that his tenuous hold on Dunrath remained subject to Rynert's whim, and had said as much. He was getting out of the Empire's sphere of influence as quickly as he could.

While he still could . . .

He should have been aboard the Elherran ship. Before God, the rendezvous had been arranged for long enough. And indeed, he would have been had not the sheer chance of an early morning canter led him to the crest of the ridge which towered high above Kenbane Haven, the only place along several miles of coast from which he could have seen the bay beyond the harbour wall—and thus the Imperial battleram which had come scything out of the dawn mist like a patrolling shark.

Kenbane had been one of five points of departure agreed in secret with Rynert and with Dewan ar Korentin. Now he wondered who else was privy to that supposed secret, for surely the warship's inopportune appearance was no coincidence? Even if it was, Aldric no longer cared. The threat had been enough.

But that had been almost two months past, near a Vreijek port many miles south-west of here. The passage of time, and the onset of the autumn gales, must surely have made even the Imperial fleet if not exactly careless, then at least a little less enthusiastic. He would see, when he tried again to leave. Tomorrow.

What profit in an enterprise, Lord King, Aldric rehearsed silently for perhaps the hundredth time, *when all chance of completing it is already lost?* Rynert probably had a hundred valid answers to that rhetorical question.

Or the single answer which was all a king required.

A young man had entered the tavern without attracting anyone's attention; indeed, had any noticed him at all, they might have been much impressed by the pains he took to avoid that notice. He was nondescript to a studied degree—dirty, tired, and with an air of boredom as though occupied by a repetitive and so-far-unrewarding task. The gaze with which he swept the common-room had more sleepiness in it than anything else. Until his eyes reached Aldric. And then the weary half-yawn which had begun to carve notches in the corners of his mouth stretched much, much further as it changed to a wide grin of self-congratulation.

The grin did not go unnoticed by the innkeeper at least, for he sidled up the counter to draw the young man's drink and to wonder casually—in the fashion of innkeepers—just what was tonight's cause for such obvious happiness, and did it mean a celebration?

'I think,' murmured the young man, 'that I may just have come into some money.' He drank thoughtfully, savouring the fine vintage which right now he felt fully justified in ordering, and jerked with his chin towards the drunkard in black. 'That one isn't a local, is he?'

No more than you, was what the innkeeper almost said aloud; but considering what this new arrival had just spent on a single bottle of imported wine, he thought better of it. And there had been something about the idly asked question which struck him as peculiar. Nothing he could pin down, but it had been there all the same. 'Him, local? Not by a long ride in whatever direction you care to choose!'

'I thought not. You must have many travellers from the seaport coming in here to drink, eh?'

'No—too far for most, I fancy.'

'Indeed . . . 'Another grin split the young man's face. 'Or too far to stagger back, maybe?'

The innkeeper laughed. 'Something like that.' Then he moved away to serve another customer and left the inquisitive young man alone with his wine, quite missing the intent expression which had settled on the dusty but no longer bored features.

Left in peace, the young man set down his cup with its contents barely tasted and began an unobtrusive study of this foreigner who didn't like to do his drinking in the port of Tuenafen. It had taken ten hours and forty taverns to reach this stage—that and a sizable outlay in undrunk drink. Now, however, the whole thing seemed as if it might be worth the effort. When the Vixen was pleased, she had definite ways of proving it.

The sketch she had shown him was a good one: detailed and probably most accurate. An excellent likeness of the man he was looking at. Not as alike as two peas in a pod, maybe, but close. Very, very close. Moreover he was in the right

place, give or take the few miles to Tuenafen, and behaving—
bar this unfathomable determination to get drunk—in the
right way. It was enough at least to let the young man
proceed as he had been instructed.

A beckoning finger summoned the innkeeper and brought
him leaning confidentially over the counter, full of ill-disguised
curiosity. *You can smell a juicy scandal in the offing, can't
you*, the young man thought, keeping contempt off his face
with an effort. *And you can't wait to hear all about it.*

'That foreigner'—he used the insulting Drusalan word
hlensyarl—'is to stay here.' There was a flat power in his
voice which had not been there before.

'What?'

'Keep him here. Don't let him leave. I don't care how you
do it—just *do* it!'

'But that sword . . . I can't!'

'I think you can.' The young man straightened his back,
squared his shoulders and shot a sidelong glance at the innkeeper. 'Because if he isn't here when I get back . . .'

He didn't bother to complete the sentence.

Far steadier on his feet than he had any right to be—and far
clearer in his mind than he would have liked to be—Aldric
settled his bill with the innkeeper. For one who had tried at
first to eject him from the premises, and then a little later to
confiscate his sword, the man now seemed strangely reluctant
to let him go. He fumbled more than usual as he made change
from the fistful of florins which Aldric had slapped onto the
counter, and as an apparent apology of sorts pressed a gratis
bottle of wine into the Alban's hands.

Aldric turned it over and squinted at the letters etched on
the green glass; then blinked twice, very fast, and tried again
with the conviction that his eyes were tricking him. This
'apology' was a bottle of sweet white Hauverne, *matherneil*,
the Kingswine which changed hands in Alba—if it ever got
there—for rising thirty marks a time. At first he said nothing,
but with his free hand dug into the pouch at his belt and
poured a shining, chiming stream of silver coins over the
counter and on to the floor, no longer caring that *silver* was a
mere courtesy title where the Empire's money was concerned. In economic matters as in all else, Tuenafen was a

part of the Empire. Let the useless currency buy something here, if nowhere else.

'For everyone,' he said, a frown insinuating its notch between his brows as he concentrated on the slurring High Drusalan diphthongs; but the words he sought eventually fell into place. 'Fill all the cups. And—' the bottle of Hauverne thumped onto the bar-top—'open this and bring two of yonder good glasses. One for me.' His eyes locked with the innkeeper's as his left hand freed Widowmaker's shoulder-belt, and the slithering noise as the *taiken* dropped to battle position at his hip was like the sound an adder makes moving through long grass. 'And one for you.'

Whatever suspicions he might have entertained about the extravagant gift were silenced as his host first sipped appreciatively, then drank with every sign of enthusiasm and none at all of hesitation. Aldric smiled thinly and followed suit. The wine was remarkable; rich, fruity and as fragrant as honey. Its fumes rose to the Alban's head as the harsh corn spirit had never done—perhaps, observed the analytical part of his mind, because one was being drunk in the hope of its effect while brooding on the need for that effect, while this Hauverne was being drunk for the sheer pleasure of drinking it. If there was more than one road to oblivion, he thought, then this was the one he would choose. If he could afford it.

The tavern doors slid open then, and stayed open while the cold, cold night flowed in. Heads turned and a voice was raised in protest—but it cut off short as armed men crossed the threshold. Six of them, wearing crest-coats over light mail and with crossbows cradled capably in their hands. They fanned out to either side of the door with a crispness that bespoke drill and discipline.

Then stopped.

She glided into the common-room like an empress, wrapped in furs against the bitter air outside and with raindrops beaded on her high-piled auburn hair which flamed like rubies in the firelight. If the arrival of her guard—for such the soldiers were—had drawn a few eyes, then her own appearance summoned all the rest. Conversation ceased; the rebec's thin music fell silent; everyone stared.

She was well worth staring at, and knew it; easily as tall as any man in the room, her willowy elegance gave unconscious grace to every movement. Nobody in the tavern had seen her before, nor was such foreknowledge necessary to realise what she was. Either the pampered daughter of some high and noble house, wilful enough to travel the Imperial roads alone. Or a courtesan of the highest rank.

The young man at her side provided a stark contrast to her finery, for he was nondescript to a studied degree, dirty, tired—and not entirely unfamiliar to the barkeep, whose tongue licked at lips which had gone far drier than his cup of wine would ever quench. The two men looked at each other; one plainly apprehensive, the other with an air of malicious satisfaction and a confidence which he wore like a cloak.

When the woman snapped her fingers the innkeeper jumped despite himself, then emerged from behind his counter to bow judiciously low. Still unsure of her station, he preferred to treat her as high-born rather than make a dangerously insulting error. And there were the half-dozen troopers of her escort to reinforce his choice.

'You have rooms here.' The fox-haired lady spoke even that simple fact in a smoky contralto purr. 'I wish to rest here. See to it.'

If the innkeeper was startled by her decision to grace his establishment—which though clean enough, was certainly a class or more below where she would normally have chosen to stay—he concealed it well. Such an occurrence was rare, but not unheard-of; on any road there were those travellers who despite riches and importance—or maybe because of them—preferred for various reasons not to advertise the fact. His inn was only one amongst many which maintained two or three fine state-rooms in anticipation of the day when Wealth might step through the door. As it had plainly done tonight.

It was not any innkeeper's place to wonder the whys and wherefores of it all, merely to make from it everything he could. Bowing lower than ever, the man went about his business buried in calculation—which had less to do with setting a fair price than with how much he could safely overcharge.

The lady and her companion made private conversation for a moment, mouth to ear; then the young man nodded, smiled slightly and went out, taking the soldiers with him to the unspoken but obvious relief of the entire tavern. Aldric watched them go, but found his gaze tending to slide back towards their mistress.

Mistress. His mind toyed caressingly with the word as he sipped wine and rolled the soft, sweet liquid over with his tongue. *Sweet.* The adjective in his native Alban—and the thought in his head—had nothing much to do with wine at all.

Granted, she was totally inaccessible. Granted, he had a failing for a pretty face and an attractive figure. Granted, that same failing had tripped him up more than once. And granted, finally, he was heading out of Tuenafen in the morning.

But he too could rest here for the night.

In the beginning there was fire, and a dream of fire; a dream of gazing down and down into the liquid seething of the world's hot secret heart; a dream of rumbling, almost sub-audible sound and a dream of the smell of burning, incongruously slashed by a sense of unbelievable blue-white cold.

The great Cavern on the Island of Techaur, and a thing of power exchanged for his given Word. Granted for a promise made to . . . Made to . . .

Speak and say, kailin *Talvalin. Name my name.*

'Ymareth!' Aldric shouted the name aloud in his troubled sleep and so awoke, eyelids snapping back so that he stared straight up towards the darkness of the ceiling. Or at where the darkness should have been, for the ceiling was not dark any more. Light moved among the beams of rough-cut timber and it was not the light of dawn. Dawn did not flicker so; it did not roar beyond the shutters so; and it was not that awesome, awful amber.

Then there was awareness and full awakening, and the knowledge that this time his dream was real.

Aldric flung back the quilt from the narrow bed, rolling sideways to plant both feet square together on the floor—then clutched wildly at the wall as the whole room continued to roll around him. For just an instant, a few heartbeats, for the second which it took his naked skin to film itself in icy sweat, everything plunged sideways and only his fingernails gouging painfully into the plaster kept him from pitching onto his face.

There was a sourness in his throat, a queasiness in his belly and a pounding headache behind his eyes. He knew only too well what had caused *them*—but the bitter stink of fire, and the smoke which was making him cough? Steadying himself with an effort, Aldric crossed the room and flung the shuttered window open.

Heat slapped like a physical blow across his face and chest, the bellow of a fire out of control assaulted his ears—and mingled with that bellow was the squealing of terrified horses. To any ears it was a ghastly noise, but to an Alban horse-lord it was infinitely worse than that. 'Lyard!' he gasped in horror, staring with wide, bloodshot eyes towards the stables where a solitary ribbon of flame was fluttering up its wall, a little insignificant thing no more than a handspan wide.

But the stable wall was wood—and the stable roof was thatch.

The Alban wasn't sure afterwards just how he managed to scramble into his clothes so fast; certainly there were straps and laces left undone, secured too loosely or too tight, but shirt and boots and breeches were all in place before the little flame had grown much larger. He thrust his *tsepan* dirk into his belt, wincing as its pommel nudged his nauseated stomach, then scooped up Widowmaker and made for the swiftest exit he could see. It happened to be the open window.

Betrayed by his wobbly legs, Aldric went over when he landed and rolled like a shot rabbit while dirk and longsword went each in different directions. Just after the bone-jarring impact came the nasty realisation that in his present state he was as likely as not to have broken his neck. There was no time even to shrug.

A swift glance told him what had probably happened: the flames were billowing from an incandescent framework where the tavern's kitchens had once stood, and even in the instant that his eyes were on them they bridged the gap between courtyard and tavern proper. Thatch exploded like tinder; sparks and smoke filled the air, stinging and choking; a dense grey cloud rolled across his line of sight and something unseen collapsed with a tearing crash.

Where in damnation's bloody name is everyone? He saw them, someone, anyone, black silhouettes in the firelight, running about aimlessly or flinging meagre buckets of water. Some, more practical, were carrying their belongings clear of the doomed building.

No more time to watch.

Get the horses out!

All of them—can't let them burn.

Why won't it rain that deluge it's been promising all day?

The thoughts tumbled through Aldric's confused brain even as he ran towards the stable-block, staring apprehensively at that ribbon of flame which—in the few long strides which took him to the door—had expanded to a flickering yellow scarf tipped and trimmed with dark smoke. Confused or not, they were the last thoughts of any coherence he was to have for a long, long time.

The stables were built to a familiar Imperial pattern: tall sliding doors at either end of a broad, paved walkway which was flanked on each side by cedar-faced loose-boxes strewn with deep, comfortable—and fiercely inflammable—straw. The animals were normally free to move about in these; but tonight of all nights, someone had secured their headstalls to the iron holding-rings in the rear wall of each box. A spasm of anger shot through Aldric at this evidence of some groom's thoughtlessness; not so much because of the fire, and because his own task was immediately more difficult than simply flinging all the doors wide open, but for the simple reason that—tied up all night—none of the horses could reach food or water until someone came to release them.

It was simple; simply nasty. And had he the time, the 'someone' responsible would be rooted out and made to dance for his neglect. Except that time was in very short supply.

Lyard knew his master and it was just as well. The Andarran's rolling eyes showed little but white, and he was streaked with the sweat of his terror and the foam from where he had champed uselessly at his halter; but he still allowed Aldric to lead him out at a steady pace, even though the flames of his own private hell skipped eagerly only a plank's thickness from his heels. Another minute, though. Another minute, and the big stallion would have pulped anybody in his path.

The pack-pony was next; Aldric flung the saddle-frame and then the boxes which contained his armour any whichway across the sumpter gelding's neck, then jerked aside hastily as it barged after Lyard directly it was loosed. As it always followed Lyard—he coughed as smoke throttled what might have been wry laughter—but a damn sight more willingly than usual!

It was the other horses which were the problem, even

though they weren't highly-strung, battle-schooled and consequently dangerous bloodstock like his Andarran courser; just a matched pair of carriage ponies and half-a-dozen riding hacks. But they were unfamiliar, and therefore risky. Scared, too; the laidback ears and bulging eyes would have told anyone that, even were they deaf to the piteous noises of fright. But it was just fright—not pain. Not yet.

Not ever, if he could help it!

The thatched roof caught as if hit by an incendiary just as Aldric went into one of the horses' stalls—and in that same second he slammed backwards and then down to the floor as if hit by a mace. It was close enough to the truth: the horse had lashed out in a paroxysm of fear and its iron-shod hoof had clipped his thigh, stunning the big muscle and tearing his heavy leather riding-breeches like paper. Another inch and it would have ripped flesh from bone and crippled him.

Muttering something under his breath, Aldric clambered back to his feet and cuffed at hindquarters which swung round to pin him against the partition. The horse flinched away—then thumped back, and stars inside his head joined the sparks already floating through the air.

Something—a dark outline against the fireglow—swam into view. No, some*one*. Aldric shook glowing motes from his eyes and the world snapped back into focus. It . . . he . . . was a man, big and broad-shouldered. One of my lady's escort? The man shouted something, but roaring flames made nonsense of the words.

'Get them out!' the Alban mouthed at him, enhancing his unheard words with mime, then returned his attention to the plunging horse. Its frantically jerking head had drawn the headstall's knot far tighter than human fingers could hope to loose, but—a knife appeared in his hand from the scabbard down one boot—there were other ways than untying . . .

No point now in trying to quiet the beast; it had gone beyond the stage where gentle words would have any effect. All he wanted now was to free the ropes which tied each horse—they would make their own way out faster than he could—and then get clear himself before the roof came in.

As if stimulated by his thought, the blazing thatch overhead creaked ominously and seemed to settle on its rafters while a drizzle of sparks percolated through the tight-packed reeds and straw. Aldric spared a single instant to glance up, then sliced his blade across the braided halter just as the horse threw all its weight into a final, desperate heave. The hemp went taut as wire, humming with strain, and the first touch of the razor-whetted knife jumped and skittered across its fibres. Then the edge bit home and it parted with a deep sound like the strings of a great-bass rebec.

The horse floundered back on its haunches as the rope let go, then wheeled to bolt headlong from the stable.

And Aldric sat down sharply, yelping with pained surprise as blood welled from the scar beneath his right eye, three years healed but laid open like an hour-old cut by the whiplash strike of the severed rope. He barely noticed the brief sting at the nape of his neck which might have been a spark. But was not.

As he darted from stall to stall, severing ropes and dodging horses as if taking part in some crazy rustic dance, he could hear the roof groan again as it settled further. Chunks of its structure fell away and the drizzle of sparks became a deluge, a torrent of burning fragments pouring onto the floor. A floor that, except for the paved walkway, was knee-deep in loose, dry straw. It ignited with the roar of a hungry animal and filled the confines of the world with fury. Heat washed over Aldric as he stumbled from the last stall on that side and into the main aisle of the stable, almost trampled as other horses— all the remaining horses—galloped past him on the way to open air and safety, and his mouth stretched into a tight grin. The trooper, if such he was, had been busy.

There was unknowing irony in the way that thought coincided with a rub at the sore spot on his neck—a rub which dislodged the tiny dart imbedded there.

He could see no trace of the man: too wise to linger in this incinerator, most likely. Aldric knew he would be wise to follow suit, for worms of smoke were already writhing from the wooden walls as they heated towards flashpoint, and the doorposts were already on fire. At each end of the building. The only other occasion when he had seen anywhere burn like this, it had been set ablaze deliberately.

His thought led nowhere; with this much straw about, no wonder the fire had spread so fast. But even so, the tavern wasn't full of straw.

That too meant nothing; it drifted across the surface of his mind even as he tucked his head down and sprinted for the nearest doorway. His legs were unsteady beneath him and once-solid objects were shimmering in the haze of hot light and smoke. Then all concerns and idle notions were swallowed in the vast rending as the stable caved in on itself. And on him!

The surge of heat made his senses swim as it consumed what little air remained, and a searing gale tugged at his hair as it funnelled through the blazing doorway; a doorway that receded down an endless corridor of fire even as he ran vainly towards it. He was conscious of the rush of movement at his back as something came scything down like a headsman's sword—

—heard the impact as it smashed between his shoulders like a giant's fist—

—saw the sparks exploding like a halo around his head—

Too late! You left it too . . .

And that was all.

'How did you find him in Tuenafen?' The man in scarlet-lacquered armour planted both his hands palm-downwards on the desk and leaned forward, his spade beard jutting pugnaciously. 'How did you know?'

'I told you.' Pinched between finger and thumb of a black-gloved hand, the scrap of parchment looked utterly insignificant and the writing on it was minute. But it afforded a certain degree of pleasure to the man who held it, for all that his glistening metallic mask concealed whatever smile might have curved his lips. Yet the smile was there, and plainly audible in the smug coloration of his laconic words: 'I told you long ago—'

'Three weeks—'

'And now I too have been told.'

'I didn't somehow think it was coincidence.'

'I abhor coincidence.' The masked man might have shuddered theatrically at the very thought, had he been prone to such gestures; but the armoured man could see no tremor in the misshapen bearded face that reflected back at him.

'Of course.' There was the merest touch of acid in his voice. 'Except when you create it. I know.' He straightened, pressed hands palm to palm and touched their steepled fingertips thoughtfully to the end of his hawk nose as he pondered a moment. 'Now, Tuenafen.' The hands clapped decisively.

'The quickest route is by sea. I'll put a battleram at the disposal of your squad.'

He stalked to the window and looked out, then turned back to the masked man who had not stirred from the highbacked chair in which he lounged with such elegantly irritating indolence. And the armoured man smiled thinly. '*Teynaur* is moored in the estuary,' he said. 'Use her.'

His smile widened as the masked man sat bolt upright, his lazy assurance gone in an instant. '*Teynaur* . . . ? But she's an—an augmented ship.'

'Of course. Why not?' There was a long beat of silence. 'Of course, if you don't like the idea, then let Voord go alone. Such things don't worry him—rather the reverse.'

'To an unhealthy degree!'

'No matter. He is efficient—you employed that very word when he was sent to Seghar. Why—have you changed your views?'

'No.' The reply was sullen. 'He is still most capable, regardless.'

'Good. Then it's agreed.' The armoured man gathered up his rank-marked helmet and settled it comfortably in the crook of one arm, obviously preparing to leave. Then he hesitated. 'You want Talvalin alive?'

'Of course. Why?'

'So do I. And untouched. There is a distinct difference. Make sure that Voord remembers it.'

'The wound is new. And he has a beard.'

'The *beard* is new—and it isn't so much a beard as a need to shave. That's something I'm better qualified to know than you, my lady. But the wound was old when I saw it.'

'When you saw it? When you thought you saw it—or when you saw what you wanted to see?'

'I saw what I saw. Look for yourself and then say I was wrong.'

Paper rustled crisply.

'Close. Very close. This is an excellent likeness . . . of somebody. But is it close enough?'

'Close enough for me. I sent the messages last night and this morning: one by courier, one by pigeon. The usual.'

'Without consulting me?'

'I saw no need; I thought you would approve.'

'Never presume what I will or will not do. But yes, I do approve.'

'And the Lord-Commander? What will Voord say?'

'Voord will be . . . very pleased.'

It was surely a dream; a soft murmur of sound that droned like insects on a warm summer night. The sound took shape and became voices, a man's and a woman's. They ebbed and flowed, weaving patterns of words. But whatever language it was that the voices spoke, none of the words made sense.

The dream faded. His eyes remained shut; other than the slow rise and fall of his chest and the never-ending tic of pulses beneath his skin, he did not move. But with a swiftness that fell between one breath and the next, Aldric was totally aware of his surroundings.

There was softness above and below him; that was the yielding warmth of quilts, and it was comforting in its familiarity. Light surrounded him, for he was conscious of its brilliance beyond his eyelids. A faint taste of bitter herbs left a flavour like steel in his mouth, and there was a scent of flowers in his nostrils—the arid, delicate fragrance of dried blossoms set out to perfume the air. He opened his eyes to see them, to see where he was—

—and saw only featureless white, and knew that he was blind.

Sweat beaded on Aldric's skin and now he could not, would not move, even though each breath was coming faster and faster and the blood-pulse in his ears was running wild. *The fire!*

Memories crashed back into his brain: monstrous heat, smoke and flames surging in his wake as he fled for ever; the roof coming down, the blow across his back and the midnight embrace of oblivion. The long fall into the dark which had never reached bottom.

A fall as black as blindness . . .

His skin was no longer beaded by perspiration, but slickly sheathed in it. Aldric could feel each droplet forming, running down his ribs, his jaw, his temples. What had happened could never, never have been so subtly selective as to destroy only his sight. Not that inferno. And if blindness was black, as the proverb claimed, then was this flaring whiteness—

Death . . . ?

With that thought came the great uncontrolled intake of breath which could only return as a scream.

Or a gasp; for in the same instant someone took the light bandage from his face and pressed a cool, moist pad against each eye in turn, and when they opened again Aldric's world lurched back to reality and equilibrium with a vertiginous jolt. The unborn cry became a hissing exhalation that trickled out between his teeth, for he was shamed by the sleek lac-quering of fear that glossed his skin and by the—surely audible!—thudding of his heart. But the woman who sat by his bed and gazed down at him either did not or courteously feigned not to notice.

Without her furs and her guards and her imperious air, she looked very different. Her hair was unbound now, and in the lamplight which filled the room it was the deep rich russet of a fox's pelt. She was smiling.

'I thought . . .' he faltered; the admission was going to sound foolish, or cowardly, or both. 'I thought that I was dead.'

'Quite so. There was a time, indeed, when we thought that we had lost you.' She spoke in the purring Jouvaine language and her voice was as Aldric remembered it: soft, throaty, surprisingly deep. A purr indeed. If foxes purred.

'Lost me?'

'Lost you,' she repeated. 'You were lucky—very lucky. The timber which hit you wasn't properly aflame, as you were running hard in the right direction. Otherwise you would never have got out.'

'I should never have gone in,' he muttered, deciding not to sit up as his stomach gave a little warning heave. His words, indeed his thoughts, were forming easily and that surprised him; he had been stunned before and the concussion had jumbled brain and stomach both. As she said: he must have been very, very lucky. He knew that he had certainly been something else. 'Stupid—'

'Unselfish, courageous. You didn't have to stay after you freed your own horses—but you did, and you saved mine. That was typical, I suppose. You are fond of horses.' Again the smile. 'I know a little about Albans.'

If she had hoped for some sort of reaction, the lady was disappointed. Aldric had never tried to conceal his national-ity, because it was both difficult to maintain such a deception and immediately suspicious if discovered. His identity, though, now that was quite another matter. But the mere possibility of an ulterior motive behind her casual remark was enough to coil another worm of nausea through him, masked only by a smile of sorts to disguise whatever else might be read from his features. 'Most people do,' he replied carefully.

Or think they do. The words were on the tip of his tongue, but stayed there. For one thing, he was in no mood for opening his mouth more than was absolutely necessary, and for another this lady was his hostess—or so he guessed the lady to be, and the house around him, hers.

There could be nothing left of the tavern in which he had awoken last night, nothing at all. Of that he was certain. Even though he was very far from certain that it *had* been last night, or even the night before that. Aldric closed his eyes and shivered as he wondered how many days and nights he had really lost. And what had happened while they passed him by.

Who are you? Where am I? What is this place? *What day is it?*

The questions were all there, waiting—needing—to be asked. Banal questions, obvious questions, stupid questions. But all lacking the answers which he needed to start making sense of what was going on.

'You are plainly still far from well, *'tlei,'* said the lady gently. 'Sleep now. We can talk again later.' Her hand was cool on his brow. 'Sleep.'

He slept.

He slept.

He dreamed.

He died!

He woke. And woke knowing that he had been drugged, for this time he was wide awake and in full control of himself, his totally alert senses insisting on the fact and emphasising it with that faint metallic, medicinal flavour lurking under his tongue and at the back of his throat. It was a flavour he remembered, but had been unable or unfit to identify before; now it was unmistakably the after-taste of herbal soporifics. Mandragora, poppy—he was in the Empire now and the possibilities were endless, for the Drusalans had raised herb lore to an art-form and a science, whilst at the same time lowering it to a particularly unpleasant vice. Swallowing in an attempt to clear away the bitterness, Aldric realised just how very dry his mouth had become.

At least—his gaze slid left—there was an evaporation-cooled terracotta jug of water on a table near the bed. He rolled over and reached out, then hesitated momentarily with the thought of more drugs filling his mind. A brief consideration put paid to that idea; if he was to have been drugged, then he would never have woken up to worry about the fact. He ignored the cups to grip the jug itself, put the vessel to his lips and disposed of its contents in half-a-dozen rapturous gulps; stared for several seconds into the pitcher's brick-brown interior; then tilted it that few degrees further and allowed the last drops of water to patter coolly across his face.

Only then did the questions once more play follow-my-leader across the conscious surface of his mind. Who, and where, and when—and *why?*

There were various answers to that one, few of which were appealing.

But the lady . . .

She of the fox-bronze hair and the purring, feline voice. The lady had something to do with all this. Yes, all of it. The fire and the trapped horses. The grinding roar of falling timber and the shower of sparks before the lights went out.

And how in the name of nine hot hells did I survive?

Aldric's eyes raked the room, noting the understated elegance which plainly displayed the wealth and taste of whoever owned it—and by that intimation, owned the house as well. If it was intended to impress, then despite his cynical efforts to the contrary it succeeded. A quick grin bared his teeth as he saw those things which at first glance reassured him above all else; but it faded swiftly as comprehension of detail gave him cause for a deal of thought.

His saddlebags were set on a chair by the far wall. There was nothing wrong with that, although he was sure they had been opened and the contents carefully scrutinised. A garment of some sort—not one of his own—was draped across the linen chest at the foot of the bed, obviously meant for his use; well, his own clothes were either still packed away or in a smelly, smoky, unfit state unless someone had washed them. Or, he amended, caused them to be washed.

But his weapons . . .

Whoever was responsible for their disposition had known exactly what he—or she—was doing, for Isileth Widowmaker was not merely laid horizontally across a fine sword-stand of fumed oak as might be done by anyone who . . . what were her words? 'Knew a little about Albans.' Oh no. This was much, much more.

The *taiken's* weapon-belt had been wrapped closely around her black-lacquered scabbard in the interlacing style of *hanentehar*, as was proper for battle-furnished longswords; and his *tsepan* dirk had been placed on the cushion of a three-legged stool, then set close in beside the bed. It was an insignificant thing; but it meant that the honour blade was within the arm's-length of its owner which tradition and the Codes required.

His own weapons told Aldric that whoever he was dealing with knew more than he liked about his homeland, his background and quite possibly himself. And that they were confident enough to flaunt the fact.

He glanced towards the door, the speculation in that glance born more of optimism than any real hope. If they—or he or she or whatever—were so sure of themselves, there might just be a remote possibility that the overconfidence could extend further. Into foolishness.

The thought was no sooner completed than he was out of the bed, Widowmaker scooped neatly from her sword-stand; and the scabbard had been shaken from her long blade before he paused long enough even to consider wrapping himself in the garment which someone had so thoughtfully provided.

It was a *cymar*, heavy and fur-trimmed, Vlei-style. The dense fabric was the colour of autumn maples, the fur red fox; and it hung from Aldric's shoulders as loosely as a riding mantle. Clothing of any sort meant much more than simple modesty right now: in this potentially hostile environment his bare skin felt horribly vulnerable, and even a single layer of cloth could give an illusory protection.

Or should have done. If anything this sleeveless, side-slashed, open-fronted and monstrously oversized *cymar* seemed to emphasise with every movement that he was stark naked beneath it; which was subconsciously worse than having nothing on at all. Aldric glanced at himself and exhaled a soft oath. This was deliberate; and the robe had probably been selected with a deal of care to unsettle him so successfully.

Isileth's equally naked blade gave him more comfort; at least with the *taiken* in his hands, then armoured, unarmoured or newborn naked he could give a good account of himself to anyone, or any thing . . . no, *Thing*. His mind reconsidered that last, and an inward shudder raised the hair on arms and neck as he regretted tempting fate with such a thought. The events in Geruath's citadel at Seghar were still far too recent for such an idle jest, if jest it had truly been at all.

Smiling a mirthless smile, he very gently closed his ringed left hand on the door's iron handle and increased the pressure to an inward pull. Nothing happened. He relaxed a little, then pushed out. Again nothing. Tentatively he tried sliding it sideways.

Then shrugged with resignation and wrenched back with all his strength and weight behind it.

The door wasn't stiff, unoiled or jammed as he had allowed himself to hope. It was, as he had feared instead, locked and bolted top and bottom—and the jolt of his failed attempt to open it sent silver spikes of anguish into every joint from wrist to shoulder.

Aldric shrugged again, although this time it was really more of a suppressed wince, and would have sworn had swearing helped at all. Then as he considered the matter and flexed his arm to work the twinges out of it, he swore anyway. Gently—but with sincerity.

'Idiot,' he muttered under his breath. 'Should have known. Now after all that racket, who else knows?'

It was talk for the sake of hearing a familiar voice and nothing more. Despite his self-accusation, Aldric suspected—no, he was quite sure—that whoever wanted and needed to know he was awake knew it already. If he was a prisoner—or a guest, though to his knowledge not even the Drusalan Empire required that guests be kept under lock and key—then it was unlikely that the past few moments' activity would have gone unnoticed for long.

But who would notice? And who would they tell?

The Alban grimaced and recovered Widowmaker's scabbard from where his unsheathing flick had sent it; the *taiken*'s blade ran home with a steely whisper as he sank to both knees on the floor. Laying the weapon across his thighs, he sat back on his heels, drew the *cymar*'s folds more closely around his chest and composed himself to wait.

He did not wait long—and had not expected to.

Privately, Aldric reckoned that no more than ten minutes had passed from the first signs of life in his room to the series of metallic clicks as its door was unlocked. At the sounds he rose smoothly, swiftly and silently, and as he regained his feet and spaced them for balance his right hand tightened on the longsword's hilt, giving it that minute twist which freed the locking-collar. Widowmaker seemed to tremble with eagerness in his grip, like a poised falcon; she would leave her scabbard at a touch now, as blindingly quick as a striking snake.

And as deadly.

The woman in the doorway knew it. She stood quite still, not in the least afraid if the smile on her full red lips meant anything; but she had been told, indeed, warned at some length, about how fast and dangerous this young man was, and she had taken note of that—as she now took note of many other things about him while her gaze swept with dawning speculation across his exposed-yet-tantalisingly-concealed and at last so very *alive* body. She had unashamedly drawn back the covers as he lay unmoving in drugged sleep, and had been mildly attracted to him then; but how very different this Alban looked now that lithe, powerful muscles slid and shifted purposefully under his tanned skin. Yes. Different indeed. For just an instant the hunger in her eyes was as naked as his body, beneath the *cymar* which she had spent a quarter-hour selecting from her brother's wardrobe. *And not a minute of that time was wasted.* She decided to treat this one with all the caution he deserved, and a little more besides. For the present, at least.

Aldric stared at her with eyes that were narrowed and watchful in a face which he had schooled to expressionless immobility. His whole demeanour was as poised and wary as a startled cat, ready to lash out or sidestep at a heartbeat's notice, because although a blurred and hazy memory told him that he had seen this woman twice before, it was only the first sight of her that he recalled with any clarity. She had been entering a room on that occasion too; but flanked by armed and armoured guards.

Well, there were no guards this time. And that was her mistake, because if need be he could reach her and seize her, and lay the persuasive length of Widowmaker's bitter edge against her expensively scented throat before that throat could start to shape a cry for help.

And then, *then*—though the idea repelled him with its total lack of any honour—he could bargain for his freedom. With her life.

'You are awake.' *Lord God and the Holy Light of Heaven, what a voice she had!* The fact was self-evident and made her words unnecessary; but their very triviality did something to ease the taut silence which clogged the bedroom's atmosphere like smoke.

'I am.'

'Good.' It was scarcely a conversation sparkling with brilliant wit. She hesitated, studied him from head to foot again with the same frank appraisal as before and nodded to herself. 'You look very well . . . rested. And healthy.'

Aldric felt uncomfortable under that stare. 'I would feel more at ease with my clothes on, lady. Where are they?'

'They were foul. Stained, torn.'

'—And mine. I asked where, lady, not what. I want my own clothes, not this—this horse-blanket.' A very superior horse-blanket and one of considerable value, but that no longer mattered. Aldric knew he was trying to be ironically humorous, and knew too that he was not succeeding very well, for the emotion which his not-quite-humour concealed insisted on bubbling to the surface. That emotion was anger.

Anger directed at her, for the way in which his memory jarred with what he saw and heard. And anger which fed on itself as his uneasiness made itself manifest in an abruptness which was not the courtesy expected of a guest. Or was he a prisoner after all?

'My clothes,' he repeated more quietly. Then, softly, 'Please.'

'Better.' She said it with a sort of gratitude, not in the bantering tone of one who has scored a point. 'Of course you realise, *'tlei*, that such a request can be fulfilled quite easily.' The purring, husky tone was back in her voice and added a honeyed darkness to her words which had not been there before. She clapped her hands together twice and stepped to one side.

And a man came in: a man who made Aldric take an instinctive snap-step backwards through no more than simple caution. Not because of who the man was—just a liveried serving-man, no more—but what he was: huge. He stood head and shoulders taller than the Alban, and those shoulders were of a piece with the rest of him—bulky with corded muscles whose outlines were plain even through his clothing. He was the sort of excellent bodyguard whose presence alone was a weapon, the kind of man it would be wiser not to cross. And by the expression on his face, he had both understood and disapproved of the way in which his mistress had been addressed.

In his arms, precisely folded, were clothes which Aldric recognised: They were black, and leather for the most part—tunic and breeches and boots. But there was something else as well, and it was not leather but fur: a *coyac* of black wolfskin. Aldric stared at it and felt a small, strange, unaccountable roiling deep in the pit of his stomach. In his secret heart of hearts he had hoped. He had wished . . .

Of everything I own, I would as soon that one was burned to ashes. And the ashes scattered on the western wind.

And yet he could not think of any reason why.

With utter disregard for their neat folds, his clothes were dropped unceremoniously onto the bed, and one boot slid with a thump to the floor. The right boot, of course. It balanced upright for a moment, then toppled over. And a knife fell out of it with an accusing tinkle which drew all eyes.

It was Aldric who looked up first, with a feeling that despite their expressions of astonishment the throwing-knife's presence came as no surprise to anyone. The whole affair had probably been stage-managed from the start, as deliberate as the choosing of the overrobe he wore. Stooping, he set the boot upright again, picked up the knife and turned it over in his fingers once or twice, then unconcernedly returned it to the sheath stitched inside the long moccasin's laced and buckled top.

'Thank you.' The remark was addressed to nobody in particular, and so neutrally voiced that it was impossible to tell if he was pleased, or amused . . . or blazing with anger.

The big servant glowered at him, and though he had known it all along, Aldric noticed as if for the first time the diagonal belt crossing his chest which was the shoulder-strap of a wide-bladed regulation army pattern shortsword. So she has an escort after all, he thought. Of sorts. But one I could take easily. Just meat. He met the other stare for stare and it was the bigger man whose gaze dropped first.

Not a flicker of satisfaction at the small victory showed on Aldric's face, because he was growing more and more certain that someone, somewhere, was testing him for a purpose of their own.

But what was it?

'Get out.' His command was so quiet that it was little more than an exhalation of breath. The servant hesitated; then, although it required a glance towards his lady and her nod of assent, he left without further protest and closed the door behind him as a good servant should. But the woman remained.

Aldric paused in the act of laying out his clothes on the bed and flicked a look towards her, then gestured with one finger. A little circle, drawn horizontally on the air between them. 'Turn around, lady,' he amplified, and waited until she had complied.

'I had not,' she said to the wall, 'expected a man of men who value honour to be also a man who threatens unarmed women.' There was just a hint of disapproval in her voice.

'I didn't threaten you. Not even once.'

'You did—and I saw you. You held your sword and you looked at me, and you wondered if maybe you might have to put the blade to my neck before you could get out of here. Oh yes.'

'Was I so obvious?' Aldric made the concession sardonically. 'Ah well . . .'

'I hadn't expected it of a guest in my house,' she repeated.

This time Aldric said nothing. He dropped the *cymar* to the floor and drew fresh linens from one of his saddlebags, then busied himself working one leg into the tight-fitting trousers of heavy cotton he wore beneath his riding-breeches.

'And I hadn't expected such a one to need long underwear.'

The Alban froze, balanced on one leg with the other raised beneath him like a stork, half in and more importantly half out of the garment in question, and he blushed all over. Apart from his left leg from the knee downward, that 'all over' was patently beyond dispute. His head snapped round and it almost certainly turned faster than the Drusalan woman had expected, for he caught the vestiges of an expression which later and calmer consideration insisted that he had not been meant to see.

She was looking over one shoulder and there was an impish smile on her lips. But in her eyes there was a glitter of truly malicious amusement. It wasn't honest good-humour, rightly created by her ridiculous, inaccurate but very apt observation. Oh God, no. It was a nasty wallowing in the undignified embarrassment which her words had caused. That wallowing, and the pleasure which stemmed from it, were stifled even as Aldric became aware of its existence—but the very fact that he had seen and recognised it troubled him.

'Not underwear, my lady. Trousers. Proper trousers.' He hitched the trews up and fastened them firmly at his waist. 'Try wearing combat leathers next your doubtless-so-tender skin some time,' he continued waspishly, 'then ask again about why I wear these. If you still have to.'

Without further comment, or indeed further insistence that she look away since it was plain she had no intention of doing any such thing, Aldric finished dressing in clean clothes from the skin out. Somebody had been decent enough—if that was really the word he wanted—to shave him and bathe him whilst he was unconscious, so why not? Loose white shirt and knee-length hosen were followed by the black leather of breeches, boots and tunic. And then finally, unwilling to wear it but more unwilling still to let the woman see his reluctance, he pulled on the wolfskin *coyac*.

Its fur was as he remembered it on that rainswept day when it had first been pressed into his armoured hands, as a payment for the death of a man who might at another time or in other circumstances have been his friend: deep, rich, warm, and redolent of the herbs which Drusalans liked to strew in their clothes-chests. Yet underneath it all was the faint reek of fire. And of spoiled, rotting flesh.

She watched in silence, impressed despite herself as he enclosed himself in a black that was made still deeper by the few points of contrast against snowy fabric or burnished brightmetal. On someone else it might have approached the melodramatic; but there was a melancholy about this man, an introspection and a brooding which stifled ill-chosen remarks at source. Instead the woman said, '*Combat* leathers, Alban? Surely you don't . . . ?'

'. . . intend to do without them, or my weapons? No. Not until I'm clear of this place. And much more confident of the company that I keep.' His eyes met hers, feline grey-green and gemlike sapphire blue, each probing for reality beneath the façade of studied, obviously false ironic humour. 'May I be entirely open with you, lady?'

'By all means.' That sardonic undertone was not a pleasant thing to hear in any pretty woman's voice, and especially hers. Because she was so pretty. No—beautiful. Naturally beautiful; and expensively beautiful.

And she knew the power it gave her.

'I don't trust you, lady—I'm sorry, but there it is. I have what you might call a feeling about this whole affair, from the fire at the tavern to your apparent generosity. For which I thank you. But I can find no proof. Nothing I can hold, nothing I can be sure of. So I must accept your motives at face value.'

'Now that is uncommonly kind of you.' Her words were flat and the thought behind them vicious, but even though her tone scoured his ears like ground glass Aldric was glad he had made himself quite plain. At least he had proved that he was not quite as naïve as she might have thought. Though she was still so very, very beautiful.

'And if you did not accept, *hlens'l*?' It was the first time he had heard her use that particular Drusalan word amongst the smoothness of her Jouvaine, and it jarred. 'What would you do?' Now she was mocking him, subtly but not so subtly that it passed him by.

'What would I do?' he echoed, picking up his *tsepan* with the ghost of a respectful bow, no more than an inclination of his head, before thrusting it through his snugly-cinched weapon belt. There was a moment's hesitation, as though he was considering his next words; and in that hesitation he lifted Isileth and looped her cross-strap across his shoulder, hooking it low so that the longsword rode diagonally across his back. Her hilt reared alongside his neck like an adder poised to strike, but for all her threatening appearance the *taiken* was being carried in peace posture. It was a courteous gesture and a compliment of sorts, one which would be understood by whoever had set the longsword on her stand with her straps wrapped just-so in accordance with lore and ritual.

But it was also an insult, one so subtle that only the same knowledgeable person would appreciate it—if 'appreciate' was the right word with insults. For wearing a fighting sword like that, in the presence of a suspected enemy, proclaimed unconcern and disdain and announced *I consider you no threat* in elegant cursives clear as the noon sun to those who knew how to read them.

'Do?' he said again, almost tasting the word. The grin which followed was a pleasant thing to see, all white teeth and sparkling eyes—unlike the words which went with it. 'Truly, lady, I have no idea. But I would ask you, now and later—do not press me into finding out. I doubt that either of us would enjoy the revelation.'

He bowed from the waist and it was a false, theatrically elegant sweep of movement which was not an Alban obeisance and was therefore another insult to any who chose to regard it as such. 'And now,' Aldric lifted his saddlebags and hefted them into a comfortable carrying position on one shoulder, 'I thank you for your kindness towards me and I take my leave.'

'Leave, Alban?' Surprise and shock; if they were feigned, then she was as much a talented actress as she was a seductively beautiful woman—and it was undeniably for the latter reason that Aldric wanted to be out of her house, out of her city, out of her circle of influence. One of the worldly-wise savants of history had said: 'It is a wise man who knows his own failings.' Aldric knew his, only too well. 'In the name of the Father of Fires, what are you running away from? Why leave so soon?'

'Because, lady, as you say: I am Alban. I want to go home. And if this is Tuenafen, as I believe, then there should be a ship to suit me in the harbour.'

'I . . . think not.'

Had her voice been amused, or mocking, or sardonic—or indeed, any of several things which Aldric had no desire to hear, then he might just have dropped the saddlebags and drawn on her. Woman or not, pretty or not. Beautiful or not.

But she sounded, looked, perhaps was, sincerely annoyed and regretful. Sufficiently so at least to still what was as reflex a fear-born action as the hunched and bristling back of a wildcat. A *kourgath* of the Alban forests.

But even then he had to draw in a slow, deep breath so that the thunder of his heartbeat would not come vibrating up to leave a tremor in his voice when he said softly, 'Explain.'

'There have been no ships in Tuenafen harbour these two days past. I'm sorry. Truly. Had I but known. With the blow on your head and the drugs which my physician recommended, you were unconscious for almost three days and nights. Oh, Lord Father of Fires, if I had *known*!' Her expression changed, altering as the eddies of several consequent thoughts and considerations fled across it. 'But after all,' she said at last, 'this is really for the best.'

'Is it? What is?'

'You being here with me, and I in your debt.'

'For those damned horses?' The foggy recollection of their earlier and rather one-sided conversation was growing much clearer. 'All I did, lady, was to make a reasonable attempt at killing myself—and to no good purpose.'

She tut-tutted at him and waved one finger in the air, as reproving as any tutor. 'Not without purpose, I insist on that. Those horses weren't just damned, especially the carriage ponies. They were—are, thanks to you—damned fine, damned expensive and damned healthy. I owe you, Alban, yes. Say it is because of the horses.'

'Lady, I don't understand what you're trying to tell me.'

'If there was a ship in the harbour today, now, this very minute, and you went aboard to buy passage for yourself—oh yes, and for your *own* horses—then you would be wasting your time. Because you couldn't afford to. Not since the fire.'

Though he made no sound and had not even formed the words with his mouth, Aldric's question was plain enough in his eyes for her to answer it at once.

'Your money is gone. All of it.'

A chill like the touch of an ice-dipped razor slithered down the Alban's spine and he seemed to see the bars of a cage closing around him. But there was still one possible key that no one knew about. If only . . . He forced his voice to a flat calm. 'How much damage was done? I . . . missed the end of it.'

'Enought and to spare,' she said quietly. 'The tavern was gutted, burnt to a shell. Stables, kitchen, tap-room—and most of the guest-rooms too. Yours among them. Somehow your saddlebags weren't there.'

Yes, they bloody were! He caught the snapping contradiction just in time; let her think she was playing him for a fool a little longer. But his saddlebags were invariably in the same room where he slept, even disregarding the presence of money; they contained the clean clothes and the razor which he needed first thing every morning. So who had moved them?

'. . . they were found at last, and investigated—'

'Of course!' This time he did interrupt aloud, but his sarcasm seemed almost an expected response to her confession and consequently went unremarked.

'Investigated,' she spoke with heavy patience now, 'for some idea of who you were, no more. Because there was a stage when my concern was only to find some true words for your grave-marker.'

Aldric stared at her and his mouth twitched slightly without completing any one of the dozen possible expressions which it might have formed—and not one of them an expression the Drusalan woman would have liked. But for her part she lifted both shoulders in an ostentatious shrug and let it go at that. Why start to worry now? the shrug said. You're still alive, aren't you?

'There was no money in the saddlebags, none at all. Nor in your pockets. If there had been, it would have been given to me for safe-keeping. And yet the innkeeper kept insisting that you were rich. "Free with Imperial silver", were his exact words. Not any more, I'm afraid. Whatever wealth you might have had is melted slag among the ashes of the inn. Now do you understand what I mean when I say that I owe you?'

'I understand that I can no longer pay my own way in the Drusalan Empire,' Aldric returned a trifle frostily. Either the silver in question *had* been destroyed—which was unlikely to a degree—or it had been stolen afterwards to convey that impression.

'Quite so.' She refused to be baited by his tone, which was natural enough in the circumstances anyway. 'Until I repay my debt, you are my guest, Alban. Because otherwise—here at least—you are a pauper.'

'Oh.' That was all. Aldric set his saddlebags down again and allowed his shoulders to sag. Not all of it was pretence; everything was far too neat, far too obviously planned in advance. And far too obviously planned for his especial benefit, if benefit was quite the word he wanted.

But for all her pretended omniscience, the woman didn't know everything. And in that lack of knowledge lay his one hope and his one chance to get himself clear of this mess before the cage was fully shut.

'I want to see my horses, lady; and to check that all my gear is as safe as you assure me. And then I want a look at the harbour anyway.' It felt odd not having used her name once, for all that they had spoken together for so long; but then he didn't yet know it—nor she his. Well, maybe that was for the best. Time enough for names—even assumed names—when they were going to be of some use.

'I'll have a servant escort you,' she said quickly. Too quickly for Aldric's liking.

'I'd sooner go alone.'

'No!'

'No . . . ?'

'No. It would be too dangerous.' He quirked one eyebrow at that. 'You are a foreigner. *Inyen-hlensyarl*. And people are uneasy about foreigners right now.'

His mind went back to the attitudes displayed in the tavern common-room. 'I've noticed that much already. Why?'

'*K'shva sho'tah, 'n-tach chu h'labech.*' 'They fear you, because they fear spies.'

Strange that she could not trust the explanation to Jouvaine, for all that they had spoken it comfortably up until now. Or maybe not so strange at all. In a strange country, inhabited by strange people, the strange becomes ordinary. Or at least acceptable. Without doubt he had found that to be true, in the Jevaiden at least.

'Why,' she asked softly, as if the answer was obvious, 'do you think that your bedroom door was locked?'

Aldric blinked once. He had planned to spring just that very question on *her* and glean what he could from the expression it provoked. But not now; indeed, it required an effort of his own will and facial muscles to prevent the position from being reversed. 'To keep me from running away?' he hazarded flippantly.

The woman stared at him: Was that contempt he saw in her eyes, or was he just imagining it? 'No.' the denial was flat and toneless, 'It was to keep everyone else out. Otherwise . . . Oh, Father of Fires, I don't know. Call it too much caution and let it go.'

'Understood,' Aldric lied, very reluctant to let it go at all. 'Now. To stretch my legs and check my horses. The harbour?'

'Of course.' She turned to leave, then hesitated and swung back with one hand extended. There was something nestling on the proffered palm, a thing of looped steel and silver, partially wrapped in snow-white buckskin.

The spellstone of Echainon.

And Aldric's heart came crawling crookedly back up his throat.

'This is yours. I kept it safe—as I would with anything belonging to a *guest*.' Aldric thought privately that she came down over-heavily on that last word, but passed no remark. 'It's a beautiful gem.'

Gem?

She had called it nothing more; the meaning of the Jouvaine word was plain enough. So the stone had somehow kept its own secret, concealed the eldritch blue glow which would have marked it as much, much more than just a gemstone. Even though he couldn't fathom how or why. Aldric's mind worked rapidly to make his position more secure, to explain away what she might have read from his eyes.

'Not even a gem, lady. Just semi-precious quartz, without intrinsic value even if it is a pretty thing. Of course, it *is* very old and there are those who would set a price on that.'

The glibness with which the lies came to his tongue unsettled him. Almost as if someone—maybe the stone itself, for all he knew—was prompting him and guiding his reasoning for its own protection.

'But it's an heirloom of my family, nobody else's. I inherited it—'

Or stole it? The conjecture in her eyes was plain enough.

'And though nobody else might, yet I consider it to have some small worth.'

His fingertips closed on the talisman, pincering it neatly off her hand and confirming repossession even as he bowed courteously to her. This time there was no suggestion of any insult; there was nothing insulting about a formal Alban Third Obeisance, even this abbreviated version. But the bow gave him opportunity to relax the muscles of his face, which felt as if they were cramping permanently into an expression of careful neutrality. Only the palms of his hands might have betrayed him with their light film of sweat, but the shaking of hands was Gemmel's custom, not his. 'I thank you, lady.'

The meaning of his hesitation was obvious enough. 'Call me Kathur, Alban. Everyone does.'

'Apt enough,' said Aldric, allowing himself to smile. 'Kourgath-*eijo*, of . . . south and west of here.' Now it was Kathur's turn to smile at his small double witticism, both of them content with their exchange of lies. He had told her only that he was named for the lynx-cat on his heavy silver collar, and anyone with wit would realise that this was no more than a nickname; south and west took in a sizable slice of the Empire, as well as Vreijaur and the independent city states of Jouvann. An answer, in truth, that answered nothing.

Her reply had been as vague, thought Aldric as he took his leave. Kathur, indeed! So she had been named—or chosen a name—for the rich colour of her hair. Because *en-K'thar* in Drusalan meant 'the fox', and she had given him the feminine equivalent with its soft shift of vowels. *In-K'thur* meant no more or less than 'female fox'.

The Vixen.

FOUR

The Hour of the Fox

Aldric reached out and gave the door a single firm push. It swung inward, silently, and a broad bar of dusty golden light speared past him into the gloomy stable, pinning his shadow against the deep straw on the floor. He remained in the doorway for several minutes, not moving, saying nothing, just watching the hard-edged contrasts of sunlight and darkness and half-expecting sudden movement.

More than half-expecting. Widowmaker was hooked in battle position now, close in to his left hip on her silver-plaqued weaponbelt, and his right hand had returned to her hilt after opening the door with a blurred flick that was too fast and precise for accident.

His caution was not required, for slowly—as his eyes became accustomed to the dimness within—they were able to see that everything was in order. Exact order. And that very neatness made them go narrow and flinty.

The horses were safe. The harness was safe (*good!*). The pack-saddle and its armour-boxes were safe—though doubtless carefully searched.

All safe. Everything he owned—except the silver which would have taken him out of here at a time of his own choosing. Yes, a selective fire indeed. Who set it? Not a flicker of the sardonic thought showed on his face for the interested scrutiny of the man who stood nearby. The promised escort.

And the expected spy.

All of his suspicions were confirmed now; not that they were meant to be allayed for long, or indeed at all, by so transparent an excuse. But if the inn had indeed been fired deliberately as the first step to getting him right where somebody—*who?*—wanted him, then it was an act of such casual ruthlessness as to take the breath away—the act of somebody who cared nothing for consequences. Or because of who supported them, didn't *have* to care. And that thought was the most frightening at all.

Aldric walked lightly inside and patted Lyard's questing muzzle as the big Andarran courser shifted in his stall, recognised the one man in this whole place he trusted absolutely and demanded attention. Aldric gave the black stallion an apple, autumn-wrinkled but still sweet, which he had filched from a fruit-bowl as he left Kathur's house, then for fairness' sake gave another to the pack-horse and crunched into a third himself as he scanned the stable building. His gaze swept over fresh bedding, noted new grain and clean water; he smelt the sweet and slightly dusty aroma which told him the place was well-aired and dry, and nodded faintly with reluctant approval, honest enough with himself to admit that he had wanted to find fault somewhere. He watched as the horses noisily consumed their presents, then walked slowly towards the tack set on a wooden frame at the far wall, turning his head to stare arrogantly at Kathur's servant.

'How far to the harbour?' He asked the question around a mouthful of fruit, deliberately rude.

There was no answer and Aldric tentatively considered repeating himself in Drusalan—even though the apple clogging his mouth could prove a challenge when speaking that guttural, slipshod language, especially when it was a language he had been at pains to prove he neither spoke nor understood. He decided not to bother. 'I'll walk anyway.'

He neither knew nor cared if he was understood, for as he spoke he stroked the flat of one hand casually over the elaborate, expensive tooled leather of his high-peaked saddle. More expensive than any footslogging or carriage-riding Drusalan could understand; his touch was that of a man sliding his hand across the naked body of a lover, and with reason.

He was still in control of his own fate.

The embossed pattern was a formal, elaborate and classic design for horse furniture, an abstract design of interlacing arabesques, and it would have required a more expert eye than existed outside two or three centres of scholarship—or else the systematic and absolute destruction of a plainly undamaged saddle—to discover the single welt which was fractionally thicker than all the others. Its very presence—*and* ensuring that nobody, not even Gemmel his own foster-father, knew of the discrepancy in the pattern—had cost Aldric three and one-half pound's weight of raw gold ingots. He had paid for the work two days after a particularly unpleasant conversation with no less a person than King Rynert himself, and had considered the metal well spent.

For within the slightly-too-thick-for-authenticity length of leather was a cylinder of parchment, rolled as thin as a goose-quill. A letter—and no ordinary letter, even on this far from ordinary mission for the king. Its very presence set the young Alban's mind a little more at rest. Let my lady Vixen say whatever she pleased about the state of his finances: he could afford to buy a rapid, secret passage after all.

Or a ship. Aldric thought a moment and consciously had to will the grin from his lips. Ship, nothing! The realisation had not occurred until now. He could buy an entire merchant fleet!

For the letter was indeed very far from ordinary; it was credit scrip drawn on what Aldric had decided was the largest and wealthiest merchant guild in the northern Empire. A note of hand good—if need be—for thirty thousand Alban deniers' worth of bullion gold.

Despite what Rynert the King had opined on that subject, Aldric had been undisputed master of Dunrath and *ilauem-arluth* Talvalin for long enough—just long enough—to make good use of the fact. He wondered if anyone had yet noticed the guild-stamps in Dunrath's treasury which effectively depleted it by one-third; and had to resist the desire to laugh out loud.

Despite his reconfirmed wealth, Tuenafen made Aldric uneasy. Anywhere in the Western Empire would have had the same effect. Young Emperor Ioen and his rebellious Grand Warlord were heading inexorably towards an armed confrontation after the sudden and mysterious deaths which had struck the Imperial Court like a plague—or, as some fanatics proclaimed, the retribution of an outraged Heaven. The deaths had begun with Crown Prince Ravek, killed in a hunting accident which many believed was no accident at all, and had moved like a scythe in wheat through courtiers, councillors, advisors and ultimately to the Emperor himself who was found dead—of poison, said some; of another sort of excess altogether, said others—on a concubine's couch in the Pleasure Palace at Kalitzim. And until their sudden demise, all had been puppets who danced most obligingly when *Woydach* Etzel pulled on the appropriate strings.

The Emperor's surviving son, Ioen, had suddenly found himself thrust to centre stage in a political drama for which he was totally unrehearsed; and that had raised certain suspicions about the passing of his father and his brother, for all that four years had separated their deaths. Not that the boy himself was accused; at the time of his accession to Crown Prince he was sixteen and hardly capable of such ruthlessness. But his guardian and mentor was: Lord General Goth was capable of anything he could justify—and recent months had shown him remarkably able to discover reasons for what he did.

Reports were rife of an assassination here, a kidnapping and imprisonment there and of skirmishes far more serious than the clashes between partisan gangs which Aldric had witnessed once or twice in other towns. It had already happened in Tuenafen, for the consequences were plain: broken windows, smashed doorway lanterns—and those as yet undamaged screened from harm by shutters or by grilles of heavy mesh. Minor streets were sealed by barriers and main thoroughfares had checkpoints manned by the city militia— armed men empowered to stop, search and if need be detain any who aroused their suspicions.

The atmosphere was tense, strained, brittle as thin ice, yet to Aldric's surprise people were going about their business in an ordinary way. It was only when he surreptitiously listened to a few conversations that he realised how false that first impression had been. They talked about what was happening in the Empire: the political divisions, the religious schism of the Tesh heresy—but always in roundabout terms that were vague, ill-defined and comfortable. "Dissent'. 'Difficult times'. 'Troubles'. But never the obvious.

Civil war.

Almost as if by not naming the actuality, they could deny that it existed. But their laughter when it came was forced and over-loud, and they had an unpleasant tendency to follow strangers with their eyes while never looking fully at them. Aldric had caught such sideways glances more than once, out

of eyes that flinched away directly his own gaze met them.
And it made his skin creep.

Somebody, somewhere, had told him why, and it was a
reason so ridiculous that he had given it no credence then.
Then. Now, he wasn't so sure. His taste in clothes was the
problem; his preferred black and silver garments apparently
reflected partisan support—for *Woydach* Etzel the Grand Warlord, of all people!—and that, with his foreign air, was
enough to influence any who saw him. No one in the Empire
was neutral; either they approved of the way he dressed—or
somebody, somewhere, would find him so provocative that he
would end up knifed. Purely as a form of political statement,
of course, and with no personal animosity intended, as if that
mattered.

The fact that any political extremist attacking Aldric while
Isileth Widowmaker rode openly across his back would find
himself sliced in half—purely as a reflex defensive response,
of course, and with no personal animosity intended, as if that
would carry weight with an Imperial court—was small comfort. That was not the way to fade unobtrusively into any
background.

But it would soon be Aldric's name-day, and he planned to
be alive and healthy on that day to celebrate it properly. If
that meant borrowing enough money from Kathur to buy
himself new clothes, then so be it; after all, she did keep
insisting how much she was in his debt.

In twenty-three days he would be twenty-four years old: a
quarter century, near enough, although there had been many
times when both he and others had doubted aloud that he
would ever attain so venerable an age. It would be ironic,
therefore—no, it would be downright stupid—if some fanatic
with a belt-knife managed to accomplish what Duergar, and
Kalarr, and Crisen (and all their respective minions) had
failed to do, all because of an unfortunate choice of dress.
Light of Heaven, the Alban thought as he mentally reviewed
the list again, *were there so many?*

Then all of his random thoughts jarred to an abrupt, shocked
standstill as he strolled around a corner and took in his first
view of Tuenafen harbour—and the things that had got there
before him.

Battlerams. Three of them, for the love of . . .

Feeling like a cat gone mousing in an occupied kennel,

Aldric slackened what had once been an eager pace and shaded his eyes with one hand, scrutinising the anchored warships sourly and remembering his encounter with the *Aalkhorst*. That memory was anything but reassuring.

No, not three, he corrected silently as another predatory shape slid with heavy grace around the sea-wall. Four. Four fully armoured first-rate ships-of-the-line, each of whose seven steel-sheathed turrets contained a chain-geared repeating catapult capable of reducing an enemy vessel to matchwood and drifting splinters. He knew; he had seen what they could do.

Aldric watched the new arrival as she came into harbour. Although long manoeuvring sweeps had been deployed from oarlocks near her waterline, they were extended clear of the water and served only to give the battleram the look of some monstrous, malevolent insect. Only her spritsail was rigged. But that small white sail was puffed like a pigeon's breast by a wind from astern the ship, despite the offshore breeze which raised choppy ripples and sent them straight toward the oncoming bow.

It appeared that, despite the Empire's stringent legislation against sorcery, the Fleet's requested waiver of such restrictions was still effective. This warship, and perhaps her consorts as well, had a witch-wind charmed into her sails. She could go wherever she pleased, whenever she pleased, regardless of the irritating vagaries of real weather; and she could do it far, far faster than any honestly propelled vessel could hope to match.

Now if only he could see whose side these brutes were on . . .

But they had stowed their sails, struck their colours and displayed no marks of allegiance anywhere on their reptilian hides. There was a nameplate clamped to the flank armour of the new ship's hull, but that was of little use for two reasons: firstly, it would require a knowledge of the Imperial fleet from coastal tenders up, to work out whether Emperor or Warlord owned any given vessel; and secondly——

Aldric couldn't read Drusalan. Oh, speak it—at least in the formal mode—yes; that was straightforward enough. But the language was written in a different alphabet from that shared by Alban, Jouvaine, Vreijek—for no other reason than sheer perversity, he thought sometimes. And they only wrote characters for consonants; vowels were represented by dots, bars and chevrons, nothing more.

At least the merchant guilds had more sense. A swift glance along the waterfront revealed what he had come to check: a painted wooden sign above a doorway which bore the same crest as his credit scrip—and as that stamped into a great many bars of Talvalin gold. The glance was very quick indeed, for Aldric could feel the escort/spy close up behind him, doubtless watching for anything worth reporting back—such as excessive interest in routes of departure from the Empire. Well, he would have little to tell apart from the fact that Albans were unsettled by the presence of the military. Since that held true for most Imperial citizens as well, it was not information with a great deal of use.

Until he knew more about the whys and wherefores of what had brought the warships here at such an inopportune time, Aldric considered that it might be prudent if he got off the public street and awaited developments somewhere more secluded. Kathur's house was one such place—indeed, so far as Tuenafen was concerned, it was the only place he knew.

There was a splash and a clatter of anchor-chain from the harbour; sailors yelled instructions at each other as they secured the new battleram at her moorings and began to warp her alongside the others. Aldric looked incuriously towards the men as he began to retrace his steps, then at the ship itself. Dear God, but she was huge!

The salt-stained carapace of armour had been thrown open in many places now, and two crewmen emerged from a hatch to unclip the vessel's nameplate and carry it below. By now he was close enough to see the three uncial characters which spelt out the warship's name, and to catch a brief glimpse of the geometric patterning of vowel values. It meant more to him as abstract art than as a written word, and he was reluctant even to hazard a guess at how it would be pronounced aloud.

Something like *Te'Na'R*, probably.

In the early evening a bank of fog came rolling in off the sea, and as it overlaid Tuenafen with a damp grey blanket the deep boom of a warning gong began to throb up from the harbour. Sitting cross-legged amid the rumpled quilts of Kathur's bed, Aldric listened to its sonorous single note and sipped at a glass of wine he did not want or need, trying far too late to ignore the warm and silky skin which pressed against his own, languid and apparently sated at long last. He was acutely aware of a sensation which might have been his own shame.

Kathur rolled lazily onto her back and scored one long-nailed finger up and down his naked thigh, watching him intently through the tangled fringe of her copper-gold hair as she inhaled the sweet smoke curling up from burners near the bed. Something about his expression made her giggle drowsily. *'Ka s'lai immau-an, t'eijo?'*

'Nothing's the matter with me!' The denial came out far too hard, far too fast. 'Nothing at all.' He was lying, and they both knew it. Aldric did not look down; the Drusalan's bronze-and-milk-white body was a definite, indeed an all-consuming distraction to a mind which already had more than enough to deal with. And Kathur, following the latest fashion of the Warlord's court in Drakkesborg, had blended *ymeth* with her favourite bedroom incense.

Sex had not been his intention when he returned from the harbour; far from it. The sight of four Imperial battlerams of an uncertain provenance, and all that they suggested, had squelched any such thoughts as effectively as navel-deep immersion in a bath of ice-melt.

It had not been his intention when she stepped out of her bedroom just as he walked past in the corridor outside, even though in fairness he had already entertained the notion of a visit once or twice.

It had still not been his intention even when he saw what she was wearing: a low, clinging, sidesplit robe that blatantly flaunted her full-breasted, leggy beauty—even in bare feet she was a handspan taller than he was—and whose rich, not-quite-transparent satin clung like a crimson second skin and made it enticingly obvious that there was nothing but Kathur and perhaps a touch of costly perfume underneath.

But when she had reached out without a word and enfolded his face in palms and fingers and bent forward to lay a kiss upon his mouth, his ironclad celibacy had become a thing of wind and straw. In itself and in its apparent brevity the most chaste of gestures, that kiss had yet contained a probing pressure of her tongue between his lips and then the swiftest promissory nip of teeth, hinting at pleasures undefined but yet to come. After such a kiss even the sternest Imperial *politark* would have torn his holy books and smashed his holy ikons and gone a-running after her.

No; up to that point, when temptation had become more than fevered flesh and pounding blood could bear, he could lay hand on heart and swear that it had not been his intention to bed the Drusalan woman. But it had been Kathur's intention all along. *She* had bedded *him*—and had done so most efficiently.

Efficiently . . . ? Yes, that was the only word for it. All the others—pleasurably, inventively, exhaustingly—were true enough, but faded into insignificance beside the icy technical brilliance which she had displayed in bed. As if following the steps of a complex but much-practised dance—*is that what rankles, Aldric?*—she had known exactly when and how hard to employ the emphases of tongue and teeth and nails and closely-clutching thighs.

Riding aids, he thought cynically. But it was the detached skill with which she had aroused him that would not leave his mind—as if she had regarded his initial reluctance as a defiant challenge to be overcome, nothing more. For just once, almost by accident amid the sweaty squirming of their lovemaking, he had chanced to stare for three full seconds straight up into her eyes. That memory remained with him, and would for a long, long time. Because there had been nothing in those eyes but the spasmodic glitter of physical pleasure. That was all. The rest was an emotional blank.

Even Gueynor, once of Valden and now mistress of Seghar, had felt more for him than Kathur did—and *she* had been paying for her own much-loved uncle's quick and painless death. Something of which Aldric had not learned until much later.

Efficiently. That was indeed what rankled, what had created the tiny flutter of uncertainty beneath his breastbone. The flutter which might have been guilt at the ease with which he had let himself be manipulated, but which was much, much more. Suspicion burgeoning to certainty that there was another purpose behind what she had done to him, and for him, and only incidentally for herself; a purpose that went beyond simple lust or curiosity or—and he would have accepted the reason gratefully, had it been true—boredom on a foggy afternoon.

With Gueynor or with Kyrin—*Kyrin, O my lady, O my*

love, the words came back to him again like a religious chant,
where are you now?—he would have been lying here, but
cuddled together with a quiet affection he would never feel
for this Drusalan woman. Kyrin had been right when once
she had called him a romantic. Because Kathur made love—
and the word 'love' was itself a lie—like a whore; all was
sensation, nothing was emotion, because emotion and ten-
derness took time and to a whore time was money. Aldric's
mind flashed to the first time he had seen her, that night when
she stalked into the tavern common-room in her furs and with
her guards to either side. He had thought then that she was
either noble or a top-rank courtesan; now his opinion was
more certain.

'*Ai, irr' hem ymau tleiyan.*' The spiked fingernails coursed
his spine. 'Care killed a cat, my Kourgath. What's troubling
you?'

He shivered—only a marble statue would not—and set his
glass aside before suddenly-trembling hands spilled its contents all across his lap. Not, he thought with another luxurious shudder, that such an accident would inconvenience Kathur
in the slightest. Not in her present mood.

'*Dakkoyo-do, h'lau-ei,*' he said quickly, releasing himself
from her embrace. 'I told you: nothing's the matter. I was
thinking, that's all.'

'*Ehreth kraiy'r hla, Kourgath-tlei.* Then think about me.'
She made the suggestion in a voice like cinnamon and hot
honey as she relaxed into an inviting sprawl of naked limbs.
Aldric looked, and swallowed hard, and closed his eyes and
took a deep breath—instantly regretting the last as a double
lungful of dreamsmoke hit him, daubing rainbow patterns
across the insides of his eyelids and through the echoing
caverns of a suddenly all-too-spacious skull.

'*Doamne diu!*' he snarled softly. It needed no translation—
one blasphemous expletive tends to sound very much like
another—and Kathur laughed at him, then sprinkled another
pinch of *ymeth* on the nearest censer. 'Lady, stop that . . . !'
Aldric began to protest, then turned it into a half-hearted
shrug. 'I'm not as used to this stuff as you are.'

'But it should take your mind off those battlerams in the
harbour.'

'Battlerams?' His face was a masterpiece of innocent in-
quiry, a reflex reaction that was entirely wasted because her

spy had been with him at the time and had apparently managed to make his report already.

'Battlerams,' she repeated laconically.

'The Imperial military doesn't like Albans much,' Aldric said, as if that explained everything.

'To the Black Pit with the military! I like at least one Alban very much indeed.'

'Thank you, my lady. But . . . whose ships are they anyway?'

Kathur's mouth went very thin for maybe half a second and her heavy-lidded eyes flicked wide open, but Aldric, staring pensively at the crawling glow of sparks in one of the incense burners, missed it all. 'Curiosity,' she said carefully, 'killed a cat, *hlens'l.*'

'Care, now curiosity,' Aldric smiled, a smile as bright and false as paste jewels. 'What have the Empire's proverb-makers got against cats anyway?'

Kathur didn't seem particularly amused. 'And why the sudden interest in battlerams?' she wanted to know. 'You've been fretting over something ever since you came back from the harbour. Tell me about it; a sympathetic ear might make you feel better.'

'And sympathetic lips?' It sounded evasive even to him, and Kathur didn't deign to respond; she merely stared, and waited for an answer. Aldric met that stare for maybe a minute; then he gave up, lay down with his head cradled on crossed arms and told her . . .

Not what she wanted to know, but what he wanted her to know, which was not the same thing at all. Nearly—but not quite. He knew from previous experience that a carefully edited version of the truth sounded more convincing than the best-thought-out lie. And right now he had no honour-bound compunctions about misleading her. None at all.

'In the spring of this year,' he began, 'I was a passenger aboard an Elherran merchant galion. Unarmed, of course; it's well known that none of the Elherran vessels carry weapons. But we were attacked nonetheless—by a battleram. She was sailing under the Grand Warlord's crest and colours, but I doubt that had much to do with what happened. Her commander claimed that the galion was running contraband; we were somewhat shot up by then and in no mood to argue. But the marine cadre who boarded searched the Elherran from keel to mizen top without finding a thing. So did the *hautmarin* apologise for his high-handed action and offer recompense for the damage? Did he, hell! Arrogant bastard didn't give a damn!'

'Calm down, Kourgath. It doesn't matter now.'

'No. Not now. Of course not. You're right. But can you wonder that I was . . . uneasy, shall we say?—when I found that pack of bloody commerce raiders in the harbour?'

'I don't wonder at all. But it's better not to wonder about what *They* do—not aloud in public anyway. *They* have many ears. And contacts in the most unlikely places.' Kathur's lips curved in a small, cold smile redolent of many things, and she studied his face for a while as she toyed absently with the silver crest-collar encircling his throat. 'You worry too much,' she concluded, and her voice carried a mocking severity. 'And about other people's problems. That's a bad thing. Positively unhealthy while you're still within the Empire's borders. So we'll have to find something to occupy that over-busy mind of yours. Something to help you relax.'

'Other than *this*!' It was perhaps as well that most of the more subtle nuances of Aldric's intonation were muffled by his own right bicep, so that all Kathur heard was a real or feigned incredulity. That, and the widening of his one visible eye, was enough to make her laugh aloud.

'This, as you so coyly put it, is mere diversion. A pleasant way to . . .' her words faltered for the merest beat—an intake of breath as of something almost but not spoken that the Alban failed to notice—and then resumed smoothly, '. . . to pass the time. And also, if you want to view it so, a way for me to convey a little of my gratitude. And a way which you seemed to appreciate.'

Aldric had heard reasoning of that nature before, and didn't much like to hear it again; but given the present circumstances, he forbore to comment.

Kathur nodded, rolled over in bed and reached for a slender silken cord which ran up and out of sight through a brass-rimmed hole in the ceiling; tugged it twice, then twice again, and lay back as if exhausted by the effort. Aldric had watched her, despite his other reservations enjoying the way her sleek body moved; now, as she flopped against the pillows, he hid a smile. 'By the looks of you,' he said virtuously, 'shuttering those incense burners might be a good idea.'

For just a moment Kathur glared at him, ready to be angry if his baiting should be more than just a joke. She had taken quite enough criticism of her private affairs and conduct from her own brother—who didn't know the half of it—without more of the same from this, this *hlensyarl* who was no more than a part of her work. She willingly conceded that he was both a better-looking and a more enjoyable part than many who had preceded him; but ultimately that concession changed nothing.

Her instructions had been concise, straightforward and most certainly not open to other interpretations. *Find. Identify. Hold.* They had been delivered twofold, as was the custom; the first no more than a cursory cipher borne on a pigeon's leg, but the second . . . Ah yes, the second. That had been carried by no less than a weary, dirty horseman in the yellow crest-coat of the Falcon couriers. The very use of a Falcon had told her much about how this mission was regarded even before she read what he had brought her, sealed by lead in a leather pouch.

The whole thing had Voord's touch about it.

The arrogance which had employed a despatch-rider forbidden to all but the Imperial Household; that sense for the dramatic which had prompted the risky gesture. And the arid, clinical precision of the prose which told her in graphic—no, Father of Fires burn it, pornographic—detail, what it was she would be expected to do. But then, that was Voord's way.

He had always been fastidious, had Voord; excessively neat in all that he did, no matter how perverse. Kathur's mind unwillingly recalled the whimpering, agonized, ecstatic night of her recruitment by the Vlechan, and she shuddered with revulsion at the memory even as conscious effort crushed it back down into the dark and dirty part of her subconscious where it was confined.

Then he had been *kortagor*; now he was *hautheisart*, promoted again at the end of summer for something which even yet remained unspecified. What it might have been, the Drusalan woman didn't know and would not dare to guess . . . because if the rumours spoke the truth, Voord was stranger now than ever.

And if so, then what did that make her?

The thoughts tumbled through her mind like images glimpsed on the flicking pages of a thumbed book, so swift as to approach the subliminal. And during those few seconds the Alban's one-eyed gaze remained locked with hers until at last she looked away, almost flinching from the expression on that part of his face which she could see. It was an expression Kathur had not seen before and would as soon not see again, for it seemed cynical, knowing and cold, and it made her feel truly apprehensive of him for the first time in their brief acquaintance.

No. More. It made her feel afraid.

And yet there was another side to the coin, another reason for her to be frightened which had nothing to do with any threat Kourgath-*eijo* might pose to her. Rather the reverse. There was a warm, delicious quivering within her that was more than the familiar aftermath of loving. Much more; she knew that sensation well enough to recognise that this was somehow different. It went beyond the physical, beyond a fever in the flesh and into something which she knew was impossible in so short a time. But which was also unmistakably true.

She was becoming involved.

It was a sense such as she had not felt for any man since . . . since a very long time ago. A sense of responsibility, a feeling that might in time become—Kathur shied away from letting the word form in her brain—love. It was a sense she neither understood nor wanted.

The idea of disobedience crossed her mind for the first time ever, and brought in its wake a nauseating spasm of terror. Disobedience would mean a reckoning later—with Lord-Commander Voord.

But if she obeyed, as she had always done before; if she followed her orders, as she had always done before . . . Then she would have to meet her own eyes in the mirror for ever afterwards, and admit to the guilt and the betrayal and the dishonour she would see reflected there.

She was thinking the unthinkable. And she did not know why.

But had she thought to search amid the tangle of Aldric's discarded clothing, the Drusalan woman might have found a

reason for such unlikely thoughts as those which troubled her
so deeply. For there, concealed from sight in a tunic pocket
yet close enough for her to touch had she known of its
presence, was the spellstone of Echainon.

Had she known, and had she touched, she would have
found the crystal's surface strangely warm against her skin.
Not hot, not painful, but comforting as the sun on a summer
day or the body of a lover in the night. And had she thought
to listen she might even now have heard the song of the
stone, a melodious humming half-heard on the outer edges of
awareness; the sound never heard by concentration, only by
chance.

Had she known, or heard, or touched, or merely looked,
she would have found the crystal suffused with a misty blue
radiance from the hair-fine spiralling of sapphire flame deep
down at its core; and that above all would have answered her
unspoken question as to the source of her strange thoughts.
For the spellstone's light pulsed with a rhythm Kathur would
have recognised at once.

It was the beat of her own heart.

Two men walked slowly through the twilight along a fog-
bound road.

Slowly, for one was no longer so strong as his burly
appearance might have suggested, and his face wore the grey,
haggard look of a man recovering from a grave illness.

Slowly, because the other was white-bearded, old, and
moved as if every one of his many years was a lead weight
borne in the pack strapped to his drooping shoulders. He
leaned heavily on the black walking-stave in his right hand—
yet at the same time appeared to cringe away from any but
the most necessary contact with it. As if the thing was hot
and had burned him painfully, and was only awaiting its
chance to do so again. There were beads of moisture on his
forehead which had not condensed from the fog.

Suddenly—but with a note in his voice which bespoke
resigned anticipation—he cried out and dropped the staff with
a clatter to the ground. Both sounds were flat and dead,
muted by the fog-thick air. He stared at the fallen staff with
something close to loathing on his bearded face, but made no
move to pick it up. Instead he looked wearily at his companion.

'Again?' asked ar Korentin. There was sympathy in his voice.

'Again.' Gemmel rubbed his hands together, trying to soothe away the burning nerve-deep pain. 'It keeps on drawing power. On, and on. Never so much at once as to do me lasting harm, always with enough rest between times for me to recover. And then . . . !' One booted foot shifted as though he considered kicking the fallen Dragonwand; then settled again as he plainly thought better of the idea.

'Why? What does it want with so much power?'

'Your guess, Dewan, is as good as mine. And I don't know. It no longer obeys me. You saw that on the beach in Alba.'

'Then give it what it wants,' said Dewan savagely. 'Give it more than it can swallow. Choke it to death!'

'No! I think not. I have no idea what Ykraith's capacity for stolen energy might be—and I'm frightened to find out. Because I might not survive the experience.'

'Then . . .' The Vreijek hesitated, his brow furrowing as he tried to make sense of the alien concepts of sorcery in a mind not trained to its rules of logic, before committing his idea to the irrecoverable spoken word. 'Then *give*. Not much: just that little you say it always takes, that it has always taken before, despite all you do to prevent it. This time, don't resist.'

'An interesting proposition.'

'Try it. What have you got to lose?'

'My life, perhaps.' With an open hand Gemmel forestalled Dewan's protest—if protest it was, and not another untutored attempt to verbalise the workings of magic. 'But as you suggest—I'll try it. Because anything is better than this. I daren't use the Dragonwand and I'm growing afraid to carry it—but I can't just walk away and leave it. Not here.' He stooped to recover the spellstave, but in stooping caught an odd look of puzzlement on Dewan's face and hesitated: 'What's the matter now?'

'A thought, no more. Before you volunteer the power it so obviously wants, shouldn't you try to work out an answer to what I asked before? *Why?*'

Gemmel jerked his hand away from the Dragonwand as if it had changed to a venomous serpent, and the glare he directed at ar Korentin was equally venomous. 'You con-

tradict yourself as easily as my son!' he snapped. 'Do . . .
then don't do. Make up your mind!'

His earlier reply to that same question—that Dewan's answer would be as right or wrong as his own—was not . . .
quite . . . true. Because Gemmel's mind's eye could recall
the summoning on Dunacre Beach as clearly as if its colossal
bulk was hanging overhead right now. A summoning whose
form was not that which he had intended, but which was most
shockingly appropriate to the name and nature of the talisman
which he had used. A dragon. Summoned by Ykraith.

The Dragonwand.

Gemmel lifted the spellstave with his left hand—the one
which didn't hurt—and stared at the design which patterned it
from end to end as if seeing the inlay of adamant and gold for
the first time. Or as if gaining a new insight from its shape.
And he wondered.

Then in fear and hope, not knowing which feeling was the
stronger, he supported the talisman's dark length on the
palms of both his outstretched hands and built the structure of
an opening-charm in the forefront of his mind. And let his
power, that concentrated inner selfness which made him a
sorcerer first and foremost, rather than a harper or a scholar
or so many other things—although he was all of these and
more—let his power surge through the opened channel into
the fireshot dragon-shape that was Ykraith.

This time there was no pain. Only a sensation of warmth
on his open hands, and a slight tiredness. That was all.
Gemmel raised his eyebrows and turned to ar Korentin with
the beginnings of a smile on his face. It was a wary smile,
but for all that it was a smile which the Vreijek felt justified
in echoing.

'Was I right?' he wanted to know.

'Well done, the untrained mind! Maybe sometimes I'm too
subtle for my own good. Yes. You were right. It didn't hurt
me—and it didn't drain more than I offered, even though the
channelling was wide open.'

'So what use can it make of the power? Have you answered that yet?'

'I think so. Dewan, you know as well as I what this
talisman is called; and where it came from. And what else
was there.'

Ar Korentin's jaw sagged slightly and his gaze jerked south

and west, towards the distant sea lost in the mist and the yet-more-distant island lost over the unseen horizon. 'Ymareth! *Vakk' schh ke' hagh trahann' r da?*'

'No, not awakening. It is awake already; indeed, it has slept lightly if at all since the day that Aldric took this,' he patted the Dragonwand, 'from the Cavern of Firedrakes on Techaur. That young man gained a deal more than he can imagine when Ymareth—'

The spellstave hummed softly, a vibration more felt in the air than heard aloud, and he fell silent. Both men stared at the talisman, Dewan with awe and wonder, Gemmel with anticipation. Neither was disappointed.

There was a soft, expulsive sound like that of a great breath held in too long, and white force burst from the crystalline flame of its carven dragonhead to hang like a captive star between them, bleaching the fog to silver upon which their shadows were smeared with the clarity of charcoal on new paper. A surge of power which even Dewan felt pulsed outward, an unseen ripple in an unseen pond. An instant later there was only the afterglow of a bolt of energy which had ripped through the fog with stunning speed and fled out of sight to leave the dull day duller yet. But both had seen the direction of its flight. South and west. Towards the sea and that which lay beyond.

'Lord God,' breathed Dewan ar Korentin, with respect and disbelief all mingled with the oath.

'No,' Gemmel corrected him, and if he smiled the sad smile which his voice suggested, it was gone when Dewan saw his face again. 'Not "Lord God" at all. Lord Dragon.'

The island had never been an inviting place, not even in the time when it was lush and green with growing things. That time was long past. Now it was black and grey and desolate. What few trees remained more than a memory were charcoal stumps. All else was ash and blasted naked rock.

A thin plume of smoke drifted lazily from the island's solitary mountain, vented in gusts like exhaled breath from the yawning crater where once its tapered peak had been. But there was no other sign of a convulsion in the bowels of the earth: no black rivers of once-molten rock, none of the great bubble-pitted cinders flung out by such activity. There was only the aftermath of heat.

And an air of expectation.

As the short evening of late autumn drew night towards it like a cloak, a star began to brighten in the northern sky where no star should have been. As it brightened, so it moved, until this star that was no star was sweeping across the heavens in a glare of light that laid hard-edged black shadows behind wave-crests and fire-scoured rocks alike. Had any been insane enough to anchor in the island's bay, they would have seen the not-star descend in a great hissing parabola, dragging a tail of silver flame in its wake for all the world like a burning missile shot from some impossibly huge catapult, and they would have seen it plunge with unerring accuracy into the smoking crater, and they would have heard . . .

Nothing.

The silence was absolute; a silence that could almost be touched, as if it were made of heavy fabric. In the course of that long silence the true stars began to glitter in the void, a scattering of splintered diamonds strewn broadcast on a mantle of black velvet.

Ymareth reared from the throat of the hollow mountain with a whisper of iron scales and the single hard, bright clank of a talon striking stone. Wings blacker than the night were unfurled in the trembling air—a huge, leisurely stretching which could seldom be indulged in the confines of the cavern far below. The firedrake's head curved up and back on its great sinuous neck, between the canopy of the wings, and was still.

Ymareth waited for the dawn.

The shudder came from nowhere and from everywhere, a single jolt that was violent enough to bring Aldric's teeth together with a click. His eyes opened very wide, and had he been able to glimpse their pupils in a mirror he would have seen the drug-shrunken pinpricks dilate to huge black discs which were set fair to swallow all the grey-green pigmentation of the irises around them. But he did not need to see, for he could feel—and it was a feeling that he had known before.

Then it had been caused by his own nightmares, dreams strong enough to shock him from his own determined drunkenness. But this sudden surge of heat, as though hot oil was running through the marrow of his bones: this was stronger still. And he didn't even know the reason why.

But one thing he did know was that despite the sweet fumes of *ymeth* in his lungs, despite the strong wine coursing through his blood, despite what should have been a heavy lassitude in all his muscles and which was instead a tingling of urgency, he was in control of his own mind again.

And with that knowledge came the shameful awareness of something he had chosen to ignore, or to blame on other things. His own monumental stupidity! He had been duped, he had been dazzled, he had been trapped—and there had never truly been any excuse for it, though he had always found one.

His own failings. Lord God! They were vices that any man—his mind defined it sickeningly: any *honourable* man—should have ignored, as he might the pain of wounds or fear in battle. For the sake of nothing more than his own pride and private dignity.

Aldric felt the queasiness of self-reproach too long held in check come gurgling to the back of his throat like the dregs of bitter wine. His gaze shot to the silken cord which Kathur had pulled—twice, then twice again: a signal without doubt. But how long ago? Seconds? Minutes? Hours? No, a minute at the very most, for he could still remember that strange, reluctant softness stealing into the Drusalan woman's hard blue eyes just as she turned her face away from his. A minute? He flung himself out of the bed and scrabbled for his clothes.

Kathur rolled over and raised her head to stare at him. Without any surprise. She had been crying, and she was crying now, the great tears gleaming like gemstones below those sapphire eyes which Aldric would have doubted had the ability to weep. And on her face—that beautiful, imperious, wanton face—was an expression of aching loss and desolation such as the Alban had seen only once before.

*Go now, Kyrin-*ain. *The words were all said long ago.*

'So you know.'

He stamped savagely into a boot and began to fight with its lacings. 'Yes-I-*do*!' The last word came out on a grunt of effort. 'And I should have known it long ago!' There was something very close to panic in the way he moved—and it was a panic only barely held in check, for when part of his shirt caught on something he took no time to work it free but simply jerked with all his strength. There was a quick rending noise and he swore viciously in Alban. As he tucked the ripped shirt into his leather riding-breeches, he turned a narrow watchful stare towards Kathur. 'When will they come for me?' It was an idle question, and he had not expected an answer, but . . .

'At—at the Hour of the Fox.'

Aldric lifted an unamused eyebrow. 'How apt, dear Vixen. How bloody droll. And your own idea, I suppose?'

'No, I . . .'

'But that's—' he hurriedly converted the clumsy Drusalan reckoning in his head, '— ten at night. Two hours from now. So how was I to be kept here? By you? Or by . . .' His eyes flicked once towards the slender signal-cord, and his voice hardened. 'Who did you call?'

'One of my servants.' Kathur paused, but once she had begun the weight of her own guilty confession drove her into saying more. 'My—my bodyguard; the man you met before.'

'Ahh . . .' It was no more than an exhalation of breath, but it came out past an icy smile which grew fractionally wider once Aldric had lifted Widowmaker and looped her shoulder-strap over his head. There was a minute click as he thumbed the *taiken*'s safety-collar clear of her scabbard mouth. 'Then I might just test a theory which crossed my mind when we met before. But only if he gets in my way. Because I'm leaving, lady. Now.' A final glance about the room confirmed that nothing had been left behind—except for the large measure of self-respect which would take him such a long time to regain. Aldric turned to go, and then looked back. 'Anyway, he's late. Just when did you expect him to appear?'

The bedroom door behind him was wrenched open, and above the sudden frantic clamour of alarms inside his head he heard Kathur's response quite clearly:

'Now.'

Aldric didn't pause to marvel at that perfect cue. He convulsed sideways at right-angles to the line from his back to the doorway, and he did so with the thickness of a wolfskin vest to spare. Literally.

Something monstrous plucked a puff of black fur from the right shoulder of his *coyac* just as it wrenched out from underneath the blow, and he heard the *whutt!* of parting air as that same something continued down to smash into the floor.

It was a mace: a flanged, iron-headed horror on a haft almost as long as he was tall, and as it tore free of the floor

with a groan of ruptured timbers he could see that it was
being wielded as easily as he might use a riding-quirt. This
footsoldier's bludgeon was meant to flatten fully-armoured
men like beetles, and if it struck squarely against his unprotected body it would . . .

But that didn't make any sense! Kathur had taken a deal of
trouble to hold him here of what amounted to his own free
will, presumably to deliver him intact and healthy to . . .
someone. So why was this hulking servant so set on smearing
him across the floor? Jealousy? Never mind wondering why—he
was trying to do it and that was enough.

Aldric flinched clear of another ponderous swing; this one
ploughed through a dressing-table, stinging him with splintered wood and the perfumed shards of cosmetic jars. His
eyes went cold. Long years of training took the place of an
instinctive fear-reaction and his right hand flicked to Widowmaker's hilt, gripped, drew, and then faltered with no more
than a double span of blade clear of the scabbard.

Yet completing that draw would have meant a certain kill.

Completing that draw would have extended into *achrankai,*
the inverted cross, first of the classic *taiken* forms and a
movement so ingrained by constant practice that it had become almost a reflex.

Completing that draw . . .

Would have whipped an unseen blur of steel beneath the
servant's chin and down between his eyes. Would have opened
his throat spine-deep and split his face asunder from hairline
to chin in a single splattering instant long before he could
have dodged or blocked. Or even realised what was happening.

Completing that draw would have solved many problems.
So why not?

So why? Aldric shook his head as if dislodging a cobweb
and looked again at Kathur. 'Call him off, lady!' There was
no fear in his voice, nothing that might have been prompted
by cowardice but a faint, elusive undertone that might have
been compassion. And yet the woman said nothing. 'Do it!
Teii' aj hah, tai-ura!'

Kathur returned the stare with blank eyes for just a moment, seeming not to notice his sudden perfect command of
High Drusalan. Then she surveyed the tableau that was her
shattered bedroom: all harsh light and shadow now, the bright
corridor beyond the open door a stark contrast to the inti-

mately dim interior. One of the gilded lamps had been upset, and the thick sweetness of its scented oil was another element of the nightmare which assaulted all her senses. She blinked.

And the stone of Echainon went dull. Perhaps it was the woman's sudden distraction towards her own possessions; perhaps it was Aldric's concern with survival more than personal honour; perhaps it was the weariness of a firedrake and a sorcerer in places far away. Perhaps it was none of these things. But when the stone's light died it was result, not reason, that was important.

Kathur blinked again—stared at Aldric—then said crisply, 'Commander Voord be damned. Kill him.'

A heartbeat's worth of utter shock slowed the Alban's reaction, and maybe the man with the mace had been deliberately, deceptively clumsy in his earlier attacks. Because this time when the great iron cudgel moved, it moved far faster than it had ever done before.

And Aldric dropped on the spot.

If he had moved in any direction other than straight down the weapon would have caught him—and pulped him—somewhere along its horizontal arc; even then he felt a tug at his hair which was not the wind of its passing but the metal shaft itself. The mace-head had gouged deeply, uselessly, across the wall where he had been standing; but it would have gouged there anyway, heedless of the meagre resistance offered by his chest.

'You fool! Kill him now!' There was ugliness in Kathur's voice, the audible equivalent of that expression he had not been meant to see, and as he rolled to his feet with Isileth Widowmaker fully drawn at last, Aldric's lips curled back from his teeth in a snarl of almost animal intensity. It might . . . must . . . have been that wild scramble across the floor which lifted the pelt of the black wolfskin *coyac*; but for just an instant its fur was bristling across the Alban's shoulders as though it were a part of him.

And for that same instant—a freezing, burning, malicious and utterly dishonourable sliver of time—Aldric's mind was flooded with just one consideration: whether he could spare the fraction of a second needed for a snap-step right and the lashing backhand which would carve a memento of his company on Kathur's face that she would carry to the grave.

Then he squashed the notion, dismissing it. Because it was

unworthy of a *kailin-eir*; because it was unAlban; because it was unTalvalin. And because consideration said he couldn't spare the time to do it after all.

The moon is only five days clear of new, dear Aldric. The accusing voice inside his head had Gemmel's intonation. *What would you have done had it been nearer full?*

Aldric exhaled through his nose with a sound like an angry tomcat's hiss. He couldn't have said against whom the anger was directed, and had no wish to dwell on it.

Circumstances forbade that, for the servant was ready for him with the mace poised in what, had it been a sword, would have been middle guard centre. He eyed the man's posture with a gaze that was still flinty with concentration but which had lost the gem-like killing glitter. It had leached out—or something was holding it well in check. Who or what, and why, he neither knew nor questioned. 'Don't blame me for this,' he said in the Jouvaine language, his tone almost regretful.

Then he moved.

Isileth Widowmaker thrust out as precisely as a pointing finger, in low line beneath all the blocks and parries that might have been made from mid-guard, and met only the slightest tug of resistance from firm flesh.

She drove deep, and twisted half around as she withdrew.

The big servant's eyes bulged from his skull and his mouth gaped wide even though he was too shocked to utter more than an unstructured whine. The mace was louder, clanking against the floor as his hands released it to scrabble at ruptured tissue. Then he too fell sideways to the floor. Aldric watched him fall, then flicked blood from his sword with a whipping, economic gesture and returned the *taiken* to its scabbard with an arid whisper of metal on wood. He was smiling.

Through the scarlet-shot grey mist of pain clouding his vision, the fallen servant saw that smile and knew the reasoning which lay behind it. His body, uselessly tensed against the follow-through that would finish him, relaxed. There would be no killing blow. He tried to smile in turn; only a small, twisted grimace, but enough to show that he understood.

He was meant to live.

Widowmaker would make no widow tonight. She had pierced the Drusalan's leg rather than his body, and had passed outside the bone to avoid the great blood-vessel which

ran through the muscles of the inner thigh. It was a fierce
wound, and one which the man would remember for a long
time: the sort of injury which aches at the onset of damp
weather. But he would be alive to remember it, and feel it
ache. And he would recover.

Eventually . . . but not now. Now was for bleeding, and
for hurting—and for realising that the dead do neither.

The man's smile went slack and crooked as his senses left
him, but Aldric had seen the faltering expression and he
nodded, once. His shoulders sagged a little with relief; something which had shown already in his smile and had been
recognised as such. Relief at his own survival; and relief that
Isileth Widowmaker, that ancient and sometimes wilful blade,
had done no more than he intended her to do.

Kathur was still staring at him as he straightened his back,
but now her eyes were blank and held as little emotion as the
sapphire gemstones they so much resembled. Her mouth
worked, trying to form words or maybe curses, but no sound
emerged.

Aldric passed one hand across the ruffled fur covering his
shoulder, and the action was not so much that of settling a
disarrayed garment as of stroking something alive. He remembered, coldly and calmly, how he had wanted to mark
this woman. To hurt her. It was like the memory of actions in
a dream, without weight in waking life. There was a place for
such behaviour, and a time, but it was neither here nor now.
Seghar citadel under the Geruath overlords was both long ago
and far away; but as a small shudder crawled through the
Alban's body he realised that it was not yet long or far
enough.

Inclining his head curtly towards Kathur the Vixen, Aldric
walked from her room without a backward glance.

Thus he did not see the *telek* snatched from a hiding-place
under the mattresses and levelled at his back.

Nor did he see the weapon waver and then drop from hands
which were as powerless to squeeze its trigger as they were to
stem a flow of silent tears. Had he seen, or had he heard a
sob, it might have made some slight difference; or it might
not. But he did not see, and did not hear, and it did not.

Somewhere in the too-quiet house a clock chimed the triple
note which marked the turning of another hour. Unlike their
Alban counterparts, Imperial Drusalan timepieces did not—

indeed, by reason of the named hours, could not—strike a number; they merely drew attention to whatever image was indicated by their single ornate pointer. Aldric did not enter the room to look. He already knew as much as any Alban ever wanted to know about the clumsy, inexact system. But because he did not look, he did not know what hour it was. Or how much time he had to spare for making his escape.

Two hours from now, he had told Kathur. But he had slept a dreamsmoke doze with the sweet smell of *ymeth* in his lungs and her hands and mouth upon his body, and at the instant he spoke the words it had not been two hours but much less than one. And from the striking of the clock he had no time at all. Those chimes had signalled the end of the Hour of the Cat.

And the start of the Hour of the Fox.

Kathur's head drooped over the discarded *telek* and tears coursed down her cheeks, falling onto the weapon's polished maple stock where they humped on the lustrous wood like pearls of great price. She stared at their translucence as if she had never seen a tear before. Not such tears as these. She did not know why she wept, unless it was in fear. The cry of the distant harbour gong rang mournfully in her ears—a one-note song of warning—and Kathur knew she had good cause to be afraid.

Hautheisart Voord was not known for his tolerance towards those who had failed him. And as if her thoughts had power to summon demons, she heard soft feet in the corridor outside.

Kathur looked up, saw the flitting of shadows beyond the door and reached out with one hand for the robe of crimson satin which was now such an inadequate covering. She was wrapped in the flimsy garment as best she could contrive when the first *taulath* drifted like smoke into her room. In the space of a single intake of breath another had joined him: both clad from head to heel in a close-fitting charcoal grey that was almost black and which blended most unnaturally into the shadows near the wall.

Hooded masks left only a narrow strip of facial skin exposed—and their eyes, which to Kathur were like those of night-stalking reptiles. Those eyes stared at her, and for a moment it was not difficult to read the expressions flickering

within them, for they studied—no, they consumed—a woman
whose single garment exposed or emphasised far more than it
concealed.

And a woman whose right hand gripped an Alban *telek*
with every appearance of knowing how to use it.

The *tulathin* exchanged significant glances, but they did
not come any closer. Nor did they say anything to her,
although it was plain despite the masks that they had not
expected to find Kathur alone. The wounded and unconscious
man sprawled on the floor quite as plainly did not count.

Then there were more footfalls, and these were not soft—
they were the firm, decisive steps of one who by reason of
power and authority had no need for secrecy. No order was
spoken aloud, but each *taulath* shifted with disciplined precision, flanking the doorway; they paused one beat, then
snapped to attention and executed the rhythmic movements of
a full parade salute. The hard smack of open palm on chest
and thigh sounded like a premonition of Kathur's future. And
then only if that future was kind.

A back-lit silhouette paused deliberately in the doorway for
dramatic effect before crossing the threshold, and lamplight
danced in sparkling motes from silvered rank-marks on a
vermilion helmet as this third man turned his head slowly to
survey the room. The helmet's deep cheek-guards, nasal and
lowering peak effectively masked his features, but Kathur had
no need to see his face to know who he was.

'Well, my dear lady.' *Hautheisart* Voord spoke with a
deceptive softness. 'And where is he?'

Seconds crawled past, eon-slow, before Kathur could swallow enough terror for her acid-soured mouth to form the
words of a reply. 'Gone,' she said. What else was there to
say? 'He realised—somehow—that he was being kept here.'
Then in mitigation, 'But it was only minutes ago: I was able
to hold him until then . . .'

Voord stared at her, saying nothing, eyes unreadable through
the jagged shadows filling his helmet. 'So. Then you tried to
be clever rather than practical after all.' Another dreadful
silence. Then he turned, ignoring her. 'Tagen, Garet, hear
me: is the perimeter secured?'

'Sir!' The response was simultaneous, that of automata.

'Then go. Both of you. Trawl the nets and bring any catch

to . . . to the harbour. To *Teynaur*. And sail at dawn—whether I am there or not. Understood?'

'Sir!' Another salute and they were gone. Kathur watched their departure with resigned, sick despair in her eyes. The troopers were familiar to her: Voord's honour guard, men who accompanied him everywhere. The executors of his will. Their dismissal was an insult like a slap in the face. She was no threat. Nobody.

Nothing.

The street had been dark and silent, swaddled by layers of grey fog. A figure emerging from the shadows at the far side of the street had walked with quiet purpose towards the shuttered façade of Kathur's house; a house identified at last as the culmination and the goal of a long, weary quest. The figure was cloaked and hooded—nameless, faceless, sexless. But there was the merest suggestion of a sword's outline beneath the folds of that heavy cloak, and the faint scraping of metal that was the sound of armour.

Then the silent stillness was shattered like a flawed glass mirror by the quick hard beat of hooves on stone, and a man on horseback erupted from the stable entry near the house at near-enough full gallop. Before the hooded one could do more than flatten for safety against the nearest wall, the black horse's rider had gathered his mount and slewed it around in a metallic slither as iron shoes all but lost their grip on the slick pavement. Then man and horse were past and away in a swirl of sound and speed.

The figure by the wall straightened rumpled garments and still more rumpled dignity, stared for a few thoughtful seconds in the horseman's wake, then studied the blank house-front as if considering whether to enter and possibly become embroiled in whatever was going on there. A fold of the cloak was flicked aside; and now the presence of both sword and armour was more than mere suggestion.

Two grey-clad men flitted down from neighbouring roof-tops, crouched warily for a bare instant and then flicked into the house through a front door that was plainly left unlocked for just that purpose. Unseen, unsuspected and concealed by the fog-dense shadows, an outline made vague and uncertain by the mantling of a too-large cloak watched with fascination—but wisely made no attempt to interfere.

Especially when a third man, helmeted and clad in full splint-mail, stalked arrogantly towards and inside the house.

'Give me that.' Voord's right hand, gloved with sable leather and red-enamelled steel, was already extended palm uppermost as if a refusal was so unlikely as to be unworthy of his consideration.

But such a consideration had already passed through Kathur's mind with the speed and brilliance of a lightning-flash: not merely refusal, but *use!* Now, suddenly, without any hint of warning. The *telek* was already loaded and cocked, its safety mechanism disengaged, and the crook of her first and second fingers had already exerted three of the required five-pound pull. It would shoot on one pressure, and there was no need even to aim.

And the thought of that two-pound pull turned her belly sick. She could no more kill a human being—even one so patently inhuman as Voord—than she could turn the weapon on herself. And that was something which might be preferable to Voord's company in this next hour. The possibility and the chance of success were gone now, all gone; only acquiescence remained. Kathur's thumb secured the safetyslide; then she reversed the *telek* and laid it softly into the *hautheisart's* waiting grasp.

His fingers closed, and with the weapon's bore pointing at her Kathur half-expected to feel a dart strike home even before she had let it go. But there was no dart. Instead Voord hefted the *telek*'s weight, and its sculpted stock settled as snugly into his hand as a falcon onto a familiar wrist. Carved and shaped for a right-handed grip, it fitted well, and he looked at it with something as close to admiration as any Imperial officer would grant to a thing of Alban manufacture.

'Very fine.' He was speaking mostly to himself. 'Yes. Very fine indeed. But then the Albans always were good at creating things to kill each other.' His eyes met those of the woman and locked with them, like a snake with a sparrow or a weasel with a mouse, and though there was a smile on his lips it did not warm those eyes at all. 'Tell me . . . does it work?'

Now the dart . . . Kathur's body spasmed in anticipation of the tearing impact and her eyes snapped shut in a useless reflex that was no defence at all against the death she faced.

Only when nothing happened did their painted lids flutter open again, reluctantly; she was terrified lest any movement at all would invite the response she dreaded, but more terrified still to remain in the dark.

'I said, does it work?'

'I . . .'

'Does it work?'

Her gaze dared to tear away from the weapon's blank, black muzzle, but Voord's own eyes were as implacable. Whatever answer she gave would be the wrong one.

'*Does it work?*'

'Ohhh . . . dear God, I don't know!'

Voord's teeth showed briefly in a shark's smile. 'Then let's find—' A soft sound at his back broke his words off short and he snapped around with the *telek* poised and ready; then both it and he relaxed. 'Ah . . . You.'

Kathur's servant tried to lean his weight on one elbow alone, unable to take his other hand from the hole which Widowmaker had left in his thigh. Regardless of how tightly those fingers were clutching his own flesh, blood still seeped slowly through them. He stared at the two by the bed, barely seeing them through his pain and not understanding what was going on. But he recognised one at least; and was full of shame. 'M-my lady? I f-failed you, my lady. I failed. Forgive me . . .'

Commander Voord's head came round with the slow deliberation of a weapon-turret on a battleram, and his mouth formed the same silent *O* as the *telek*'s muzzle. The woman made no response by either word or gesture; she already knew how Voord's mind worked. And because she knew, she reached out with a crazy courage that was near to suicidal and clutched the *telek* by its barrel-shrouds. The *hautheisart* stared at her hand, and then at her face with the expression of one confronted by some noxious vermin.

'No!' Her voice was soft, her intonation vehement, pleading. 'Don't. Even he saw no need—'

'He? Meaning the Alban. Didn't what?'

'Didn't kill. Not even in the heat of a fight. Because it wasn't necessary. And it still isn't . . .'

Voord's thin lips moved, stretching to a brief smile before once again forming that sardonic *O*? He blinked, lazily as a cat, and in that feline blink reminded Kathur for just an instant of Kourgath who had shared her bed.

'No need. For an Alban. No need for a man who can hide behind his oh-so-very-flexible code of honour. No need where any excuse will do instead, so long as it can be couched in the proper terms. Oh yes. It's easy then. But I too have been honoured, lady, and in a better way. I have earned my honour, lady: I wear it for all to see. But I have no elegant little knife to let my life out if I fail. No. I must bear failure as I bear success. As I bear *these.*'

His left hand reached up to touch the rank-marks on his helmet and on the high-collared black robe he wore over his red armour, and Kathur stared. Not at the *hautheisart*'s double bar-and-diamond worked in silver on black velvet collar tabs and scarlet steel, not at the jagged-lightning insignia beside it—for though the thunderbolt of the Secret Police served to frighten the ignorant, it was still no more to Kathur than the branch of service in which Voord held his command. As, indeed, did she.

No . . . She stared at his hand.

When she had last seen it, when it had last touched her, it had been slender and graceful like the hand of a musician, its contact soft as a butterfly's caress. Now . . . Now it was twisted, and crippled, and hooked like part of a military machine, a claw of distorted bone and sinew that was mercifully hidden by a leather glove. Now it was the sort of disfiguration which made men wince and look away and thank whatever gods they worshipped that they were still whole, untouched by war, or accident, or—whatever had done this.

'Yes indeed, dear Vixen. It is as I say. I wear my honour—whether I want to or not.' The frightful talon lowered from her line of sight, but its presence, and its shape at which the concealing glove had merely hinted, remained in her mind and made her skin crawl.

Voord watched it crawl. 'I suffered this, my dear, and so earned my present rank. Now I suffer the responsibilities of that rank. I am *Hautheisart Kagh'Ernvakh*. Concerned with internal security; espionage; counter-insurgency. And with the enforcement of—' a jerk of his wrist wrenched the *telek* from Kathur's grip, 'discipline.'

She flinched at the flat, vicious whack of the weapon's

discharge, and shut her eyes again; but she could not shut her ears to a crisp, moist sound like a melon hit by a mallet, or the hollow thump of bone on wood as her servant's head was slammed back against the floor as if it had been kicked. Nor could she shut her mercilessly precise mind's eye to the image that was seared into it as if by red-hot irons; an image that she could still see now. An image that she would always see. The instant of a man's death.

He lay on his back, one hand thrown wide and the other still uselessly endeavouring to staunch the wound in his leg. But there was no longer need. And there would be no staunching of this latest wound, for it had already ceased to bleed. Blood and mucus was spattered across his cheek and forehead; his left eye-socket was a pit of oozing mush; a triangular chunk of his skull lay feet from where it had burst from the back of his head. But what expression could be seen on his ruined face was no more than faint surprise.

'Yes. It does work.' Voord spared a glance for his handi-work, looked back at Kathur as if analysing her reaction and then at the *telek* with the beginnings of an idea that was as swiftly concealed as it was to blossom. 'It does work indeed. And so do you, Kathur. Most of the time. Like another woman I once knew. But Sedna failed as well. As you failed this time—and by disobeying my direct command. You must remember in future. Punishment should aid your memory.'

He made the weapon safe and laid it carefully aside; then removed his helmet and dropped it to the floor, gazing at the woman with his head cocked quizzically to one side. Sweat-darkened hair was plastered flat against his skull, and there were shadows in the sockets of his eyes that were not created by any light or lack of it in Kathur's room. 'The customary sentence is a bowstring—or impalement.'

As the meaning of his words sank in, Kathur stared blankly at him and then slowly cowered away as comprehension dawned. The only sound to pass through her loose lips was an unstructured whimper of raw fear.

'Yet it could be said—in your favour—that you tried. You were told to keep him drugged and bound. But you still succeeded until . . . what was it you claimed only minutes ago? Then if there was a plea for clemency on your behalf, the sentence might well be commuted. Would you have me consider such a plea?'

Though Kathur did not, and in her extremity of terror could not make any coherent sound, Voord watched her with a sort of cold appraisal and nodded at last. 'I am content. The plea is accepted.' His hand reached out to stroke along her face and slowly down the rigid muscles of her neck.

The left hand. . . .

Kathur cringed within herself, but dared not let her revulsion show. Not even when that dreadful claw settled like a gross spider on her shoulder and then with a bitter, self-mocking sensuality smoothed the heavy satin of her robe aside. The garment fell free of its own weight and whispered down to puddle in crimson folds about her ankles, leaving her naked and shuddering before Voord's rapacious stare. Even then she did not move, did not attempt the classic cliché of one arm across her breasts and the other hand hiding her crotch; she merely stood with both arms hanging limply at her sides and her eyes lowered in a shame at her nudity that she had never felt with the Alban. She stood like a condemned prisoner facing the block, passively awaiting what fate chose to send her; and she heard the slow creak of leather as some effort of ruined muscle and tendon forced Voord's fingers open; and she waited for the degradation of its contact on her body.

There was no such contact. Instead the crooked fingers clutched at the back of her head, tangling in the locks of auburn hair, tilting her face up until Voord could lean forward to kiss her on the lips. A faint scent of some perfume such as courtiers used hung about him, and his breath had been sweetened by the recent chewing of lancemint leaves. Other than that, he smelt simply clean.

And that was the worst of all.

Had he foul breath or his body a sour, unwashed reek, Kathur knew she could have prepared herself better; even though *Kagh' Ernvakh* had required her to seduce enough men to know that it was those with dirty bodies who had straightforward notions of vice, and the clean-scrubbed sophisticates who were inclined towards what even she thought foul, yet the contrast always shocked her. As Voord shocked her. For though he was fresh and pleasant in his person, his mind was warped and vile.

She could feel his kiss grow more intense, more passionate, and almost by reflex she responded with a pressure of her

tongue against his lips. Then she felt his teeth close, and felt
the stab of pain, and tasted blood—her blood—and knew that
even though her 'plea' had been accepted she was still to
suffer punishment after all.

Voord's left hand—talon—locked in her hair as Kathur
wrenched away, and she jolted to a halt at the length of his
arm. He grinned at her, and there were streaks of dark red on
the white of his so-clean teeth, and the glitter in his eyes was
like nothing she had even seen on any man's face in all her
wide experience.

'Oh yes, my lady, dear Vixen my own, you *are* to be
punished after all. Surely you knew, surely you expected it?
Surely you looked forward to it as you did before? And who
am I to disappoint a lady?' He was struggling with his own
clothing as he gasped the words at her. 'I spare you the
cord—but I think impalement is appropriate.' He flung her
face-downwards on the bed and pinned her with one hand and
his straddled legs. 'Relax, lady'—a weight of hot bare flesh
and icy armour descended on her back and buttocks—you
might even enjoy it. But even if you don't,' Voord shifted a
little and then plunged like a man riding an unruly horse, '*I*
will!'

There was a gasping interval of some few seconds.

Then at last Kathur began to scream.

In the street outside, a figure wrapped in a hood and cloak
heard the hoarse, outraged, anguished shrieks. And wrapped
the cloak a little closer and perhaps shivered in sympathy,
and waited until the three men counted into the house had
become three men counted out of it even if the waiting took
this whole foggy night.

But did nothing else at all.

If it was stolen, then why only one and not both? Aldric
smacked pettishly at the butt of his sole remaining *telek*; there
was still no sensible answer to his unvoiced question, and
perforce he set the matter aside yet again. Reining Lyard to a
standstill, he stood in his stirrups to glance back the way he
had come, but could see nothing except the mist, deepening
to fog that darkened to blackness and night. And yet . . .

He was certain that somebody was watching him.

It was gloomier here than he had expected. Oh, an unlit

city was as dark as any place not actually buried beneath the
earth had right to be, but Imperial cities were not unlit. Not,
at least, in normal circumstances. But at some recent stage in
Tuenafen's past, some political group had felt it necessary to
their cause to smash nearly all the doorway lanterns in the
seaport's Old Quarter.

Nearly all? They had probably destroyed the lot, thought
Aldric, and what he now saw were the very few which had
been replaced. Not that there would have been many to begin
with: most houses in this part of the city were eighty years
behind such modern affectations. The architecture told him
that much; above his head the upper stories of both sides of
the street leaned conspiratorially together, so much so that in
places one householder could lean out and rap upon his
opposite neighbour's window. Even at midday they would
block out most of the light. Now. . . Now the effect was
stifling and claustrophobic. Ominous.

Aldric forced a smile at his own fretting, knowing even as
he did so that it would look more like a snarl. Lyard shifted
beneath him; the big horse was uneasy too, maybe uncomfortable on the smooth pavement which had been greased by a
film of condensation, or because of his rider's mood, or
simply because he too disliked the fog and dark and oppressive
stillness. The courser's hooves clanked noisily—too noisily,
thought Aldric—as he moved into the false comfort of the
light from a surviving lantern, itself muffled by the watery
yellow halo of fog which surrounded it. He was wondering if
he could have spared the extra few minutes needed to load the
pack-horse with his gear and—most especially—his armour.
But the arguments he provided both then and now were
specious, lacking the weight of conviction: bits of equipment
and pieces of metal, even such metal as the battle harness
given him by Gemmel, were things which could be replaced.
Time lost now would be time gone for ever. Time which
might well make the difference between . . .

What and what? There had been more than enough wasted
time in the way he had spent the earlier part of the evening,
enjoyable though that had been.

Aldric's gaze flicked from side to side, taking in what
meagre detail he could see through the darkness and the
drifting fog. Potential ambush points, escape routes and the
like. *Escape routes!*—and myself none too sure of even how

to get back to Kathur's house! His hand freed Widowmaker from where she rode obliquely across his back and secured the *taiken*'s scabbard at his hip before he gathered up the reins again and kneed Lyard forward. And if there was moisture in the palm of that ungloved left hand, then surely it was because of the foggy moisture in the air and no other cause at all.

Then . . .

A clock somewhere nearby ground harshly into life and began to strike for the hour—many, many minutes late, though Aldric at that instant was in no fit state to notice it. The sudden noise had shocked his highly-strung, already-nervous mount and sent the stallion skittering sideways.

Towards the ragged granite facing of a wall.

Aldric saw the stonework loom out of the mist and spat an oath; then kicked his nearside foot out of its stirrup-iron and up across his saddlebow before foot and leg together could be crushed, and twitched back on snaffle-bitted reins to get the warhorse back under control before his flank ground into the fanged abrasive surface. Lyard stopped instantly at the brief pressure on his velvet mouth; nothing more was needed. His rider disliked and was loudly critical of the vicious metal used by some who styled themselves horsemen to dominate their steeds. Aldric had not time for such brutalities as spade or curb or bradoon, and held that schooling was of more value than the infliction of pain. His opinion was justified now.

As he leaned forward to gentle the Andarran, and to coax calm into himself as much as the horse, Aldric admitted privately that it would take just one more fright like that—whether real or false—to send him wheeling about on another route. Any other route but this one. Yet to retrace his steps—a necessary evil, if he was to reach the last junction he had crossed—would bring him back to a certain high-walled court-yard which seemed now, as it had never seemed before, an ideal place in which to set a trap.

But it was not the only ideal place in Tuenafen.

As if summoned by the striking clock and the clattering of Lyard's hooves, boots slapped the wet paving-stones behind him: many feet, running men closing on him fast. And a voice: *'Dah'te ka'gh, hlens'l! Doch'taii-ha!'* It spoke in Low Drusalan and its words were an all-embracing order to stop, dismount, drop all weapons. Surrender. And they were enough to send Aldric's sole stirruped heel—the other still around his pommel where it had been hooked clear of the wall—jabbing into Lyard's flank. The horse responded like a clap of hands, snapping from immobility to a surge of acceleration towards the concealing darkness of the nearest alley.

Lyard's laid-back ears were barely tickled by the rope stretched taut across its entrance, so precisely had its height been calculated.

But it caught Aldric across the chest and plucked him clean out of his saddle in a single uncoordinated backward roll, pitching him winded to the wet ground with a flare of shrill stars inside his skull where his brain had been. Black against the grey of the foggy night, a weighted net whirled down towards him, opening like a predatory spiderweb just before its mesh enveloped him in clinging folds.

Aldric flopped backwards onto the ground with the crisscross pattern of the net-cords harsh against his face, and fury spasmed through him; fury at whoever had set this up, fury at the delay for which he and he alone was to blame and which had brought him to this, floundering like a landed fish in a Tuenafen street. Blind, crimson fury whose heat would not be quenched without the shedding of blood. His, theirs, anybody's!

Had Isileth been drawn he might have cut the net, might have butchered the men who even now drifted silently out of the shadowed fog, might have escaped . . . But the long-sword was still sheathed, her presence a dull pain against his side where he had landed awkwardly on the loops and bars of her hilt. He could not touch her; and when some swine pulled on the drawline and the net tightened its embrace, he could not even move enough to ease the ache.

When they loosened off the mesh he kicked a few times, uselessly, and then gave up as heavy hands were laid on arms and legs to tie them up in what seemed an entirely excessive quantity of rope. Even to Aldric's dazed mind, coherent thought still fighting for precedence against the swirling sparks of mild concussion, all this care and consideration seemed overly elaborate. An arrow from the darkness would have been much more efficient.

And then as his wits began to trickle back and things fell into place, confusion was replaced by the beginnings of fear. He was to have been held in Kathur's embrace until he was collected by . . . someone. Her servant's attempt to kill him could be dismissed; it was not a part of the pattern. But now he had been captured and secured virtually unhurt. For someone.

Who? And why?

These men were dressed in grey; they wore hoods and masks; like *tulathin*, the Alban mercenary assassins. And that realisation was as horrifying as any, for Aldric started to remember all the people—or the friends, supporters and surviving relatives of people—who might pay the sort of money *tulathin* demanded, just to have him caught alive, unharmed and healthy.

Just to make his death their personal and very lingering pleasure. There were several such—too many for just one man.

Despite the chill of the night a droplet of sweat coursed down his face. They had taken all his weapons by now, including the three hidden daggers which were evidently not hidden well enough. And the spellband with the Echainon stone set into it, which no more resembled a weapon than his crest-collar. They checked that too, and the scar across his cheek, studying them by the light of a dark-lantern and comparing all with a sheet of paper one man held in his hand. Everything was done without a surplus word or gesture, although one cuffed him across the face when he attempted the only action left open to him and tried to bite. It was a petty gesture—on both sides—and the retaliation was no reassurance. It was far too gentle.

'Close enough! He'll do. Take him.'

A hood dropped over Aldric's head; no mere blindfold, it reeked with some soporific drug. He was growing, if not familiar with, then at least accustomed to the offhand, casual employment of such things within the confines of the Drusalan Empire. It was as if, forbidden sorcery except where the granting of permission was convenient to those in power, men who would have been enchanters had instead become apothecaries and chemists, jugglers not of power but of poisons. As he breathed the aromatic reek within the bag, Aldric's mind went back five years to the last time he had smelt this smell.

Then . . . He was armoured to the neck—Heaven and the Light of Heaven alone knew where his helmet was—and he lay flat on his back as he lay now, but instead of stone pavement beneath him there was grass, and instead of grey *tulathin* looking down at him he could see his brother Joren. There was concern on the big man's face. Behind and beyond was the wreckage of an assault-course jump; Aldric's horse was grazing unconcernedly a little further on. And there was pain.

Pain like and yet unlike that he felt now—a grinding, gnawing pain which worsened when he moved. Aldric tried to lift his head, but it seemed as though there was some great weight strapped to his brow, pulling him back and down. Someone—*was it Joren?*— leaned over him and slipped darkness firmly past his eyes. The same someone fumbled to hold that darkness shut beneath his chin. 'I fell off,' Aldric tried to say apologetically, 'and I think I've broken . . .' The words in his head came out as no more than a drowsy mumble, but he made no attempt to correct them.

As the drug took effect, he did, and saw, and knew, nothing more at all.

FIVE

Dragonship

Kathur lay where Voord had flung her at the last, after he was
sated, after all that fevered, slimy, endless night. She was
sprawled inelegantly across her bed—a bed which she would
hack apart with her own hands if need be, rather than leave it
and the memories it contained under her roof for one more
day. And except for the bloodied, befouled, sweat-streaked
tatters which had once been silken quilts, she was naked.
Against her stripped skin she could feel the obscene pressure
of the pillows which Voord had wadded into place to give
support to and prevent retreat from his inclinations of the
moment: beneath buttocks, beneath belly, behind head. And
she wept.

Kathur's tears were not those of shame, even though she
felt it for the first time now in five years as a first-rank
courtesan; no, these tears were born of the harsh sobs which
racked her, sobs which held more of frustrated rage than
anything else. She had been terrorised, agonised, subjected to
a cynical and systematic degradation, and she knew that there
was no way in all the world that she could gain requital for it.
The Drusalan woman dabbed a wincing hand at her mouth for
perhaps the hundredth time since Voord's laughing departure;
a mouth once merely lushly full and the colour of ripe
cherries, but now puffed and split and bruised plum-purple.
She felt that she would never be truly clean again.

There was a pallid light beyond the shuttered windows that
told of oncoming dawn. Soon the house-servants would appear, with their mask-like faces which betrayed nothing of
thoughts of disapprovals within, and their quick, capable
hands which would tidy the aftermath of the night without

117

any reaction to what they might have to touch. Just as they had done so many times before.

Except that now was not like all those other times.

None of those other times had ever left her feeling as she was feeling now. None of them had left a dead man stiff and cold on the floor at the foot of her bed. None of them had left the contents of a shattered skull soaked darkly into the rugs. None of them had left the foetid taint of death hanging on the air.

Kathur felt a churning looseness in the pit of her stomach and tried to close her nostrils to the reek, her mind to its source; rolling onto her side, she stared at the blankness of the wall beside the bed—stared anywhere, indeed, just so that she would no longer have to stare at the corpse with its smashed half-expression of surprise, or at the door which still gaped wide like the corpse's slack-jawed mouth, or even at the side of the room from which her snug and sybaritic world had been so totally torn asunder.

As she lay there, trembling, her skin slick with the icy sweat of nausea, her hearing seemed to grow uncannily acute and she could hear the most minute noises with utmost clarity. Noises distant: the tick of a bird's claws and the rustle of its feathers as it perched to preen on the sill beyond the window. Noises close: her heartbeat and breathing, and the whispering of silk disturbed by the rise and fall of her own rib-cage.

And the noises of soft movement at her back.

Kathur's heavy, drowsy eyelids snapped wide open and her very eyes seemed to bulge out of sockets that were no longer deep enough to contain them: sapphires inadequately bedded in a mask of carven ivory. For this was no sound made by a servant; they were quiet—but this was stealthy. Hope and horror fought for precedence in the half-dozen slams of her suddenly-racing heart. Because it might be Kourgath. Or equally it might be Voord.

Her head jerked up and around to look over the obstruction of her own shoulder, but flinched backwards in the self-same movement with a shrill small mew of terror, away from the glittering point of a sword which hung unmoving on the air less than a handspan from the fragile bubble of her eye. Had she sat up more abruptly—! The very thought of what might have happened turned her belly sick again. Even now, the most minute forward thrust of that implacable steel and . . .

Her eyes focused beyond the weapon's point, and it was neither Voord nor Kourgath after all.

The intruder was cloaked, and hooded so deeply that the swathing of cloth resembled the cowl of a holy man. All that could be seen of the face within the hood was an inch or two of smooth chin; and it was impossible for even a gaze as experienced as Kathur's to read anything from that. But the thrusting-sword drew back a considerate inch or two, and its tip swung to one side so that it was no longer aimed quite so directly at Kathur's eye. The small motion which shifted it was accompanied by a dry metallic scraping, and that told her something at least. Whoever and whatever this person was, they wore armour.

'No noise.' The figure's free hand moved across the hood's opening in a gesture which Kathur had never seen before, but understood at once: A quick, neat blending of the sign for silence and the threat of throat-cutting. She swallowed down a gullet that, though sore from screaming and . . . screaming, was still intact, and nodded hasty agreement while trying to fit a nervous smile onto a face which plainly didn't want to carry it. The cowl studied her. Nodded once in response. Then a finger jerked out at her with a suddenness that made Kathur jump. 'And no movement.'

Feeling like a mouse beneath the flight path of a kestrel, movement was the last thing in her mind.

As Kathur lay quite still, her anonymous visitor stalked about the room, dabbing inquisitively at things with the murderous point of that long sword, and despite the voluminous folds of the oversized cloak still contriving to move with all the mincing, lethal grace of a hunting cat. Kathur could see that it would take little provocation—probably none at all—for this particular individual to respond with a burst of killing violence. Whatever else the cloak concealed, it made a poor job of hiding tension, apprehension—and rising irritation. The dead man on the floor was inspected with no more than cursory interest. Until the *telek* dart which had killed him was found embedded in a panel of the wall.

'So.' A glance—a sweeping glare from the blank blackness within the hood—studied distance, trajectory and penetration,

and drew some conclusion from them all. 'So, and so, and so
. . . Did the Alban do this?'

The question snapped out harsh and clear after the muted
introspective muttering of voiced thought, and again Kathur
jumped. At first she did not answer, and for her hesitation
was lashed by a volley of words in a language which she had
never heard before. 'Answer, damn you!' The voice returned
to Jouvaine again, more heavily accented than before and
using the most basic mode; each word's meaning was une-
quivocally clear now, and the speaker knew it. 'Did the
Alban do this—and if he did, why?'

Whatever patience there had once been in that voice was
eroding fast, and as the cloaked figure took two long steps
forward, it led with a levelled sword. Now not only accent
but tone and timbre were impossible to ignore. There was
something wrong about all three, something very wrong indeed, but still Kathur could not place what instinct said was
obvious.

'Why, and when, and where is he? What is going on here?'
The hood was pushed back, then shaken clear of its wearer's
head.

And Kathur knew at last what was wrong. Except that it
was *right*.

'I can't help but think,' muttered Gemmel half to himself,
'that *I* may have caused last night's fog.'

'You . . . ?' Dewan ar Korentin flexed the big muscles of
his shoulders and back in a huge yawn-and-stretch. Gemmel
had been uneasy about entering a tavern and Dewan had
given way to the old man's doubts; they had spent a chilly,
uncomfortable night in some farmer's hay-barn, and now
there were kinks in Dewan's spine which felt as if they would
be there forever. He was getting too old for this, too old and
too soft. Tonight, like it or not, wizard's objections or not,
they were going to sleep in beds like human beings, not like
rats in a rick. 'Why say so? And why worry? It's gone.'

Gemmel glanced at his companion and said something in a
voice so low that Dewan made more sense from the movement of his lips. 'I say so because I believe so—and I worry
for the same reason. You saw what happened with this thing
just as well as I.'

Dewan looked at him, then at the Dragonwand, and grunted

expressively. 'I wonder what else you might believe, old man. And what else might happen because of it.'

'That, friend Dewan, is something we may find out before much time has passed us by . . .'

The morning bloomed around them like a flower. Dewan had been right: the fog was gone, leaving in its wake a cloudless, chilly blue sky which toned through pastel shades of rose and saffron towards where the sun rose on their landward side beyond a screen of tree-clad hills. They were still very close to the sea, moving north-east towards Tuenafen Port on the Inner Coast-Road; the Outer Coast-Road ran a hazardous course along the crest of the limestone cliffs which marked the Empire's western boundary, and in rough weather was prone to lose stretches of itself to the hungry sea.

'*Yo!* Look there!' Ar Korentin pointed with the full length of his right arm towards the ocean—or more accurately, towards the black speck scudding across its beaten-metal surface. 'Warship,' he pronounced with such authority that Gemmel didn't quibble his opinion.

Not aloud, anyway; but the sorcerer reached into his satchel, withdrew a long-glass and studied the speck with it before uttering his agreement. 'As you say: warship. And a big one. Bigger than I've ever seen before. Look.' He passed over the long-glass. 'What is it?'

Dewan squinted, and held his breath; the wizard's glass was more powerful than any he had used before, and just the beat of his own pulse was enough to send the magnified image dancing wildly about. It took him a few moments to fix the distant vessel in the circular field of view, and some seconds more to adjust its focus for his eye. Then he said something malevolent in his own language, something which provoked a raised eyebrow from Gemmel and suggested a certain familiarity with Vreijek oaths.

'Apart from that,' he said, 'what is it?'

'A battleram.' Dewan's 'of course' was unvoiced, but there all the same. 'I should have guessed. Anything else would be too small to notice at . . . what, a mile-and-a-half?'

'Nearer two. He's bearing north. Out of Tuenafen?'

'There isn't another port on this stretch of coast that can take battlerams; not unless they've built one in the past few years and managed to keep it secret. Which,' he slid the long-glass shut and handed it back, 'I very much doubt.'

Then he stared at Gemmel, guessing from the old enchanter's face that they were sharing the same thought.

'Aldric . . .' Gemmel said it first.

'We're too late.'

'That . . . that depends.'

'On what?'

'On whether he's aboard that ship; if he is, on who put him there. And on its destination.'

'You know more about this business than you've let slip before, don't you?' Dewan accused, watching the sorcerer's reaction closely.

'More—but not enough. Rynert is very good at keeping secrets.' Gemmel said nothing more for a while; he was watching the distant battleram dwindle beyond sight, and thinking unguessable thoughts about kings and conspiracies and other matters which were of importance only to himself. Then he glanced at the sky. The sun was well up now, though still concealed by the wooded high ground, and its glow was already giving a suggestion of warmth to the late autumn morning. 'It's going to be a good day,' he said idly, unslinging his satchel and taking a pack of biscuit and dried meat from it. 'Breakfast?'

'Thanks.' Dewan took a helping of the food; jerked beef like strips of leather, and twice-baked sheets of wheaten bread which both looked and felt as if it had been sawn from the trunk of a tree. It and the meat required as much effort to eat as if they had been in very truth what they merely resembled; breakfast was an exercise in chewing rather than a meal. 'By the way,' the Vreijek said after finally disposing of his first mouthful and washing it down with a swallow of black, bitter beer, 'I'd sooner you said nothing more about the weather.'

Gemmel squashed the beginnings of a smile. 'Because it might be unlucky? I hadn't thought superstition would be one of your vices.'

'Call it caution; I've grown very . . . very cautious since I met you. And since the beach beyond Dunacre. The Valhollans have a wise proverb: don't praise the day until evening—'

'Or ale until it's been drunk. Pass the beer.' He drank, and made a face. 'This Hertan brew doesn't travel well, does it? Yes, I know the proverb you mean. It goes on and on rather. Don't praise a maiden until she's been married—and don't praise a wife till she's dead. Quite . . .' He laughed softly. 'Well, I can praise my wife and will if you want to listen— but why that proverb in particular? You're not known for quoting things.' He stared sharply at the Vreijek. 'Especially words from Valhol. What made you think of it?'

'Just a thought. An idle notion. Nothing more.'

Gemmel looked at him and smiled, and drank more beer, and said nothing at all.

When they stopped again the day hung on the cusp of noon; and with ill-concealed dismay Dewan surveyed a scene which he had not expected. For the past hour he had been praising the tavern where they planned to stop for a midday meal, and maybe rent the use of horses. Except that the tavern was no longer there. Oh, it had been until recently, and parts of its structure remained—but most of these were blackened, char-coaled wood and the rest were shanty reconstructions. Everything else was gone.

'So much for dinner,' said Gemmel drily. 'I still have some beef and biscuit—if you want it.' He did not even trouble to feign enthusiasm at the prospect. Dewan made an expression of distaste and stalked across the seared ground to find out what had happened—also to ask what might be left that was worth rating.

He found out rather more than he had been expecting.

Dewan supplied speculative details himself, when relating the innkeeper's story to Gemmel. Both men knew enough to make educated guesses whenever blank spaces in the second-hand story gaped too wide; and Dewan in particular was able to draw on his Imperial and Alban military service to suggest answers.

'It seems,' said Gemmel around a mouthful of excellent spiced beef stew—the tavern was making a determined effort to get back on its feet, and its more loyal patrons were chivalrously undeterred by the state of the place—'that we are going to Tuenafen regardless, and once there to find someone who can tell us a thing or three.' He swallowed, and drank good red wine with an air of satisfaction.

'Find someone who might need persuasion, you mean.' Dewan broke bread into his own portion, Vreijek-style, and sank a chunk or two idly with his spoon; then tapped for emphasis on the bottom of the bowl. 'But if this is the work of *Kagh' Ernvakh*, both the finding and the persuading will be difficult.'

'*Kagh' Ernvakh?*' Gemmel repeated the Drusalan words carefully; their literal meaning was clear, but what Dewan meant by them was a mystery to him. It was a mystery easily solved.

'The Honourable Guard. The Guardians of Honour. Translate it into Alban however you like, Gemmel—it still means nothing more than the Secret Police.'

'Ah. And by "persuading" you mean torture.'

'Don't lose your appetite, old man.' Dewan grinned briefly. 'Persuasion covers more than you think: bribery, coercion, blackmail . . . I don't want to hurt anyone, any more than you do.' He lifted another sheet of bread and stared at it thoughtfully, then ripped it across and across with unsubtle emphasis. 'But if I must, then—'

'You will.'

'Yes.'

Gemmel wondered how sincere that threat might be; Dewan was not an Alban, and owed nothing to the Alban codes of honour. But then—if one was brutal and bore recent events in mind—neither did King Rynert. The wizard found that his mind was tending more and more towards considerations of honour and personal worth; towards how these might be valued; towards how his own honour might be weighed in the balance and found wanting. The thought was an uncomfortable one. If only it was possible to turn back time and undo past events . . .

For the briefest instant he found himself thinking about the great hold beneath Meneth Taran, and about the things which lay there. Then he dismissed the notion; that way was more dishonourable than to go on and try to recover what had been lost by his own efforts. Gemmel looked down at his own food—good beef and fresh vegetables, inventively blended with herbs and fiery spices—and despite the enticing aroma rising from the redware bowl he felt his hunger fade to no more than a faint emptiness. 'So what is going on, *eldheisart?*' His use of Dewan's old military rank was no accident.

Yet the Vreijek was—or seemed—unruffled by it. 'Someone wants Aldric Talvalin. Someone is prepared to pay a very large amount of money for the privilege—witness the presence of the battleram, which we both suspect might have him aboard. Or—or they have the rank to authorise such an action. And I don't know which would worry me the most.' He drank more wine; not much, just enough to flavour his mouth which, if it was anything like Gemmel's, had the sour dryness of failure in it. 'And *why* would they want him? I should have asked Rynert that much at least.'

'What? The man who tried to have us both killed? What a waste of breath *that* would have been!'

'At least we know that he was taken from here alive.'

'Yes—but how many days ago?'

'Two, three . . . ' Dewan hesitated, a quizzical expression crossing his face. 'Would Marek Endain know anything about it?' He threw the demon queller's name abruptly into the conversation; it had been Gemmel's idea to send the Cernuan after Aldric, as much to keep an eye on him as to help or protect him, and Dewan had acceded reluctantly to the idea—an idea which had seemed to him more full of risk than of use. But Marek's last report had been a garbled thing, full of wild surmise, which had ended with the information that he was now—involuntarily—first councillor to the new Overlord of Seghar. And that the Overlord was a woman.

'Marek has his own troubles.' Gemmel had read that last report as well, and had found it mildly amusing. The demon queller had been no more than a casual professional acquaintance, a sharer of scholarly interests, and to think of his rotund silhouette as the power behind any throne—no matter how small—was a notion which provoked a thin smile even whilst Gemmel's mind was occupied with more serious matters. Matters touching what even the Albans would regard as personal honour . . .

Dewan stared at him a moment, then shrugged to himself and drained his cup, throwing back his head to let the last fragrant drops flow into his mouth, and to allow the brilliance of the day to wash his face with azure heat. Then he choked.

And dropped the cup.

Its explosive thousand-sharded smash on the table right in front of him snapped Gemmel from his introspection, and he stared at the Vreijek with an expression that was half anger and half a fear that Dewan might have been stricken again with illness. But the big man's head was still tilted back, his mouth hanging open and stained to the chin with a dribble of red wine that hadn't quite reached its proper destination. Yet

there were none of those signs which Gemmel had so feared:
no shock of pain, no clutching at the chest. Only undiluted
awe.

The wizard stared skyward in his turn. And remembered:

> *. . . Long, long ago the firedrakes flew,*
> *And flaming flickered in the sunlit sky.*
> *But firedrakes fly no more within the sight of men . . .*

Until now . . .

The sky was blue; pure, pale, late-autumn blue, unblemished
by any cloud of black or white or grey. But across it ran a
wisp of white, fine as a hair and so straight as to almost be a
silver seam in the vaulting firmament. And at its uttermost
tip, like the perfect barb of a perfect spear, was a minute
black filament of darkness, momentarily flowing from cruci-
form to no more than a dark scratch against the heavens with
a rhythm that was the beating of great wings. No one else had
seen it. No one else could have known what it was . . .
except for Gemmel and Dewan. And neither of the two
considered for a moment that it could be other than . . .
Ymareth.

'Splendour of God,' breathed Dewan ar Korentin, and
there was much more than just an oath born of disbelief in his
reverent voice. He was now as Gemmel had been then—years
ago; lives ago.

As any man would be, possessed of an ounce of imagination or an ounce of romance in a soul no matter how
prosaic. Any man, any woman, any child would want to see
this wonder above all wonders of the world: a beast, a
creature, a being from the depths of legend of many people,
alive and magnificent in the clear cold air that was scored by
the vapour-trail of heat pouring from its own mouth, glinting
dark and glorious against the azure arch of Heaven. Fifteen
thousand vertical feet separated it from its sutnned audience
of two, so that details were indistinguishable through a haze
of distance and the glare of the noonday sun; Gemmel did not
subject it to the indignity of close scrutiny through his long-
glass. All of those who mattered knew already—that this was
a firedrake. A dragon. *The* dragon.

Ymareth.

And it was scything northward on the track of the battleram

which they had seen that morning, flitting out of Tuenafen on the wings of urgency across the sea of hammered steel. Not knowing that greater, darker wings were driving in its wake.

'Innkeeper!' bellowed Dewan, 'bring me the best wine that you have left, and drinking vessels worthy of it if you still have any!' The man did, and had, and brought them all: tall, slender goblets of rock crystal and burnished silver, stemmed so that they stood a foot above the table's surface. The wine was golden Hauverne, *matherneil*, bottled in green glass; but Dewan cracked the battle open on the table's edge with a single snap of his wrist that sent both cork and bottleneck flying off to somewhere at his right-hand-side—then countered such brusque soldierly impatience with a mannerly flourish worthy of a courtier as he filled first Gemmel's glass and then his own with the rich rare vintage. His grin, all white teeth and curling moustache as he lifted the goblet and stared at Gemmel across its rim, was filled with such pure, happy mischief that it stripped ten years from his weathered face.

'Drink hail and health, *purcanyath* sorcerer. To Aldric. And to aid unsuspected by all. Including, I think, the lad himself. *Hail!*'

Gemmel drank: once, twice and then to drain the cup. He began to laugh so hard that tears streamed from his crinkled emerald eyes. Or was the laughter only to conceal those tears which would have flowed in any case?

Gemmel didn't know.

Aldric's eyes opened sluggishly; there was a throbbing in and behind them, and he knew both instinctively and from bitter experience that if too much light startled that throbbing, he would be very, very sick. There was an acrid, vinegary sensation in his mouth and nostrils: the taste and chemical smell of whatever had put him to sleep—yet again!—and it occurred to him through a spasm of mild irritation which had nothing to do with the peril that he might be in, that he had spent the greater part of the past few days either drunk, or drugged, or knocked unconscious.

It was . . . undignified.

Aldric Talvalin was not a religious man; he had ceased to believe in the so-called benevolence of Heaven on the day his father died, and since that day—whether through an ostentatious grudge against deity or a private reluctance to be

hypocritical—he had refused to cross the threshold of any
holy house. But there were times, and this was one of them,
when he had the distinct feeling that Someone was trying to
make some sort of point.

Just now his whole sensory world seemed to be moving in
a dozen quite illogical directions at once. Then things fell into
focus—more or less—and sounds which had meant nothing
bare seconds ago enhanced his realisation of reality. His
world—or at least his immediate surroundings—*was* moving.
He could see the rolling of reflected light across a ceiling that
was far, far too close, far closer than it had any right to be,
and in his ears was a constant liquid rushing, blended with
the multiple notes of half-a-hundred different creaks from
wood and cordage. And he knew at once where he was. Or at
least, he knew as soon as the narcotic clouds had cleared
sufficiently from the dazed organ which did duty as his brain.

He was on board a ship.

With that conclusion, someone at the back of his mind
broke into ironic applause. But it was true enough; he was
aboard ship, and a ship not only under way but—if the
sensations transmitted through his spine were any judge—
moving at considerable speed. Flank speed, the Imperial Fleet
called it, and Aldric thought to himself that Imperial terms of
reference were all of a sudden highly appropriate, because the
only vessel he knew of within several leagues of coast that
was capable of such immediately apparent speed would be
one or other of those he had seen in Tuenafen harbour.

An Imperial battleram!

The exhalation of breath which hissed out between his
teeth was also a sigh of resigned defeat. So they had him after
all—whoever *they* were. Kathur had won. Had the pleasures
of her company been worth this and what was doubtless to
follow? Aldric doubted it.

He had no need to move overmuch, or even to look
around, to know that he was completely unarmed; completely
helpless. That memory was clear enough, beyond the soporific fog: the hands which had stripped him of every blade
which he carried, and which had sought out and removed the
belts and laces from his clothing for fear they might become
nooses or garottes.

Whether they feared that he would use such makeshift
weapons against them or on himself had either not been clear

or had been forgotten. Certainly if he was being carried to a lengthy and unpleasant death, then suicide whether in the form of *tsepanak'ulleth*, or something less formal but just as final, would be a preferred solution to be sought without delay. Certainly if he was *kailin-eir* of the old school, then they would have good reason to fear that he might kill himself and thus cheat them.

But he was not.

Aldric stared at the ceiling and admitted a fact which he had secretly known this long, long time: he would sooner live than die. No matter that it might well be true of most men, it was not true of Albans and especially high-clan Albans, *cseirin*-born, like himself. And yet unlike himself. 'Where there's life, there's hope,' Gemmel Errekren had told him once. Then, he had snorted in derision. Then, it had been the accepted and expected reaction. Then even then, it had been only a mask to the way he truly felt. Had he truly followed the beautiful, savage, bloody Honour Code of the *kailin*, how many times should he now have been dead by his own hand?

Too many. He remained alive through his own choice alone, and that was not cowardice no matter what might be said, or what had been said—though grant the truth, no man had yet been so in love with death to say it in his hearing. No. Cowardice was running away—not tactical withdrawal, but turning tail in flight whether that flight led to the woods or the hills.

Or the dark lands beyond the stab of a *tsepan's* blade.

Courage was standing fast, setting to rights, taking the hard path. Courage gained and justified trust from friends and from companions—and from self. Aldric stared at the ceiling and grinned momentarily. *I must remember not to trust you near complaisant, pretty women*, he told himself sternly. *A most lamentable failing*.

Except where one is concerned.

But—his thoughts came back to present reality with a jolt—who commands all this? He could think of none among his possible enemies with such power and wealth and resource as had been so arrogantly displayed here. And there were not so many enemies, at that: the enemies of Aldric Talvalin showed a tendency to get themselves killed. But even so, a courtesan of the first rank as bait, the firing of an expensive tavern to close the trap, and the use of both a squad

of *tulathin* and at least one battleram complete with crew and
marine contingent! That bespoke either a disgusting private
wealth, a stranglehold on someone with power and privilege—or
power and privilege itself.

Power that involved politics, rank, status and an independently controlled unit of the Imperial military. Power that
suggested the Emperor himself . . .

Or the Grand Warlord.

Woydach Etzel was one of the very few who fulfilled all
the present criteria. He had access to a quite obscene amount
of money—for which he had no need to account; he had the
rank to discourage idle questioners; and he had the power
necessary to manoeuvre warships like pieces on a gaming
board.

So this was what a pawn felt like when a crown piece was
hammered down on it and it was flung back into the box until
next time. Except that carven bone and ivory felt no pain
when the end came, whereas Aldric doubted he would be so
lucky.

The cabin door rattled, then clicked, betraying the presence
of a lock on the outside. It slid open and the young man who
came in was wearing a marine's half-armour flashed with the
single rank-bar of an officer-cadet—*en tau-kortagor*, in the
Empire's cumbersome system of named ranks. Improbably
enough, the young man was smiling. 'Ah, good—you're
awake.' More improbably still, he was speaking in good—
well, passable Alban. 'No ill-effects, I trust?' Most improbably of all, he seemed genuinely concerned. Solicitude from
such a source was so improbable . . . no dammit, so totally
unlikely that Aldric thought his ears were playing him tricks,
and he stared blankly at the pleasant-faced *tau-kortagor* until
the question was repeated. Then, and only then, did he blink
and shake himself back to some sort of sense.

'Ill-effects . . . ?' He too spoke in Alban, with something
approaching relief after so long contending with Jouvaine and
Drusalan. 'None. None at all. So far. I'm fine. I suppose.'

'Excellent. My name is Garet—on *Hautheisart* Voord's
personal staff.' He hesitated, as if anticipating a reaction, but
the name was only one among many to Aldric and meant
nothing significant. 'And I've been assigned to your care.
So—food?'

Aldric shrugged. His mind was still having difficulty in

assimilating the situation, for he was not being treated as he
had expected a prisoner of the Empire might have been. Far
from it—except in one respect. For it was only when he
shrugged that he realised—with a nasty start barely concealed—
that he was still bound at wrist and ankle. He had spent so
much time lost in thought, staring at the ceiling and wander-
ing through his mind rather than exploring the narrow confines of the cabin, that he had not noticed the bindings until
now. Unlikely as it seemed with hindsight, it was not so
surprising after all, for they were not ropes but soft wide
bands of woven silk, far beyond his strength to break but
secured with such care that their presence was not a constriction of his limbs. Just an unsettling inability to move.

'What about these things?' He lifted them: snug, almost
comfortable wrappings that were as secure as any wrought-
iron shackle—and stared pointedly over his crossed wrists at
Garet, who at least had the good grace to look uncomfortable.

'Oh—I, ah, I don't have authority to release you.'

Aldric made a small, faintly disgusted noise which managed to suggest he had expected no other response, and that
seemed to embarrass the cadet still more.

'But—but I could ask the *kortagor-ka'-tulathin* on your
behalf. He brought you aboard, so he might just . . . '

And that small kindness was not something Aldric had
dared to expect at all. Where there's life, he thought, . . . and
lay back on his bunk to watch the play of light across that
too-close claustrophobic ceiling. But he didn't dare to hope.
Not yet.

The order to release him was not long in returning down the
command chain from whoever authorised such things aboard
this battleram; but it was an order wrapped in so many
conditions as to negate its usefulness. Ultimately it was obeyed
more in spirit than to the letter, as might have been expected
about Drusalan orders.

His wrists and ankles were released, but he was not allowed on deck, and his left leg had been locked into an
elaborate harness of steel and leather strips such as might be
worn by one with a weakness in their muscles. Except that
this was not meant as a support, but as a restriction; the
hinging at its knee-joint was so tight that each stride was
reduced to a rolling, stiff-legged hobble. He could walk,

more or less, but his briefly entertained notion of pouncing on
someone was reduced to no more than a wry joke. Aldric
hadn't tried the experiment yet; but someone, somewhere,
had suspected that he might and he could recognise the signs
of being outmanoeuvred yet again. The addition of a thumb-
thick rope leash which secured him to a bulkhead was downright insulting.

Nevertheless, the food brought to him from the warship's
galley went a long way to compensate for injured dignity. No
prison rations these: the various dishes were uniformly excellent and another pointer to instructions laid down for his
continued well-being. There was a thin soup; charcoal-broiled
fish which he guessed was not long out of the sea; meat and
vegetables in a rich sauce of herbs and cream; and a sharp
white wine—cooled by a water-jacket—with which to wash it
down.

But like the over-elaborate security measures, the food's
very presentation was influenced not so much by himself as
by his reputation—or rather, by whatever highly coloured
version of it had preceded him aboard. It had certainly lost
nothing in the re-telling, for every piece of vegetable, meat or
fish had been cut up in advance so that the only eating
instrument he required—and was given—was a kind of wooden
spoon with rounded, blunt fork-tines carved into it. The sort
of thing given to very young children, so that they couldn't
possibly hurt themselves.

Or to supposedly lethal Alban *kailinin*, so that they couldn't
hurt anybody at all. The idea of a precaution lest he try to
take over an Imperial battleram with his dinner service was so
ridiculous that he sniggered himself into a fit of hiccups;
although afterwards, as he ate, Aldric reflected ruefully that if
he was less well known—or his reputation not so awesome—to
whoever had arranged all this, then he might by now have
had a chance to get away. *Off a ship in open ocean? Be
reasonable!* Even so, it would have gained him a little more
freedom. Notoriety might be flattering to some of the people
he had met; he personally could do without it. And he
wondered if the officer cadre of the Drusalan Empire had ever
heard of the concept of a gentleman's parole.

The meal was good, and he was hungry. Those two facts
led to empty dishes—and a stifled belch as Aldric lay back
and composed himself for an after-dinner nap. It was not

something in which he indulged given normal circumstances; but the thirty-odd pounds of strapping around his rigid, awkward leg was a constant reminder of abnormality. Besides which, he had eaten far too much.

Up on the command deck a sandglass was turned over and its turning was marked by a bell struck at the changing of the hour. Just after noon, thought Aldric drowsily: just after lunch. That makes it—the effort of thinking was such that he almost gave up—the Hour of the Hawk becoming, becoming . . . He yawned hugely and snuggled into the rolling, swaying, comforting embrace of the bunk as sleep overwhelmed him.

Becoming, he might have finished, the Hour of the Dragon.

It seemed that he had barely closed his eyes before they snapped open again, and he was jerked from an uncomfortable slumber by a sound that he had heard before: the clangour of an Imperial warship's alarm gongs sounding battle-stations. For just the first few seconds it was as if his strange, troubled dream had carried over to the waking world; then reality in the form of clattering footsteps outside and overhead gave the lie to such a notion. There was another clattering, harsher and more metallic, and the cabin's interior went abruptly dark as armoured screens dropped over the two small, thick-glassed ports. Aldric found himself in twilight, his only illumination the wan trickle of daylight which filtered through shrouded weapon-slits in each screen.

It was no longer a dream—it was a nightmare, that same recurring nightmare of helplessness. Once more he was aboard *En Sohra;* once more the First Fleet flagship *Aalkhorst* was shearing down on him with white water boiling from her prow; once more he could only hope that she would turn aside.

And she did. The bunk beneath him heeled abruptly from the horizontal, its angle so steep that he all but tumbled off. A rushing of water filled his ears and the feeble light beyond the screened ports turned green and then black as the battleram in which he was an unwilling passenger executed a vicious evasive snap-turn. Aldric knew what was happening: he had seen such a manoeuvre before, from the outside—it *had* been the *Aalkhorst* that time—and he knew too that as the warship turned, part of her hull submerged under the sideways pressures of having her helm put hard over at speed. But Lord

God! He hadn't known that such a turn could be so bloody *steep!*

Twice more the vessel lunged, and twice more Aldric dug his fingernails into the planking and tried to avoid being flung helplessly to the deck. Already there was blood on his face and a ragged gash at his hairline, as mementos of violent contact with one of the bulkhead uprights.

Then suddenly, between one rolling turn and the next, the watery light outside flushed a rich, rosy amber. Just for an instant: slower than the brilliant flicker of a lightning-flash, but much much faster than the blue-white skimmed-milk glow of a break in clouds crossing the moon. And the warship stopped.

Not dead in the water—there was too much momentum in her great bulk for that—but she lost way, ceased to be a vessel cutting through the ocean and became instead no more than a mere decelerating hulk. And Aldric could smell burning.

There was a dreadful stillness as if everyone aboard—officers, crewmen, marines, and even the ship herself—drew in a great breath and held it in expectation of something monstrous about to happen.

Aldric's barely-relaxed fingers tightened again as the battleram heeled—then clamped more convulsively still when the angle changed and he realised she hadn't heeled at all. She had *tipped*, her stern rearing out of the water as her beaked prow plunged down. He had never, ever watched a ship sink, much less had one go down beneath him, but he had heard it described and knew well enough what it was supposed to feel like. Like *this*!

The cabin door slammed open and outlined by its frame—indeed, clinging to its frame as Aldric clung to his bunk—was the young officer-cadet Garet. No longer friendly and no longer concerned—except perhaps for his own safety. Even—impossible though it seemed—no longer as young. Yet in the shadows of his close-fitting helmet his boy's face still seemed no more than sixteen, blanched white as bone with shock, or fear, or disbelief—as white as the knuckles of the hands which gripped the uprights of the cabin door.

'You!' He gasped the word, Drusalan now and guttural-harsh as only that language could achieve. 'You—get on deck! Now! *Move!*'

Aldric stared at him and as if the officer's fear played

counterpoint to his own emotions, felt the unknowing fear of
the past minutes fade and freeze over until they were sheathed
in an icy armour that was all dignity and pride and honour-
born courage. Which was not the same as true courage at all,
and Aldric knew that even if no one else did. But they
appeared the same and that was enough. He slapped the brace
on his leg with an irritable, careless gesture, as a man might
swat at an insect he can't quite reach.

'I go nowhere with this. Remove it. *Now.*' And he spoke
the words with studied malevolence in the highest mode of
the Drusalan language that he knew, quite aware that the
insult of implied superiority was a killing matter. Usually.
'Well?'

Garet stared at him, gaped at him for half-a-dozen heartbeats—and then ripped the dress dagger that was one of his
marks of rank out of its scabbard. Aldric thought that at last
he had miscalculated, pushed a little too far, at last had
overstepped the mark—thought that this would be a killing
matter at any time, in any place.

The dagger point paused, glittering nastily in the cabin's
subdued light, the silvery striations of honing on its cutting
edges sparkling at him as the weapon trembled in an unsteady
grip.

'I should gut you for that, *hlensyarl*,' Garet whispered.
'And maybe I will. But not just yet. I have my orders. Later
. . .' He sucked in a deep breath, trying to regain a degree of
self-control. 'But . . . but you're going nowhere unless I
have your Word. Your parole. You do understand "parole",
Alban, don't you?'

It seemed that he, too, knew how to use language for
subtle insult.

Aldric hesitated. Even though he had already considered
such a possibility, and would have welcomed it half an hour
ago, things had changed. The warship seemed under attack—
seemed, he reminded himself—and he might well have a
chance to escape during any confusion which might arise. But
not if he was bound by an intangible thing that was harder for
him to break than the shackle on his leg.

His mind began to hurt with the swirling rush of variables:
without his given Word, the brace would not be removed;
without its removal, his chance to escape was nil; with his
Word given and the brace removed, he could not escape

anyway. But locked up down here, with iron about his leg,
the only certainty would be of drowning if the battleram
rolled over and began to sink.

'All right. All right . . . ! I swear. On my Honour and on
my Word, I do swear that I will not endeavour to escape or
yet take flight without permission granted by those who hold
me captive.'

The cadet watched him coldly, his expression easy to read
framed as it was within the rank-barred helmet. *Tau-kortagor*
Garet was wondering, and not troubling to hide his doubts, if
the Alban's oath was worth more than the exhaled air which
carried it. Aldric returned the stare with interest, and that
interest was hatred.

'*So-ka, Drus'ach arluth'n*. My parole is given. Satisfied?'

The edge on Aldric's voice was as sharp as that on the
knife still aimed at his throat and slowly, slowly Garet nodded. Just once. 'I am content.'

'Then,' Aldric gestured with one hand, 'take this bloody
thing *off*!'

The restraint fell away to the oak-planked deck with a
clatter that was very loud in the silence which had settled on
the warship, and as the bands of steel and bullhide released
their grip on his thigh Aldric felt the agonising tingle of blood
as it poured back into vessels which had been constricted for
far too long. He stretched the limb and flexed it, again and
again; from hip to ankle it felt as if each muscle had been
dipped in boiling brine, and despite Garet's ill-concealed
impatience it was only when the leg felt and worked more as
it should that Aldric nodded curtly and agreed to do as he was
bid.

The inner belly of the battleram was much as he imagined
a rabbit-warren might look to a rabbit: a maze of passages
which branched off from one another, each low-ceilinged and
constricted, each leading somewhere that was unknown to a
stranger. He followed the *tau-kortagor's* disapproving back
along walkways, through heavy doors edged with greased
leather that was obviously meant to keep water at bay—and
always, always upward.

The Imperial warship was truly a huge vessel; doubtless
she was not so monstrous as she seemed to him right now,
but before God and the Holy Light of Heaven she had no

right to be so big and so powerful and so armoured and still defy the sea by floating on it.

Daylight through a hatchway hit him like a blow in the face and he flinched from it, shielding his outraged eyes with one arm. It was only the impact of the light from outside that brought home to Aldric just how dim it was on the lower decks where he had been confined. And he knew why, too: no lanterns. They had all been stowed away in case of fire.

So why, why, *why* could he smell such a reek of smoke and burning?

Aldric stopped in his tracks, suddenly afraid of the urgent summons, and equally suddenly there were two marines at his back, called up from God-knows-where or merely poised just out of sight against this very hesitation, ordinary troopers—if one could dismiss men so tall and strong as 'ordinary'—and they hustled him inexorably through the hatch and out onto the open deck.

The sun shone down without heat from that sky of limpid blue which seems only to appear in autumn or winter, and Aldric shivered in air which by its very freshness felt chilly after the closeness of below-decks. Under the unsympathetic scrutiny of that bright, pale light, and despite the taint of smoke which stung his nostrils, he became aware of two things—and was disgusted by them both.

The first was his appearance, and the second was his smell.

He was wearing the same clothes as when he had left Kathur's house—clothes which since then had come into violent contact with a wet Tuenafen street—and they were filthy. Those same clothes, unchanged after the sweaty exertions of fight and fright and flight, and the capture which had brought him here, went beyond grime into foulness and the heavy stink of stale perspiration. Any Alban would have found such a state of affairs intolerable; to one so fastidious as Aldric, it was revolting. He felt his skin crawl as if it shrank from contact with his grubby shirt, the lank oiliness of his hair, the crescents of dirt under his fingernails. Light of Heaven, to have eaten a meal with such hands . . . ! He barely choked back the heaving spasm that would have spewed his late lunch all across the deck, and tried hard to think of other things. There were plenty such to think about.

For all that the air was fresh and at first cold, under its crispness was a strange medley of odours—even setting aside

for a moment the aroma of unwashed Alban! Most powerful
was the astringence of scorched cloth and wood; but under it
was a warm, metallic tang reminiscent of the atmosphere in a
blacksmith's forge. Aldric had smelt it before—but not in any
forge.

The man who stalked across the quarterdeck to face him
was close to raving; whether with fear or fury, Aldric didn't
know. Most of the raving was in a Drusalan dialect which
meant nothing—and given the few recognisable words which
came through, ignorance was probably just as well. But
inflection and tone conveyed enough for him to guess the gist
of the captain's complaint, even before his language changed
to something more intelligible. Yes, this was the captain, for
all that wild eyes and a fear-pallid complexion detracted
somewhat from the *hautmarin*'s rank-marks on his green and
scarlet Fleet armour.

'Look at my ship! Look what's been done to my ship!
You! Alban! Damn you! What do you know about it, eh?
Devil burn you black! What do you know about *that*!'

Aldric's escort seized him by the shoulders and wrenched
him around, swivelling him in the direction of the captain's
outraged, outflung arm. The warship's deck was a shambles:
shattered yards, torn rigging and the charred shreds of what
once had been its sails littered the vessel's planking and
drooped wearily over the plates of its armoured hull. An acrid
film of thin grey smoke hung over all. And he saw for the
first time what was on, what was all over, what was coiled
massively around the semi-sunken turrets of the battleram's
bow.

For just that instant, until he took a mental grip of himself
that was as much a physical dominance of involuntary muscles, Aldric's lower jaw sagged just as far as that of anyone
else aboard, because of all the situations he might have
expected to face, this was the least likely. And of all the
emotions he might have experienced, this was by far the most
utterly impossible.

For it was *recognition*!

Because although he had looked at one before, spoken to
one before, fought down his disbelief when facing one before, the last thing that he had expected in all this wide and
wonderful world was to meet a—*the*—name-known and
familiar Goddamn firedrake!

Except that here it was!

'Ymareth,' he said, very, very softly. And perhaps his voice was not so quiet as he thought; or perhaps the fire-drake's hearing was far more acute than he believed—or perhaps the huge glow of delight that rose within him was strong enough to carry clearly to its cause. Whatever the reason might have been, it didn't really matter. Because the firedrake heard him, or sensed him, or . . . something.

And it moved.

There was a dreadful languid grace in the way that the horned and jagged head curved back, elegant as an iron swan, but at the same time there was an arrogant flaunting of incalculable might and a pride that Aldric could appreciate. He heard sounds that he knew well, sounds that he recognised as if he had last heard them yesterday: a steely slithering of scaled coils and the slow bass surge of a vast respiration. The sounds of a living dragon.

As the ornate, elongated wedge of Ymareth's head swung towards him, Aldric prudently lowered his eyes—not merely through respect, for all that this huge being was deserving of such courtesy where many men of rank were not. As the firedrake's phosphorescent stare raked over all the men who lined the armoured railing of the warship's quarterdeck, only one among them knew that he *had* to look away or be entrapped as much as any little bird before a snake. Aldric knew. No man born of woman could meet such a gaze and hope to walk away unscathed—or if the circumstance was wrong, hope to walk away at all . . .

The dragon exhaled gently and Aldric smelt again that harsh, clean furnace wind. The hot gust carried words in a voice that few had ever heard—a voice which held the sounds of steam and falling water, the sounds of stone-stroked metal and storm-waves on a rocky shore, the sounds of the sifting of blasted ashes. A voice that none save Aldric understood, and he only by virtue of the Charm of Understanding laid on him at their first meeting, months ago and miles from here.

'I give thee greeting, man. Well met, Aldric Talvalin.'

Aldric shook free from the hands which held him and they fell away slack-fingered, the marines who flanked him struck dumb and witless by Ymareth's gaze.

He knelt, paused and then bowed forward to place his crossed hands against the deck and press his forehead briefly onto them in the Second Obeisance which he had given when he first met the dragon in the Cavern of Firedrakes on Techaur Island. Here and now it was perhaps not quite appropriate—Second Obeisance was properly due an equal or superior under the roof of his own hall and nowhere else—but overly elaborate manners were always better than insufficient, if sincerely meant. Then he sat back neatly on his heels and composed himself as best he could. Ymareth, watching in reptilian stillness, had not moved.

'Well met indeed, Lord Firedrake,' Aldric returned; then, greatly daring, 'But why—and how?'

Flame licked momentarily between the dragon's parted jaws and Aldric flinched despite himself. He felt like a man walking a tightrope, balanced precariously between the perils of ignorance and that insolence which comes of importunate curiosity.

'Which first, O man—the "why" or the "how"? Thine is the choice.' Insofar as it was possible to attribute human reactions to something so manifestly un-human, Ymareth was amused and gently teasing. This was enough to make Aldric marginally bolder.

'Try the "how", my lord. I already know that Techaur and your abiding-place lie many leagues from here.'

There was another quick spout of flame, that harmless incandescent swirling which Aldric had already come to recognise as laughter—and which he had already guessed was responsible for the state of the battleram's sails. Even though he was only half-way right . . .

'I am Ymareth. I am dragonkind. I searched for thee: I found thee. Such is our way.' The dragon's head swung leisurely towards the sea, staring south along the now-vanished track of its passage through the upper air. 'Yet verily, any task is made as nothing when there is a true guide with that searched-for. As was the Eye of the Dragon with thee, *kailin* Talvalin.'

'The Eye of . . . ?' Aldric's voice trailed off with its question incomplete, for in his own mind's eye there was an image of Gemmel Errekren with the Dragonwand Ykraith in one hand and the azure-glowing stone of Echainon in the other. The spellstave's carven dragonhead had an eye already; but only one, and that an ordinary sapphire gemstone. Its other socket was empty. Then the wizard's hands came together, and when they parted the Dragonwand looked out on the world with two eyes, one of them alive and throbbing with the glow of its own internal energies. The Eye of the Dragon indeed!

And the self-same talisman which Aldric had carried these months past, in ignorance of the truth.

There were a great many things which he might have said, and probably an equal number which he should have said. But what at last came from his mouth was no more than a barely audible exhalation of, 'Oh *God* . . . !'

Which served no real purpose whatsoever.

Ymareth watched him and again seemed to derive amusement from his confusion. Its thin-lipped mouth stretched back and back in a grin, that foxy smirk which Aldric had seen before; and though then he had thought it no more indicative of real humour than any other so-called "expression" on an animal's face, now he wasn't quite so sure. There was a certain precision about the way in which the firedrake's facial muscles moved which suggested that Ymareth was deliberately copying something observed and noted by its icy draconian brain, something which might be used to reassure the nervousness of humankind. If that was indeed the reason, it failed: there was no reassurance to be found in the shocking armoury of fangs which the dragon's grin put on display.

'And the "why", Aldric Talvalin? Does "why" not begin to pique thy curiosity?'

It did. So much so that for just an instant, just the merest breath of inattention, Aldric's gaze flickered speculatively upwards as the many possibilities of that *why* crossed his mind. And in that momentary glance he met the smoking amber mirrors that were the eyes of Ymareth. Truly the Eyes of the Dragon. Aldric's own eyes met them and locked with them. And were caught.

Time stops as it stands still. The voice was within his head, as Ymareth's had been—but this was not the dragon's voice at all. It was, or seemed to be 'Gemmel?' Aldric's mind alone shaped the word, for his mouth and tongue could not. There was no reply—no repetition of the voice that had no place here, no reason to be here, and no reason to say what it had said, for all that the words were right and proper in the here and now. If here and now there was.

For time ceased to have meaning and reality ceased to

exist. There was only himself and the two great glowing orbs
that stared and stared and never, ever blinked. He was laid
bare before their gaze: not naked *unclothed* but naked *without
concealment*, stripped of the screens and shields men use to
disguise the truth from one another. He was stretched out
before the coldly burning scrutiny of the dragon, and what
was there was all that he was. Without rank, without privilege, without title. Without anything to hide behind.

And he was ashamed.

He could see, as Ymareth could see, all the ugliness that
was within him; all the unadmitted secret vice that might be
indulged if only he dared to do so, all the carefully-forgotten
sins that at one time or another had been indulged, all the
things that any and all but the very purest carried deep inside,
buried under manners and courtesies and outward show like
the slimy life under a rock. Always there and known, but
never revealed even to the closest of friends.

Until now.

The questions were not asked in any way that ears might
hear or mind might comprehend; they merely formed, resolv-
ing from the grey mist of sadness that surrounded him. But
once they had taken shape, they struck and flayed like iron
whips. Questions which he could not answer—simple questions which in their simplicity probed with pitiless directness
deep into his soul.

Aldric said nothing—and could say nothing—in his own
defence. Guilt sickened him, rose choking in his throat,
raised scars that would never heal. Then something snapped;
he heard it snap, or felt it snap—a sound and a sensation like
the breaking of a leash. And the world came back to him with
a jolt.

Nothing had changed; he was still kneeling on the deck,
straight-backed, sitting on his own heels. But his face was
wet and chilled by the cold breeze. One hand came up—oh,
so slowly—to touch the wetness. Tears. He had been crying,
for no reason and for every reason. Because he felt dirty,
soiled by having those things which were secret drawn out
into the light of day, and yet at the same time he felt
strangely cleansed as though that same drawing-out had purged
him and somehow made him whole. Blinking the blur of
unshed tears out of his eyes and dashing them away with his

knuckles, Aldric focused on reality again. On the ship; and on the dragon.

Ymareth's huge head was right above him, an arm's length over his own, ponderous as the raw stone roof of the Kingsmound and as redolent of great age. He could feel the arid scouring of the being's fiery breath on his skin, and could smell the heated-metal tang of it. For the flames and the death they carried were so close now. And he was not afraid.

The fear had always been there, whether he admitted to its existence—tempering such an admission with mockery, as if to prove he wasn't really scared at all—or kept it locked away, nestled deep within him. Aldric had always imagined that fear of Ymareth as heavy and foreign and cold, a lump of ice-sheathed lead tucked underneath his heart; but now both lead and ice had been taken from their hiding-place and washed with dragonfire until they were melted and left not a trace behind.

'Know now why I came, Aldric Talvalin. Honour awakened me. Honour summoned me. Honour bound me as it binds you.'

'Honour? What honour have I left? I threw it all away in Seghar long ago!'

'So say *ye*. I say *not*!' Flame gouted above his head—not the flutter which indicated humour but a blasting torrent of irritation that slapped heat down at him like a physical impact. There was an edge in the great voice, a steeliness like crossed blades; Ymareth was not accustomed to dispute. 'Hear me, O man. I have such wings as may bear thee to thy liberty, if such is thy desire. Speak and say, will ye escape thus? Speak!'

Aldric closed his eyes, feeling his heartbeat quicken and the breath begin to catch in his throat. Escape? An hour ago, yes, and willingly. But now? Now he could not.

The dragon blinked once and he heard the metallic click of its eyelids clearly in the silence. 'Speak,' it repeated, more gently now.

'I cannot. I *must* not. I—' He looked up, deliberately seeking the dragon's eyes. 'I gave my Word.'

'The Word of one who by his own admission is without all honour?'

Aldric shrugged. 'The right to keep a promise is all that I have left.'

'So, and so, and so. Thou art more worthy than the Maker ever was, *Kailin* Aldric-*eir*.'

To my eternal shame. Again Aldric heard the voice inside his head, and again it was not Ymareth but Gemmel who seemed to speak.

'To his shame,' echoed the dragon.

Aldric listened, and heard, and at last a minute flower of understanding began to blossom in his mind. But it was a flower with sombre petals, for the only meaning made possible by his understanding was such that his senses began to swim with the enormity of it all.

Ymareth's wings unfurled, dwarfing the Imperial warship, and Aldric realised with a jolt that which he had unconsciously known since he came out onto the deck: now that he could see the firedrake against a background of normality rather than within the Cavern on Techaur, it was far, far bigger than he had dreamed. Wingtip to wingtip, Ymareth's span was more than sixty yards; from nose to the flattened spade-shape which ended its tail—aerodynamic in section, like the horns and crest of its head—it was another forty yards in length. Weight . . . ? Enough to all but sink the bow of an armoured battleram, more than enough to make flight impossible.

But then, everything to do with dragons seemed to be impossible: their speech, their intelligence, their flaming breath, their unnatural extra limbs—for surely it would be more right and proper for their wings to be like those of bats, an alteration of the forelegs—and above all the fact that at least one of these legend-bound creatures was alive and here before him, for all that logic said they could not exist in the natural scheme of things. Even though many men might desire dragons, the reality was overpowering. Inexorably the processes of Aldric's thought sheared away surmise, reducing possibilities one by one until only the last remained. If dragons could not exist in a natural world, but one at least unquestionably did, then . . .

Who was the Maker?

And the answer to that was such that Aldric could not bear even to let it shape within his brain.

'I go.' Ymareth crouched low on tensed hindlegs, wings arcing up and up above the lean, scaled body until their

uttermost tips met and crossed, then poised for the barest
moment as the set of their membranes shifted to cup the air.

'Go?' Aldric asked the question hurriedly. 'Go where?'

'From here. From this shell. They scarcely will forgive my
flaming of their sails, for all that I bade them to stop ere harm
befell. So. But the Eye will watch thee as it has watched
aforetime. As I will watch thee, Dragon-lord. And I will
know that which it is needful for me to know. Until that time,
farewell!'

Ymareth's hind-limbs straightened like the throwing-arms
of a catapult, flinging the dragon's armoured bulk into a great
bound towards the sky. An instant later and the wings swept
down, their thunderous whack of displaced air ripping away
what shreds of sail remained and all but blowing Aldric on to
his back as they transformed that prodigious leap into true
flight.

The battleram's deck kicked beneath him as it plunged still
lower in response to the dragon's take-off thrust, then reared
up past the horizontal as Ymareth's weight was abruptly
removed. Great concentric ripples rolled away from the ram
bow as it smashed back into the sea in a cloud of spray and
creamy foam, mingling with the rings of disturbed water
where the pressure of the dragon's wings had slapped brutally
against the surface. And then all was still.

There was only a rakish black silhouette in the sky, and the
feather touch of that cold breeze from the north. It was a
stillness that was all too brief: Aldric had barely risen to his
feet, legs weak with reaction and knees sore from the impact
of the oak-planked deck, before the two marines behind him
shrugged off their firedrake-induced drowse and laid hard
hands on his shoulders again. He glanced from side to side,
looking at the troopers without really seeing them, and then
relaxed in their grip without so much as a token twitch of
either arm.

The warship's captain glowered at him, all of his earlier
frantic anger quite gone now and replaced by a deadly control. He reached out one armoured steel-and-leather hand,
twisted up the front of the Alban's shirt and used it to lift
Aldric onto tip-toe, almost eye-to-eye at last with the tall,
lean *hautmarin*.

'It is as well for you, *hlens'l*,' he said quietly—too quietly—
'that I have my orders. Otherwise I would take great pleasure

in supervising your protracted death. Oh, but I would. . . .'
He said what he would do, in elaborate detail and at length.

   Aldric stared at the officer, hanging in his grasp as limp
and unconcerned as a kitten in its mother's mouth; stared at
him and through him as if he wasn't there. Ignored him
completely. He had heard all the threats before, more or less;
some of them were original, indicative of a nasty mind, and
some were commonplace. But all, because of those so-important
orders, were just onion-scented air and the occasional passion-
driven speck of spittle. Nothing more at all. In Aldric's mind
right now were two words and two words alone, words which
had nothing to do with threats or Drusalan naval officers, or
anything so mundane as that. They were words he understood
in the literal sense, but did not dare to recognise as a title.
Yet.. Words that should have been repeated as a question:
Dragon Lord?

   But once the *hautmarin* had run out of breath and inven-
tion, he let himself smile slowly and deliberately full in the
officer's face. 'Despite all that you say, shipmaster,' and he
used the civilian rank as a clearly understood insult, 'all that
you can do is write in your report. Yes?'

   The Drusalan smirked. 'No. Not quite. Take him below.'

SIX

Recruitment

'That's the house,' said Dewan. He didn't stop, didn't even slacken his pace, and most certainly did nothing so obvious as to point. But he sounded entirely certain and Gemmel was impressed.

Impressed not only with the results of his companion's ability to extract information—from people who often had not known that they were answering a question—but also by the house itself. Gemmel had tried to avoid preconceived notions of what they might find, but once he had heard that the woman they sought was a courtesan, his mind had replaced the word with all of its uglier alternatives. It was both unusual and uncomfortable: he was normally a most tolerant man.

But once formed, those preconceived notions had led to further misconceptions, errors that were now shattered like glass. None of the *sluts*, or *harlots*, or *whores* of his imaginings would or could live in such a dwelling; at least, if they were still to justify such names as his ungenerous subconscious had supplied. He altered the angle of his stride a fraction, intending to walk straight in—since surely gentlemen callers were familiar at this front door—but without apparent deliberate intent, Dewan was suddenly in the way.

'Not so hasty!' The Vreijek's voice was crisp and commanding, as it had been since first they passed through the Landwall Gate; Dewan could have donned the uniform and half-harness in his laden pack at any time, and not have drawn a second glance by incorrect demeanour. 'Take this carefully, man. Remember the battleram. Somebody was here before us—if we're guessing right—and I want to make sure they're gone before we go barging in. So gently does it, eh?'

They walked on, idly curious about their surroundings and
no more until Gemmel felt—*sensed* Dewan go tense. 'In the
stable entry. Don't *look*! One man. Minding his own business. Too much so, I think.' There was the faintest whisker
of hesitation in Dewan's stride, and Gemmel knew that violence and sudden death were being considered in that instant.

Then the Vreijek relaxed. He even chuckled—a deep, rich
sound unusual right now for its incongruity. Now at last
Gemmel chanced an over-shoulder glance at the source of
such conflicting reactions—and stifled a laugh in his turn.
'Ah,' was all that he said at first, for all that there was a
paragraph of meaning in his tone. Then: 'He was minding his
own business after all.'

'His, and nobody else's.'

The man Dewan ar Korentin had seen—and might have
killed, had he not chanced that swift second glance—walked
past them with no more than a nod and a muttered word of
inconsequential greeting. He smelt somewhat of beer and he
was busy fastening his breeches.

Gemmel watched him until he passed out of sight around a
corner, leaving the street empty but for himself and Dewan.
Then he turned a little, and his smile was gone as though it
had never existed. 'Now—do we stay here, or do we get this
matter done with and out of the way?'

'I told you before, don't worry about it. You still talk as if
I'm going to put someone's feet in the fire. I'm not.'

'Unless you have to. And then you will.'

'Not if I can get the information any other way, old
wizard, old friend. I served with the Bodyguard Cavalry, not
with the Secret Police. But I can still talk a good threat when
I have to.'

Kathur's head jerked up from the travelling-trunk she had
been so frantically packing and turned towards the door of her
room, a door that once again framed the back-lit outlines of
intruders. Her eyes flickered from one man to the other, back
and forth, and the garment in her hands slithered from its
folds to hang in an untidy limp tangle like a wet flag. There
was a hunted, persecuted look on her face, and it deepened to
something near terror when one of the men took the single
step necessary to bring him across the threshold; he was
broad-shouldered, moustached, the younger of the two and

the bigger in all but height, and he looked by far the more likely to hurt her.

Hurting had been very much at the forefront of the Drusalan woman's mind this past few hours. Hurting—and confusion, and misery, and regret, and all those other emotions that early yesterday she would have sworn that she was done with feeling. But now all of those lesser emotions were subordinated by an all-consuming fear.

To his credit, Dewan ar Korentin read her face and her eyes and stopped what he knew must be a threatening advance at once. 'Gemmel,' he said, using Alban, 'best I think that you talk to her and I keep out of it. For now, anyway.'

Gemmel shot him a quizzical, eyebrow-lifted glance, but followed the request immediately; he too had seen how terrified the woman was, and from the first glance had been appalled at how she differed from the description Dewan had cajoled from one of the local people. He was more appalled still by the all-too-plain reasons for that difference.

Only the fox-red hair remained unchanged; for the rest, although there was still an eroded beauty in her face and figure, it was masked by her expression and by the purpled tissue of a carefully-administered brutalising. Gemmel's mind refused to accept the lesser alternative of *beating*, because although what he could see was bad enough, the flinching, careful way in which she moved implied that worse was hidden by her clothing. Maliciously, sadistically, much, much worse. And to his own private shame both then and afterwards, the first words which left his mouth were an unjust accusation that he could only blame on shock and the cynicism of one who has seen too much cruelty to too many people to believe that even the most familiar might be incapable of it.

'Lady—did Aldric Talvalin do this to you?'

The battleram limped towards harbour; as she had limped heavily, leadenly, since her fiery encounter with Ymareth. Aldric, on deck and under guard, was limping too, Important prisoner or not, gentleman or not—both matters stridently if uselessly protested—he had perforce assisted the warship's crew to bring their vessel safely into port.

He had not known that the witch-wind enchantment was woven into the pattern and the fabric of the sails. He had not

known that destruction of those sails meant destruction of the
spell, and consequently of the battleram's ability to move at
speed wherever her captain desired regardless of the vagaries
of wind and weather. And he had not known—although he
had suspected—that without the charmed sails at her mast and
bowsprit, an Imperial capital ship became lumbering, un-
gainly and above all slow.

He knew it now, and the information had been docketed at
the back of his mind for possible future reference.

Just as he also knew now—for it was engraved in every
muscle of his body that hurt individually and collectively in a
symphony of discomfort that would flare to real pain as they
cooled and stiffened—how such a vessel must be propelled
when the wind was in the wrong quarter for ordinary sails.
By such aching muscles as his own.

Not muscles pulling oars, which he might have understood
at once had not the lack of oarlocks along the battleram's
armoured sides denied any such notion. The ship's design
was not that of a galley; and in any case her half-dozen
close-manoeuvring sweeps were too few in number for lengthy
propulsion on the high seas. Instead there was some arrangement of shafts and cranks deep in her belly, enhanced by
gears and cogs and wheels such as were so beloved by the
Drusalans, which ultimately spun a seven-bladed thrust-screw
at the vessel's stern. That much the captain had told him with
a degree of relish as he was escorted below-decks to the drive
chamber which ran almost the full length of the warship's
keel and—he alone—shackled by neck and waist to ringbolts
in the hull cross-members.

He had at first been advised, not ordered, to strip; and at
first he had refused, thinking that it was just another attempt
to humiliate him. And had continued to refuse until he saw
the conditions in which he would be working. Then he had
undressed quickly enough, down to the brief trunks which
were the last step before nudity. He kept those. Albans were
a modest folk, except in those situations where modesty was
an affectation and which situations usually involved women—
but he had been grateful that nothing warmer than the too-hot
air was pressing on his skin.

That inferno of sweat and stink and nauseous motion would
remain one of his choicest nightmares for a very long time.
Not being slaves, the men in the drive chamber were not

flogged as they worked; Aldric escaped only because of those wonderfully restricting orders. But they laboured achingly hard for all that, feet buckled into stirrup cranks that were like and yet unlike a treadmill, using the big muscles of their thighs and their body weight as well to turn the flywheel-weighted subshafts which led at last to the grinding, greasy main drive. After only a few minutes wrists and arms and spine and legs were all trembling with the strain of the incessant pumping push-and-pull, heads aching and giddy with the constant bending and straightening, hands flayed raw against the brace-bars for all that they were fitted with rotating sleeves against just such an occurrence; backwards and forwards, up and down again, and again, and *again,* hour after hour amid grunts and cries of effort, the constant squeak and clatter of machinery that was so wearing in itself and so unusual to one familiar only with the noises of a sailing-ship, the rush of water against the lead-skinned underwater hull and always in the background like the beating of a weary heart, the whap-whap-whap of the great rotating blades.

But it was over now and Aldric felt a certain glow of satisfaction, even of pride. Having been forced to the work and given no other option, he had done as well as any of the others who, he fancied, were more used to it. He had neither vomited nor fainted, although he had witnessed both, and he had completed his 'shift', as the drivemaster-serjeant termed it, without flagging behind his fellows. Maybe he had been lucky, because he had been right below one of the shafts which drew cool fresh air from the open deck—by means of yet more bladed propellers, these turned by boy-sailors—but even so, that was not to say he would be in any haste to repeat the experience. Nevertheless it had crossed his mind that the underwater drive-screw at least preserved the integrity of the warship's armoured shell, and that if there was another way than manpower to propel a ship in that fashion, it might well be worth a closer study . . .

It was then that somebody—some evil-minded bastard! —had sluiced him down with a bucket of icy fresh-drawn seawater all over his naked, sweat-scalded skin, and in the sudden horrific-becoming-glorious shock Aldric forgot everything else.

That had all been half an hour ago. Now, dressed in borrowed clothes and feeling at least marginally cleaner—if also hellishly tired—he stood on the battleram's foredeck in the shadow of one of her weapon-turrets and watched as she was teased with a delicacy that approached art into a stone-walled holding bay little wider than the ship herself. Evening was approaching, and both his own vessel—he smiled wryly at that unconscious usage of the possessive—and the five or so others either in fortified docks like this or riding at anchor out in what seemed an estuary, were showing lights. That understatement scarcely described the hulking armoured vessels which were illuminated like so many ocean-going mansions; or rather, like the floating fortresses they were.

'Alban?' It was *tau-kortagor* Garet again; one of the several men aboard who had treated him with markedly more friendliness since his unstinting efforts down in the warship's drive chamber. 'You disembark here, Alban. *Teynaur* is going into dry-dock for repair after . . .'

'After what happened?'

'Yes.' The expression within Garet's helmet might conceivably have been a grin. 'You're being talked about.'

'I can't say that I'm surprised. What do they say?'

'Do you want the polite version, or the truth?'

This time it was Aldric's turn to grin, even though the expression looked stretched and uncomfortable. 'If that's the way of it, forget I asked. But . . .' He hesitated, knowing that he was about to presume on a tenuous bond of acquaintance—not even friendship!—which probably didn't exist at all. 'Where are we? And who had me brought here?'

The questions seemed to make Garet uncomfortable; at least he turned his head away as if fascinated by non-events at the far end of the harbour, and Aldric could no longer see his face. 'The first I'm not allowed to answer,' Garet said without looking back, 'and the second, at my rank'—he touched a finger pointedly to the solitary rank-bar at his collar—'I'm not allowed to know.'

Aldric shrugged. It was the sort of response he should have expected, even if more courteously phrased than it might have been; but a waste of time and breath for all that. With a nod of acknowledgement to the officer-cadet, he squared his shoulders and walked—not slowly, but not especially fast—to a boarding-ladder where the crew of the ship's cutter were waiting to take him ashore. Ashore!

Lord God! Beyond the quays and the loading-cranes that

were commonplace on any waterfront whether military or civilian lay a sprawling structure that had nothing whatever to do with wharves or warehouses. It was a fortification, walled and turreted, gated and grim, and its courtyards were alive with troops of horse and foot moving purposefully to and fro. Even to one accustomed to such things it was an unnerving sight.

Teynaur had put into harbour three days late. This was the first day of the tenth month, the first day of the beginning of winter, and the evening sky was grey as woodsmoke. Despite the many lanterns which bejewelled its massive walls, the crouched shape of the stronghold was ugly and ominous beneath that sombre canopy of cloud. Its spired turrets were stark against the lowering heavens and the banners which they bore—indecipherable in the dusk—flapped listlessly from their poles. There was no elegance in the place, none at all; not even that austere grace sometimes born of pure functional design. This looked like no more than it was: a fortress—and a prison.

Aldric stared out over the bows of the cutter and tried to keep real and imagined terrors under control. The sort of power involved here was appalling, and he could not imagine who would want him so badly that a fully-crewed battleram could be sent to bring him back. He fancied that he was soon to find out.

'*Hlens'l?*' One of the marine escort tapped him on the shoulder and proffered a leather bottle of the regulation pattern which all Imperial troopers carried as part of their equipment. If there was one thing Aldric would never refuse at a moment like this, it was a drink—even the notoriously rough, sour ration red. But at least it was cool in his dry mouth and warm in his belly and head; that was enough reason to gulp it down. He drank a little more, stifled a nasty acid belch—there was nothing but the wine inside him, and his stomach was complaining about both matters—then handed the bottle back and tried to snuggle deeper into the wolfskin *coyac* that someone had returned to him. While it didn't make him feel much warmer, it did make him wonder for just a moment about something other than his own imminent fate.

What phase was the moon just now?

Then the cutter bumped against a wooden jetty and he all but fell off the upturned barrel which was doing duty as his seat. The marines laughed, but not unkindly, and made observations about Albans and army-issue wine which Aldric preferred to ignore. He had in his time downed enough alcohol to float the *Teynaur*, and never before had he tasted stuff that was so obviously rented for re-cycling.

Two soldiers—regulars in crimson armour and full-visored helmets, not Fleet marines—came clattering down the steps of the jetty and lifted Aldric bodily, as if he was a sack of meal. He wasn't pleased. Directly his feet touched the lowermost step, weed-covered slimy wood but dry land for all that, he shrugged himself free.

'Thank you both, gentlemen,' he said, 'but I *can* walk quite well without you.' For once he managed to achieve the right tone of injured dignity rather than dangerous rudeness, but that was not why the soldiers laughed—a hollow, metallic sound inside their closed helmets.

It was because, as Aldric discovered, legs that were both tired and grown accustomed to the constant motion of a deck found the immobility of solid ground a far from certain footing.

But he managed. Just.

The first two soldiers flanked him, presumably in case he did fall after all, but several more who had remained atop the jetty formed up behind and in front before setting off at an unsettlingly rapid march-pace. *Teynaur* was late, therefore he was late, therefore his presence was required at once. The Imperial *at once* did not leave room for excuse or further delay.

Their destination was one of the largest buildings within the fortress complex, and as they approached its door up a flight of broad stone steps, the sentries to either side of the door flung it open so that the little group could pass through without breaking stride. The sullen boom as it was slammed shut behind them had an unpleasantly final sound, but Aldric was given no time for reflection and little enough in which to look around.

This place might have started life at some time in the past as a palace or a mansion—before the military took over—and it remained a building where the high-born of the Empire would not look out of place. But there were no aristocrats in the handsome panelled corridors this evening: just soldiers, some in half-armour but most in tunics with both their arms full of paperwork. Even when the passages were briefly free of hurrying figures there was an air of furious activity, a tension which made the atmosphere tingle.

The boots of Aldric's escort awoke echoes in a vaulted hall as he was quick-marched through, neither pushed nor forced but simply hemmed about so closely that he either matched their pace of his own volition or had his heels trodden by the rearguard. They rounded another corner, entered a short, well-lit corridor which had only one doorway at its end and then stopped dead, for this passage was lined with soldiers.

These were big men in full battle harness, and their faces were uniformly blanked by the featureless closed visors of their helmets. There were six of them across the double doors, razor-edged gisarms carried at the port; but when two of Aldric's guards continued to advance, all of the sentries took a single well-drilled forward step—a step so precise and simultaneous that Aldric half-expected to hear the whirr of machinery—and levelled their spears, three at each chest. There was something cold, something automatic about their manner; something chilling. It was a suggestion that these men had their orders, and if those orders involved killing comrades-in-arms, then the killing would be done with dispatch and without a second thought. Only when the senior-ranked soldier of the escort spoke a password did the wicked points withdraw, and as if the word had set off a new series of signals, four of the gate-wards stepped aside while the remaining two threw all their weight into opening the ponderous bronze-sheathed doors.

The room revealed beyond the threshold was long, and low, and wide; lamps burned in sconces along its walls, striking reflections from the polished table which dominated the centre of the floor, from the crystal goblets which rested on it—and from the gold-worked crimson armour of the twenty Imperial officers who sat along its sides and who turned as one man to stare at the intruder in their doorway.

Escort or no escort, Aldric froze in his tracks. At his back there was a rippling clatter of parade salutes, and only after they had been completed did someone give the Alban a much-needed shove between the shoulder-blades to send him stumbling into the conference room.

As he halted and straightened up a little, he eyed the officers dubiously—for their part, nineteen-twentieths of them

regarded him with open curiosity—but at the same time he
felt the stirrings of relief. There was real power here, the kind
of power he had thought to find at the back of all—that of the
Imperial military machine. Oh yes. Aldric knew the yellow
metal bars and double diamonds of general-rank insignia
when he saw them, and there were several right before his
eyes. But he also knew the Emperor's crest of the eight-
pointed star, and that was worked in precious metal on the
temples of each man's helmet, resting on the table among the
wine-cups. Emperor Ioen's supporters had no grudge against
King Rynert's men—he had been assured of that, and it was
one of the reasons which had brought him here to the Empire,
what seemed so very long ago. Not caring who could overhear him, Aldric released a gusty sigh of held-in breath.
Whatever he might hear from these granite-faced gentry would
never be as bad as his imaginings.

There was one officer in particular who drew his eyes; the
man was seated at the head of the table, gazing at him
steadily, saying nothing, his only movement the slow tap-tap-
tap of one index finger. His rank-marks were of a type of
which Aldric had only been told and had never seen: the twin
bars of commissioned rank, and over them a pyramid made
up of three diamonds. All in bullion gold soft and pure
enough to scratch with a fingernail. This was the most senior
of all Drusalan military ranks, before political significance
took over: *en-coerhanalth*, Lord General. But which one?
With a perfunctory gesture of his hand the officer dismissed
Aldric's escort—all but two who closed in to grip the Alban
by wrists and biceps—before he rose and strode down the hall
to confront his captive at close quarters.

He was a stocky man, this general—Aldric's own height,
but with an already-broad build made massive by the armour
which encased him. Though his grizzled beard and balding
iron-grey hair were those of a middle-aged man, there was no
dullness of age in the pale eyes which glinted below his
heavy brows. Those eyes drilled through Aldric as if, like
Ymareth's, they probed the innermost recesses of his mind.
Except that this officer appeared more plainly to disapprove
of what he saw there.

Aldric swallowed and refused to meet that piercing stare.
Even without the guards, the other officers, the armour and
the marks of rank, this man had a forbidding presence of his

own. One blunt-fingered hand reached out, closed on Aldric's chin and lifted it up and back from where instinct had tucked it low over his throat. A finger of the other hand tapped—as it had done to the table—against the heavy silver torque of the Alban's crest-collar, and the general grunted softly to himself as if satisfied. That same finger touched lightly against the scar on Aldric's face, and this time the tone of the grunt was displeasure at the wound's apparent newness. A moment more and the general turned away. 'Release him,' he said over his shoulder, and Aldric felt a muscle in his face tic involuntarily. Because the language of the order was his own.

Massaging his arms more for something to do than because they hurt—even though the sentries's grip had been tight enough to stop the flow of blood, and it tingled in his fingers as it returned to them—Aldric watched all the officers surreptitiously from under drooping eyelids. And the general who spoke Alban most of all.

'My lord,' he said, cringing inwardly at the loudness of his own voice in the silence, 'I thank you.' He bowed a little, as was polite; then looked straight at the general, as was not polite at all, and tried not to care that his direct gaze might be considered insolent and dealt with as such. 'But I would thank you rather more if I knew what the hell was going on!'

Nineteen high-ranked officers growled their displeasure—suggesting that each and every one of them was familiar with colloquial Alban—but the twentieth merely inclined his head. 'Talvalin,' he said. The statement was neither confirmed nor denied by so much as the flick of an eyelid, but he nodded again, seeming content. 'Aldric Talvalin. Yes. Your file suggested that you might react like this.' Aldric didn't miss the inference, delivered with all the subtlety of a battleaxe: *We know all about you, boy.* 'And I,' the bearded lips allowed themselves a thin smile, 'am Lord General Goth.'

At last. At long last.

Aldric did the most sensible and indeed the most appropriate thing he could in the circumstances—he knelt and offered Goth the elaborate courtesy of Second Obeisance that was due to him as senior officer here and thus technically Lord of the place. It also gave him a chance to get his betraying facial muscles under control, so that when he sat back he was hiding behind a cool, inscrutable, half-smiling mask.

Goth half-smiled as well. 'There is a proverb among my people, Aldric Talvalin. It refers to your people: "Be wary of the Alban when he bows to hide his face." Should I be wary of you, perhaps?'

Aldric shrugged; he doubted it. Doubted indeed if there was much this man had to be wary of, anywhere at all. Lord General Goth was third man in the Drusalan Imperial hierarchy, and paramount military commander—for despite its martial title, the office of Grand Warlord was more political than anything else; recent events had made that all too clear. Equally, or most likely more important, he was virtual father to young Emperor Ioen. Much as Gemmel was to Aldric, but for years longer. He was a man of honour, although it was Drusalan honour and more flexible than most Alban *kailinin* would have tolerated. Goth, in doing what he considered necessary for the good of the Empire, had been required to twist his vaunted honour almost beyond recognition.

'Then be seated, Aldric-*an,*' the general invited. 'Properly.' It wasn't really an invitation at all, and Aldric did as he was told. 'First,' continued Goth when the Alban had settled himself, 'I ask pardon for the means which brought you here.'

Since the verb he used for 'ask' was in an imperative mode, it seemed unlikely to be just a linguistic slip. That kind of accident was only made by such as Goth for its effect. So Aldric nodded and smiled, and made all the courteous little wordless gestures of one dismissing a paltry inconvenience.

Rather than an experience which had been terrifying at the time—he admitted this without hesitation, if only to himself—and which had still done little in the way of reassurance.

'Now, as to the reason for it all.' Goth leaned back in his chair and made ready to talk at length; Aldric had seen such expressive body language before, too many times, for both Gemmel and Dewan were great preachers when the mood was on them. 'You must realise, of course, that you were in what we regard here as debatable territory—most seaports must perforce be. . . .'

Locking an expression of polite interest onto his face, Aldric let five minutes of speculation and political theory wash over him. Either he had heard it all before, or he hadn't been interested in finding out about it the first time around.

Then Goth said something which jarred him back to full awareness.

'. . . and more than my men knew of your presence there.'

Something of what he felt must have shown on Aldric's face despite his endeavours towards guarded neutrality, for Goth leaned forward and wagged a disapproving finger at him—a tutorial gesture much in keeping with his tone of voice.

'Come now, you didn't really think the goings-on at Seghar went unnoticed, did you?' He stared more closely, spade beard jutting pugnaciously. 'Or *did* you?'

Aldric said nothing.

'Well . . . !' There was a deal of private opinion in the way that Goth exhaled the word, but he elaborated no further and instead lifted one armoured shoulder in the beginnings of a shrug. 'No matter now. But given the situation—and your apparent frame of mind—you would scarcely have paused for conversation had you been approached by armoured regulars like those who brought you here. Besides which, their presence would have made my hand too plain. As I say, there were more eyes than mine in Tuenafen. So I was forced to resort to—shall we say, other means? Despite some opposition.'

As if on cue one of the other officers got to his feet, snapped a perfunctory salute and began to address his superior in what Aldric could only think of as a polite shout—if such a thing were not a blatant contradiction in terms. Certainly it was very different from the muted voices at King Rynert's war council before the Dunrath campaign.

Another man rose, nodded to his equals, saluted his superiors and joined the discussion—if discussion was really the word for it, and Aldric was still not sure that it was. This man's oration carried more shouting and less politeness, so that the tapping of Goth's finger began again. Both speakers employed dialect, as Geruath of Seghar had done all those months ago—and for the same reason: so that the foreigner present wouldn't understand.

As indeed he couldn't. Aldric was curious to learn how they knew this fact; eager, too, to find out the other score or so of things which were perplexing him right now.

'Gentlemen,' Goth said finally, his tone indicating a full stop to the discussion, 'gentlemen, we voted on this matter when the plan was first proposed.' He spoke Drusalan, and though the drawling accent which seemed to be a trademark of the military made understanding difficult, what he said was clear enough to Aldric. All too clear.

Plan? a voice was yelling in his mind. *Nobody told me about a plan!*

The first officer jumped up, scowling, and barked out a few words before making an indignant gesture in Aldric's direction.

'We have not been *forced* to anything,' returned Goth. 'This was a choice made by the whole council. And yes, Hasolt, I do remember your views at the time. Do you want to make your objections formal—a matter of record?'

'*Kham-au tah, Coerhanalth Goth!*' The officer glanced around the table, shot another unfriendly glare at Aldric and began to count off points on his fingers. '*Ka telej-hu, sho'ta en kailin tach; cho-hui k'lechje-schach hlakh t'aiyo? Teiij h'labech da?*'

This time, either because of his passion or because he no longer cared who understood him, the officer called Hasolt used Drusalan. Even without it Aldric could have taken meaning from his words and waving arms; and his complaint was one with which the Alban could—almost—sympathise. He had been led to expect a warlord, a *kailin,* and Light of Heaven alone knew what picture Hasolt had created in his mind. What he got, and what he was being asked to accept on the same terms, was a singularly scruffy *eijo*. A man who, as he said, could as easily be *h'labech*. A spy.

'Hasolt.' Goth's voice was sharper now, and the officer fell silent. 'That's quite enough. If you want to continue in this vein, then at least have the courtesy to speak so that our *guest* can understand. He may well wish to challenge you as a result.'

Hasolt licked his lips, then bowed curtly and sat down; he was aware that he was in the wrong, but at the same time he was trying to retain some face by an air of respectful defiance. One thing was certain: he wanted no challenges from *eijin*. What Drusalans knew of the landless warriors was crude and melodramatic; it made them artificial, characters from a cheap play rather than the honour-bound self-exiled men they truly were. Seldom heroic, often villainous, always lethal. The perfect anti-hero. Not all of it was fact.

But not all of it was fiction.

Aldric suspected that Goth knew much more about his guest than he had confided to his colleagues. He wanted—needed—to know how much more; to know where the general had obtained his information. And there was one other question which, discourteous or not, seemingly cowardly or not, he had to ask.

'*Coerhanalth* Goth-*eir*?' The Drusalan glanced in his direction, eyebrows lifting in query. 'Sir, what plan is this?'

'Ah. So Rynert didn't tell you after all? That was most remiss of him.

The reply sent an apprehensive shudder scurrying down Aldric's spine, and he felt his mouth go dry as the fear he had suppressed so well came flooding back. 'Tell me? Tell me what? I was requested to deliver messages of—of some delicacy to Lord General Goth, in a place of his own choosing. Nothing more.'

'Indeed.' Goth steepled his fingers and stared at them in a very Rynert-like gesture. 'Ah well.' He seemed to come to some decision and looked past Aldric at the escort who had brought him from the harbour. 'Return him his black knife,' he told the escort leader, 'then dismiss.'

Aldric looked at the *tsepan* where it had been laid gently—the soldier had either been warned in advance about disrespect, or knew anyway—on the table before him, and heard without hearing the clatter as the armoured troopers took their leave. His *tsepan*. The Guardian of his Honour. A blade whose scars crossed his left hand, scars he would carry to the fire. He lifted the weapon gently, almost between finger and thumb, and felt its black lacquer cool and comforting against his sweaty skin as he pushed it through the belt which closed his borrowed shirt-tunic. 'General,' he spoke Drusalan himself now, for sincerity's sake, 'again I thank you. For returning my,' the proper word eluded him, '. . . my self-respect. But—what plan?'

'Was no mention made of certain favours you might do for me—you and your sword?'

'I don't . . .' Aldric closed his teeth on the excuse. Rynert's words were months in the past, but he had an uneasy feeling that the king had indeed said something of that sort. What was it? 'If there is any favour you—and Isileth—can do to further prove my friendship, then I expect it to be done.' A mere courtesy phrase to indicate cooperation with tacit allies,

or so it had seemed at the time. Now he wasn't so sure.
'Suppose you hear the messages?' he wondered at last, hopefully. Those messages had been locked within his skull by
sorcery, and only those for whom they were meant knew how
to release them. Which meant they *had* to be important;
Rynert had said his messenger's rank alone served to make
them so, and Aldric was about to say as much when a
hollow, metallic voice spoke right behind his head—where
nobody had any right to be without his knowing of it.

'Tell him, Goth—then perhaps we can get on.'

It was probably impossible to get out of such a deep and
well-upholstered chair with quite the speed that Aldric managed then, but when he was as startled as he had become in
the past few seconds impossibilities ceased to concern him.

The man who stood far too close for comfort at his back
was almost six feet tall, and though he was leanly built there
was altogether too much of him to enter any room without
someone as nervous as Aldric Talvalin at least suspecting he
was there. Yet he had done so, with absolute success, and
now stood with his arms nonchalantly folded as if proud of
the fact. Grave and elegant in crimson and silver beneath the
dragonsblood cloak of the Imperial military, he wore its hood
drawn part-way over his head. But it was what that hood left
exposed that started Aldric's pulse-rate jumping.

For it was a mask of mirror-polished steel.

There were far too many deeply-ingrained images from his
memories of cu Ruruc and the demon-sending Esel in that
tall, silent figure; enough, and more than enough, for him to
jerk his newly-regained *tsepan* from its scabbard. Even though
the suicide dirk was no fighting weapon, it had killed before—
Overlord Geruath of Seghar, that had been, and at the hands
of his own son. And anyway, it was all that he had. His own
warped, miniscule reflection stared back at him from the
surface of the mask. There was nothing else to read from that
blank visage: no threat, no anger, no amusement. Nothing at
all.

'Aldric!' Goth's voice was sharp with urgency. 'Aldric, it's
all right. This man is a friend.' Tense seconds passed before
the younger man relaxed enough to move from his attack-
ready posture, and even then it was only to retreat on stiff,
poised legs from an immobile would-be opponent. Not until

Aldric was content with the separation space did he chance a single glance at Goth.

'If he's a friend, then make him show his face.'

The masked head shook from side to side, just once, unspeaking but quite clear. No.

'He won't do that at your command, Aldric-*an*,' the general said. 'Or mine. This is Bruda. Prokrator Bruda, the other man your king commanded you to meet. *En Hauthanalth Kagh' Ernvakh*.' Aldric stared, not understanding until the general elaborated further. 'Call him Commander of the Guardians of Honour.' Everyone caught the Alban's eyes flick from the glittering mask to the glittering blade of his own *tsepan*. 'Or call him Lord of the Honourable Guard. He's Chief of the Empire's Secret Police.'

Aldric returned the *tsepan* maybe a finger's length to its scabbard and hesitated, glancing thoughtfully from the slender blade to Bruda's cold steel face; then he shrugged and slid the weapon home. 'Secret Police.' There was a world of unvoiced insult in the way he sneered the words. 'So. Now I begin to understand.'

'Perhaps you do.' Bruda unfolded his arms, seeming quite unruffled by the display of open hostility. 'And perhaps you merely think so.' Snapping his fingers, he pointed in a single sweeping gesture to the officers who sat at each side of the table, and ended it with an over-shoulder jerk of his palm towards the door. 'By my command,' he said, 'out.' And that was all.

To Aldric's slight surprise they did as they were bidden at once, without question—and without a word of protest at the Prokrator's high-handed manner. That in itself told him a thing or two about the power of the Secret Police. But as he turned his head to watch them go, he caught his first glimpse of three men who stood silently in the lee of the doorway; men who by their appearance had nothing to do with the military conference but everything to do with Bruda. Only one he recognised: Garet, the officer-cadet who had been his gaoler aboard *Teynaur*. The others he had never seen before.

There was a man in armour, flashed with *tau-kortagor*'s rank bars like those Garet wore, and alongside them—also like Garet now, though they had not been there before—silver thunderbolt insignia which meant nothing to Aldric other than that Bruda wore them prominently at the collar of his robe.

Whilst the third stranger was strangest of all, for he was a replica of the Prokrator himself, with a mask—this of red-enamelled metal etched with patterns that seemed to mean more than simple decoration—and a wide-shouldered scarlet over-robe stiff with matching silver-worked embroidery. Aldric's first impression was of some reptilian creature which only incidentally resembled a man; and it was an impression which refused to go away.

'My chief lieutenant, *Hautheisart* Voord,' said Bruda in that resonant metallic voice of his, and Voord bowed with a courtier's grace. 'I think you know his action squad already. *Tau'hach-kortagorn* Tagen and Garet.'

Aldric looked steadily at the two officer-cadets, guessing privately that such a low rank in the Secret Police was far from low at all. Garet's profession of ignorance had been no more than that. 'We have met, yes—but not socially. And without formal introduction.'

A wintery smile crossed Goth's hard features. 'We'll be talking for a while yet; I think refreshments would be in order. See about it, and bring Lord Aldric's gear and equipment.'

'All of it?' Voord's voice was plainly quite youthful—and petulant—despite the hollow echoes of the mask.

'All. Do it. Now.'

Aldric suppressed a smile; he had sensed from the very first that Voord probably didn't like him much. The reason didn't concern him, and it certainly wasn't going to cause any sleepless nights since it was plain that as Goth's 'guest' he enjoyed a somewhat privileged position. The situation was one he was fully prepared to use. Then his hearing plucked a familiar name from the background mutter of conversation, and without thinking he echoed it aloud.

'Kathur?' Heads turned, and though he could see only one face of the three that mattered, all were probably alike in their quizzical expression. 'Then I was right.'

'Right about what?' Voord was the first to voice everyone's question.

'About the woman, Kathur—in Tuenafen. That it wasn't a coincidence, when she and I . . .' He stopped, embarrassed, but his meaning was clear enough.

'*Kagh' Ernvakh* regard coincidence as useful,' said Bruda, 'only when we create and control it. At all other times I dislike it intensely. Though it does seem that the woman in question—'

'Went beyond her instructions rather,' finished Voord, and had his face been on show it would have been stretched by an unpleasant salacious grin. 'She was ordered to contact you, to keep an eye on you. The fact that she chose to keep much more than an eye should be a source of some amusement, *hlens'l*. It most certainly was to me.'

'Kathur wouldn't talk about—' Aldric burst out, and was promptly silenced by a wave of Voord's hand. There was something wrong with that hand, something horribly wrong.

'Kathur would,' the *hautheisart* said with a nasty air of authority. 'And did. After the proper persuasion. At considerable descriptive length. She gave you a very, very good report—one you should be proud of.'

'Voord!' Goth really had no need for the added emphasis of a flat-handed slap against the table; that an Imperial Lord General had cause to raise his voice was emphatic enough. 'I earlier had cause to warn *Eldheisart* Hasolt about insulting talk. Stop it. At once!'

Voord swung round on the general and, secure in his own power and the power of what he represented, paused just long enough for insolence but not so long that it was obvious. Only then did he salute. 'Of course, sir. Immediately, sir. But these are merely facts related to me by one of my own agents. Sir . . .'

'Whether they're merely facts or your own opinions, Lord *Commander* Voord, be good enough to suppress them. Because regardless of your arm of service, Lord *Commander*, three gold diamonds outrank one in silver, and any *junior* officer can be broken by a *superior*. Do I make myself perfectly clear?'

'Eminently so, sir!' Voord was at attention now, and very likely sweating inside his mask. 'But I would point out, sir, that this agent, this *woman* thought enough of the prisoner—'

'Guest, Voord, not prisoner. Guest.'

'Thought enough of him to threaten me with a weapon later proved to be both loaded and lethal.'

'And were you disturbed by this threat, *Hautheisart* Voord? Did it frighten you?' Goth's voice was silky.

'Frighten? Not for a moment, sir!'

'Then you were a fool. If you spoke to her as you have

spoken to me, I'm surprised she didn't at least mark you just
to teach you manners!'

'Lucky for her that she didn't.'

Goth stroked his beard a moment and stared at Voord
without troubling to hide his dislike. Then he smiled with a
quick gleam of teeth and no humour at all. 'But luckier for
you.

It was perhaps as well that at that point the chamber doors
were opened to admit several retainers. Most carried trays of
food and drink, but two bore benches, on which were items
that Aldric had thought he would never see again. His armour,
left behind in Tuenafen—or so he had thought. His saddlebags and saddle, suggesting that just possibly Lyard had been
transported here as well. It was not beyond the bounds of
possibility. Then he saw what was tucked like an afterthought
into the facial opening of his helmet's warmask; a cylinder of
papers, bound with tape and sealed with the crest—he could
see it even at this distance—of the Imperial Fleet. It had the
look of a report about it; the sort of report that a warship
commander might put in concerning certain irregularities on
his last voyage.

Voord—Voord, Voord, Voord: where had he heard that
name before?—stepped forward and plucked the scroll from
its resting-place, snapping away the seal with his left hand.
Aldric looked at that hand and shivered; something most
unpleasant had happened to the *hautheisart* at some time, to
leave him with such a claw, and it made his own few scars
entirely insignificant. After only a moment scanning the sheets
as they uncoiled from their tight roll, Voord nodded as if they
had contained no more than he expected, glanced with his
expressionless masked face towards Aldric and then laid them
with a flourish on the table before Goth.

'Will you take wine?' Aldric jumped a little; the voice at
his shoulder belonged to Bruda, who moved with uncanny
silence for such a large man; the sight and sound of this
sinister figure playing the courteous host—and playing it
well—chilled him with a recollection of where he was.

'I . . . I would rather something with more strength, I
thank you,' he replied, cursing his jumpiness, cursing his
shock-born stammer and taking refuge in slightly stiff formal-
ity. When he was offered Elthanek malted-barley spirit, he
didn't for once pause a second to wonder how it had passed

through the various blockades between its source and his hand. Instead he put the glass to his mouth, feeling and hearing its rim clink against his teeth, and let the liquid fire within it run down his throat to light a small, comforting furnace in the pit of his stomach. There he took another swallow; and a third.

There was a small metallic click behind him and Bruda removed his mask before helping himself to some food. Voord did likewise, and there was a third and more final clatter from the door as Garet and his companion secured it to keep unauthorised eyes from the faces of the Empire's Secret Police.

Aldric's eyes might well have been regarded as unauthorised, but special dispensation had left him on this side of the door so he stared his fill. First at Voord, he being closest—and also most likely to be annoyed by the scrutiny. The *hautheisart*'s features were those of a young man, sufficiently so to be remarkable when set against the markings of his rank. He was only a couple of years older than Aldric, most likely, and he looked thin, stretched, gaunt—although it was difficult to be sure about that, for there was armour beneath his patterned overrobe and it gave his body a bulk it probably lacked in the flesh.

Voord's hair was fine and washed-out blond, almost colourless; he wore it brushed straight back from a high, intelligent forehead that gave him a disdainful air. Hooded light-blue eyes returned Aldric's gaze with an apparent or well-played lack of interest—his mask, as was its purpose, had concealed an initial monstrous curiosity about the Alban's wolfskin jerkin, a curiosity born of reluctant, unbelieving familiarity. His whole attitude was one of studied indifference, and only his mouth was wrong; to match his languid expression it should have been full-lipped and decadent. Instead it was little more than a flaw in a clean-shaven face carved of white alabaster.

Bruda, for all his seniority in rank, seemed rather more approachable, more likely to make that small effort which bridges the gap from acquaintance to—however superficial—friendliness. It was a small thing, but one which experience had taught Aldric to regard as important. The Prokrator's face, that of a man in his early forties for all that he moved like one fifteen years younger, was . . . ordinary. Totally ordinary. Aldric was disappointed at first; he had expected drama, an angular jaw, high cheekbones, distinctive, icy eyes. Something to make this man look like what he was.

And then he realised that Bruda was *perfect* for what he was. Apart from his height, and there was nothing unusual about it for there were many who were taller, there was nothing about the Prokrator to hang a memory on. His features were regular, symmetrical; neither scar nor blemish nor any other distinguishing mark marred the smoothness of his skin, which in itself contrived not to be so smooth as to be worth remarking on. Even his sweeping moustache meant nothing, because moustaches could be shaved—or false. For all that he had the necessary eyes, and nose, and mouth— which themselves were neither large nor small nor irregularly shaped—Bruda to all intents and purposes had no face.

Aldric took another mouthful of spirit, fully aware as he raised the refilled glass that this and the ration red he had downed earlier were the only things in his stomach. He was equally aware how quickly that would make him . . . relaxed; and the prospect concerned him not at all. There was nothing now that would better his situation, and probably nothing short of an armed assault on the three officers could make it any worse. All of this hospitality hadn't fooled him; he knew the honeyed bait before a trap when he tasted it. The Alban *eijo*—for if that was what they wanted, that was what he would be—grinned on one side of his face with an expression he didn't trouble to complete, and drained the glass instead.

Made bolder by the alcohol which had already percolated into his system, he studied the discarded mask: those metal screens that were the public visage of *Kagh'Ernvakh*. Then he lifted the nearest—Bruda's—for closer inspection and looked up from his own face reflected back at him to meet the Prokrator's curious gaze. 'Why?' was all he said.

'The masks? See for yourself. Status, and a mark of rank; secrecy, and somewhere to hide my face.' Even Bruda's voice—and he was speaking Alban now—had no accent. No accent at all. Neither the underlying throatiness and sibilance of one whose first tongue was Drusalan, nor the nasal purr of the Jouvaine; not even any of the Albans' own regional colourations. The words emerged and were understood, but their source remained untraceable.

Aldric set down the mask and saw how even the lamplight

seemed to shudder from its polished curves and angles. Or maybe that was just the slight movement of his own touch. 'Yes. I see. All too well, I think.'

'Bruda!' General Goth spoke from the head of the table, where he held a sheet of paper at arms' length with the plain wish that it could be held further still. 'Bruda, read this if you would. The rest of you: Voord, Tagen, Garet, be seated. We should begin the business which has brought us here.'

'Myself included, Goth-*eir*?' asked Aldric, lifting his eyes from the steel mirror of the mask.

'Especially yourself. This concerns you—both as a man and as an agent of your king.'

'Of course.' If there was a faint edge to his voice, it was not directed at the general. 'But have I a choice—whether to accept or to refuse involvement?' Even as he asked the question Aldric heard Bruda's soft, inhaled oath as the Prokrator read what a certain Imperial ship-commander had to say about a certain passenger aboard his vessel; and that inhalation told him what the answer would be. *Had* to be. And he was right.

Out of the three who might have given a reply, it was Goth who voiced it. 'I regret not, Aldric,' the general told him, but for all that there seemed to be little regret in the man's tone.

'Then I'd as soon not hear your plan at all.'

'You misunderstand, *hlensyarl*,' said Voord unpleasantly. 'What the Lord General means is that you have no choice at all.'

Aldric favoured him with a neutral glance. 'We'll see. Afterwards. But for now,' he deliberately turned his back on the *hautheisart* and inclined his head courteously towards the two senior officers, 'whenever you wish to begin, sirs, I will be ready to listen.'

'Our Emperor,' said Goth, 'has a sister; Princess Marevna. And she has spent the past two months under lock and key in the Red Tower at Egisburg.'

'A princess,' echoed Aldric in an odd, small voice. 'Imprisoned in a tower. Yes. You did say, tower?'

'I did. The Red Tower. At Egisburg.' Goth looked at him curiously, wondering just a little; but it was Bruda who tilted back his chair and hid the start of a smile behind one hand. He could see what way Aldric's thoughts were tending, and what their reaction might eventually be; and it was something which the sober, serious general might not like—even though it tickled Bruda hugely.

'It was her misfortune,' that Prokrator continued, once his twitching mouth was under control, 'to be on the wrong side of what is really a truce line (although nobody will ever dare to call it that) when yet another of those damned interminable so-called demarcation conferences—peace talks, if you really want to know—when yet another of those wrangles fell apart and the borders were closed. Marevna and her people were stopped well short of the frontier, taken into custody, and there they've been ever since.'

Bruda pushed papers to and fro on the table, then flicked a glance at Aldric from under his lowered brows. 'I don't know how Etzel's cavalry patrol came to be where they were at so opportune a moment. But I do know that the breakdown of the conference was engineered; I was there, and I saw it happen. Someone, somewhere, is playing a double game and when I find out who . . .'

'Knowing or not knowing does little to help the Princess just now,' Goth said stiffly. 'She's a political prisoner and her continued well-being is the Emperor's responsibility.'

Aldric nodded; this was a standard enough ploy. 'What was the threat this time?' he asked blandly. There had to be a threat, there was *always* a threat.

'This.' Goth set a tiny, elegant box on the table. Made of ivory, it was covered in a fine mesh of carving, openwork so that the red satin of its lining could peep through in contrast— the sort of thing in which a lady would keep her choicest gems. 'This contained the letter by which Emperor Ioen was informed of his sister's abduction.'

'And how many boxes did Grand Warlord Etzel promise to return the Princess in, if her brother didn't behave himself?'

'Enough,' said Bruda flatly, all his humour quite evaporated. 'And he isn't bluffing. Never in all the years of the Sherban dynasty has any Warlord made an idle threat.'

'I can imagine,' said Aldric. 'Yes indeed.' What point in making ferocious noises if the violence they promised was never carried out?

'For the sake of political balance it is vital that the Princess be rescued,' Goth was ticking points off on his fingers now, 'and equally vital that the Emperor should have no connection with anything irregular.'

Aldric looked at the general and fought back yet another crazy, humourless chuckle. Typical, he thought, that outright war was preferable to subterfuge. But then subterfuge of another kind had brought him here. As Goth explained further, he—Aldric—represented Alban support for the enterprise as no words ever could. An enterprise that was potentially lethal and which had at all costs to be resolved without unnecessary bloodshed. Neither side wanted a war if it could be avoided—but if it came, each would prefer the other to have started it.

'So then, my lord Aldric-*arluth* Talvalin,' the general gave him his title for the first time, in much the same way any wheedling request is preceded by flattery, 'what think you of our predicament?'

There was silence up and down the table; heads turned to stare at Aldric, waiting expectantly for his reply. And Aldric did as Prokrator Bruda had expected that he might.

He laughed . . .

'You mean—You mean to say that this is why I was dragged halfway across the Empire? For a story I might tell to children! Princesses and towers and wicked lords, by God!' He kicked back from the table, a jolting violent movement which brought Voord's honour guard out of their seats with swords half-drawn. 'Sit down, you two!' the Alban snarled. 'I won't bite!' Neither man moved, and he shrugged. 'Then please yourselves. I no longer care.'

'Aldric! Hear us out, man.' It was Bruda now, the one man among the lot of them whom possibly he might listen to. That at least was what the Prokrator was hoping. 'At least, listen to *me*.' Bruda had not risen to his feet—had not, in fact, changed his posture in the chair at all. He radiated calm as a fire radiates heat, and when Aldric looked at him he caught the younger man's eyes with his own and held them for a moment, then gestured with his hand. 'Sit down. Be still. Hear what we have yet to say—then be angry if you wish.'

Aldric stared, glared rather, through eyes that had gone narrow and vicious, and the black wolf-pelt *coyac* covering his shoulders seemed for just a moment to . . . bristle? *No*, thought Bruda, *I'm imagining things*. Some inner prompting made him glance at Voord, and what he saw on the *hautheisart*'s already too-pale face made him revise his opin-

ion. The ship-captain's report had been bad enough, but the
implications of this were just too . . .

Then, very slowly and carefully, Aldric Talvalin resumed
his seat.

He had been told many things already, Bruda knew, but
not the unpalatable truth behind his being brought here. No
one had yet decided how and when he was to learn that, but
Bruda had once expressed the wish to be there when it
happened. Now he was no longer so sure. He knew a great
deal more than he had any right to know about this Alban
clan-lord, but it was the way in which he and Goth and Voord
had come to know such things that lay at the bottom of all.
For all that it would be of benefit to the Empire which he
served—and loved, though that was only admitted on rare
occasions, in private, when he was in the maudlin stage of
drink—the transfer of information had been a distasteful thing.
Dishonourable. If there had been some other way . . .

But there had not.

Bruda was not *Hauthanalth Kagh' Ernvakh* for nothing. He
commanded the Guardians of the Emperor's Honour, as old
and respected a position as any in this young Empire, and to
do so he was truly a man of honour and self-respect. Unlike
Goth, with his plots and stratagems—and especially, unlike
Voord. But very like the young man who sat bolt-upright not
the length of his own ash cane away, sat and stared and dared
him to try to make some sense out of his disrupted life.
Aldric too was an honourable man; honourable not only as
the Albans defined the word, but also as the Prokrator himself
regarded it. He was consequently deadly—a whetted blade
poised and ready to fall. But where? On his captors?

Or on the king who had so totally betrayed him?

'Aldric,' said Bruda very quietly, 'Princess Marevna was
taken captive twelve leagues from the frontier. More than
thirty miles inside hostile territory. So tell me—why is she
held in Egisburg, a city only three leagues from the line?'

'Well within range of a mounted storm-column,' expanded
Goth.

Aldric looked from one to the other and whistled thinly
through his teeth. ' "Here's your sister, majesty—come and
get her." And if the Emperor does send in a force—'

'Then the Empire will go up in flames from end to end.

War, to justify the Warlord.' Bruda leaned forward, his face taut. 'Will you help us, Aldric? As your king desires?'

The Alban settled back into the padded embrace of his own chair and looked from face to face with hooded, unreadable eyes. His own mind was already made up—duty demanded it—but curiosity and alcohol were beginning to get the better of him. He wanted to know what these allies-to-be really were, beneath their eager, dutiful, would-be heroic expressions that were concealed by masks of metal, and he knew a certain way of finding out.

'This whole affair,' he said, no longer looking at anyone in particular, 'is so twisted that merely trying to work through the basic permutations gives me a headache. And it stinks of intrigue. That's not a perfume I'm too fond of. So, just for your so-comprehensive records, king or not, duty or not—no, I won't.' He allowed the small sounds of astonishment, anger or downright disbelief to fade away, then glanced bleakly towards *Hautheisart* Voord. 'But I imagine you volunteered to change my mind. So. Convince me.'

He had expected threats of violence, such as those uttered by *Teynaur*'s captain; what he had not expected was the exultant smile which stretched Voord's razor-cut mouth, a smile which sent a tiny shiver of apprehension across the Alban's skin. The pressures of the Imperial Secret Police, he guessed far too late, were likely to be more than commonplace. What could they be? Or promise? Or do?

He learned.

'The report from *Teynaur* is quite enough for this man to be handed over to the secular authorities on a charge of sorcery. That, however, would be time-consuming and ultimately a waste of our investment. In any case, mere straightforward death is no threat to a *kailin* of Alba.' If drunk enough to tell the truth, Aldric would have differed with that opinion; but for once, and wisely, he kept his mouth tight shut.

'So instead,' continued Voord, 'I considered the dossier which we acquired. It gave me a means whereby this pride and honour—stubbornness, no more—could be turned to our advantage.' He tapped one finger on the table and Garet slid a folder towards him across its polished surface. Voord opened it, flicked through the contents twice—an operation made clumsy by the bone and leather talon of his left hand—and extracted two fragile sheets.

'One: the steading of Tervasdal in Valhol.' Aldric's head jerked up. 'Two: the citadel at Seghar.' A harshness darkened Voord's voice as he pronounced the name, and he arranged both sheets on the table with fastidious neatness, their edges parallel and just-so. Then he seated at Aldric. 'And three: a certain very fine Andarran stallion, presently in the stables of this very stronghold. Kyrin and Gueynor and Lyard,' he grated, all the mockery leaving his words as he slapped his right hand flat against the documents. 'Do you really want to hear the details of what I have in mind?'

'You *bastard* . . .' All colour had drained from Aldric's face, and his fingers were gripping the arms of his chair so tightly that the knucklebones shone ivory through the stretched skin.

'Think of everything your mind can compass, *hlensyarl*,' hissed Voord. 'And even then you won't have guessed the half of it.'

Aldric came to his feet slowly—very slowly, like a man oppressed by some vast weight—and only Bruda was close enough and quick enough to catch the brief, bright malice that glittered for a moment in the Alban's eyes. He turned, shoulders sagging like those of a man broken in body and spirit, a man with no defiance left, spreading both hands helplessly wide as he bowed his head to Goth. 'The . . . my . . . sir, the decision is concluded. When do we go?'

'Tomorrow,' said Goth, 'will be soon enough. First you need clothing and armour.'

Aldric waved one hand—a weak, indecisive gesture—towards the bench behind him. 'Armour I have already, sir,' he said.

'But not for Egisburg. Ride through that city's gates in Alban harness and you would never leave again. You'll need our cavalry equipment.'

'I am keeping my own weapons.' This time there was a hardness in his voice which had not been there before, an edge that left no room for argument.

Goth heard it and looked past him towards Bruda; Aldric's peripheral vision caught the Prokrator's nod of consent and also a hand-sign which meant nothing at first. It was the sort of gesture he might have used himself, if signalling that something be increased, but here and now it seemed right out of context—until Goth spoke again.

'Prokrator Bruda concurs with your choice of weapons,'

said the general, and Aldric almost let his thoughts be heard aloud. *Choice*, said his mind; *as if I gave you any more choice than you gave me.* 'But he also points out that to warrant such blades you must also carry high rank.'

Aldric heard the clatter as Voord shot out of his chair, knocking it over in his haste and this time didn't bother to conceal the smile summoned by the sound—a smile which widened to a grin of honest pleasure as the first few words of an outraged protest were silenced by Goth's upraised hand. 'What . . . what rank, sir?' he ventured at last.

Both of the senior officers considered for a moment, but it was Bruda who answered at last. 'A brevet of *en-hanalth* should be quite sufficient,' he said, accompanying the words with a look which dared Voord to argue with him.

Voord did. 'You can't do this!' he blared, all affronted dignity now. 'You can't hand out such a high rank as if it was—'

'Voord!' Bruda's voice was sharp. 'I just did.'

'But . . . but that means . . .' Disbelief struggled with the reality of the situation and reality won. 'He's superior to *me!*' Hoping that he was wrong, that this was perhaps some black joke played on him for his earlier foul manners, he stared at Bruda and then at Goth in the hope of seeing an eye twinkle or a smile begin to spread. Instead he saw the Lord General nod his head in agreement.

'Effectively, *hautheisart*, yes,' Goth said. 'He is superior.' There was something about the way he said it which suggested that the superiority lay in more than merely rank, but Voord was past noticing subtle nuances of tone.

He flinched visibly at the general's words, for such a statement from such a source was not open to question—not after what had been said bare minutes earlier about the differences in their rank. But this was more important to Voord than even caution, and his next words were addressed, pointedly so, to his own commander. '*Prokrator Hauthanalth*,' he said, his use of Bruda's full style and title being for exactly the same reason that Aldric's had been spoken by Goth: to preface and emphasise a request. 'Sir, tell me that I don't. . . . I don't have to obey his orders, do I?' The abject 'please' was unspoken but patently obvious for all that.

On another occasion, or in a different situation, or even if Voord had not been so discourteous—no, bloody rude!—earlier,

Bruda might have said what his lieutenant wanted to hear.
Instead he too nodded, with finality. 'I'll be the final arbiter,
of course; not,' with a significant glance at Aldric, 'that I
anticipate anything of the kind. But this is a step taken for
protective coloration, so if *hanalth*-rank should by any chance
give a command to *hautheisart*-rank before witnesses who
might otherwise be curious, then *hautheisart*-rank will obey.
Without hesitation or question. Is that understood?'

Pallid even at the best of times, Voord by rights should not
have been able to grow much paler; but as Bruda spoke what
little colour there was drained from his face to leave it as
white as chalk. An instant later he slammed his hand against
the table-top—his maimed left hand—as if, needing in his
rage to hurt someone, he resorted to the only person present
he could hurt with impunity. Himself. It was a gesture redolent of such monstrous perversity that Aldric cringed inside as
he saw it.

'*I will not!*' Voord's voice was shrill and tremulous, though
it was impossible to tell how much of this was caused by pain
and how much by fury. 'I will take no order from that . . .
that fatherless son of a whore, that—'

However much he might have been accustomed to abusing
prisoners and subordinates, Voord plainly had had no previous experience of high-clan Albans. Otherwise he might have
been more guarded in his choice of insult, or at the very least
been sure of how close he was standing to Aldric Talvalin
when he uttered it. Instead he made both of those mistakes
simultaneously, and had not properly drawn breath to say
more when the still-forming words were smashed back into
his mouth by a fist that was backed by all the focused power
of a swordsman's trained muscles.

Aldric's face had frozen over as Voord spoke, and long,
long before anyone could cry halt he had swivelled at the
waist in a half-twisting movement which put all of his upper-
body weight behind the punch. It didn't quite lift the *hautheisart* off his feet, but it snapped his head back on his neck
and staggered him so hard and fast that his feet shot from
under him and he crashed to the floor amid a clatter of
harness and weapons, with blood smeared on his face and
chin from lips that had not so much been split as burst by the
hammer-and-anvil impact between Aldric's bunched knuckles
and his own teeth. As Voord's mouth sagged open and he

gaped dazedly up at the Alban standing over him, splinters of one of those teeth gleamed whitely amid the blood.

'Sharp teeth,' remarked Aldric to no one in particular. 'Though I doubt that they're poisonous.' He sucked the oozing, ragged skin across his knuckles for a moment to ease the stinging, took the hand from his lips and stared at the wound for a moment, then worked his jaws and spat a mingling of blood and saliva onto the floor a bare inch short of Voord's right hand. 'But then, you can never be sure with snakes.'

'Schii'aj!' The obscenity was a clumsily articulated shriek as Voord scrambled upright and slapped hand to short-sword hilt—then jolted to a standstill with the blade still sheathed. Again he had miscalculated where Aldric and speed and distance were concerned, for in the time it had taken him to regain his feet the Alban had sidestepped to the bench which carried his gear and had snatched up just one very particular item. Isileth.

The fur of the wolfskin *coyac* that Aldric wore moved like wind in a field of wheat. *'D'ka tey'adj, Voord,'* he said softly, ominously. *'Cho taeyy' ura.'* The longsword in his hand was levelled at Voord's windpipe, so close that a handspan's worth of thrust would let his breath from it to mingle once and for all with the air; and that hand was far, far steadier than the hand of a broken and defeated man had any right to be. Far, far steadier than the hand of any man whose eyes glittered with such a force of leashed-in violence. Voord looked at the blade, at the hand, at the eyes, and knew that in the sum of these three things he looked at his own death.

'Stop!' Goth's voice, parade-ground harsh, slashed through the room and created for just an instant the necessary hesitation in Aldric which saved Voord's life. Neither the Alban *eijo* nor the Vlechan *hautheisart* had moved, but something— some tingling, vicious thing—was gone from the air.

'You heard him.' Aldric did not take his eyes from Voord's face, nor his *taiken*-point from the man's throat; but at least he spoke instead of driving that point home. 'You heard what he said. All of you. He is dead.'

'No. He's too valuable.'

Aldric coughed a single humourless laugh at that. 'Valuable! You mean, he's an investment like me? Then, general, he should have invested a few seconds' thought in what he said before he said it!'

'But look at his face, man—look at what you did! Isn't that enough for one ill-chosen word?'

'No.' Aldric sounded vindictive. 'Not yet.'

'Ach, let them fight!' Bruda's words drew everyone's attention, flying as they did full in the face of a superior's direct command. 'But let it be with wooden foils. *Taidyin.* I can see a sheaf of them yonder, in the Alban's gear.

'Or, at least,' he amended after the silence had grown heavy but before anyone else could speak, 'since Voord is as you say worth more undamaged—so are they both, general, so are they both—then let Aldric fight with somebody else. Anybody . . .' That was as much a challenge as a suggestion, but no one reacted by so much as the flicker of an eyelid. 'You say to him, look at Voord. I say to you, look at him: right now he's wound up like a crossbow. He's dangerous. Lethal. And besides . . .'

Bruda settled into the padded embrace of his chair and propped his feet up on the table, crossing them casually at the ankles; and suddenly he no longer looked approachable. Instead, in that single languid motion he was transformed into all that an Imperial *hauthanalth* and a Chief of Secret Police should be—something arrogant; sinister; menacing. 'Besides,' and he tapped a folder cradled in his lap, 'I'd like to see if he's really as good as they say.'

'If you think for an instant that I'm going to entertain—' Aldric bit the words off short as *tau-Kortagor* Garet stood up.

'You talk of insults, Alban—the sort of thing your honour thrives on. Have you forgotten how you insulted me, aboard *Teynaur*? Because I still remember even if you don't, and if you truly want a fight . . .' he spread arms sheathed in fine ringmail, 'here I am.'

Aldric stared at him; this was the same youngster, the same baby-faced cadet who had seemed almost friendly as the warship came into dock. And yet he was not the same. If this was Drusalan friendship, then it was as transient as snow in springtime. No matter; if that was so, he had no need of such friends.

And he knew that Bruda had spoken no more than the truth about him, because hide it how he might for the sake of manners and his own self-respect, he was taut and hot and

trembling with fury inside. Angry enough indeed to fight with
anyone. That was the cumulative effect not merely of verbal
insults, but of being used and abused by these so-called allies,
of being treated like a chattel, like something bought and paid
for, like an inanimate investment—lord God! how that word
burned like vitriol—rather than as a human being who could
be and had been bruised in body, mind and soul.

But the cold, cold killing rage shuttered behind his eyes
was still reserved for Voord alone. Widowmaker whispered
back into her black scabbard and was laid gently on the table.
Aldric uttered no redundant hands-off warning, because it
was unlikely in the extreme that anyone would dare to touch
the blade in Goth's and Bruda's presence, and they had too
much sense to permit it . . . he hoped.

Garet had already selected a *taidyo* and was whipping the
four-foot length of oak from side to side in what seemed a
most experienced manner. It was unusual for anyone other than
an Alban to be familiar with *taiken'ulleth,* classical longsword play—his foster-father Gemmel was a notable exception, as in much else—and as he watched Garet's posturing
Aldric wondered if this too, like so many other things, had
been arranged; another test which had merely waited a long
time before the proper circumstances for its employment
arose. He didn't really care.

'I'm not allowed to damage you permanently,' Garet said
as he stalked across the floor, 'but you'll remember how to
address Imperial officers properly—next time you're able to
say anything at all.'

So was this set up by Voord? Aldric hefted one *taidyo* after
another, seeming oblivious to the threats or at least selec-
tively deaf. Then he chose one whose chequer-carved grip
fitted his hands comfortably and tugged it from its canvas
sleeve to test its weight and balance with a flex of his wrists.

Garet was still talking: threatening, boasting, casting doubts
on Aldric's ability and on the worthiness of fighting with
sticks. But Aldric knew these 'sticks' of old, and knew—
intimately—the damage they could do; on an occasion, not so
long ago that the pain of it had yet been forgotten, a 'stick'
just like those they carried now had snapped one of his ribs.
That was why he laid his own *taidyo* aside and buckled on the
sleeves of his battle armour—an action which provoked yet
more scathing comment from the already-mailed Garet and a

certain amount of muttered observation from the others present. It didn't concern him; the long steel plates of the vam-
braces made a better shield against percussive impact than the
best linked mail-mesh ever made, and if Garet was so inexpe-
rienced that he didn't already know that, then he was likely to
find out.

Lifting the *taidyo* again, Aldric raised it slowly in centre
line, low to high above his head, then equally slowly across
at the level of his eyes. It was *achran-kai* again, the first and
simplest form, but executed this time more to check the fit of
the armoured sleeves than for any other reason. Garet watched
him, and Aldric could see incomprehension flit across the
young Drusalan's face. Now that was very interesting—
enlightening, almost. If he failed to recognise an inverted
cross in slow time, then maybe—just maybe—he didn't know
as much about Alban longswords as had first appeared. And
if that was so, then . . .

Cramp suddenly stabbed at one shoulder-joint and Aldric
gasped audibly as its silver bolt of pain bored down the
marrow of his bones. A legacy of being unhorsed in Tuenafen
perhaps, or of helping to propel the battleram *Teynaur* to
port; the reason was of no account. But Garet had heard him
gasp before he could silence the involuntary sound, and had
seen him wince.

'I'm better than you, Alban,' the *tau-kortagor* said. 'I'm
better because I'm faster, and I'm faster because I'm younger. That's why I'm going to really hurt you, Alban, and why
there's not a thing you can do about it.' As he spoke he
shifted into a stance that Aldric recognised; it was one of the
ready positions for duelling with the long Jouvaine thrusting-
sword, the *estoc*—a weapon as different from the *taiken* as
night was from day.

Only then was he convinced; only then did he allow himself a small, contemptuous smile, for only then was he quite
sure who would win and lose. Who would be hurt—and who
would do the hurting. Words came to his mind, heard or read
somewhere far from here, a quotation from a play; not one of
Oren Osmar's classics but something modern, terse and striv-
ing for the new ideal of realistic speech. The sort of laconic
line that often sounded so wrong—and yet, just once in a
while, so very, very right.

'Garet,' Aldric said, 'you talk too much.'

An instant later, there was a *taidyo* lashing at his face. He didn't bother to block the cut—which was no true cut at all, but the kind of slash he might have expected from a man with a club—but merely sidestepped it without even bringing his own foil to guard. It was done with a studied lack of effort, and that was unusual for Aldric in such circumstances. The first rule—and the last—in any weapon-play was that to toy with an opponent of unknown capabilities was to invite disaster, and it was a rule he usually obeyed; yet now, though the opening for a devastating counter was there, he held back and instead merely grinned at Garet.

The Drusalan answered with a thrust—pure *estoc*-practice, that—aimed straight at the eyes.

Aldric said, 'Idiot!' in a loud, clear voice that sounded almost annoyed, and did something he would never have risked with live blades unless in full armour. Enveloping the incoming point with a circular parry, he deflected it out to his left and then stepped inside the weapon's compass to snatch it back in again—pinned now in the angles of left upper arm and elbow. All that was required and all that he did was to make an edge-handed chop across Garet's fingers and a side-wise twist away.

The trapped weapon was wrenched from its owner's hand almost as if he had presented it of his own free will, and Aldric grinned again. 'What was that you told me? That you're better?'

Prokrator Bruda clapped his hands slowly together in ironic applause, but whether it was at the swordplay or the dialogue Aldric didn't know. At least he had proved his point—and proved himself as well, both as a skilled and as a restrained fighter. There was no purpose in continuing this farce and he turned away to return the *taidyin* to his gear.

Then a voice behind him said, 'Garet.' Aldric scarcely recognised it as Voord's once-so-urbane tones; but then, apart from a single shrill expletive he had not heard the *hautheisart* speak since . . . since silencing him. He looked back and saw the other escort—Tagen, was it?—on his feet with one hand resting negligently on the pommel of his sword. Aldric tensed for an instant, then saw that none of the attention here was directed at him. Instead Voord was staring at Garet over a bloodied kerchief that concealed most of his face, and though no further words were uttered by that muffled, mangled mouth, the young *tau-kortagor* seemed able to take meaning from his commander's eyes alone.

Aldric too could guess easily enough what this little tableau was all about. Having volunteered—if he *had* volunteered—to punish this Alban upstart, ostensibly for his own reasons, Garet was not going to be permitted to stop. Not while he also fought on *Hautheisart* Voord's behalf. Nor, Aldric fancied, would failure be well regarded; Voord did not look the sort of man who had a forgiving nature.

Altogether more serious now, he bowed courteously as he returned the captured *taidyo* to Garet's hand, and was conscious of more attention along the conference table than there had been before. It was as if they all knew that the next exchange would be more than a mocking display of technique; and as if they knew still more—something of which Aldric was yet ignorant.

That 'something', whatever it might prove to be, was already enough to raise the hackles on the Alban's neck. 'I will not draw this man's blood,' he said, because it was something that had to be said no matter who it annoyed. If Garet had not been forced to this, then maybe he would have had fewer scruples; but Aldric had been King Rynert's—assassin? Executioner? Duty-bound, honour-bound, reluctant slayer . . . Once. But never again; not for any man.

He tried to think of some stratagem with which to end this matter quickly, before someone was hurt. Before *he* was hurt, since Voord wasn't going to be satisfied with just seeing a few welts and bruises. Not with his broken face to remind him of what Aldric had done.

They took guard again, but slowly now, warily and with a deal more care than the nonchalance of their first exchange, and the *taidyin* touched. Clack. Wood ran against wood, notched surfaces ticking as the pressure of wrists increased. There was a shuffling sound—someone's feet—and a moment's stillness. Clack. Another stillness, when nothing moved but mind and eyes. Then clack; clack-*stamp*, and Garet launched a cut—a proper cut this time, downward and diagonal to strike neck or shoulder, hard, fast and direct.

It was easy.

Aldric moved not back but forward, dropping to one knee, intersecting the arc of Garet's cut with his own *taidyo* as it whirred up and across. Gripped in both hands, his wrists counterflexing on the long hilt for leverage, the last six inches of the hardwood blade jumped from near-immobility to an unseen blur. And it hit squarely home within an inch of his aiming point—not on Garet's own weapon, to block, but on the Drusalan's tensed, extended forearm. To break. He shouted, once: '*Hai!*'

The mail that Garet wore was no protection, no protection at all; transmitted all the shock of the blow clear through whatever minimal padding was beneath, and even over the harsh rasp of oak against linked metal Aldric heard both forearm-bones give way.

Garet yelped thinly and released his *taidyo* to clatter across the floor, but before it had come to rest he followed it, crashing headlong to the ground as the follow-through accelerated down and all but tore the kneecap from his braced right leg.

He lay there, squirming and trying not to scream, while Aldric cat-stepped backwards with an expression of distaste stamped into his features. The other *tau-kortagor*, Tagen, barged past him and knelt at Garet's side to check his injuries. Aldric could hear his muttered curse quite plainly, for it had grown very quiet in Lord General Goth's great conference hall: quiet—and expectant.

'Well?' Voord asked it, his thick voice free now of all passion, anger or even interest.

'The arm is cleanly broken, lord; it should heal. But . . .' Tagen hesitated, and looked up at Voord before saying any more. 'But he'll not walk without a stick, if he ever walks again.'

'So. Small use to me, then. Why am I surrounded by incompetents?' he demanded of the air. No one troubled to supply him with an answer and he flung both arms wide in an exaggerated shrug of disgust and dismissal. The blood on his face was drying black. 'At least they only ever fail me once. *Tagen, sh'voda moy: ya v'lech'hu, kh'mnach voi! Slijei?*'

'*Slij'hah, hautach!*' Tagen jerked his shortsword from its scabbard and rammed two inches of its point into the nape of Garet's neck. The injured man's eyes opened wide, all whites with just a pinpoint spot of pupil, and his mouth gaped silently; then his legs went kick-kick, kick . . . And he was dead.

Aldric forced his own bunched muscles to relax, quite sure

that he was the only one to even react. That was worst of all, for in his innermost heart he had anticipated something like this and then dismissed it as beyond even Voord. It had been the 'something' in the atmosphere which had disturbed him before they began to fight. He should have been on his guard, responded differently, not given Voord a reason to . . . to do what had been done. Then maybe a life would not have been wasted, spilled without purpose across the polished floor.

But what better way in all the world to impress a man known to be careless of killing—a man even nicknamed Bladebearer Deathbringer, by the holy Light of Heaven!—than to prove oneself more careless still. That was how Voord's mind had worked, even to the extent of having his own guard killed for the failure of losing a duel. Just to impress! It was appalling. But that was Voord, and at the last that was the Secret Police. And that was the Drusalans, for they had all connived at it, Goth and Bruda both, knowing what might happen—no, knowing what *would* happen—but saying not a word against it.

Aldric looked at them, and looked at the blood—dear God, so very little blood to mark a death!—and for once kept his thoughts entirely to himself.

SEVEN

Shadow of the Tower

'I often wondered why you had such an interest in *ymeth*,' said Dewan. He was trying to strike up a conversation again, for what felt like the hundredth time. Even an argument would be better than the gloomy silence which had settled over Gemmel since their interview—and 'interview' scarcely described it—wih the Drusalan woman who called herself Kathur the Vixen. If ever anyone talked too much, she did; and Dewan suspected that Gemmel's use of the dreamsmoke drug was no more than a contributory factor.

She talked, he thought idly, staring at Gemmel's back as they rode along on tired, hired horses. Well then, some of the men who had shared her bed must have been regular speech-makers, and it had all come spilling out, as unselective as an up-ended bucket. They had heard about the governor of Tuenafen; about the governor's son and his stableboy; about two of the seaport's magistrates and how they liked to relax after a hard day administering the Empire's justice. All of it had been fascinating in a small way, even though Gemmel obviously disapproved of most of it, and it would have been most useful had they planned to stay in Tuenafen and set up as professional blackmailers. But they had also heard about Aldric, and what *Kagh' Ernvakh* had planned for him.

Dewan had laughed, as he felt certain Aldric would also have laughed at the notion of rescuing a captive princess from a lofty tower. But the laughter had been of short duration and Gemmel had not joined it. This matter ceased to be a child's tale and a source of amusement when it involved a friend and the risk of that friend's death. And Dewan was well aware that Gemmel regarded Aldric as much more than a friend; he had heard the title *altrou*—foster-father—used by the younger man on more than one occasion.

The risk was greatly increased by a factor which Kathur had named several times: the Imperial officer called *Hautheisart* Voord. She had been Voord's lover once, and then his mistress, five years ago—for all that even then his tastes had tended to the exotic, rather than the conventionally erotic. Voord, Dewan had decided, was peculiar. But to be promoted *hautheisart* at the age of twenty-seven bespoke a mind and an ability that was out of the ordinary in much more than merely sexual preferences.

They knew now where that warped genius lay. Voord was a gamester, a gambler, a player of one side against another and both sides for himself. His games extended far back, beyond the death of old Emperor Droek and the division of the Empire. They continued through that division and right up to the present day: complex, selfserving and often murderous. Voord still played both sides, although there seemed of late to be a marked preference for one over the other—but Voord still worked hardest for Voord. There had been vague talk from Kathur about an attempt to control an isolated province on the Jevaiden plateau and transform it into an independent, neutral city-state—supporting and supported by the Emperor and the Grand Warlord both. It was a plan which had come to nothing for various reasons.

One of those reasons had been a certain Alban clan-lord, sent there about his king's business and still ignorant of what he had upset.

Not that this was the first time Aldric and Voord had crossed paths in ignorance. Oh no. Voord himself had evidently talked far too much in bed in his younger days; presumably less mature, less confident—but quite certainly just as coldly cynical. He had talked about his first-ever great stratagem, originated solely by himself; the plan which had gained his first promotion, that long, long leap of one rank that so few men made—from *kortagor* to *eldheisart*, and with it the transfer from infantry to secret police.

That plan had broken half-a-dozen of the Empire's notoriously strict laws against sorcery by its very inception, and was pushed through by—significantly—Grand Warlord Etzel's personal intervention. And no wonder he supported it; at that time the plan was certain to attract him, in his then-current uncertain position with the Imperial dominions at peace and questions being asked in the Senate as to whether the rank and title of Grand Warlord should in fact be done away with. It was a simple plan: the despatch of a man to a place, with instructions to create sufficient havoc for military intervention to be justified.

The plan which, four long years ago, had sent Duergar Vathach to Dunrath.

It was an operation which Kathur should never have known about, because it was a failure. That failure had done something to the way in which Voord's mind worked; it seemed now that failure was the worst sin in his canon and the one most drastically punished. But she had heard all about it—maybe because it was his first, maybe because despite its lack of success it had done no damage to his career—and maybe because in those days there had been no such thing as *sides* within the Drusalan Empire. Emperor and Warlord had been twin figureheads on the one ship, Dewan knew that much: he had been a part of it, and knew that the oneness was that of a puppeteer and his doll. But it explained Voord's openness as nothing else could.

Only fear had kept Kathur's mouth shut, and it had needed sorcery-assisted drugs—or drug-enhanced sorcery, Dewan was uncertain of precedence—to open it again. The great question now in his mind was: what would happen if, or when, Aldric found out? If he hadn't found out already. Either way, if he was still alive he would need help—all the help that they could bring to bear.

Gemmel rode on, sagging in the saddle and looking far from comfortable. He was usually a good horseman, certainly better than some Dewan had seen—although as an ex-*eldheisart* in the Bodyguard at Drakkesborg, he conceded that he was often over-critical—but right now the old wizard's mind seemed occupied by more than even the elementary, instinctive knee-grip and balance which kept him on his rented pony's back. Gemmel had been subject to broody periods like this ever since they landed in Imperial territory; indeed, ever since they had seen the white contrail of the dragon scratched across the cold blue vault of heaven. For the life of him Dewan could not understand why, because even he—unimaginative military crophead that he was—had been thrilled to the core of his being by the sight. It had not mattered that he had seen Ymareth before; in the Cavern of Firedrakes it had been somehow appropriate. Just—*just?*—one more strange and mar-

vellous thing among so many other marvels. But in the open
sky, with nothing to detract from its distant grandeur—although
in truth, at two miles above his head it had been no bigger
than a sparrow, and only the stately leisure of its wingbeats
had shown it for what it truly was; that, and the condensing
trail of heat from its mouth—the sight of a dragon in flight
was another matter entirely. Dewan's drinking of a toast to
the great being's mere existence had been sincere, not mockery.

So what was wrong with Gemmel? Dewan looked at him
again and wondered idly if it was worth-while wasting more
breath in yet another attempt to cajole the old man into
speech. Deciding not, he hunched himself deeper into the
furred hood of his cavalry cloak.

There had been no dragon in the sky today—nor, for that
matter, any blue sky for one to fly across. Only an overcast
that was as grey and featureless as new-split slate. By the
Alban calendar it was *Hethra-tre, de Gwenyer;* the Drusalan
reckoning, for once, put it in more simple terms: the third day
of the tenth month, and three days into winter. The year was
winding down—and the weather just at present was trying
hard to prove it. Today had started badly and grown steadily,
malevolently worse, progressing from a nonexistent dawn lost
in slanting rain, through a chill, and sleet, to a proper fall of
snow. That at least was over for the present, but it had
already transformed the countryside through which they rode
into an ink-wash study; all light and darkness, chiaroscuro.
Everything was either black or white, stark, toneless, without
any subtlety of shading beneath that leaden sky which was so
heavy with the promise of more snow. Dewan glared at it,
and was answered as he might have expected by a quick
flurry of fat, soft flakes. And it was cold. The breath of men
and horses alike went smoking from their nostrils to drift like
skeins of fog on the bitter, barely moving air. Like the breath
of dragons.

Dewan ar Korentin wiped a crust of hoar-frost from his
moustache, itself become as black-and-white as the land-
scape, and exhaled a soft oath on his next billow of breath.
Cold, he thought, watching the vapour twist heavily away
from his face. *So cold.* His eyes abruptly shifted focus as
something drew their attention to the middle distance. A
movement, or a suggestion of movement; a flickering, like a
gnat's dance on warm summer air, caught at the edge of

sight. Except that this was by no means summer, and whatever he had seen was no gnat. *There, look!* No. It was gone again—if it had ever been there. Dewan blinked; maybe it was a speck of moisture caught on his eyelashes, or a bird—although he had seen no birds today, they had too much sense to travel in such foul weather—or maybe no more than a trick of his imagination. He turned his head away, dismissing it.

And then snapped back, not believing, to gape as the thing he was convinced he had not seen came scything out of the low cloudbase like some monstrous bat with a ribbon of black smoke scrawling like charcoal to mark its line of descent.

Firedrake! Dragon! Ymareth . . .

Or—not Ymareth at all, for it was so *big!*

His fear was spawned by the thing's size and by the steepness and the speed of its approach, for with wings half-closed like those—Gods! too like those—of a falcon stooping upon fieldmice, the dragon reached them in the space of a single racing heartbeat. Too fast for evasion; too fast even for prayer.

It slashed past, right to left, twenty feet above the ground—and because they were both mounted, that was a shocking less-than-twelve above their heads—in a great rush of hot wind, moving far faster than any creature, even one born in legend, had any right to move. The thump of displaced air tore at their clothing, whipped up spirals of snow that melted even as they left the ground, and went whirling off in the dragon's wake as it climbed away, returned to its patrol height like the swinging of a pendulum by the awesome dive-created speed which had flicked it past them like a beast seen in a dream—or a nightmare . . . Huge dark wings, horned and crested wedge of head, armoured serpentine body and a long, grinning, fang-crowded mouth whose trailing scarf of smoke brought with it the bitter reek of burning.

And the ponies which they rode went mad. Kicking and squealing, bucking and plunging, the animals tried to throw their riders, to throw their saddlebags, to flee in abject terror somewhere, anywhere, as far away from this airborne horror as their legs could carry them. The beasts' eyes were rolling crazily—all whites, as white as the foam which creamed on bits and bridles. And Gemmel, who had patently lost interest in staying mounted? He too had gone a little mad—Dewan could think of no other reason why he might be laughing.

Crowing with glee, the old man tumbled—very neatly, granted—to the ground, landing on his feet, and with a quick, casual gesture of the Dragonwand froze both of the fear-crazed ponies in their tracks. Only their eyes *could* move now; the rest, even to ears and tails, were struck still as equestrian statues in cold bronze. Dewan looked at the Dragonwand, then at the wizard, and thought *how very appropriate* to himself. He was too tactful—and wise—to voice the thought aloud.

But the dragon seemed to hear him; a quarter-mile away and three thousand feet up, the great wings beat once, twice, three times, accelerating its climb until it was rising almost vertically like a pheasant rocketing from cover; then no longer like a pheasant but as negligently aerobatic as a rook, it yawed, half-looped, rolled—then *twisted* snakewise in the air as no bird ever hatched from egg could do—and was coming back in the same instant.

The approach was slower now, a wide-winged glide rather than the previous attack dive, but no less ominous for all that. Dewan could see plainly that the smoke wind-dragged from its mouth was thicker now, denser, as if the fires of the creature's belly were fully alive. As if to prove the fact, the dragon's head vectored a few degrees off-line with a deli-beration that reminded him nastily of a battleram's weapon-turret, and then—with a whistling roar which reminded him of nothing in or above or under the whole wide world—its mouth opened to unleash a gout of yellow-white flame, glar-ing and brilliant against the dullness of the day.

Dewan flinched at its brightness, and at the heat which slapped at him as if a furnace door had been flung open; but at the same time drew a breath of awe and wonder. If he was to die, then surely there were more squalid ways than this brief, bright glory. Another instant, and he was wondering at his own morbid turn of mind. The hundred-yard-long plume of fury faded and choked in a swirl of dark smoke and once more the dragon was upon them.

This time it moved slowly, so slowly that it barely main-tained a flying speed. The great membranous wings flared and shifted to control the air which flowed above and below them, then scooped down at last in a great braking arc as Ymareth—if this *was* Ymareth, and Dewan was still far from convinced—rounded out its final descent and settled onto the ground with all the daintiness of a hawk returning to a familiar wrist, a delicate grace odd and eerie in something so huge. Dewan, still astride his motionless pony, was reminded more of a cat in wet grass than a hawk. Except that this 'cat' was one hundred and twenty-odd feet long, radiated a warmth that he could feel from where he sat—and right welcome it was, too!—and where the plate armour of its belly touched on patches of snow, those patches melted amid clouds of steam and fast-forming pools of water.

The dragon's head swung leisurely from side to side, considering them both: old man and young, mounted and afoot, shocked-silent and still chuckling. Its eyes . . . such eyes: pools of yellow phosphorescence which drew his gaze and held it . . .

NO!

That *would* have held it, had he not torn away with an effort like that of lifting some great weight. His face darkened, flushed with blood that was not summoned by either of the contrasting stimuli of dragon-heat or winter-cold; it had been pumped there by a heart which the strain of looking away had provoked into a spasm of furious beats, a muffled drumroll which filled his ears and made his senses spin. It felt briefly as if his whole chest was about to split wide open to give the frantic organ room; then the hammering died away, and the world stopped swaying, and Dewan drew a normal breath again.

By that time the dragon had transferred its attention to Gemmel. The wizard stopped laughing at once and instead raised the Dragonwand before him as if to fend off the advancing head. Or to deflect the spell that burned in those great, glowing eyes. They regarded him, Dewan thought, with more than a touch of scorn—with what on a more human visage might well have been contempt. Then it spoke.

And Dewan understood what it was saying.

For all his years of service in the Imperial military, Dewan ar Korentin remained at heart what he had been born: a Vreijek. Not a Drusalan. It meant that he had been dismissed— more than once in his own hearing whether by accident or not—as a 'mere provincial'. It meant that he had never reached a higher rank than *eldheisart*-of-cavalry, and never would. It meant, too, that he was—though usually veneered by Imperial stiffness or Alban courtesies, both so studied that they cried out their falseness to all—one of a vehement, sensitive, imaginative race some said, inclined like peasants to superstition and who found the forbidden art of sorcery most attractive. It was much like what those same 'some' said about Alban *eijin;* the stories were only partly true—or conversely, only partly false.

But most importantly, it meant that where a Drusalan or a Tergovan or a Vlechan—any of those who arrogantly styled themselves the Imperial races—might have retreated from the impossibility of comprehending dragon-speech into the ultimate, irrevocable refuge of madness, Dewan himself—after an instant's total nerve-shock, like that of a man jumping into a pool supposed warm but in fact icy—accepted what his brain told him as he accepted all else in this life. As no more than another facet of reality.

'I give thee greeting, Maker-that-was.'

The words were within Dewan's head and understood there, nowhere else; because the voice itself, borne on a soft, hot wind, sounded no more like words than the hissing rumble of some huge fire. Above that rumble he heard the click, click as the dragon's eyelids shut and opened in a leisurely, insolent blink. 'And this? In thy hands is it then a whip, a crop, a means to master such as I? I defy thee to dare use it so.'

Gemmel looked from the dragon to the Dragonwand and back again; then lowered the spellstaff with a small, jerky, embarrassed movement. 'I would not . . . I would not use it like that. You should know.'

To Dewan's ears at least, he sounded somewhat ashamed. Just as he had done after he had assumed that Aldric had beaten the Drusalan woman Kathur so viciously when all sense, all logic—even a moment's pause for thought before he spoke—would have spared him that error. Not so much ashamed of being wrong, as of being obviously so before witnesses. What, wondered Dewan ar Korentin, could have the old man so preoccupied that he made such mistakes? The dragon? Maybe; because there was a tension between the two that Dewan sensed should not have been there.

'Why should I know, Maker? Upon thy word? Not so. Only the Masterword of Governance holds such weight with me. That—or the given Word of a man of honour. I am Ymareth. Dragonkind. Thou knowest well that which I am. In very truth, none should know it better.'

Dewan watched and listened to the exchange sitting stock-still in the saddle of his stock-still horse, aware that he looked painfully obvious while he remained where he was and equally aware that directly he made the slightest move to dismount or in any other fashion become less obvious, he would only make himself still more so. He considered this; felt stupid; and stayed just where he was.

'Or perhaps,' the dragon continued more softly, 'I should know indeed, and should not have tried thee so, with denial and with doubt. We are of a kind, thou and I. There should be trust between us.' Ymareth's great wedge head swung lower. 'Why, therefore, is Aldric Talvalin held a prisoner by those who are his enemies? Know this, Maker: he is a man of honour indeed, for though I might have aided his escape out of this captivity he, having promised that he would not, did not. Think thou on that.'

'Prisoner! Where?' For all his wish to avoid attracting attention, Dewan blurted out the question without thinking—and found himself staring down the dragon's throat an instant later.

'Aboard a vessel of this Empire's warfleet,' Ymareth replied. 'There at least I found him.'

'Then I was right! Gemmel, I was right! It was that battleram after all—it must have been—'

'Dewan!' The wizard's voice was sharp with reproof. 'Dewan, control yourself! How many battlerams are there in the fleet—in each fleet, for the love of Heaven—and how many possible destinations might each vessel have?'

Ar Korentin matched stares with the older man for a long five seconds; then looked away, subsided back into his saddle and closed his mouth.

Ymareth the dragon had watched this brief byplay with what might well have been dry amusement. 'Maker,' it rumbled softly. 'Maker, if ye be yet so uncertain of this warship's abiding-place, why therefore do ye ride inland and from the sea where such vessels pass?' There was a knowledgeable mockery in the words. 'Know this—the Eye of the Dragon sees much that is hidden, and mine own eyes can watch from such heights that the sight of men cannot know my presence. Even,' the dragon neatly pre-empted Dewan's unspoken thought, 'if they should have the aid of far-seeing lenses.'

That suggested the sort of altitude which ar Korentin, still a

Vreijek soldier at heart, preferred not to dwell on; he and his upbringing still had too much superstition about them for him to hear such things with anything like true peace of mind.

'And this I saw,' Ymareth continued. '*Kailin* Talvalin was brought to a strong place that was filled with many soldiers. Time passed, and I saw speech among men who by their garb were of rank and power. There was a killing, to no purpose. Aldric Talvalin rides now with the soldiers of the Empire, clad in red even as they.'

'To the Red Tower,' breathed Dewan.

'To thy destination. Yea or nay?' Either Ymareth knew without being told, or was guessing—or was giving a command veiled as a suggestion.

'Aye, Ymareth dragon, Maker to made. But we know already of this matter concerning the Red Tower.' Gemmel's voice was just the merest trace pompous. 'And we travel there now.'

'On these?' The dragon-voice inside Dewan's head was wholly sarcastic, no longer veiled by irony or allusion. 'Then of a surety, thy need for haste must be small indeed.'

'They were all that we could acquire at short notice,' snapped the wizard impatiently, and it seemed to Dewan that he was speaking with the ease of long familiarity. Nothing else could explain such a casual approach to a creature which could roast him, or flatten him, or snap him in half as a man bites a biscuit. No matter, any of that—the implications behind it all were enough to lift the short hairs on the nape of ar Korentin's neck.

'But now there is a swifter way, if ye dare it.' Ymareth did not elaborate further and had no need to do so. Verbally, at least. The dragon's wings spread out to either side of the bridle-path, enormous fingered sails more vast than those of a fully-rigged Imperial capital ship. Their silent invitation was plain, and chilling. Flight.

'What about . . .' Dewan's voice faltered. Sitting on one of them, the problem of the ponies was plain enough. Until he looked at Ymareth and at Ymareth's fanged, smoked-fuming mouth; and knew exactly *what about* the ponies. He was no Alban horselord, with a perhaps excessive love of that particular animal, but even so the prospect of, of feeding them to a dragon was enough to make his war-hardened stomach turn over.

'Take off the harness and all the other gear,' Gemmel said dispassionately. 'All of this must be done. Whether you like it or not.'

'And would you be as quick with your orders if I was Aldric?' returned Dewan, his temper flaring up for an instant. It was an uncalled-for remark, known and regretted the instant that the words were spoken—directly it was too late to recall them.

'You're like him enough, Dewan ar Korentin. More than enough. You know how to hurt with words. Now—do it, and let's get this thing over.'

Ymareth watched and waited with a dreadful patience, saying nothing, aware perhaps of how these men felt about the beasts they had ridden, aware that there was no place for words here and now. There was nothing to be gained by speech on either side; indeed, if the situation was looked at with the sort of honesty that was little short of brutal, this was a kindness. To abandon the ponies in this wilderness of scrub and snow and desolation would be to condemn them to a lingering death by freezing and starvation. Better the . . . what had Dewan's own thought been? . . . brief, bright glory of a dragon's fire.

So at least the Vreijek persuaded himself, as he loosened the cinch on the last saddle and lifted it away. As he lowered it gratefully to the ground a little way off—with all the gear strapped around it, that saddle was heavy—Gemmel's hand, feeling just as heavy, came down on his shoulder.

'Stay there,' the wizard said. 'You won't want to see this.'

Dewan stiffened and looked up at the old man, while pity fought with contempt for room on his face. 'You are like a king,' he said softly. Which king was not specified. 'You can command death by war, by assassination, by execution—but you'd as soon not watch it happen.' Aldric had told him once about a killing before Dunrath; about how Gemmel, master of theoretical swordplay, had been shocked and horrified to see his theories put to practical use. This was the same. Dewan straightened up and shrugged the wizard's hand away, then turned around. 'Maybe if you watched, if they *all* watched once in a while, you and they would be less free with such commands in the future.' The ponies were still immobile, still frozen by whatever spell had been laid on them—as incapable of escape as prisoners trussed for the block. Or soldiers drawn up in line of battle. You've lived among the Albans for too long, he told himself, to be so concerned about the fate of a pair of nags. But still he gripped Gemmel's shoulder as the wizard had gripped his. 'You gave the command, old man. It's only right that you should look at the consequence. So look. I said, *look!'*

He swung Gemmel around by main force just as Ymareth's huge head descended on its prey. At least the attack was merciful, for neither pony could have known what happened with each head chopped off at the neck like someone swatting the blossoms off dandelions. One instant they were alive and whole, and the next . . . not. Even the blood which gouted onto the snow was no worse than the mess which followed a successful hunt, nor the wet ripping noise of rending tissue any more dreadful than the sound of dogs at their meat. No, not dogs—cats. Ymareth ate with all the dainty fastidiousness of a feline—or a certain young Alban of Dewan's acquaintance.

There was a few minutes' digestive silence as Ymareth swallowed down the last fragments and considered their flavour. Then a lance of yellow-white fire billowed from its mouth, scouring away the last residue of blood and flesh from the dragon's teeth. Dewan understood now why it did not have the foetid breath of a carnivore; any stink was seared away by that cleansing gush of flame—which was just as well.

'Now,' said Ymareth, and even though the words were unheard, forming as they did within the Vreijek's head, Dewan could detect a well-fed satisfaction in the dragon's tone. 'Now, gather that which thee might need, and mount to my neck.'

As he bent again to lift the pack of gear and armour to its accustomed place across his shoulders, Dewan hesitated and braced his weight against his knees until the pounding heartbeat in his ears had once more died to a murmuring of blood. A cold sweat had broken out across his forehead, and there was a hot throb of pain running down the very core of his left arm. For just a moment the world gyrated around him, mocking his self-imposed stability with its movement, and then grew still again. Dewan ground his teeth until his jaws ached and drew himself upright again with such a shudder as the Albans said was caused by someone walking across a grave. He no longer found that superstition funny. Not now. Dewan ar Korentin had begun to realise what it might be like to die.

*   *   *

For the tenth—or was it the hundredth?—time, Aldric swivelled half-around in Lyard's saddle to glance back at the men
who kept him company. This glance, like all those others,
made him feel no easier. It was certainly not the kind of
company an Alban gentleman would prefer to keep—rather
the sort of company that he personally would have made
considerable efforts to avoid—had he the choice, which he
hadn't. It was not Bruda, not even glowering Voord with his
killer Tagen at his elbow, but the half-score of heavy cavalry
who made up the honour guard for this group of staff officers
and adjutants—the gold insignia were staff, the silver not—
and thus gave credence to their supposed rank. Their armour
was the full lizardmail of *katafrakten*, and that in itself was
what Aldric found unsettling, ridiculous though the feeling
was. But he had ugly memories concerning *katafrakt* armour
and about the demon-sending Esel who had filled such armour
when he—it?—had been sent by Duergar Vathach to kill him.
Those memories were only six months old—nothing like old
enough for him to live easily with them. Not yet.

It was not merely the escort which disturbed him, for all
that. Even granted that, apart from Bruda, he wore the most
senior insignia of the little commissioned-officer squad, at the
back of his mind Aldric knew that the bars and triangles and
diamonds were only badges, only insignia which he had no
right to wear. If put to the uttermost test they would be no
protection. No protection at all. Even wearing the things made
him feel uncomfortable.

At least the armour which in part bore those rank-tabs was
comfortable enough. Senior officers, Bruda had taken pains
to inform him, did not wear issue harness like an enlisted
trooper. Their armour was tailored for them with the same
care as a fine suit of clothing—indeed, with more care: unlike
cloth, metal and leather was unforgiving of careless measure-
ment. It didn't stretch . . . For all that what he wore now had
been assembled from available parts rather than forged especially for his limbs and body, it was—he conceded reluctantly—as good a fit as his own beloved black *an-moyya-
tsalaer*. Right now, in very truth it was a better fit altogether,
for what with one thing and another he had lost maybe twenty
pounds in weight and it showed. Alban full harness had a
tendency to hang loose when it didn't fit its wearer properly,

and Aldric's harness would have hung very loose indeed just
at the moment.

This was red-enamelled, rather than lacquered black; it was
made of small plates and splints, but linked by strips of mail
rather than the lacing of lamellar; and yet for all the differences, it was not so dissimilar after all. Except for the
helmet. The Drusalan officer's high-crowned *seisac* had a
peak, a neck-guard and cheek-pieces like the war-mask of its
Alban counterpart; but everything fitted so much more closely
that it was claustrophobic just to think about it. And it had a
nasal. That nasal bar had made Aldric squint for nearly three
days now, so that he was playing host to the mother and
father of all splitting headaches—although he was generous
enough to admit that if he came out of this particular venture
with his head split by nothing more permanent in its effect,
he would be more than happy.

The roads were busier than Aldric had expected they might
be; either the Empire was in less internal trouble than he had
been led to believe, or its citizens were making a laudable
and convincing attempt at normal life. Only one thing disturbed him a little, and that was the reaction of ordinary folk
to the military presence of which he was perforce a part. He
had seen something similar before, in Alba, when he had
ridden as an *eijo*. But there, though timid, people had responded with no more than cautious, courteous, mannerly
respect. Here it was just fear.

Not knowing the meaning of all the insignia splattered in
gold metal and coloured enamel on his helmet, overrobe and
armour, he was half inclined to ask somebody on that first
day of the ride to Egisburg. Then the inclination died. He was
hanalth, and that rank was made plain by two horizontal bars
beneath an inverted triangle surmounting a diamond made of
two more triangles joined base to base. All in gold. And that
was all he needed to know. All he really wanted to know. For
the rest, whether they meant he was pretending to such rank
in an élite, heroic regiment of cavalry; or in the political
police whose action squads might execute a man for treason
when his only crime was to empty rubbish wearing a ring
bearing the Emperor's—or more likely the Warlord's—likeness
still on his finger, thus insulting them by implication, Aldric
had decided that ignorance in such matters was best.

But there was one matter in which he remained most

interested, and moreover most secretive—it was not something he intended drawing to the attention of his companions. Once, twice, maybe three times he had sensed—and then seen—a mounted figure far off on the horizon. Maybe he was wrong, and maybe he was just guessing, but he did not yet need a scholar's spectacles and was still ready to swear that it was the same person every time. A long-glass might have confirmed that notion one way or another, but Aldric had none in his gear and though Voord carried one—a good one, Navy issue—he was the last person the Alban was going to ask. And maybe he *was* wrong, anyway; he could fathom no reason why a solitary rider would want, or dare, to shadow a column of heavy cavalry.

Aldric had once heard Gemmel use a word which described how he was feeling, and the word had stuck somehow in his memory. *Paranoia*. It was an odd, cumbersome, unAlban word, but once its meaning was explained it described exactly how he felt right now—how he had felt ever since the Imperial military had begun to take an interest in him. Nervous and suspicious of everything and everybody which didn't have an instantly discernible motive.

But why shouldn't someone else be riding this road? Egisburg was a large city and there were many more reasons to go there than—than his own. And any reluctanace to get too close to Imperial soldiers was scarcely grounds for suspicion; it was, rather, something to be applauded as laudable caution. For himself, he would as soon have the breadth of a province—at the very least—between himself and Voord at any time.

Except that he had given his word to help in this enterprise—given it not only to Goth and Bruda, who were only foreigners after all, but to Rynert as well. He was the king's man and it mattered not a whit that he had been pledging himself only in the very vaguest sense. A given word was a given Word, and a Word given was a word honoured. Even if it did complicate his life exceedingly. He would hold to that Word to the best of his life's ability.

But he would have dearly loved a friend nearby—Gemmel, Dewan, someone, *anyone*—just to confide in now and then.

Lord General Goth had been right in his remarks about how close Egisburg was to the Emperor's part of the Empire—a

distinction which he made clear with a sardonic smile that
Aldric thought would have looked more at home on the jaws
of a wolf. The Alban had *seen* a wolf grin just like that and
he knew exactly what his thought meant.

By the straight Army roads it was two, or maybe three
days ride from Goth's fortified headquarters; certainly no
more. The journey would have been still quicker had they
used the Falcon courier routes, but those of course were
forbidden even to senior officers. And still more to those only
pretending to such a rank.

Throughout that last long afternoon, four cold hours that
were at one time crystalline clear and at another blurred by
falling snow, Egisburg coalesced from a smudge on the horizon to the hunched, jagged reality of a city. Even then, it was
only as evening folded its grey wings about them that they
had their first clear view of the place which they hoped to
enter—and leave—unseen and unscathed. Aldric sat up very
straight in his saddle, aware that the sporadic conversation at
his back had died away. It was scarcely surprising; but it did
suggest that the reputation of the Red Tower carried a degree
of weight even with the Secret Police.

There were larger fortresses in the world, he knew that—
and had no doubt of the knowledge, having seen some of them.
Datherga, Segelin, Cerdor, even his own hold of Dunrath was
bigger than this; and they in their turn would be dwarfed by
some of the Imperial fortresses, like the Grand Warlord's
recently completed citadel at the heart of Drakkesborg. But
for all their size, none of them could have looked so forbidding to intruders.

He had expected a slim spike of masonry, maybe something like that in the old story of the Elephant Tower which
he had loved so much as a child, or like that which the holy
men of Herta were said to build and in which they could hide
from sea-raiders. The Red Tower of Egisburg was none of
these. Somebody, once, long ago—at least two hundred years,
if he was any judge of fortified architecture—had decided that
they would build themselves a strong place here at the junction
of two rivers. 'A 'castle', as the Drusalans would have said.
And this somebody had spent lavishly, unstintingly on the great
keep that would be the core of his fortress; so lavishly that he
apparently had no money left to do more. There were no
curtain walls, no river-fed moat, no outer defences at all.

But there was the Tower.

From base to rampart it was two hundred sheer feet of worked granite, and its stones were sheathed in the thick glaze which gave the place both its name and its colouration: a deep, vivid crimson that was unpleasantly like the hue of fresh-spilled blood. It reared starkly against the iron clouds like the tower Aldric remembered from his dreams, distorted by an errant swirl of snow; and at the same time an amber ray from the setting sun stabbed from the west over his right shoulder and seemed to lick against the stonework. For that brief instant, until the rent in the overcast closed again, the tower glistened with a sheen that was almost sticky. Aldric would not have been surprised to smell the sweet, salty tang of new blood. And within his borrowed armour he shivered just a little.

The Red Tower's history was such that its name was used beyond the Empire as a threat to frighten naughty children. Beyond, but never within. Within the Empire, such threats frightened more than children. For within the borders of the Empire, the Red Tower's threat was real.

Aldric's guess had been right. It was to have been the most splendid, the most imposing and the most impregnable fortress in Drusul; and then the money ran out. No one but historians and scholars even remembered its builder's name now; he had been disowned by his infuriated family for committing the near-capital offence of squandering inherited wealth, and they wanted nothing more to do with him. He had died an unmarried, childless, nameless old man.

Eighty years passed, and the tower became a fortified residence for the hereditary Overlords of the rapidly growing new city-state of Egisburg, a place made rich by the traffic passing along its twin rivers and by the ironworks which were already passing into proverb. 'As good as Egisburg steel' had been a token of approval more than a century ago. In those days the Sherban emperors had been more tolerant of autonomous city-states than they were now.

During the early decades of the Sherbanul dynasty's rise to absolute power—before the coming of the Warlords—it had become necessary to find a secure place where important prisoners, political hostages and 'guests' of the Drusalan Empire could stay pending an ultimate decision on their fate.

That decision could be a reprieve, or the signing of a favourable treaty—favourable to the Empire, naturally—or legal execution. Once in awhile it was just disappearance.

The Red Tower—which had acquired its name and its
glazing when the city first declared its support for the Emperor ten years before, during that delicate few months when
the second autocrat of the dynasty was considering who were
allies and who enemies and what to do to each—was just
such a place. Created as a fortress, finished as a home, it had
all the necessary requisites and had been handed over to the
then-current Emperor on the instant that his speculation passed
from the cerebral to the verbal. Red being the preferred
Imperial colour (a fact made known to those who had chosen
the tint of the glaze, and everyone was aware of it) the gift
was accepted at once. Since then a considerable number of
people had passed through the tower's lowering portals, and
though most of them were accounted for in one way or
another, there were still a score or so who had never been
seen or heard from again . . . as if the sombre crimson
building had swallowed them. Yet in keeping with the façade
of safe, comfortable accommodation for individuals of
consequence—and since a few of them were indeed restored
to their full rank and privilege with apologies of varying
sincerity—conditions within the Tower were said to be little
short of luxurious. And the guard contingent was supposed to
be downright polite!

Dewan ar Korentin had told Aldric about this place over a
drink; one of the many, many Imperial subjects which they
had discussed in the short time available for Aldric to learn
about them. He had said that a posting to duty in the Red
Tower was regarded by most regular troops—and granted by
their officers—as a kind of good-conduct award. That meant
several things; most of all, that the attitude of the entire small
garrison from its commander down tended to be somewhat
lax. Quite apart from anything else, the construction, reputation and appearance of the Red Tower was such that it
deterred all but the most determined escape attempts. Not that
any of those had ever succeeded, of course—and for the same
reasons, nobody should be mad enough to want to get *in*.

Except, reflected Aldric sardonically, that several otherwise rational people apparently were . . .

And somebody, somewhere, seemed to suspect as much. Why else would all the streets leading to Tower Square be blocked by army checkpoints? The soldiers manning them wore *Woydach* Etzel's crest and colours—Aldric was growing very tired of seeing that jagged four-pointed star disfiguring what he still regarded as his own clean black and silver, for all that he wore Imperial red right now—and they were turning away any who lacked the proper written authority to pass through their blockade, even those who, by the sound of their protests, actually lived in the sealed-off streets.

'What's the meaning of all this?' Aldric wondered quietly out of the corner of his mouth. 'They can't be expecting us. Can they . . . ?'

'No.' Bruda's reply sounded confident and unconcerned. 'This is standard practice. A drill. A precautionary measure.'

'Precaution against what?'

This time Prokrator Bruda made no answer.

There was a travelling fair in town: jugglers, musicians and acrobats—and knowing the Imperial Secret Police a little, Aldric guessed that some of them, the acrobats at least, were as likely *taulathin* as not. It was only a guess, because nobody had told him or even hinted that it might be so. But then, they probably hadn't told Lord General Goth either. The fair was keeping company with the more respectable and socially acceptable entertainments of professional storytellers and a theatrical troupe; altogether an expensive-looking show, drawn here for some festival or other to make the last few performances of the season before winter closed in, which had attracted more people than Egisburg seemed able to comfortably hold. One or two more strange faces would hardly attract attention; Bruda or whoever was behind this venture's planning must surely have known, and it explained much of the tight timekeeping involved.

For all the crowds, it proved easy to find lodgings; the cavalry escort were billeted at once with the city's garrison— for despite tensions among the politicals, there was no similar internal breakdown in the Army. Yet. That lay behind the arrogant ease with which they had travelled from Goth's headquarters, and was why the Lord General had insisted Aldric wear Imperial armour. It made him just another part of—the Alban sneered inwardly as the thought took shape— one big, happy army. And a part who was of such rank that he need not fear casual questioning; no military policeman or checkpoint serjeant would dream of questioning a *hanalth* of Armoured Cavalry without a triple-thick, lead-lined, copper-bottomed damn good reason to hide behind. And if he had one, and was already so suspicious as to ask questions, then it was already far too late.

Officers of rank naturally did not live in barracks with their men when there was better to be had, and in Egisburg there was much, much better. For all the teeming host of visitors, and regardless of the fact that they were the best in the city, there were still rooms vacant in the inns lying directly beneath the brooding shadow of the Tower. Vague, forbidding rumours of just who might be held in the citadel—and those rumours varied widely from the unlikely to the downright impossible—were enough to persuade all but the boldest and the wealthiest to seek rooms elsewhere in the city—anywhere elsewhere. Those who remained, other than high-ranking military officers, were men and women cushioned by money whose boldness was directly proportional to their wealth. And some were very, very *bold* indeed.

The explanation had come from Bruda, prompted by Aldric's voiced doubt that they would find anywhere to stay other than barracks and that he most certainly wasn't going to live and sleep in a place where his slightest error would show up like a candle in a cellar. They were riding easily through the crowded streets, letting the throng part before the horses in their own time rather than forcing a passage as they might have done; to do so would have been unnecessary, and obviously so. A casual drifting was much more natural in Egisburg's holiday atmosphere; as natural as the smile which it created on Aldric's face when he began to appreciate the citizens's cheery mood. It was the first such mood, and the first unforced smile, which he had experienced in far too long. More interesting still, the leisurely pace gave him time to overhear such of the storytellers as were close enough to avoid drowning in the background babble.

Aldric had long known that these professional storytellers were rather different from the Alban equivalent—like, for instance, the old man who had harped and sung at his *Eskorrethen* feast almost four years ago. *Four years ago this very month!* he realised with a slight start. Albans were conservative in many things, preferring the old ways to any innovation; that was not always a good thing, whether in the matter of literature or in wider world affairs. One might lead to a degree of cultural stagnation, but the other could be much more dangerous. Of course, King Rynert's new approach—as typified by his presence here—could be equally chancy. To Aldric!

That old man had memorised scores of old legends, old stories, old folktales and even the old, approved way in which to tell each one. But all, like their teller, were *old*. However, the Imperial word for a storyteller translated literally into Alban as 'one who makes tales which entertain', and indeed they spent as much time creating new material as they did in learning the classics. It was no accident that, though Jouvaine by birth and Vreijek by inclination, the playwright Oren Osmar had produced some of his most enduring and popular work under Imperial auspices. Even *Tiluan the Prince*, a play still widely regarded as original, daring and controversial more than eighty years after its first performance.

Not, of course, that such daring controversy touched on anything to do with the Empire's policies; generations of hard-working theatrical censors had seen to that, and Aldric was not so naïve as to forget it. Still, it was intriguing to hear not only stories which he knew already—though in a foreign language which required a degree of concentration for him to understand—but also tantalising snatches of tales entirely new; although some of these were familiar and popular favourites here, if the noisy approval of their audiences bore true witness.

'. . . As long ago as forever, and as far away as the moon . . .'

'. . . Know, O Prince, that between the years when the oceans drank . . .'

'. . . be sure that you return before the stroke of midnight, for otherwise . . .'

'. . . proud, pale Prince of ruins, bearer of the rune-carved Black Sword . . .'

'. . . the falcon struck thrice upon the ground and became a fine young man . . .'

'. . . I shall clasp my hands together and bow to the corners of the world . . .'

Aldric was jolted violently back to an awareness of his purpose in this city by a slap between the shoulder-blades

which observers—had their eyes been keen—might have noticed struck him far, far harder than any *hautheisart* had a
right to strike a *hanalth*, no matter how close their friendship
might have been. But there was no friendship at all in Voord's
grin when Aldric swung round with a stifled oath to glare at
him. The man's thin, bloodless lips were stretched back far
too tightly from his teeth; it was an ugly rather than an
amiable expression, and both men knew that the other was
meant to know it.

'There will doubtless be a time for sightseeing, *sir*,' the
Vlechan said. 'But later. Not now.'

Drinking white wine from a flagon sunk in compacted snow
to keep it cool, two Imperial officers sat in the otherwise
deserted withdrawing-room of a fine tavern and regarded one
another over the rims of their goblets. Two others were
absent. *Hautheisart* Voord had gone out for an ostentatiously-
announced walk, and if there was any ulterior motive behind
his decision—coming as it did so closely on the heels of
certain observations regarding sightseeing—not even Aldric
Talvalin considered it worth commenting on.

Aldric himself, typically enough, had settled himself into
his assigned room for some five minutes, then had gone
looking for the tavern's bath-house. Bruda had shown no
surprise; he knew the Alban people and their customs slightly,
and this young man rather more than that. It was of course
possible that Aldric was being subtly insulting, trying to
imply that the company he was forced to keep made him feel
unclean, but any insult so delicately subtle that it went unnoticed failed to be an insult at all. Instead Bruda and Tagen sat
drinking their chilled wine, chatting about inconsequential
matters in a relaxed way which would have shocked officers
of a similar difference in rank who were unaware of the
informal rank structure within *Kagh' Ernvakh*.

Aldric came in before the flagon was more than half-way
empty, looking pinkly clean, still a little damp behind the
ears and smelling the merest touch scented—in short, like any
other officer of the Drusalan military on an off-duty evening.
He was out of armour now and back into his own clothing as
far as his pretence allowed; only the rank-flashed brassards on
the upper arms of his tunic, and the wide embroidered shoulder-
tabs resting uncomfortably on the densely-furred *coyac* he

wore over it, gave any outward indication of what he was
supposed to be. The severe haircut inflicted on him before he
left Goth's headquarters was no different from that of any
other man, officer or other rank, and the overrobe bearing his
other insignia was doubled carelessly over the arm which
carried his sheathed longsword. In the instant of his taking a
seat, that robe was flung casually across the chair-back—and
the sword leaned respectfully against its arm.

'You should be wearing that,' said Bruda reprovingly.

'The sword?' Aldric misunderstood deliberately, then reached
behind him and pulled the rank-robe further down to make a
better cushion for his head. 'Or this thing? Because you
aren't wearing yours,' he pointed out with impeccable logic
as he poured himself some wine.

Bruda smiled thinly 'Your point,' he conceded without
rancour. 'But then again, I'm entitled to my rank; I earned it.
Yours is merely borrowed. So wear the robe whenever you
go out of this tavern: understood?'

The request was acknowledged—just—by a lifting of eyebrows and wine-cup, and by the faintest of nods.

You do know how to be annoying, don't you? thought
Bruda. He said nothing of that sort aloud, and instead turned
back to Tagen and the conversation interrupted by Aldric's
arrival. 'So—now that you've seen the Tower, what do you
think? Any ideas about getting in?'

'What?' Aldric sat up very sharply, flinched, swore and
shook cold wine out of his sleeve. He was none too pleased
by the import of Bruda's words; playing things by ear was all
very well in the proper time and place, but this was neither.

Bruda's gaze flicked unemotionally from the spilled wine
to Aldric's face and back again in any eyeblink. 'Mop that
up,' he said, taking a drink of his own. 'And I wasn't talking
to you. Tagen—you're from the hill country. Opinions?'

'I think, Prokrator,' said Tagen, after taking a moment to
gather his thoughts, 'that hill-climbing and the Tower don't
go together. No natural toe or finger-holds, thanks to the
glaze; and if you tried to hammer in a spike you'd have the
whole garrison out to answer your knocking.'

'Conclusion?'

'As well try to climb a mirror as go up that bitch by normal
means. Sir.'

'I see.' Bruda shifted in his chair. 'Well, Aldric: no comments yet?'

'No. Not yet.' There was more on Aldric's mind right now than being sarcastic; and granted, that did make a change.

'Sir? said Tagen in the voice of one struck by a sudden thought. 'Sir, I might be able to get a grapnel on to one of the parapets.'

Glancing at Tagen, Aldric opened his mouth to say something like, 'What, ten-score feet straight up, and in the dark?' then closed it with a snap as the *tau-kortagor* idly flexed one arm and gave a hint of the heavy muscles hidden by his sleeve.

Yet Bruda did say much the same out loud—although not scornfuly but with regret. 'Not even your strength could manage that feat, Tagen,' he said.

'Oh, not throwing it, sir.' The man laughed a little, flattered that his commander had given such a possibility sympathetic thought. 'No, I was thinking of a crossbow.'

'You'd have to pad the hook,' said Aldric. 'Those things must be noisy when they hit stone. And you'd have to get it first time. Could you?'

'Not first time—not in the dark. Nor second, most likely. But I could promise third or fourth.'

'By which time the—what was it?—the whole garrison would be out to answer your knocking, eh?' Aldric echoed Tagen's own doubt softly and the Drusalan grinned, amused by the word-play.

Bruda was not amused. He set down his goblet with a sharp click that drew all eyes and turned it slowly around and around as silence fell. 'Well done,' he said acidly. 'You're skilled at picking holes, Aldric-*erhan.*' The Alban 'scholar' suffix was more an insult than anything else, the way he used it now. 'But let's hear something positive for a change.'

Aldric stared at the two Imperial faces . . . hard faces, foreign faces—and knew quite well that he was taking a risk even to voice his thoughts aloud. But he did, at last. 'Try sorcery.'

The door opened and Voord came in as if on cue. Or as if he had been listening outside. 'Sorcery?' The *hautheisart's* voice was disbelieving. 'Alban, you deserve credit for sheer gall at least—thought little enough for wit. To recommend the use of the Art Magic to a Chief of Secret Police must rank among—'

'Look at the warships of our so-gallant fleet, dear Lord Commander Voord!' snapped Aldric, 'Then tell me more about how magic is forbidden in the Empire!'

'So you know about the Imperial proscriptions, then,' observed Bruda unnecessarily.

Aldric stared at him a moment, and nodded; who didn't, for Heaven's sweet sake? They were only the most viciously penalised edicts ever to appear in a legal statute book, and they had been stringently enforced ever since their inception fifty years before. Enforced, that is, except where raw power could command them to be set aside.

'If you know, then perhaps you could also suggest where I might find a sorcerer?' Bruda continued in a voice of deceptive sweetness. 'Vreijaur, perhaps? Or maybe even Alba?'

It struck Aldric then that Bruda might not be quite as sober as he had first appeared. 'Your lieutenant has already pointed out that you are Chief of Secret Police,' he returned flatly. 'As *Hauthanalth Kagh' Ernvakh,* you tell me.'

There was a chilly pause, then Bruda threw back his head and laughed with a harsh bark of mirth which startled Aldric considerably. 'All right,' he said, still grinning, 'I will. There.' One hand pointed to where Voord was leaning against the door-post looking enigmatic. 'That's your wizard.'

'*Him?*' Aldric was, and let himself sound, insultingly incredulous.

'And why not?' smirked Voord. 'Where better to practise secret arts than in the Secret Police? We all of us have our little vices. I already know some of yours, and this is one of mine. You might find out what the others are some day, *hlensyarl.*' His smirk went thin and nasty. 'Or they might find you.'

'My personal staff are men of many talents, Aldric,' said Bruda. It was impossible to tell if the fact pleased him, but somehow Aldric fancied not. 'Many talents—and various.'

'So it would appear.' The Alban poured himself more wine, and flavoured the inside of his mouth with a minute sip. He met Bruda's eyes and held them with his own. 'I'll remember that.'

'Yes. Best that you do.'

'Prokrator,' cut in Voord, 'I was a little late. What are *we'*—all Imperial officers together, he implied, and no play-acting foreigners—'discussing?'

'The *tulathin* and the Tower,' said Bruda, and hesitated. 'Well, would magic be of use?'

'Perhaps . . .' Voord's voice tailed off as he realised he had over-filled his cup and concentrated on bringing it un-spilled to his lips, where a long draught brought its contents to a safer level. Only then did he lower the goblet and nod slightly in agreement. 'Yes, perhaps indeed.'

'Prokrator *hauthanalth*, this is scarcely evidence of careful planning!' From the tone of his voice, Aldric was not so much surprised as angry; annoyed that a plan which in its earlier stages—the 'acquisition' of an Alban representative— had seemed geared to the fine tolerances of an expensive machine, should now have degenerated to speculations over wine. And after another half-second's consideration, he said as much aloud.

'Careful planning?' echoed Voord before Bruda could say anything. 'But it is, Talvalin. It is. All of these "specula-tions" as you call them, have been aired before.'

'And advance reconnaisance? You all talk as if you were seeing this Red Tower for the first time!'

'Most of us are; but it was carefully surveyed by one of my agents not long ago. A single man, rather than a group— attracting less attention that way, and preserving what he learned in his head rather than on paper, for the sake of secrecy.'

'So much secrecy that I see no evidence of what was learned. Who was this so-called ag—' His words cut off as he realised what the answer would be.

'Garet.'

He was right. 'Oh,' was all that Aldric said in response to Voord's statement, but inside his mind was in a whirl. It was ridiculous that so delicate an enterprise should hinge on the knowledge of one man, and that such knowledge should be carried only in the fragile vessel of that man's mind. It was so ridiculous that Aldric felt suspicion plucking at his hackles yet again. Learning that Voord—of all people—had a fond-ness for sorcery was one reason; and enough reason to make anyone suspicious without anything to bolster it. But that discovery was beginning to nudge other, deliberately sup-pressed and now half-forgotten memories into place. Memo-ries from Seghar.

'What plan for us, then?' he wondered aloud, knowing that

he was almost too elaborately nonchalant. 'Do we climb ropes like *tulathin*—or spiders—or such vermin, or do we—'

'Walk in through the Tower's front door?' Bruda finished Aldric's question for him. 'Yes, in fact we do. A bold approach. I have all the proper written authorities: genuine for the most part, where we could get them. Otherwise carefully forged.'

'Walk in,' repeated Aldric softly. 'Just like that.'

'Exactly so. What could be more realistic? And any other response would be suspicious in itself.' He caught Aldric's sceptically lifted brows; could hardly have avoided doing so, for the expression was not hidden at all and he could scarcely have missed it. 'Oh yes. You're forgetting, Aldric *ilauem-arluth* Talvalin, that we all—you too!—are senior officers of the finest Army on the face of the earth. Important people, man! We'll pay our respects to the garrison commander later this evening, and to any . . . high-ranked guests he might have. Because he knows we rode in today, and he would be shocked by the breach of protocol if we failed to walk in tonight.'

'I hope you're right, Bruda. Indeed I do. For all our sakes.' Aldric stood up and settled Isileth Widowmaker's cross-strap comfortably on his shoulder, then her scabbard to his weapon-belt. The longsword had come in with him; had leaned her hilt on the arm of his chair as a loving dog will lean its nose; had not, in fact, been allowed to stray more than an arm's length away since she was returned to him, even though it was considered most unmannerly to carry a battle-furnished—and thus threatening—*taiken* when to do so wasn't necessary. But those were manners for Alba and among Albans; here, in Aldric's view, the sword's presence was necessary. Very. And would continue to be so while Voord hovered in the background.

Then he glanced at Bruda, nodded and lifted the rank-marked black and silver overrobe from his chair. 'Satisfied now, *sir?*' he asked with a thread of good-humour in his voice.

Reasonably, *hanalth*. But the rank-robe is crumpled; it could do with a pressing. See to it before you wear it on the public street.'

'Yes, *sir!*' Aldric snapped a neat half-salute for Bruda's benefit, turned to leave the room—and found Voord blocking his path.

'Just where the hell do you think you're going anyway?'

Aldric hesitated, considering the flavours of the various responses he could make; then shrugged and put a sort of smile on his face as he brushed past. 'Sightseeing,' he said. Then he dusted an imagined smudge from the black fur of the *coyac*, where Voord's arm had touched it. 'And to have a look at the moon, if the sky's clear enough.' He sank the last barb with an unsubtle malice, sure of the Vlechan now. 'I'm tired. But you know what they say. 'A . . . change is as good as a rest.'

'Be back by the Hour of the Cat,' Bruda advised his receding back.

Aldric turned sufficiently to see the Prokrator's face, then said, 'You mean by eight of the clock, of course. Although midnight would be as appropriate.'

'The Hour of the Wolf? Far too late! Why do you——'

'Voord might tell you. But I doubt it.' Aldric smiled again, the smile of one who knows a secret, and left.

Because of clouds and darkness there had been little sensation of flight; but there had been every sensation of great speed and Dewan's face and hands were numbed and stiffened by the icy wind which had scythed past them. Only his legs were warm, where they forked the dragon's armoured neck. But for all the discomfort, and all the—he would not give the word more than an instant's consideration, even though he knew it was correct—all the terror, Dewan ar Korentin would not have missed this experience for half the gold in Warlord Etzel's coffers.

No, not for *all* the gold, because every once in a while the silvery grey blanket above, beneath and around them had parted, and he had seen the fires of countless stars mirrored by the lantern-lights of human men far, far below. It was impossible to guess the speed of Ymareth's flight, but the thinness of the cold air and the difficulty he had in breathing it told him that he was at least as high off the ground as the mountain-peak he had climbed for a wager long ago. Why the air should grow weak, Dewan didn't know; but he was intelligent enough to conclude that if he felt now what he had felt then, and the only similarities were altitude and cold, then one or the other was responsible. And he had been equally cold sitting on a horse, so . . . Perhaps the richness remained near the ground, where there were more men and beasts to breath it.

'Egisburg,' said Ymareth's voice inside his head, and with the word the dragon tilted onto one wing and began a lazy, spiralling descent. Dewan's ears popped as they were filled with the rich, thick lower air, and he swallowed automatically to relieve the pressure; but he was no longer thinking vaguely scholarly thoughts about the composition of air at different heights above ground level.

Instead he was gaping like the stupidest backwoods peasant at the sight which came drifting up towards him as he sank through the clouds towards it, knowing that he was gaping and not caring who else knew. *Egisburg,* Ymareth had said. The single word, the name, could not begin to do justice to the great strew of luminescent jewels which were spread out below him. Oh, Dewan knew what they were, and what their colours meant: the lamps of the city, yellow for the most part, bright and steady where their source was oil-fed lanterns, duller and flickering for live-flame torches. There was a cluster of sapphires—someone's house-lamps, glazed in blue glass; there emeralds; and there rubies. Further away, slipping beyond sight as they glided down and thus narrowed the angle of view, Dewan caught a brief glimpse of the wealth and reputation of Egisburg: the amber glow of her furnaces, near the silver ribbons that were the confluence of the city's two rivers. Now and again there would be a harsh glare where some ironmaster worked late into the night, and the cold wind brought with it a faint, faint reek of charcoal smoke edged with the acrid bite of white-hot metal. It smelt of . . . dragons.

The dragon beneath him banked over and away from the myriad glitters of the city, and Egisburg slipped smoothly out of sight under Ymareth's wing and body as it turned toward the darkness beyond the city boundaries in a search for somewhere safe to land.

How can even a dragon see in this? Dewan thought wildly. The thought was stifed an instant later as he learned just how a dragon could see after dark; for the billow of flame from Ymareth's jaws was as hot and white and brilliant as a lightning-flash, and threw the scudding ground below—and not so far below, at that—into a sharp-edged relief map worked in black and silver-white.

Arrogant, Dewan thought then, but not careless. Who'd be out on a night like this? And who'd believe what they saw if they saw this? And who'd believe *them?* If they were stupid enough to mention anything so linked to sorcery within the borders of the Empire!

Ymareth's flight curved around, leisurely and slow; Dewan felt the shift of muscles under his gripping thighs as they adjusted the set of the dragon's wings, and then he felt those same muscles flex like cables to drive the wings forward and down in the final landing manoeuvre he had watched earlier this same extraordinary day. The dragon's mailed spine kicked up at Dewan's unarmoured one, a sensation reminiscent of taking an assault-course jump bareback, and settled beneath him. Movement ceased.

And they were down.

Dewan climbed from Ymareth's neck—'dismount' was scarcely an adequate description for such a height as was between him and the ground—and walked away like an old man, very stiffly and carefully, his legs locking at the knees with every stride. He was aware that by rights he should still be frightened, or shocked, or at the least startled; but he knew equally well that if asked he would admit only to exultation and great wonder.

Ymareth, crouched huge and impossible in the broken moonlight a few yards from the Vreijek's back, watched him even though the man was unaware of such a scrutiny. 'He is as one who has looked upon the face of his god,' said the dragon softly, privately, for Gemmel's ears alone. 'Seldom has this form given such joy.' Yellow-white fire danced lazily in fanged jaws, but there was no threat in the gesture; only satisfaction and a great, gentle amusement.

'I did not teach you blasphemy,' returned Gemmel a touch sourly. 'And you aren't a god.'

'I did not say so—that was thy word. But now that thee makes mention of it . . .'

'Don't!' It was only after his twitchy, nervous response that Gemmel realised how he was being teased. Almost affectionately so, if the word applied to dragons.

'Thee taught me the appreciation of humour, Maker. So enjoy the jest.'

'I taught thee—you—so that you would better understand humankind. Not to make jokes. Stop it.'

'Not at thy command. Not now.' Ymareth's mind-heard voice hardened, became severe and almost reproving. 'Thou art no longer worthy of such obedience. Not now. In the future . . . Perhaps. But know: the Dragon-lord is he who refused escape and safety for his honour's sake. Remember it, Maker—that—was.'

Gemmel ignored all the strata of implication in the drag-on's speech, as much because he was unwilling to consider them just now as for any other reason. But he looked into the dragon's eyes, as few men might have done, and after several moments smiled. 'Then I commend myself to the future,' he said simply. 'But what has been done, has been done—and what I must do, I will do. Ymareth Firedrake, I am *lonely*. You know my mind as none other, yet not even you can dream of such loneliness. Always, always alone. And my son the Dragon-lord, with the face of the son of my blood; surely that is a bitter jest of the Darkness.'

'So thou namest now a jest of the Darkness. Of Fate. Of whatever name thy choice desires. But a jest—such as those I am forbidden. Is that justice, Maker?'

There was logic in the dragon's reasoning. *Do as I say*, thought Gemmel, dredging up a phrase from years past, *not do as I do*. 'Your pardon, then,' he said, as he had never thought he would. 'For my lost honour's sake, I commend thee to the Dragon-lord Aldric Talvalin. My fosterling. My son. Guard him. Aid him. Keep him safe.'

'All those and more.' Ymareth spread great, dark wings in a stretch, and yawned like a cat so that for just one instant Gemmel was gazing right down the dragon's throat. Fire slumbered uneasily within it. 'But tonight is an ill night for watching; the heat in yonder city makes confusion against the cold air.'

'What if . . .' Gemmel began to say. The dragon looked at him—nothing more—but the wizard fell awkwardly and immediately silent.

'There is the Eye of the Dragon,' said Ymareth. 'Thus he is at once within my notice—and thine also, if it is thy wish to spend again a little power. That power which the Eye has stolen betimes, these few days past, so that I at least might see.'

Gemmel looked from the Dragonwand to the dragon and remembered the stinging hurts which he had suffered will-

ingly or not; and he might well have become angry had not
Dewan's voice slashed through the chill night air like a razor.

'Now what of the Dragonwand, Ymareth, Lord Firedrake?'
Gemmel, listening, would have doubted Dewan ar Korentin
capable of such delicate courtesy as the mannered form of
Drusalan which he now employed. But though he listened,
the wizard did no more and passed no comment either then or
at any other time. 'As if in a dream,' continued Dewan, 'I
remember that Aldric Talvalin gave his promise that the gift
of a talisman of power would be returned to its rightful owner
and its rightful place. Yet I see it here. So then, what of the
Dragonwand?'

Ymareth's eerie, terrible, beautiful head turned slowly as if
surprised to hear such words from such an unlikely source.
So far as black and steel and goldbright scales could hold the
expression, there was warm pleasure on the dragon's face and
in its phosphorescent, unwatchable eyes. 'It is fine that thee
cares for such a matter here and now. But be assured, Dewan
ar Korentin,' and hearing his name from such a source made
Dewan shiver slightly, as it had made Aldric shiver before
him, 'that I am in no haste or eagerness; for such is not
required. Be at thy ease. *Kailin-eir* Talvalin gave his promise. That is enough. He promised its return when all was
accomplished and that time is not yet. Though he knows not
yet whose will he does, he knows full well the meaning of
what he does. Ykraith Dragonwand is a part of that.'

Though Dewan could sense the needle of an insult somewhere, buried deep, he was unsure if the dragon had meant
deliberate hurt by it or merely a goad to Gemmel 'the
Maker'—a title which to Dewan had many facets of significance—who had become, in the phrase which he had overheard, 'Maker-that-was'. He turned, slowly, no longer speaking half over his shoulder as he had done when first trying to
come to terms with so many enormities, and deep inside
himself Dewan—ex-*Eldheisart* of the Bodyguard, King's con-
fidant, warrior's friend, wizard's acquaintance and now most
impossible of all, dragon's rider—felt himself dwindle into
insignificance.

'Ymareth,' he said, dropping from the formal mode, 'this
is near the heart of the Drusalan Empire. Aldric, Gemmel and
myself—we are three individuals against a mighty realm.
What can *you* do?'

A gush of fire from the dragon's jaws threw down stark shadows beyond the trees of the small hollow where they had landed: a billow of pale, cool flame that was the dragon's laughter. 'O ar Korentin,' the words forming within his head had an aura of chuckling about them, fluttering like an alcohol flame, 'if thou art within a mile of what I *can* do, ask again. If asking is required . . .' Then the flickering amusement died away, fading like a morning mist in sunshine. 'Enough. For all the darkness it is but evening yet, however these Drusalans calculate their hours of night and day. Best therefore that I not remain. From thy words, good ar Korentin, I do not exist within the boundaries of this Empire. That makes me sad. But for all my sadness I would as soon give no priest of this land a conflict of belief. Yet. Later, later they will see, and know, and believe indeed. I go. But remember,' and had the words been spoken rather than heard within the confines of their listeners' heads, they would have been lost in the sounds as Ymareth prepared to rise once more into the air, 'remember that I watch by Dragonwand and Dragon's Eye. Be aware of aid uncalled-for. Farewell!'

The downward slap of air all but threw Dewan off his feet, for all that he was expecting something of the sort. By the time he had wiped powdered snow from his eyes, the dragon's lean black silhouette was no more than a scudding disruption of the cloud-occluded stars; but it mattered little to Dewan that he could see no more than a dark razor-slash interrupting the jewelled twinkle of the winter sky. He stood in silence and he stared, his head tipped right back on his shoulders, and he did not move from that position until Gemmel reached out to lightly touch him on the arm.

'So,' the old wizard said, 'how much do you know of me now, Dewan?'

The Vreijek's unwinking gaze shifted from the stars and that which flitted across them to Gemmel's bearded face, blinked twice and came to focus. Dewan smiled then, very gently. 'You are not Dragon-lord. Not Maker. Only Maker-that-was. You must explain those titles to me, Gemmel.'

'Soon. You have said what I am not—what else?'

'A—a wizard. And a scholar. A man wise in many arts. And the foster-father of, of my friend.'

'Then Aldric is your friend . . . ?'

'Yes. Because he speaks the truth—at least to me—as only

a friend can do. Because we talk as equals. And because we can insult each other!' That last was accompanied by a laugh, but Gemmel had been reading between the lines all along and needed no signal to understand. In the Alban culture, and especially among the high clan *cseirin*-born, any men who could swap insults had to be friends. Otherwise one of them would be dead.

'Then tell me,' Gemmel purred, 'what has he told you of *en-altrou* Errekren, old Snowbeard his sorcerous foster-father? For he must have told you something, surely?'

'Enough.' Dewan looked at Gemmel with a clear-eyed gaze that even in the darkness suggested much unsaid. 'He told me that you lived beneath *Glas' elyu Menethen*. I laughed at him then, but he insisted—so is it true: *under* the Blue Mountains?'

Gemmel nodded, and at that starlit acquiescence Dewan swallowed audibly before he dared continue to speak. But when he did, the words began tumbling out with all the excited eagerness of a boy maybe a quarter of the Vreijek's real age—a boy Dewan might once have been, and a man he might yet have been, before or without the Drusalan Empire and its military service. 'Under the mountain—Lord God! Under Thunderpeak.'

Gemmel had not said so—had not used the name at all— and at the back of his mind he began to wonder just how much—knowledge and guesses both—Aldric had told Dewan when they were both just drunk enough to exchange confidences. He knew that the younger man made friends quickly and thoughtlessly, in the way that often led to hurt on both sides. And hurt to third parties as well.

'He said that you travelled as well, great distances to many countries, before you came to Alba—'

'Came *back* to Alba, Dewan,' the wizard interrupted softly. It was enough to put a slight hesitation in the flood of words, and a thoughtfulness as well.

'You had a son. He . . . died.'

'Yes. Long ago.'

'You told Rynert the King, that day in Cerdor when you found out about . . . how Aldric had been given to the Empire.'

'I told him that my son died. But not how he died; nor who killed him; nor anything about the consequences of that killing. I told him only what you heard yourself. That I had lost a son—and much more than a son.' Gemmel shivered. He looked around him and fixed his attention on a tree-stump left by some woodcutter earlier in the year. 'I'm cold, Dewan,' he said. 'Cold . . . and I'm beginning to hate the dark. We'd both be better for some heat and light.'

Without waiting for agreement—or disagreement, or warning, or anything else—he raised one hand and pronounced the Invocation of Fire. A pulse of force gathered around and then sprang from his fingertips, pale as a dying candle, so weak that daylight would have made it no more than a half-sensed haze in the air; but for all that, the snow beneath its track flashed from white solid to white steam with no intervening stage as liquid. Then it hit the stump: a core of unseasoned wood wrapped in spongy, sodden rot and topped off with more snow. There was a sound like the crack of the world's biggest whip . . . and the stump burned as hot and clean as holly dried for kindling.

'Better,' said Gemmel, and scooped up a little snow to ease the blisters rising on his hand. That small discomfort was well worth it. Heedless of lingering dampness, he dropped his small pack to the ground in the lee of a clump of bushes and sat down on it, stretching chilled feet gratefully towards the blaze.

Dewan looked at him and drew breath as if to say something; then thought better of it and sat down in his turn. 'Now. Tell me. And tell me first of all: who killed your son?'

'I . . . I never knew his name. But he was the uncle of the now-*Woydach*.'

'Etzel's uncle?' Dewan stared at the fire, not understanding at first; then, still staring at the fire and remembering how it had been created, understanding all too well. 'Oh God. *That* one! The one who was—'

'Burned. Roasted alive where he sat on his horse and laughed at my dead son. Killed by magic, Dewan. Killed by me.'

'Then *you*—you're behind the Empire's edict on sorcery!'

'The Grand Warlord's edict—but yes, I am. I, and the thing I did.'

'Fifty years ago,' Dewan muttered, thinking aloud and not meaning to; then he considered his own words and turned abruptly to face the wizard—literally, for now he was staring carefully full at Gemmel's face. It was white-bearded and careworn, but Dewan was giving it more than the casual glance that was usually already coloured by preconceived assumptions concerning wizards—and those who called themselves wizards. It was an old face only until Dewan tried to set a value in years on 'old'; and then it wasn't quite so venerable after all.

A man in his fit and healthy middle sixties. Too fit and healthy for such an age. Old enough—and yet not old enough. Aldric had said how much like himself Gemmel's son must have looked; but when they had first met, the Alban was already twenty years of age and probably seeming older through the fright and grief he had experienced. Either Gemmel had been a father in his teens—not impossible, but unlikely given how strait-laced his morals could occasionally be. Or Dewan's arithmetic was at fault—which was equally unlikely in this case of simple addition.

Or something was not what it seemed.

'Gemmel?' There was a damnable tremor in his voice when he spoke, but the wizard gave no sign of having heard it. 'Gemmel, how . . . how old are you?'

'Older than I was yesterday. But not so old as I'll be tomorrow.' That there was no smile with the words chilled Dewan more than the snow-melt soaking into his clothes. 'It's all a matter of time. And time is something I always had plenty of. Except now. Now I have far too much!'

Dewan felt his skin start to crawl beneath his furs, his armour and his damp clothing, because he had a feeling—no, he *knew*—that he was about to hear things he didn't want to, yet equally didn't want to miss. He wished Aldric were here, with that healthy streak of cynical humour which was just what Dewan needed right now. Because Dewan, ex-*eldheisart*, ex-bodyguard, ex- all the rest, knew something else with absolute certainty.

He was terrified.

But not so terrified as to get up and walk away. Gemmel was gazing at the star-shot sky as though searching for something—the return of Ymareth, perhaps; or perhaps not. It was more as if he searched for that something beyond the sky that either of them could see, a something that only he might hope for.

'I should have spared him,' the wizard said at last,

'because by then his death was needless. Too late to save my son. Too late to bring him back. But I killed: in rage, in grief . . . in vengeance. Because I had the power to do it, there, then, at once—and because I wanted to, more than anything else in all the world.'

'There's nothing wrong with vengeance, Gemmel. Look at Aldric. Look at what he did—and with your help.'

'Oh yes, with my help. And with what motive? Why did I do all this?' There was a dreadful bitterness in Gemmel's voice, a shame and self-loathing which to Dewan had no business there. 'I had my reasons. I always have *my* reasons long planted and long in growing. But now they're coming to full flower and I'm afraid the price will be too high. I'm afraid I'll lose my son again.' Gemmel took a deep breath and held it, then let it slowly out and smiled and shook his head. 'And no, Dewan, you're wrong. Because there's everything wrong with vengeance—at least, for me. It can only be forgiven if it's right, if it's expected, if it's the proper thing to do. The Alban High Speech has seven different words for "revenge", did you know that? Seven words, each with its own proper circumstance for correct usage. The taking of revenge is an Alban's heritage, Dewan. It isn't mine; never has been. I was wrong to do it. It cost me my . . . my honour. And Ymareth knows.'

'Ymareth? Was that why—'

'Yes. Why it holds me in amused contempt—for being less than those to whom I was and should have remained superior. You heard it. I am no longer Dragon-lord. Ymareth respects only honour—an intangible thing which cannot be bought or forced; a fragile thing which must be earned and held, no matter what the price of its holding. I lost mine fifty years ago; I haven't regained it yet.'

'Oh, I . . . Dragon-lord I understand,' Dewan managed at last, 'for all that it's one of *Woydach* Etzel's titles too.' Gemmel glanced towards him, raising an eyebrow, but said nothing more—plainly waiting for the rest of the question, because what Dewan was trying to say had to be a question. And it was. 'But what about . . . What about—*Maker?*'

The wizard smiled. 'Another title. Concise; descriptive; accurate. And true.'

'*True!*' Anticipating something, being absolutely sure of it,

was not at all the same as having it confirmed. 'Then you
made . . . ?'

'Yes.'

Dewan had promised himself that he would do nothing
foolish, nothing which might compromise the carefully cher-
ished dignity which gave him a screen to hide behind. So he
didn't spring to his feet, nor did his mouth drop open, nor did
he swear. But slowly, very slowly in keeping with that
dignity, his right hand moved to touch himself over the heart
and above each eye in the old Teshirin blessing. 'Father,
Mother, Maiden,' he whispered, 'be between myself and
harm, now and always.' He kissed the palm and closed the
fist and only then said, 'But why would you want to make a
dragon?' in a voice whose steadiness surprised even himself.

'Because I wanted to.' The laconic answer paused on an
upward tone, so that Dewan stayed quite still and perfectly
quiet and waited for the rest. 'And because it was appropriate, and because I could.'

'Appropriate?' the Vreijek prompted, speaking as a man
might walk when all beneath his feet was made of blown
glass and tolerance.

'There are world— . . . Places where armed guards are
right and proper, and places for high walls; places for fences
made of wire with fangs like roses, and for wires with—with
lightning running through them. And there are places for
threads of light hotter than the sun in summer, threads that
can cut and kill. But here . . . Here I *wanted* to have a
dragon.' Paying no mind to the burn-blisters already mottling
his fingers, Gemmel gestured at the fire and it flared up more
fiercely still. 'Not just to guard gold—you've seen the Cavern
on Techaur, of course?'

Dewan nodded. There had been far more than gold in it,
but he doubted now that Gemmel meant silks or costly per-
fumes or any of the other things that he, Dewan ar Korentin,
would have thought worth guarding against theft.

'Then you'll know what I mean when I say that anyone not
sent there with specific instructions would probably steal
whatever took their fancy. Or try to.'

Again the Vreijek nodded. Dewan could remember his own
hands and those of Tehal Kyrin, reaching out as though of
their own volition to touch, to hold, to lift—and perhaps to
take. Only Aldric's cry of warning had stopped them; and

later events had shown what would have happened had they completed the attempted theft. He did not know, and did not ask, how Ymareth the dragon had been made, quite well aware within himself that he would neither understand nor really want to know. Dewan knew quite enough already to know he wished to hear no more.

That was not to say his education stopped there and then, for as Aldric had warned him—five, six, seven months ago? —with a slightly drunken grin of good-fellowship, once started on a topic of conversation Gemmel Errekren would pursue it until either it was explained to his own absolute satisfaction or, more usually, his audience rose in rebellion to silence him or leave. Right at the moment, Dewan decided that his own wisest course was to sit quietly and listen.

'What can a person do to control something,' Gemmel said, 'when its power is such that even the possibility of its falling into the wrong hands is an unthinkable nightmare?'

For all that the question sounded merely rhetorical, Gemmel paused so long that it seemed he was waiting for an answer, an opinion, a guess. For something. Dewan provided one, and even then his quietly ventured, 'Secrecy?' was more to end the dragging silence than because he thought he might be right.

Gemmel shook his head in a jerky way that was more emergence from a dream than denial—but denial it was, all the same. 'Not secrecy. That seldom works. Few things can be kept a secret for long. Either the secret is discovered independently, or it's betrayed by spies and traitors, or by idealists who think equality of information should be restored. And throughout the course of history, Dewan, such great secrets have usually been weapons of one kind or another—ways to kill, not ways to cure. One country learns how to heal a terrible disease, and they give the knowledge to all; let that same country discover how to reduce a city ten times the size of Egisburg to dust and cinders in a single flash of light, and they try to keep it to themselves. Fear, do you think? Or shame? No matter. Not once such countries start to think of success in war not as "win" or "lose", but in terms of what number of dead will prove acceptable. Acceptable, Dewan, not intolerable . . . '

Gemmel gazed for a long time into the dance of flames, as if seeing something else entirely in the incandescent shift of

embers and the crawl of sparks. Then he looked up again.
'The Albans place great store by honour,' he said. 'And no,
I'm not patronising you, Dewan. You're not Alban, not even
by marriage, so I can say things to you that I couldn't—or
wouldn't—say to Aldric. Honour—call it the extent to which
a person can be trusted—is a measure of that person's worth.
Of their personal ability—their power, if you like—to keep
things safe. An oath, a promise, a secret; even a piece of
gossip. But such power can be directed out as well as held in.
As magic. A person of much honour is also a person with the
capability—and no more than the capability, mind you—for
considerable magical skill. But in Alba, the concept of honour
has developed in such a way that using magic is no longer
consistent with the reputation of an honourable man.'

'Which is why Rynert has sent Aldric to do his dirty
work!' concluded Dewan savagely. 'Because one way or the
other, no one will think the worse of him!'

Gemmel applauded, making that simple gesture of striking
his hands together something laden with irony. 'Well done!'
he said. 'Except that Aldric's capability is because of, rather
than a lack of, what Rynert the King is pleased to define as
honour.'

'And Ymareth recognises it.'

All the sardonic humour disappeared from Gemmel's face
and Dewan wished that he had kept his mouth shut. 'Yes,'
the wizard said, and all the old bitterness was back. 'I
instilled a respect for honour in Ymareth when I made it. Not
a respect for me, myself, the Maker, but for—. For what I
was. I knew that *then* nobody could take the dragon from me.
Because I had given it intelligence, the ability to judge and to
reason. That was why cu Ruruc couldn't—' He bit the words
off short and blinked, but he knew that Dewan was watching
him.

'Gemmel,' the Vreijek said, and he spoke very softly now,
as if trying not to give offence. Or fright. 'Gemmel, there's a
time and a place for all things. This is the time and place for
truth. Total truth. Nothing hidden. What I think already, what
I guess, is likely far, far worse than anything you could tell
me, and look—' he spread both arms wide, shoulder-height,
and in the heavy furs he wore over his armour he looked
more like some big, friendly bear than ever before, '— I still
have my sanity. If I was going to go mad, don't you think I

would have done so long ago? I doubt that you told Aldric any of this; but credit him with wisdom and an open mind at least. After four years of your tuition, maybe . . . ? So. All of it. And on *my* honour, if you can trust such a thing given by not even an Alban-by-marriage, what you say will go no further without your leave.'

There was another silence, broken only by the crackling of the fire—and by another small sound which at first Dewan could not place. Suspicious, he laid hand to sword-hilt and scanned the clearing's perimeter for intruders; then turned very slowly back to Gemmel. Because the old man was crying.

Dewan ar Korentin was a military man and a King's bodyguard, a good drinking companion—but not someone overly familiar with emotion. For that reason, and they both knew it, he had never been a particularly good husband to Lyseun his wife. All the love in their marriage had been one-sided and at times he was glad they had no children. But not now. Now he wished they had had as many as his own parents, for then he might have had some inkling of what to do. Gemmel was crying, yes—but not as old folk will, or like a child. Instead he wept like a young soldier Dewan had once had in his command, years ago in Drakkesborg, who had committed some offence—the details were forgotten now, but it was nothing important: against a barrack-mate, probably, petty theft or a discovered lie—and instead of the small penalty his crime carried he had been wholly, unconditionally and unexpectedly forgiven for it. Dewan could only do now as he had done then; he sat quietly, neither offering useless sympathy nor, equally rude, ostentatiously pretending that nothing was amiss. He simply watched, and waited, and said and did nothing, but was there all the time—a burly, amiable-if-needed presence who took no offence and gave support merely by that.

At last—only a matter of a few minutes—Gemmel sniffed vigorously like a man suffering a drizzly winter cold and nothing more, then scrubbed his face with both hands and rammed their knuckles into his eye-sockets hard enough to bruise. 'Thank you, *Eldheisart* ar Korentin,' he said, not looking at Dewan's face.

'You know how to laugh as well,' Dewan said, and left the rest of the proverb incomplete. *No one should laugh until they know how to cry.* It was Valhollan, something he remembered from talking to Aldric's lady: Tehal Kyrin. A lady who should never have been sent away, he thought. Had I known then what I know now of Rynert-King, I would never have agreed to it. More—I would have opposed it to the limit that my place allowed. Beyond. But that page is written. *And rewritten;* it was a notion which gave birth to a thin smile, but notion and smile were both for himself alone.

'Yes,' said Gemmel, 'I know how to laugh. But not honestly—only at the foolishness of this world, or at the simplicity of humankind—' and no matter what he had said, Dewan felt something curdle inside him at the way the wizard chose his phrasing, 'or at my own cleverness. I thought I was so very clever, Dewan—so cunning, to use the king's wishes for my own ends. Remember those messages I locked into Aldric's head before he left Cerdor for the Empire? Support, and aid, and all those other things. Well, they weren't alone. I put something there for myself as well.'

'Maybe you shouldn't be telling me this,' Dewan said nervously.

'All of it, you said. So: all of it. You saw the Grand Warlord when you served with the Bodyguard in Drakkesborg, yes?'

'Yes. Many times—'

'And close? Near enough to see well?'

'*Yes!* But what has that to do with—'

'Patience. Listen: learn. He wears different uniforms for different ceremonies; of course he does, I've checked and I know he does. But one thing never changes; you must have noticed the one piece of regalia which never leaves him, the one kept closer even than an Alban keeps his *tsepan?*'

Dewan *had* noticed; though his facial muscles were under full control and did not so much as twitch, Gemmel saw the involuntary dilation of his pupils in the fireglow and nodded as if the Vreijek had agreed on oath in writing.

'*En sh'Va t'Chaal!*' The Drusalan words came out on an exhalation of grey vapour, seen as much as heard, and Gemmel nodded once again.

'As you say: the Jewel of Green-and-Gold Ice. A cumbersome name. Where does Etzel wear it?'

'At his throat—it clips as a centrepiece onto whatever collar of office he might require. But why ask? You've seen it yourself—haven't you . . . ?'

'No. Not for . . . a long time, and then not as a piece of jewellery. But I'll describe it for you and you can tell me if I'm right. And then I'll tell you what it really is.'

'What it *really* . . . ?'

'Oh yes. Because it's not a gemstone. And never was. It's a million times more valuable than that, especially to me.' Gemmel's hands sketched a quick outline on the air. 'Oblong, about so by so—one by one-half palms—and two fingers thick. Transparent, but tinted slightly by the green at its core and the mesh of gold filaments surrounding that core. Three of its edges thick with gold studs, like sunken beads. And cold enough to take the skin off an unwary hand.'

'You *have* seen it, Gemmel—or something very like it. Yes, that's *t'Chaal* as I remember seeing it. But you forgot the frame.'

'Frame?'

'Yes: gold filigree, crusted with emeralds. The jewel-not-jewel is mounted in it.'

'Of course—because of the coldness, and because of the way that it's worn. I see.'

'And what is it, if it's not a jewel? Tell me that.'

'It's . . .' Gemmel hesitated, seeming reluctant to take the final step. 'It's what my son was carrying; what I lost when he died. And what Aldric will try to steal for me.'

'*What!*'

'That was the last message I locked into his mind, because I thought—the way people and events were explained at that time—that he would be in no danger. No real danger. Then everything went wrong. At Seghar. When the killing started. And even after that I thought he would have been all right, because he would return to Alba rather than risk himself on a venture gone sour. And he must have tried—God, how he must have tried!'

'Until Rynert handed him over.'

'Because of those rotten, stupid, petty messages? Because he was determined to prove his support for the Emperor, to show how far he would go, how many loyal vassals were willing to sacrifice themselves for his cause. And because we knew the truth behind it, he tried to have us killed! Just as what I put into Aldric's mind is going to get him—my son—killed again . . .'

'Not if we can reach him first—that's why we came here,

Gemmel. But you said that you would tell me, and you're trying not to do it; *what is t'Chaal?*'

'It's a primary control. A circuit.' Just one glance was enough to show that Dewan understood no more than the thing's importance. 'It's a key, Dewan, a gateway for me to control the lightning which will . . . It's my road home.'

'Home?'

'You know—or at least you guess. Aldric does and you've spoken to him. Because when you learned for certain of my hold in the mountains, you said "under Thunderpeak". A name I hadn't mentioned even once. *Meneth Taran:* The Mother of Storms: Thunderpeak. That place has had something of a reputation for years now. And Aldric surely told you what he saw beneath it . . . within it. Didn't he, Dewan?'

'He hinted. That the mountain itself was . . . hollow. Filled with lights. And power, incalculable power—the very air sang with it. But there was something else.' Dewan's voice faded into silence and he stared at the fire as though hoping for inspiration or for strength before slowly raising his eyes to Gemmel's face. The old man's expression had not altered by even the flicker of a muscle; it remained as neutral as an unwritten page, not prompting, not pressing for a reply, just waiting. And Dewan finished at last, in simple, undramatic words that asked neither for proof nor for denial.

'Aldric said he . . . He thought it was a ship.'

'He was right. My ship. A ship that once could sail between the stars. Because I am now as I told the dragon, Dewan. Alone. And very far from home.'

EIGHT

Heartsease

Aldric stopped smiling directly the common-room door closed at his back. A smile was not the sort of expression he felt like wearing right now; raising his right hand and holding it in front of his nose, he could see—as if he needed visual confirmation—the tremor in the fingertips. The hell with that! He was trembling all over, because saying those few words to *Hautheisart* Voord had brought on as bad a fit of reaction-shakes as anything he had done these past few tense days. He leaned back against the door and closed his eyes; not in an attempt to eavesdrop, even though the conversation he had primed and left behind him would be well worth listening to, but merely to let the hammer of his heart drop to something like its normal rate. There would be no eavesdropping through that door anyway—it was oak plank three fingers thick and hadn't even shifted in its frame as his full weight was leaned upon it—but likewise there would be no hearing Aldric as he drew in huge gasps of breath. Stupid to provoke such a man as Voord—utterly crazy. But just as crazy to let him think that *everyone* was ignorant of his private dealings.

Straightening again, Aldric glanced at the long black and silver rank-robe draped across his arm. Bruda was right, of course. It was badly creased, too badly for a man of—or assuming—high rank and dignity to wear it on the public street. Not that Aldric cared overmuch about the dignity of the Imperial military, but if it likely gave the lie to what he was pretending, then best follow what had been suggested. He stopped off at the doorway to the servants' hall and handed the garment over with a few suitably terse words of instruction.

Then he made his way quickly and quietly to his own

room. No matter what he might have said to Voord, no
matter that it was still something like twelve days to the full
moon, he was not going outside with the wolfskin *coyac* on
his back. The jerkin made him feel uneasy. At another time,
in another place—and most certainly with another coat—he
would have laughed at the notion of a garment having such an
effect on a hardened cynic like himself. Except that he was
no longer quite so cynical as he once had been, particularly
where this black wolf-pelt was concerned. He had seen enough.
More than enough, far too much.

Even thinking about it was more than Aldric could tolerate
in his current frame of mind; with a convulsive wriggle of his
shoulders he squirmed out of the *coyac* as if it had suddenly
become something filthy. And maybe it had. He held it by
the scruff of the collar between a reluctant finger and thumb
while he stripped away its embroidered shoulder-tabs, then
pushed open the door of his room and threw it from the
corridor haphazardly onto a chair, not caring if it caught there
or slithered to the floor. The thing had served its purpose, as
a provocation and a flaunting of supposedly-hidden knowledge; let Voord make of it whatever he would and explain it
whatever way he could, Aldric had no intention of wearing it
again.

Without the wolfskin's weight across his shoulders, it was
as if an equal weight had lifted from the Alban's mind—a
strange sensation, like the removal of a foul smell or the
healing of slight nausea, or the dismissal of a . . . presence.

He glanced just once at the bundled darkness where the
coyac crouched, half on the chair where it had landed and the
rest dangling limply like something newly dead. Then he
deliberately turned his back on it and went to his saddlebags
to take out an object which was, to his present way of
thinking, far more wholesome: the Echainon spellstone; or
the Eye of the Dragon. Whatever its proper name, it was a
blindfolded eye right now, for the crystal was still wrapped in
its covering of fine white buckskin. Aldric bounced it once or
twice on the palm of his hand, wondering why Voord—who
had certainly either searched his gear in person or had its
contents reported to him in detail—hadn't made some comment. Or even stolen it outright.

Maybe. . . . Just maybe. . . . Loosening the lace which
held the pouch of buckskin shut, he pulled it away and the

stone lay in his hand. Completely clear, completely innocent, completely without any flaring luminescence pulsing from its heart. It was now as it had been with Kathur the Vixen, and by inference as it also must have been with *Hautheisart* Voord: nothing but a man's luck-piece of crystal or quartz, set in wrist-loops of polished steel and silver so that it could rest elegantly on the back of its owner's hand.

Or nestle in his palm. Though they were not to know that, and would not have realised its significance even if they had.

Aldric gazed down at it and felt his mouth stretch into a smile that wanted to do more—wanted to grin, to chuckle aloud, to open wide and shout with laughter. But he did nothing of the sort, knowing full well that such behaviour would have provoked all the questions which the stone had so far avoided. As he fitted it snugly to his left wrist and pulled up the cuff of a glove to cover it, Aldric saw—briefly, just enough to prove the dormant power was still there—a single twisting thread of azure fire at the crystal's core, minute and fragile as a human hair, yet bright enough for that one instant to splash his shadow harsh and black behind him on the wall and ceiling.

Then everything was dark again, a darkness held at bay only by the shuttered oil-lamp hanging from its chains above his bed. But now it was a comfortable darkness; more comfortable than it had been this long, long time. Too comfortable, perhaps.

The snow was no longer falling when he stepped outside, and the sky had cleared enough for a faint scattering of stars to show—but the air had become icy. Aldric was not overly concerned by that; he was warmly booted, jerkined and gloved and even the—freshly pressed!—Drusalan rank-robe was of the hooded, quilt-lined winter-weight issue. Dressed so, he could appreciate and almost enjoy the bite of the crisp, clean cold.

Even had it been damp and dismal, he would scarcely have noticed; and not at all after the first five minutes, for that short time was all that he required to walk briskly from the tavern to the square—and the festival—and the storytellers.

It wasn't the eaters of fire or the eaters of swords who interested him; not the jugglers, the acrobats, the singers and players of instruments. The storytellers alone drew him like a moth to a candle-flame. Aldric eased through the crowds towards them—and *eased* was right, for dressed as he was it involved no effort. The first and only pressure of his hand on an arm or shoulder drew an immediate backward glance and his rank-marked clothing did the rest.

He listened, fascinated, regretting that he could spend so little of his time with each, intriguing snippets impinging on his hearing as he moved to and fro. The gloves were off now—perforce, for like so many others he was munching on a sheet of unleavened bread which had been split and stuffed with sliced, spiced meat. Removing his gloves had been a necessity, what with the hot juices running down his fingers, but the Echainon stone remained no more than a handsome clear jewel . . . with just the tiniest, half-seen strand of blue deep down inside it. Like a flaw, he thought to himself.

'. . . a sage,' said one storyteller, 'with a slight flaw in his character.'

Appropriate, said Aldric's mind. '. . . and then,' said another further on, 'the Bridge of Birds lifted above Dragon's Pillow.' Two tellers and but a single tale. Aldric smiled; he knew that story and liked it well. Each storyteller—all of them—had a raised seat, half-ringed with benches for their audience. Every bench was full and beyond them the fringe of casual listeners who had to concentrate if they wanted to hear every nuance of their chosen story, and who tended to hear distracting phrases from half-a-dozen others anyway. Only paying audiences were beyond the range of interruption. Obviously enough: the spacing was based on professional etiquette, consideration, courtesy among . . .

Then Aldric's head jerked around, his smile vanishing; for what he had just heard had to be more than accident, more than just a tale. There was an uncomfortable coincidence between certain memories and the words.

'. . . the dragons confer honour where *they* will.'

He could feel his hackles lifting. Maybe this *was* coincidence, but it was still too close to what had happened to him, and to what Ymareth had said to him, for him to ignore it safely. Once he had traced her voice above the background babble, the speaker was easy enough to aim for: a stocky, middle-aged, matronly woman whose silvery hair was pulled straight back from her forehead and held there by a bronze clip, and who wore an unmistakable suit and overmantle of

turquoise velvet. But more important, and more noticeable
even than her own appearance, was the embroidered design
on each sleeve: a dragon, crawling from cuff to shoulder.

Moving closer, Aldric waited until she had finished her tale
of dragons. *Dragons again.* Call it a dragon in the Empire,
call it a firedrake in Alba; call it anything at all, my lady—
just tell me why, why, *why* one came looking for *me!*

There, she was done. Aldric thumb-flipped a coin towards
a nearby drink merchant, lifted two of the wooden tankards
from his counter, had them filled with the pale, frothy local
brew of beer and then made straight for the woman who
spoke with such authority of dragons.

'Your throat must be dry, lady,' he said in careful mid-
phase Drusalan, proffering one of the mugs of beer.

She hesitated, lifting her eyebrows at him and at his rank-
tabs and at his gift; then with the merest ghost of a shrug she
accepted the drink, said, 'You're right, commander,' in an
accent he had never heard before and took a healthy swallow.
After a second or two she smiled. 'But until now, I hadn't
realised just how very right that was. Thank you.' The woman
bowed politely and Aldric almost echoed it before remembering his supposed character and snapping a half-salute instead.
'I'm Aiyyan ker'Trahan; and you are . . . ?'

'Dirac. *Hanalth* Dirac.' No lie, for the Drusalan form of
his name was common enough and besides, Aldric wasn't
about to give the Alban equivalent—with or without a
surname—to anyone whose business it was to remember
names and events and the stories that went with them.

They made a strange and unlikely pair, subject maybe for a
story in itself: a storyteller and a soldier standing drinking
beer together in a city square which might have been deserted
for all the notice either of them gave the crowds. Aldric did
most of the talking, hedging his way like a cat on eggs
between one non-specific and another—as non-specific as he
could manage and still hope for a useful reply. About dragons, about honour and more warily yet, about the forbidden
Art Magic.

Aiyyan watched him all the time he spoke, and the night-
dilated stare from beneath her brows was far too shrewd for
the Alban's peace of mind. Those green eyes reminded him
of Gemmel, and like Gemmel the lorewoman seemed able to

read beyond the outward meaning of his words and to study the unvoiced truths within.

'So . . .' she said at last. 'I *see*.' Aldric felt that she did indeed, far more so than he had wanted; and he was already regretting his own rashness. 'Commander,' Aiyyan's voice was much softer now, much more confidential, 'these are hardly subjects for discussion in the public square. Especially since you chose to come here wearing *those*.' She flicked a quick, disdainful gesture at the insignia which glinted in so many places on his dark clothing. 'Undress uniform doesn't fade unnoticed into many backgrounds, does it?' Then she grinned, a flash of teeth that lit up her entire face. 'But I make my living from—such subjects of discussion and I'd like to hear more. Lots more. Safer by far if we talk later, in private. Over another drink, maybe. Either there—' she nodded sideways to where a painted tavern sign caught the lamplight, 'or . . .' The woman considered in silence, then came to some inward decision. 'I have a small library in my home, commander, dealing with'—again that brilliant grin— 'those subjects. Especially the winged, fire-breathing ones. You'd be a welcome guest on your next leave; I find your interest most refreshing.'

'Lady, my thanks for the offered hospitality at such brief acquaintance, but . . .' He was trying, and failing, to keep a back-note of apprehension from his voice. 'But this is urgent!'

'Indeed?' She glanced at him, looking hard and deep, and her eyes narrowed as once more she looked beyond the apparent to what truth might lie behind it. Not merely his words this time, but the whole man himself. And she saw. Now all the badges and the marks of lofty rank could not conceal the fact that this Cavalry *hanalth* was in all probability no older than her own second son—and most likely younger, at that. But there was an air about him, not merely an expression in the eyes and face but the whole set of his body, that spoke of . . . Not fright exactly; Aiyyan corrected her own thoughts even as they formed. More of unease. He looked—and now her storyteller's mind inserted colouration that was all too apt—like a scholar who had found logic in something unbelievable. As if he had just found a way to prove that twice two equals five. Or three! 'We really must set aside the time for a lengthy talk, Commander Dirac,' she began to say. And then stopped saying anything, since it was plain that he was no longer listening.

Instead the commander was staring off and away over her shoulder; not quite into the distance, for big though it was Tower Square could scarcely boast a view that would qualify as distant, but certainly *at* something, with an intensity that was disturbing. Aiyyan broke eye-contact just long enough to shoot a glance over her own shoulder, then turned back with the beginnings of a new respect and wariness in her own face. She had thought that this young man was interested in legends which his peers considered either peasants' fare or slightly distasteful—hence his nervous secrecy—but she had not for a moment thought that there might be something more. Now she wasn't so sure.

Already the young *hanalth* was backing away, his mind quite plainly on his own affairs once more. The focus of his gaze flicked back to her for just an instant, and in that instant he saluted her, grinning as she might have done herself on a would-be witty exit line. Except that his grin, his tight-lipped baring of white teeth, lacked the essential quality of humour. 'Lady, about what I said: this is more urgent still!'

And then he was accelerating away.

'Ker'Trahan steading, commander,' she yelled after him with all the power of a voice that had been trained for song and public speaking. 'Beyond the Great and Lesser Mountains and through the valley . . .' Aiyyan ker'Trahan closed her mouth around the unfinished sentence, knowing that to continue was a waste of breath. She looked from side to side and felt the slightest tremor of embarrassment as she met the interested—if somewhat bewildered—stares of the new audience who had begun to take their seats around her. A scarcely-formed notion of following the *hanalth*—just to see what happened; all right, call it nosiness!—took no further shape as she sat down and composed herself with a toss of her silvery head and a sweet storyteller's smile. One after another they named favourite tales: classics, rarities, her own work.

Aiyyan pushed the strange young officer and his most un*hanalth*like interests right to the back of her mind. But not out of it entirely; he was far too interesting a potential story-character for that. Then she drew breath, nodded at her audience, and began:

'Lessa woke, cold . . . '

*   *   *

What Aldric had seen, and what Aiyyan the storymaker had seen, was a man on a horse. But no ordinary man, and no ordinary horse—that, of course, was the problem.

He was an exhausted man on a lathered horse and—though neither of them knew it—he had ridden through Egisburg's North Gate at a hard-gallop less than five minutes before. His long yellow overmantle—splattered now with the parti-coloured mud of two provinces and an independent holding—bore embroidered crests at chest and cuffs and in the centre of the back: stylised blue gerfalcons, with gold-feathered wings. They were the unquestioned markings of an Imperial despatch-rider, one who might at a moment's notice be commanded to ride at a pace that involved two hundred miles between one dawn and dusk along the roads of graded dirt that were forbidden to all but those who wore the Falcon badge.

This horseman had the look of one reaching the end of such a mission: a messenger with seventy leagues and a score of weary mounts in his wake across the Empire. Both his sweat-stained appearance and the jingling crossbelt hung with warning bells attracted curious glances—mostly from those who would have done better to mind their own business, but in at least one case from one who was determined to profit from the chance which had let him see this new arrival in the city.

The Falcon courier was a source of murmured speculation; and several of those who murmured then cast would-be knowing looks towards the black silhouette where the Red Tower reared into the night sky. There could be, they ventured, only one reason for a Falcon to arrive in Egisburg in such a state and at such an hour. And that reason was the Princess in the Tower: Marya Marevna an-Sherban.

Without exception, they were both wrong and right at once.

Such a suspicion had flickered across Aldric's mind when he first saw the rider walk his stiff-legged mount around the swarming mass of people in the square. But then he had seen him halt, reining in the horse with the gentleness of skill and consideration. And that was when the second possibility took shape. His own presence in the city—indeed the presence and the purpose of the whole small group—could be another and equally viable reason for a Falcon to ride tonight into this of

all the many cities of the Empire. There was no chance of
getting through the crowds fast enough to intercept the man,
even had he been prepared to try. Instead Aldric made his
impolite and over-hasty goodbyes to Aiyyan the talemaker—
privately determining to hold her to her offer of hospitality
sometime in the future—and began the process of returning to
the inn where Bruda and Tagen and Voord awaited his return,
and the striking of the Hour of the Cat. Damned if that rider
didn't look as if he was waiting for someone! Or something.

A clock chimed somewhere at the perimeter of the square,
and Aldric's head twisted on his neck to see it and to read
what hour showed on its face. Then he relaxed a little; the
half-mark of the Hour of the Dog, and seven o' clock as
Albans reckoned time. But he didn't relax completely because that still left an hour for the courier to set everything
wrong before a 'deputation of officers' arrived at the Red
Tower's gate. When a convenient space presented itself at his
elbow, Aldric shouldered himself clear of the people in Tower
Square and, throwing the assumed dignity of his assumed
rank to the Nine Cold Winds of Hell, he began to run.

And because of that precipitate departure, he quite missed
the courier's contented glance at the selfsame still-striking
clock, and the leisurely way in which he shook his tired horse
to a walk.

Another clock was striking for the same hour as Aldric
approached the inn. Wondering vaguely and with no real
interest why the Empire failed to regulate its public timepieces more correctly, he slackened his pace. Somewhat out
of breath—a breath that fumed white in front of him as he
gasped it in and out—and stickily warm despite the freezing
night, he tugged with both hands at his rumpled clothing.
Right now, Bruda's sarcasm he did *not* need—not when at
the same time something fatally unpleasant might be brewing
in the Red Tower.

Ahead of him a door opened; snapped hurriedly open to
release a fan of yellow lamplight sliced by a fast-moving
shadow, and then as hastily jerked shut. For some reason that
was no reason at all, Aldric swivelled sideways and faded into
the darkness between two buildings. It wasn't exactly suspicion,
and it wasn't quite wariness. But it was enough to put him
where he couldn't be seen, without a pause to think about it.

Softly set-down footsteps approached and passed; and Lord-Commander Voord's distinctive profile passed him by, back-lit by the tavern's courtyard lamp. No matter that he was already near-enough invisible, Aldric flattened himself against the wall at his back and wrapped anticipatory fingers round Widowmaker's hilt. Nothing came of it and Voord strode on, but to Aldric's senses, heightened by perception or deepened by suspicion as they were, he strode too quietly for so early in the evening. Later, perhaps, and it might have been no more than an innocent wish not to disturb, but now—to Aldric at least—each step seemed furtive, stealthy . . . And worth further investigation.

Closing the black-and-silver rank-robe right up to his throat and flipping its deep hood over his head, Aldric waited for a count of ten before venturing back onto the street. By then Voord was a good thirty yards away, and hard to see except when he was silhouetted by a paler background. Aldric took note of it and was careful not to make the same mistake himself.

Voord's progress made him smile thinly at the *hautheisart's* arrogance; the man had taken not the slightest precaution against detection or pursuit, and stalked through the streets of Egisburg as if he owned them. And a jolt of sobering thought suggested that he just might. Aldric, by contrast, slipped quietly from shadow to shadow without being overly obvious about it. At least he was wearing his own moccasin boots rather than the heavy military issue; even the quality-controlled officer's pattern made tracking by ear a simple undertaking. Had Voord done the same, then in all likelihood he would have been lost before the end of the first narrow street.

Eventually the Vlechan halted. Then—and only then—he swept the street with a glare that had been signalled whole seconds in advance. Without even trying to glimpse his quarry's doings, Aldric was already hidden snugly and quite out of sight around a corner—holding his breath, and listening with the good ears that God had given him.

He heard first a soft, staccato tapping and then the slither of a heavy wooden door sliding in well-waxed channels. Aldric was sufficiently quick-witted to memorise the pattern of the tapping; and sufficiently cautious not to risk a rapid glance around the corner until the slithering sound was repeated and,

more importantly, punctuated with the solid thump of a closing door.

There was nobody to see. As he had guessed, Voord was
inside whatever door had just opened and shut. *But which
one?* Aldric silently debated for a few seconds whether to
move closer or not. Then had the choice made for him.

Don't!

Voord came out again, very fast, and Aldric wrenched
himself back out of sight with equal speed. The Vlechan had
been inside for only a matter of minutes—and what sort of
time was that to spend on a secret which involved use of the
Falcon couriers? Other than asking Voord himself, there seemed
just one way to learn the answer.

No. There were two. Either he could go back, confront
Voord and hope that Bruda could pry more than well-turned
lies from his subordinate; or he could learn it himself, in the
same way that Voord had done. Whether the *hautheisart*'s
source would be amenable to repeating himself was something Aldric might well learn within the next few minutes.
You're an idiot, he told himself. Silently he agreed. There
was really nothing else to do.

By the time he reached the door Aldric had his course of
action planned—more or less. It wasn't sorcery, and in a way
he wished that it was; there would be fewer variables that
way. It was just a virtuoso display of daring and impudent
nerve. Holding in a deep breath to calm himself—*calm? now
there was a joke!*—he reached out with one gloved and
slightly meat-spiced hand to firmly rap the door.

'*Keii'ach da?*' The voice might have been muffled by thick
timber, but its tone was plain enough: suspicion, pure and
undiluted. Voord had come and Voord had gone, but no other
visitors were expected.

Aldric paused, counted ten and then rapped again more
loudly. More irritably. More in the fashion of a man kept
waiting five seconds of which four were a compound insult.
He sifted through his mind for what he intended to say—
which was obvious enough to that same mind—and the form
in which he meant to say it, which was proving somewhat
more elusive. Whoever was on the far side of that as-yet-
unopened door would have to be impressed by and convinced
of his authenticity within two sentences and without creden-

tials, or he would never be convinced at all. And then it would be killing time.

And still the high-mode diphthongs eluded him . . . Aldric had of necessity used Drusalan as a first language for almost a month now, except for those rare occasions when he could employ Jouvaine or—luxury!—Alban. And therein lay the problem. For during that almost-month, apart from one or two anger-fuelled lapses he had been careful to avoid just such phrasing and construction as he was now pulling from his memory; because spoken by inferior to superior, the High Speech was a blood insult. And in all the Empire, there was nothing more inferior than a rankless Alban.

'Is it thy intention that I stand here until the dawn?' he snarled at last, pitching his voice low and loading it with all the arrogance that he could summon. Not that High Drusalan in its augmented mode required much in the way of tone to make it arrogant. Aldric breathed deeply once more, with a studied, calming count between inhalation and speech, then spoke again. 'I grow impatient with thee, man!' A good octave below its normal level, his voice sounded fierce, gritty—and strained, observed part of his mind. Aldric mentally commanded that part to keep quiet. 'I command: open, or there will be blood spilt!' *You're committed now, so say it all!* 'Voord commands! And I warn: I have finished speaking!'

He hadn't known quite what would follow that—whether the door would inch back or jerk open all at once. In the event it did neither, but slid smoothly to one side without any apparent haste. Playing this game by instinct, and ignorant of whatever rules might govern it, Aldric knew he didn't dare risk losing the initiative. Which was why, instead of stepping forward and inside directly there was room to do so, he stayed right where he was and let the lamplight come to him.

It worked: he heard a soft oath from inside, and as a cold smile skinned lips back from teeth he knew why. Because of his appearance. Pale from nervousness and shrouded in black from head to heel, there would be only the barest suggestion of humanity about the face revealed in the stark lantern-glow. Any other points of reflected light came from metal; the black, glinting hilt-guards of a sword, and rank-insignia so immediately impressive that even to consider it might not be genuine would feel like the beginning of a crime.

And there was always the possibility that this dark figure

really was *Kagh' Ernvakh* Commander Voord, of evil reputation. That thought in itself was quite enough.

'You grow wise—at last,' Aldric observed bleakly, and with those comforting words he stepped across the threshold, staring unblinking at the man who had opened the door until he bowed very low and slid it shut again. It was the courier; no longer wearing his distinctive robe, Aldric still recognised him by the heavy moustache swept halfway across his face. 'Better,' the Alban said, Voord-style. Haughtily. 'But your manners need mending. Take care that I don't mend them for you—because my way leaves scars.' That too was in keeping with what Aldric had guessed of Voord's reputation; but so much so that when the courier flinched from the threat, it made him feel uncomfortable. He was here to gather information, not to terrorise.

But there was a crossbow in the corner of the little room, a weapon covered less than adequately by a length of cloth. It was both spanned and loaded, its threat such that Aldric-'Voord' favoured it and then its owner with the lift of disapproving eyebrow before dismissing them both with a shrug. 'What's your message?' he demanded, resorting thankfully to an easier level of speech but retaining his air of arrogance by the simple expedient of keeping his back turned.

'Message, sir?'

'Message, idiot!' Aldric let it snap out, knowing well enough how any officer of rank, let alone Voord, would treat a subordinate who did no more than echo his questions. 'Are you deaf? Or merely impudent?' He half-turned and slapped one leather-gloved hand with loud significance—he had no time to be subtle—against the menacing jut of Widowmaker's hilt. 'Because if impudence is your problem, be assured I have a cure for it!'

The courier drew in a noisy breath to deny the allegation; and lost his chance as the man he knew as Voord swung round on him at the first sound of inhalation. 'Yes?' the officer said nastily; there was a handspan of blade clear of his sword's scabbard now. Then, nastier still and most unpleasantly perceptive: 'Who else was here tonight?'

Usually the weatherbeaten colour of old brick, the courier's face was shades paler already; and at this question it blanched as near to bone-white as such a complexion ever could. He was caught off-balance by every alternative he could choose:

repeating the question to gain time would merely further aggravate this already all-too-angry *hanalth*, and a refusal to say anything would have the effect, whilst lying to a man who most likely knew it all, chapter and verse . . . In the end he told the unvarnished truth, for safety's sake—and that was worst of all. 'Commander Voord,' the messenger faltered wretchedly.

'Yes? What?' Aldric rasped the reply, deliberately misunderstanding.

'No, lord. N-not you. Another . . .'

'Another *what?*' Aldric let his tension vent itself in feigned impatience. 'By the Father of Fires, I'll gut the man who gave a fool this mission!' His raging stopped abruptly as he decided it was 'time to understand', and he repeated, 'Another?' in a voice so soft it barely carried across the room. But the courier could guess what thoughts must now be tumbling through 'Voord's' mind.

Aldric stared at him and allowed a released breath to hiss slowly out between clenched teeth. 'There was someone else? Pretending to be me?'

The courier nodded.

He instantly regretted it, for the back of one black-gloved hand lashed him across the face. 'And you believed him.' Aldric let the words come out without inflection, but inside himself he felt sick; delivering that backhand slap might have been in keeping with the part he played right now, but it was not in keeping with the way he had grown up, or with the company that he had kept, or with the Code that still wrapped around his life more closely than he knew. How closely could one play a role like this before it became reality? Aldric was frightened of learning such an answer.

'You believed him,' he repeated—not a statement, but an accusation of guilt. 'And so you told him what should have been for my ears alone. And you let him go. But you kept *me* standing in the street!' Aldric let the feigned outrage drain from his voice, only to replace it with an equally feigned and equally realistic note of suspicion which edged each word like a razor. 'Yet you didn't think to mention this previous visitor. Was that because you hoped I wouldn't know about him? Was that it?' He purred the last, soft and cajoling, letting it fade into silence. Then: 'ANSWER ME! *F'KAAHR, SCH'DAGH-VEH!'*

Terrified by the intangible thing that was the reputation of the Imperial Secret Police, and more particularly by the less intangible and all-too-widely-known reputation of *Hautheisart* Voord, the courier fell to his knees and spilled everything he knew in a tremulous whimpering which was all mixed up with pleas and abject apologies. The very sound of it was enough to clench Aldric's stomach into a nauseous knot. He had killed men in the past, but he had never—until now—driven any man so far down the road of absolute fear. It said more than he had ever wanted or needed to learn about what Voord was really like, and about how skilfully Aldric had simulated him. For just one self-loathing, disgusted second the Alban was within a muscle's twitch of walking out. Then the preliminary babble of excuses came to an end and the true message began.

And Aldric, too, felt the icy touch of terror . . .

It was a plan of sweeping concept, of elaborate construction, of ruthless simplicity; and it reeked of Lord-Commander Voord.

As he filled in the details of the instructions which the courier relayed to him Aldric began to understand a great many things more clearly. Why so much time and money had been expanded to lay hands on him and bring him to Egisburg; why Voord had allowed himself to be overruled with so little protest from one who was—and it could scarcely be denied even now—of considerable standing and high rank. It explained, too, a reason behind the small annoyance which had troubled Aldric as he had left Kathur's house in Tuenafen as far behind him as he could—even though his own stupidity hadn't given him the time to leave it as far behind as he might have wished. The apparent theft of one of his paired *telekin*. Most people, he had discovered, knew at least a little about Albans: about their fanatical adherence to an outmoded Code of Honour, their suicide daggers . . . and about the spring-guns which were in their modern fashion as typical an Alban weapon as the *taiken* had been in the past.

Let such a weapon be found close by Princess Marevna's murdered body, and its mate found holstered at the saddle of the King of Alba's envoy, then no court of justice anywhere—at least within the borders of the Drusalan Empire—would require or search for any other evidence than that set out before them.

For this was first and last a plan involving murder.

Aldric considered and rejected the daintier term 'assassination', because he refused to let it dignify what he was hearing. There was no daintiness here. He wondered when and why and how the plan had first been mooted, and at whose suggestion, and realised that though the message was for Voord alone he could trust nobody now. He dared not fling what he had discovered in Bruda's face, for was Bruda not Voord's superior, and as likely implicated as not?

But the basic idea was so *simple!* That was what his mind continually returned to, for Aldric knew that in other circumstances even he would more than half believe that King Rynert would have someone murdered for political advantage. He knew, if certain suspicion was knowledge, why the last emperor had died so suddenly: and there were bound to be other informed sources than himself. Dewan ar Korentin, for one. That the big bear of a man who had become his friend should soon think him capable of murdering women made Aldric's blood thicken in his veins. And Dewan would believe, because he knew the ruthless rules of expedience as well as any and he had been present when Aldric swore on his Word to do what was necessary to aid the King.

Marevna, alive and imprisoned in the Red Tower, set pause to the continued strife within the Empire that brought a wary peace to Alba; the peace which lasted only for as long as the Imperial armies were turned inward. While the Princess was held by one faction as surety for the behaviour of the other, cooler heads than those of the military might prevail, and could lead to ultimate agreement that such leashed-in force might better be expended in bringing the benefits of unity within one Empire to those not yet part of the greater whole. Annoyingly, aggressively independent Alba, for one. But Marevna dead and entombed with her ancestors at Kalitzim would be no bargaining counter for any side to use. Unless by the manner of her passing.

A simple appeal to simple emotion would be all that *Woydach* Etzel's faction needed; it was he who stood to gain the most, he most likely who was behind this plot—and certainly he who would know how to make best use of such a Hell-born opportunity. Aldric could hear the speeches in his head already: not the mannered rhetoric of Osmar's plays, but the fieriness of words intended to lash up a frenzy of grief and thus create a common cause. Revenge!

That was something which Aldric knew all about. A thirst for 'justified' vengeance was a thing of frightening intensity among individuals, and none were better qualified to admit it than himself. He had felt it; had seen its blue-white burning in Ykraith the Dragonwand; had seen it burning just as hot in the blue eyes of Gueynor Evenou, now Overlord of Seghar. And such an emotion running unfettered through an already militaristic empire was not a thought he cared to dwell on overlong.

But another thought drifted, settled and took on solid form. *Seghar*, said the thought. *This has happened to you once before. To play the scapegoat, betrayed by a blade that was yours and could be no-one else's.* That was the time when Crisen Geruath murdered his own father and used Aldric's *tsepan* to do the deed. Almost-forgotten voices linked Voord's name with Seghar, and with Crisen; the details were long lost, but the connection had been made. It was enough.

More than enough.

Then the farther door slid open and another man came in, saying as he entered, 'Serej, has the Commander—' He and his voice stopped in the same instant. Aldric didn't know him, had never seen him before, and it was plain from his expression that this lack of recognition was returned. More words made it plainer yet: 'Who in the Fires are you—and what are you doing here?

Aldric didn't have to be watching to know that the courier—Serej?—had jerked himself backwards and was now staring from one to the other with shock-widened eyes. And he didn't need sharp ears to hear the soft obscenity born of sudden realisation.

'He said that *he* was Voord, Etek.'

'I've worked with Voord bef—' Again his words were cut off short—and Etek himself was within a finger's thickness of the same fate—as Aldric, without even the warning of an intaken breath, flicked hand to hilt and whipped Widowmaker's already-loosened blade clear of her scabbard and straight out into the first cut of *achran-kai* all in the one sweeping arc. Only a slight knowledge of Alban swordplay and the spasmodic quickness of the fear of death saved Etek; for while the first had given him an inkling of what to expect, only the second was fast enough to evade the terrible grey steel that blurred through space his throat had occupied a split-second before. Wisps of his beard drifted in the *taiken*'s wake, razored off without so much as a tug to show where hair and wicked edge had met.

His own army-issue shortsword came from its own sheath in the same instant as his sidestep, lifting frantically to block the downward second stroke of the inverted cross as it descended on a line running right between his eyes. At the last moment his block changed to a glissade deflection, and as metal shrieked and sparks flew from the point of contact Etek's eyes bulged with the discovery that a square impact from this intruder's blade would snap his own in half.

Serej the courier picked his moment, then lunged towards the loaded crossbow propped against the wall. All he had to do was reach it, point it and pull the trigger. Serej's hands were already reaching out when he half-heard a scuff of soft boots before that noise and all else was drowned in the sound of a shout.

'*Hai!*'

Aldric had caught the courier's move, and had broken contact with Etek's blade for long enough to spin right around before facing him again. It was movement so unexpected that Etek did nothing even though for just an instant he was offered the target of an unprotected back, and it was so swift that he had no time to use his chance before that chance was gone again. But Aldric's turn was still enough to let him cut, just one; it licked out at full force—savage, graceful and perfect.

Serej the courier continued on a lunge gone loose and uncontrolled, and it ended as he slapped down full-length against the floor. Momentum skidded him a little further forward, close enough for his outstretched right hand to reach the waiting crossbow . . . even though he no longer had a use for it. The impact of his fall had parted the last few tissue adhesions in his sheared neck—and as his body stopped, his head rolled free.

Aldric knew that the man was dead; had known it halfway through the arc of the cut, when he felt the crisp-to-yielding jolt along his arm as Isileth the Widow Maker made another. He had held no malice for the man and felt the anguish of his killing burn within him; but all of his attention was refocused now on Etek and he forced the hurting down, back from the distracting *now*. There would be more pain before he was finished here; and he would have to finish quickly, for this man had already survived two strokes more than he had been expected to. The clangour of steel was a sound which always drew unwelcome attention, and the sooner such a sound was curtailed the better.

Aldric seemed to hesitate an instant, shifting his feet and his balance; his grip on the *taiken* shifted fractionally. Then he feinted one—two—*three* . . . And the third was not a feint at all. He heard the strike go home and jerked himself to one side, away from the vivid spurt which burst out of Etek's chest like wine from a new-tapped cask. It was a jet as deeply, brilliantly, ominously crimson as . . . as a rose which Aldric had once known, and it was as thick as his thumb and as long as his arm before its arch turned downwards and broke into droplets. They spattered against the floor with a sound like rain, a colour like rubies, and a smell like a slaughteryard.

Etek looked down at the spread of gaudy stain across his shirt and tunic, at the pumping of his own heart's blood and at the pale-faced young man who had drawn it from its secret places with his blade. He tried to say something—witty, angry, a curse, a denial of death or a protest at this theft of his life, something which might be remembered for a little while. It came out only as a blood-flecked exhalation and sounded like '*h'ahhh* . . .' Then his knees buckled and he fell down, and was dead.

Aldric held that last accusing stare long after Etek's eyes had glazed—trembling, telling himself that he had done only what had to be done, that these men had been enemies, that the responsibility for choosing death had been theirs and not his; that he didn't care at all. But he did.

The days were gone when he could have pushed a killing from his mind, dismissing it as no longer of importance once the act was done, and he was glad of it. The alternative to *feeling* was to have none, to have as little concern or conscience as the weapon itself. Widowmaker would eat *his* life as readily as any, with another hand about her hilt. That change had come with awareness of what he had always secretly known, that there was an obligation to the killing of another living thing beyond the swing of a blade or the

squeeze of a trigger. It was remembrance. He stood very still
with the new-copper stench of warm blood in his nostrils,
looking at his dead; and feeling lost. *Not yet twenty-four, and
how many corpses now?*

He knew the answer: the number, and in some instances—
not many—the names as well. There were some who might
recite such a bloody list with pride in the skill it showed; and
there were some who might think that he had done the same
in the past. When he remembered . . . But that was not a
recollection Aldric made proudly. He was humbled by it, and
ashamed of it—humble that he had lived while they had died,
filled with shame that without his hand they might live yet.
But there was *self-defence,* and there was *expedience,* and
there was *necessity.* Three words which were all that any
killer needed.

They left a taste like vinegar and ashes on his tongue.

A storyteller finished, smiled acknowledgement to the courteous bows of her audience as they left and sipped at a little
more cold beer to soothe her throat. The story just concluded
was one of her own and no effort to tell, linking as it did like
a chain—or a mesh of mail, for it might lead off in several
directions at once—with other of the tales she told. Tales
whose characters were as well known to her as her own
family and friends.

Aiyyan's smile broadened at that, for often enough those
characters *were* her family and friends, their quirks observed
and embellished with humour and with love. It was a fault of
hers. No, not a fault, a privilege which those who wove tales
from the joint webs of imagination and experience were well
allowed to exercise.

She had met several such potentials in the past day or two:
that scholarly man whose fiery enthusiasm suffused everything he turned his considerable mind towards; the woman
with the string of riding-horses—Aiyyan had bought one and
left herself with an option on two more—and the string of
anecdotes. And that twitchy young *hanalth* with the dragon
fixation . . .

Something, some *thing* made her look up towards a sky
which was half dark and flecked with stars, half grey with
another band of snow-laden cloud. And she saw . . . She
would have seen nothing on a cloudy winter's night, had that

night been other than what it was: festival. Ordinarily this great city was a dark place after sunset, freckled only sparsely with the lanterns hung outside the houses of the wealthy—or the loosely moralled, which was often one and the same. But now, tonight, on this holiday, Egisburg was lit as brightly as anywhere in the Drusalan Empire—even Drakkesborg or Kalitzim—and the glow of all that extravagance reflected dully from the surface of those lowering clouds. Not enough maybe to increase the light in the streets below, but enough that their no longer totally dark surface formed a pale backdrop to . . . things in the sky.

There were two such: one was the Red Tower, and its hard-edged outline sent an unsummoned shudder up from Aiyyan's imaginative soul. There was a brooding about that dark fortress, and an expectancy which was enough to make her glad that in the morning she and her new horse—or maybe horses—would be leaving this city and returning home before the winter closed on them completely. But the other thing was smaller than the Tower, and blacker than the Tower; it was a scrap of lightless nothingness, a rent in the clouds that was blacker than black and as lean as hunger.

And it sailed through the night sky at twice the Red Tower's height above the Red Tower's topmost turret!

Aiyyan stared until small glowing motes began to swim before her eyes, and then she stared some more. She watched until the—all her mind would shape was *what I daren't believe I'm seeing,* in case giving it a name would somehow make it disappear—the winged creature drifted out beyond the grey of the clouds and across the starlit heavens. Even then she could still follow it, for those cold star-fires blinked briefly out as the great dark shape sliced between them and the world.

Another of the sparks which danced in her vision expanded, putting forth a long bright tendril that as swiftly died again. Aiyyan released a breath that was more than half a sigh; had she not been watching—what she knew now that she *was* watching—she might have thought that quick straight scratch of fire across the sky to be the track of a falling star. Except that no starfall that she had ever seen before had swirled and plumed and choked in smoke as this had done.

'*Ohh v'ekh!*' said Aiyyan ker'Trahan, and put a deal of feeling into it. '*M'nei trach'han kelech-da?*' Oh yes, Commander Dirac. I see now. I *see* . . .'

She did indeed: something she had always wanted to see, since the first tale she had ever made about them. A dragon.

But having seen this one, she wasn't sure that she wanted to stay for more. Huge and powerful though *her* dragons were, there was still an underlying gentleness in them; and she had felt nothing of the sort in her brief glimpse here. Another long talk—with a little more forthrightness in it! —with *Hanalth* Dirac would prove enlightening, even educational, but Aiyyan had no desire now to wait in Egisburg to find out for herself the answers which he had hoped to learn from her. It was not fear—a daughter and mother of soldiers, Aiyyan wasn't particularly subject to that—but it was most certainly caution, for once she started thinking about him again in connection with what she had seen, the storymaker began to notice little oddities which at the time had gone unregarded. Most important was his speech; its accent had not been that of Drusul, nor Tergoves, nor Vlech. And if he was not of the Imperial races, then he was a provincial. And if he was a provincial, then there was no way in the world that he could possibly wear the *hanalth*'s bars and diamonds. Her own sons had been in the Empire's armies, the younger just released from his term of service, and she knew of the un-official—but rigidly enforced—restrictions on promotion.

So why *was* he wearing those rank-tabs? Aiyyan didn't want to know. And because she had been speaking to him, and been seen speaking to him, she wanted to be away from Egisburg before whatever he was brewing boiled up in her face. The doings of the great, the not-so-great and the down-right notorious had a way of hurting all around them, innocent bystanders most of all.

Aldric walked slowly and steadily along the street and along his own shadow, flung far in front of him by the leaping flames behind. Those flames cleaned away the final remnants of what he had done, but he did not look back. Instead he ignored the fire and pushed it from his mind; but he did not and would not push aside the two whose funeral pyre it was. The two whom he had killed. 'Serej and Etek,' he said softly—recalling the names, the faces, the men. Because forgetting would be to kill them twice.

What to do? Stay or run? He had thought about both sides of the problem, even though all along he knew that he, what he was and what he tried to be had only one choice that could rightly be made.

There would be no point in running anyway, because somewhere in this city—whether in Voord's or Tagen's or maybe even Bruda's hands—there was a *telek* which was the undoubted match of that weapon seen by all too many people. holstered at his saddle. An unusual accoutrement for a cavalry *hanalth*—though apparently not so unusual as to be forbidden by Lord General Goth—it would have been noticed, remarked upon . . . And would be remembered. With its mate still unaccounted-for, then whether or not he was there to take the blame at once Princess Marevna would die tonight—and even if he fled, that would be explained in such a way as to compound and confirm his already apparent guilt. It could not save him, and it would not save her.

By the same token, there was nobody he could safely tell: in this Imperial city everyone was a potential enemy, a potential informer ready and willing to betray him for no reason other than what he was, if that was discovered. *Hlensyarl* and *h'labech*, foreigner and spy: the Drusalan words were probably interchangeable, even more so when the foreigner was wearing a uniform and a rank to which he was most certainly not entitled.

It left the conclusion Aldric had reached at the very beginning, when Serej the courier had first outlined this dirty little plot: to rescue the Princess—it was still a cliché, but he no longer laughed at it—but to rescue her on his own terms. Properly. At least he had a slight advantage now; he was forewarned of treachery and knew to expect it, while They— whoever *they* might be—were unaware of his knowledge. He hoped.

'One day, Aldric,' he told himself, 'all this is going to get you killed.' It was like something Dewan ar Korentin might say; and there would be those who would presume that his reason and his choice lay with what else Dewan might say. Because of Dewan, and Gemmel, and the king—yes, even the king—and all those others who would mutter and look askance if he did his duty so well that he had the death of an innocent woman on his conscience. But that was not and never had been his reason. It was simpler and more straightforward than that, a reason which would have made him continue with this rescue even if by running now, at once, as

far and as fast as Lyard's legs could carry him, he would
avoid all the consequences of his failure.

That reason was the self-respect which men called Honour.
Drusalan though Marya Marevna an-Sherban might be, and
sister of the lord of a state that one day might be at war with
his own, yet he was still bound to help her to the best of his
ability. *Honour-bound:* a term used lightly now, but when it
was meant sincerely it bound as tight as chains of steel. He
had the right to fight for it, and the right to die for it either on
another's blade or on his own. The *tsepan* he now wore hung
from his belt in the Drusalan military manner was a constant
reminder of the oath which he had taken—an oath which he
might put aside as he might put aside the black dirk, but one
whose existence he could never forget while the white scars
on his left hand's palm remained.

Aldric looked down at that hand, at the place where the
scars were hidden by his glove—and its fingers clenched into
a fist at what he saw on the wrist above the black leather cuff.
There was a flame within the spellstone: tiny, spindle-shaped,
and throbbing in time with his own pulse. Its appearance was
familiar: the slitted intensity of a cat's eye.

Or the Eye of a Dragon.

Aldric's head tilted on his shoulders and he flung back the
rank-robe's hood to stare straight up at the night sky; just as,
elsewhere in the city, a storyteller was doing at this same
moment. He saw what she saw; but in his case there was no
momentary hesitation before acceptance, no beat of disbelief.
He knew and recognised at once. *Ymareth.*

Not knowing the power of the dragon's eyes at night, but
quite willing to believe that one way or another the great
being was watching him, Aldric drew himself up straighter
and offered the shadow in the sky the courtesy of an Alban
crown salute. No matter that it was incompatible with the
uniform robe he wore, no matter that such a token of respect
was rightly due the king alone; Ymareth the dragon had done
more for him than Rynert, and had shown him more kindness
in its reptilian way than the king had ever done in his. The
dragon hung against a sky half-snowclouds and half-stars, and
vented a brief, bright lance of fire. It was a signal, a reminder
and an encouragement needed now if ever that Aldric was not
entirely alone in this city full of enemies.

And after all was done, once the Princess had been

freed—*oh, such confidence, Talvalin!*—and he had discharged his present obligation to the man whom he called 'Liege' and 'King' and 'Lord'? What then?

Aldric didn't know.

'Did you see that? Gemmel, did you see it?'

'So you're talking again. Well, thank you for that much, anyway.'

The soldier and the sorcerer stood together on a low ridge near the road which led down and across the river-plain to Egisburg's great gated walls. They had been set down something like two miles from the city—a negligible distance in fine weather, or even now had it been daylight and they able to use the roads. But it was not, and they had not, and the cautious slog in darkness through snowfields where drifts had sometimes risen to six and eight feet in height like frozen white ocean waves had taken the best part of an hour. It had been accomplished in total silence on Dewan's part, except for grunts of effort and the occasional heartfelt oath. His mouth had closed at Gemmel's final revelation and he had not spoken to the old man since; perhaps no longer sure that 'man' was a proper term of reference.

'I . . . All right, yes I am. I must. I've known you long enough before, before——'

'Before I gave you honest answers to your questions, and you found that you didn't like the sound of truth after all?'

'I—I found it hard to swallow.'

'Like the man who ate the cart-horse,' Gemmel said, and grinned. It was the old grin and the old Gemmel, and Dewan felt a deal more easy in his mind to see it. 'You mean that flare in the sky? A falling star.'

'That was no star, falling or otherwise!'

'Good. Then we can agree on something. Would you also agree that we should abandon this excessive caution just for once, and use the road?'

Dewan looked along the road for as far as he could see in both directions; which wasn't far at night, but far enough to make sure that there was no one else in the area. It wasn't so much using the road so close to the city that concerned him, but the chance of being seen emerging from concealment by someone who might take an interest in the question *why?* 'All right,' he said. 'All clear. So come on.' He floundered through another drift, noting with absent irritation that Gemmel waited until he had done so before following him through the already-broken ground. 'I must remember, Gemmel, wizard, *friend*, to let you take your turn in front some time,' he growled, slapping snow off his furs and clothing.

'As you wish,' said Gemmel, reaching the road—which so close to Egisburg was not merely paved, but also kept reasonably free of all but the heavier falls of snow. 'Then I'll lead from here, shall I?' He walked off down the road.

Dewan watched him for a few seconds and in those seconds, with snow still in his hands, the Vreijek fought a noble struggle with his own sense of dignity, the inadvisability of what he was considering—and the potential satisfaction that a well-aimed, tightly-squeezed and accurately hurled snowball would bring.

Then he dropped the still-loose snow and dusted off his hands, and set off after Gemmel without another word.

Aldric returned to the inn without making any detours; he avoided the square and its distractions and therefore didn't see one storyteller in particular gathering her gear together in readiness for a rapid departure from a city which had lost all its attraction for her. Most of all, Aldric wanted to get back and behind a locked door before he met someone who might pass comment on his appearance. He hadn't checked, but there was most likely drying blood about him somewhere; he had enough intimate experience of killing swordplay to know that its traces were hard to avoid, even when one was the winner.

The entrance hall of the inn was empty, and he was glad of it for though he might be calm and in control right now, he doubted that he could remain that way if he came face to face with Lord-Commander Voord. Later, perhaps, but not just at present. He closed the outer door noisily behind him, deliberately signalling his return to any interested ears and knowing that any such would be listening for *his* return alone, since from what he had seen of Voord's departure that worthy had not—supposedly—left the building. He would be back by now, of course. Aldric cast an eye towards the inn's big case-clock in its alcove by the stairs and hesitated, surprised. Barely half of an Alban hour had passed since he had flinched into the shadows and out of Voord's sight as the man stalked out into the night. A half-hour—or a quarter, Imperial! Then walking leisurely as seemed his custom, it was likely that Voord himself was not long through this very door—much more quietly, of course. That was a piece of luck indeed, and probably just as well.

Unintercepted by whoever might have remained in the withdrawing-room to finish up that flagon of chilled wine, Aldric reached the door of his own upstairs room without incident and put out one hand to open it. Then he paused, looking at the hand with his head quirked quizzically to one side. As he had done earlier, he raised it level with his nose and stared. It was steady, as steady as it had ever been, and not even the vibration of his pulse was enough to shake the black leather-skinned fingers. *Am I growing used to murder, then?* he thought sombrely. It was not a possibility which held much appeal. *Or is it something else entirely?*

Now that was likely indeed, for the thought of doing something worth-while at last—the rescue of a prisoner rather than the assassination of someone never met before, like those two in Seghar, would be enough to calm anyone; or at least to fill them with an excitement that was a deal more wholesome. Aldric threw open the bedroom door, noting absently that it was darker than before because someone—a servant perhaps, or simple lack of oil—had reduced the lamp to a mere glow of flame.

Once inside he turned, pushed the door shut again and ran its heavy deadbolt into place. There: all secure! And then he stiffened because something, somewhere was not quite *right!* Without moving, he analysed the brief glimpse of the room which he had caught as he crossed the threshold: the furniture was unmoved, the shuttered windows as he had left them, his gear untouched. Other than the reduced lamp, nothing had changed. Until, moving only eyes that were rapidly adjusting to the gloom, he saw it and in that instant every alarm inside his head went screaming off at full pitch.

Lying down the geometrical centre of the bed, dividing its mattress in two precise halves, was a sheathed sword. Jouvaine pattern, said some dry index of his mind through the warning jangle which filled it. *Estoc* thrusting-sword. But it was not a weapon he remembered seeing carried by any of his companions in this rescue party—even though it was familiar, somehow. More: there was a presence in the room, a living person somewhere, hidden, waiting. All the muscles and the sinews of Aldric's body tensed and his right hand flexed for the grip of Widowmaker's hilt.

But before his fingers closed on it, the sword was plucked away from his hip by knowing hands—knowing, because while one gripped the *taiken's* scabbard with the lift-and-twist which unhooked it from the weapon belt at Aldric's waist, the other unclipped one end of the cross-strap which passed over his shoulder. It passed over his shoulder now like a snake, slithering with the sound of a viper on parchment as the whole weapon was wrenched clear of his hand with frantic speed.

A voice spoke in his ear, a voice from so close behind him that he could feel the warm breath carrying every word. How did that happen? he raged inwardly. Nobody gets that close if they mean mischief! And then: but what if they don't?

'Stand still,' the voice said. 'Just answer me this: What is a woman that you forsake her, to go with the old grey Widowmaker? This Widowmaker!' The *taiken's* grey star-steel blade clanked once inside its scabbard as the chape grounded on the floor, and Aldric's eyes went wide as he stared for a long moment at nothing at all, swallowing once or twice, trying to clear his gullet of the hot throbbing constriction that was surely his own heart, pounding half-way between his mouth and its proper place. He did not hear the longsword clash against the floor; all he heard was that voice.

And all he said in answer to its question was, 'Kyrin?' He turned then, expecting to be wrong, expecting to be cheated yet again by his own imaginings; but he was right this time and he was not cheated now, because it—she—was Tehal Kyrin after all.

All the tension drained from face and body, but was replaced by a shuttered, enigmatic, unreadable expression very far from that which the Valhollan had been expecting. 'Lady,' he said, giving her the ghost of a bow, 'one moment.' Then he walked quietly across the room and adjusted the lamp until it flooded them both with light. 'Yes. Lady, your . . . your eyes are as blue as I remember them; your hair is as fair.' He did not move to touch her. 'And you have troubled my dreams both waking and asleep this six months and more, Tehal Kyrin, Harek's youngest daughter. But lady, why talk to *me* of forsaking and of Widowmaker?'

He held out his right hand for the weapon and Kyrin took the three steps forwards that was just enough for her to lay it gently, respectfully, on his outstretched palm. The fingers closed, reaffirming possession, gripping tightly, and rotated Isileth Widowmaker so that Aldric was staring at her past the longsword's looped, forked guards. 'This has been true to me, lady; I trust her and she returns that trust. It—*she* has not yet left me for another. I did not, will not forsake. I did not and w-would not forsake you. That choice was yours and you made it. You alone.'

For just a hurt heart's beat there was a look in Kyrin's eyes which Aldric had seen before; he recognised it, for he had caused it now just as he had caused it then, so many painful months ago: a look as if he had reached out and struck her across the face. After a moment she drew breath, and with it seemed to draw on some reserve of inner strength, enough at least to meet him stare for stare past the black steel of Widowmaker's hilt.

'Aldric-*an*,' she said, pronouncing it as salutation and as valediction, using the honorific rather than the affectionate form and with her Valhollan accent emphasising its vowel-shift all too plainly. 'Aldric-*an*, you've lived for too long with this cold mistress. I travelled far to find you, to be with you again. Foolish, with an uncertain reception waiting at the end of all. Or maybe not so foolish after all. Now that I know how it is between us, I can leave again—and this time be at peace within myself. Did you flatter yourself that yours were the only troubled dreams, the only sleepless nights? There were times when I lay awake in the darkness, alone, when I wondered if I had done right or wrong. Not wrong to go with Seorth; there was no wondering about that. Not after I learned that he and Elnya had been married within a month of my . . . My supposed loss, when my uncle's ship foundered off the Alban coast. Have you ever found yourself an excess number, Aldric-*an?* Discovered that you were one too many under your own roof?'

'But you said . . . !' Aldric burst out, stopped himself, considered. Then, accusingly: 'You showed me a letter.'

'Which you couldn't read. You only guessed at what it meant and because of . . . I'm sorry. There was a deal of deception with you unknowing in the middle. I said things I didn't mean, things that weren't true, because—because I

was afraid. Afraid of them, afraid of all the power they had
and afraid for you. I told them and I told you what they
wanted, because I knew that even you couldn't turn *no* into
yes, and you'd have come to harm if you tried. Because you
would have tried, Aldric, *Kailin-eir* Aldric *ilauem-arluth*
Talvalin. I know you, knew you well enough for that. As I
thought I still knew you.' Kyrin forced herself to stay wide-
eyed, staring and arrogant, because she knew that just one
blink would be enough to let the waiting tears go free.

'Kyrin.' She looked at him and the *taiken* was no longer
between them; it had been lowered and was hanging slackly
in his hand—as near to being flung aside, perhaps, as it
would ever be. 'They, Kyrin? Who are *they?*' He asked it,
but was already sickly certain that he knew the answer.

'Dewan,' she replied without hesitation, 'Dewan and the
King.' Then she saw the muscle start to tic along the renewed
scar beneath his eye and caught a stifled gasp between her
teeth and knuckles. 'But they promised that they would
explain—they would tell you everything, their reasons, their
need . . . After I was gone. Everything! They *promised* me.'

'Words—that's what promises are. Sometimes, made with
honour, they're worth the having. But mostly they're just
breath with a little sound in them. So what did you say that
they wanted to hear so much? What did you tell us all?'

'That there was no love between us. Nor ever had been.
Dewan asked me and he wanted to hear *no*, so I said *no*.
But . . .'

'But?'

'But I should have had the courage to tell him the truth. To
say *yes*.'

Aldric's hand came out slowly towards her face and she
didn't move a muscle, braced in case he . . . The leatherclad
fingers touched gently along the line of her cheekbone in the
old caress, and stroked at a stray tear which had escaped all
of her efforts.

'Truth, lady? *Yes?*'

'Truth. Then. Now. Always.' Then she saw the change in
his face, and most especially in his eyes, and began to be
afraid again—not of him, now, but for him as she had been
before. 'Aldric, you're *cseirin*-born. High-clan. They would
never allow . . . You can't fight tradition with a sword!'

Softly, thoughtfully, almost to himself: 'You said that once before.'

'But it still holds true!'

'Not now. Not for me. Not after what I've had to . . . Duty, Kyrin. Obligation—it's a two-edged sword. Our proverb cuts both ways. It's the sword to fight tradition with, because after what I've done, what I'll yet do—though before the Light of Heaven, it's more for myself now!—for Rynert the King, he owes me. He owes me honesty at least! No deception—and no broken promises. And afterwards . . . afterwards we'll see about tradition and the sword, my lady. This sword. This old grey Widowmaker.'

He laid the longsword down, delicately, respectfully, on the bed beside the *estoc* which was Kyrin's own, which he had seen her wear a score of times; which he had recognised and yet not known.

'Then it was you,' he said, wondering now that he could have been so dull as not to realize.

'Where?'

'On the road to Egisburg. Following. I thought I saw someone once or twice; and I thought I felt a presence, a watcher, many times. How?'

'Dewan ar Korentin,' she said and confused him more than ever. 'He and a Drusalan woman he told me to find.'

'Kathur the Vixen!'

'Kathur the bitch-fox,' Kyrin corrected, sweetly vicious. 'Yes. She told me enough to get here. Because when I came to Alba, looking for you, you were gone—some mission for the king. But Dewan sought me out, met me secretly and used words like *decency* and *betrayal* about something which the king had done. He didn't approve; and he had already told Gemmel. The sorcerer. Your foster-father, Aldric? Is that true?' Aldric nodded silently and waved her to continue. 'But he told me this: "Look for him; find him if you're able, help him if you can—and stay with him if he and you both want each other still. With my blessing for all it's worth. And tell him that I'm truly sorry.' "

'Dewan said *that?*'

'He told me to tell you that the old bear is getting far too old; and blind and deaf and stupid, because he should have been half wise enough to ignore the *no* when what he really heard was *yes*.'

'Kyrin-*ain*, I say yes as well. And I always will.' When he put his arms—those killer's arms—around her and held her close, it was like a dream. There was the scent of her hair, the cool smoothness of her skin, the warmth of her lips and the simple nearness of her being there—but unlike so many other dreams there was not the bitterness of waking. 'Lady,' he whispered—*O my lady, O my love*—'I missed you far more than I ever knew till now. I prayed you would come back, somehow, some day. And death strike down the first man who comes between us again . . .' He kissed her again, gently and then fiercely, hungrily—and she was as gentle, fierce and hungry and they were both trembling in each other's arms, for it had been too long, too long, six months that had been a lifetime apart.

And a fist hammered on the door, making them both jump and shattering the moment. 'Get yourself armoured up and neat, dear *hanalth*, sir,' came Voord's voice, edged with a sneer scarcely blunted by the thick timbers through which it passed. 'We leave in ten minutes for the Tower!'

Silence. Then: 'Who was that?' It was Kyrin's question, but when she glanced at Aldric's face she knew that she needed neither a name nor indeed an answer. Because for just an instant she had caught a glittering of pure hate in his eyes such as she had seldom seen before.

'Death strike the first man who comes between us,' he repeated. 'If Hell or Heaven hears my prayers and curses, I hope that one is answered.' Then he took a step away from Kyrin and shrugged out of the military rank-robe, flinging it across the bed in a businesslike, no-nonsense manner which could never be confused with stripping for more pleasant purposes. 'Did you understand him?'

'I don't speak Drusalan.'

'Damn . . . What he said was *hurry up*. None too politely, either, burn his snake's skin black. Anyway—' he jerked with his chin at the racked armour near the wall as he tugged off his own, too-Alban outer clothing, 'Could you, please?'

Kyrin hesitated just a second, still confused, then began scooping metal and leather officer's-pattern harness from the frame beside the window where she had come in. There was no sign even now that the shutters had been disturbed; but then Tehal Kyrin's talent for subtle burglary had never really left her. When coupled with lithe, slim build and a natural gymnastic ability, Hunger made an excellent trainer of thieves.

'What are you doing tonight that's suddenly so important?' she wanted to know, kneeling beside him to tighten the buckles of armoured leggings with long fingers which had a distracting tendency to wander. Those fingers told her that despite his outward air of calm, Aldric was thrumming inside like a full-drawn bow. Part of it had to do with her, but the rest . . . It wasn't fear, not even the flash of anger which she had caught from the corner of her eye. Just simple, plain excitement!

'I didn't believe it when I heard at first; so you won't either, most likely. But it seems that the Princess . . .' Between grunts and oaths and struggles with intractable red-enamelled splint-armour, he managed to get out an edited version of the story. 'But that apart, they can't know what I intend.'

His voice was muffled by the scarlet arming-tunic he pulled over his head in mid-sentence, a heavy thing of quilted cloth and leather with thick padding at the shoulders where the hauberk's weight would lie, and as his face emerged from its neck-opening—tangled with laces and nearly the tunic's own colour with exertion—there was an expression on it which told Kyrin that he had had an idea. No—an *idea*, dammit!

'Just for now, let's forget most of what they don't know and concentrate on one aspect—*push*—which even I hadn't thought of until a few moments ago. God, that's more comfortable!' He held out both arms so that she could buckle on the laminated defences running from knuckles to elbows and wiggled his fingers amiably at her to prove to them both that his hands could still move freely. 'Because since you're here,'—Kyrin looked up and arched a disdainful eyebrow— 'this is what I want you to do.'

NINE

Patterns of Force

It was snowing again as they left the inn; dense white flakes from a dense grey sky falling vertically, steadily, heavily past that dark tower brooding over the city. Hooded and cloaked, gloved and booted, muffled as tightly against the weather as any of the others, Aldric still stopped short and unwrapped enough of his helmeted head to see the fortress better. Oh, he had seen it before in clearer air and better light, but never while walking towards its gate with the intention of going inside the belly of the beast. That knowledge put rather a different interpretation on what he saw.

It was huge, and sinister as a hungry animal. A great dark block of stone set down square in the middle of the city, eyed with lamps and fanged with the iron spikes that fringed its drop-gates, it was an evil building both by appearance and by reputation. As he drew closer, Aldric saw nothing that might alter such a judgment.

They were four armoured men flanked and followed by eight more: an honour guard found by the squad of cavalry who had ridden with them. Black and scarlet, silver and gold, the soft swaddling of fabrics and the bright, hard glint of pigmented metal all stark against the fallen, falling snow. Few were on the streets to remark on their appearance, for the festival was running down, its momentum gone on this last night of holiday; it was somehow appropriate that this foul weather should have come to force the revellers indoors—there to talk, to reminisce, to drink and to become drunk against the sober thought of winter closing in.

Aldric was uneasy, made guarded and wary by what he knew and what remained undiscovered; his nerves were drawn to a fine pitch, tingling almost to snapping point, and he was

sensitive as never before to other sounds, reactions, feelings;
emotion hidden well or ill. He could sense something about
them all, and not merely because his mind had told him such
sensations should be there. Bruda, Tagen, Voord. All of
them. And they could probably feel just the same surrounding
him. So long as they dismissed it as mere nervousness and
nothing more! For under his rank-robe, pushed through his
weapon-belt and out of sight but within quick reach of his
right hand, was a *telek*. His own *telek* from his saddle holster,
its drive-spring and action greased and checked, its rotary
cylinder freshly loaded with eight lead-weighted steel darts.
He carried it now in the certain knowledge that he would
surely need the advantage given by this missile weapon.

Because he was equally aware that someone else's cloak
concealed the other one.

Hoofs beat for just a moment behind them, dull and muted
in the snowfall silence, striking in the measured cadence of a
slow walk. Not one horse: several. Then as suddenly the
sound was gone. No one turned, for no one was so very
interested. But Aldric, expecting to hear just such a sound,
smiled quickly to himself within the shadows of the rank-
flashed Imperial helmet and then composed his face again.

Bruda had not merely made encouraging noises about the
power of his forged pass authorities: they worked. Presented
at the Red Tower's perimeter wall, they drew a clashing full
salute from the sentries on guard within the shelter of the
great gate-arch. It was acknowledged in the approved manner—
Aldric half a watchful beat behind the others, to see what was
done—with right arm snapped up to chest level, forearm
horizontal and crooked in, palm downwards. And nothing
more than that. He was—they all *were*—superior.

The soldiers both at the gate and those met with increasing
frequency as they crossed the Red Tower's grounds—pairs of
men, Aldric observed, and always one of them with a crossbow slung at his back—gave them the respect of further
salutes but showed no other interest. Visiting officers, staff,
flag or line officers; they were all a common enough sight
around the Tower, brought sometimes by curiosity while they
were in the area, and sometimes on more businesslike er-
rands. Whatever the reason, their presence was not worth
noticing other than as something more needing a salute.

At last they reached the Red Tower's gate, yawning to receive them, jagged above and below with the drop-and rising-shutters which gave it that look of unappeased hunger. Aldric stepped into the shelter of its lowering outerworks and threw back his hood, stamped a time or two to rid himself of loose snow and looked about him with a deliberate curiosity. He had decided that trying to hide such interest would appear more false than indulging it to the full, so he indulged.

For all that this place was known as a comfortable residence where noble guests could be invited to stay without fear of their leaving without permission, the first sight of the maw of its gate said *prison* in black-letter uncials too big for any mistakes. The famous red glaze did not continue beyond the outer cladding, except for the big six-sided tiles which paved the floor; and that gave Aldric, already far from comfortable with his private image of this building as a ravenous devourer, the unpleasant notion that he was standing on its tongue. The walls were built of grey stone, cut and dressed in massive blocks a score of tons apiece. Grey and huge. It was not the cold, but an errant uncalled-for memory which raised gooseflesh all over Aldric's body. The memory was of a tomb which he had entered: an ancient tomb, made of such monstrous stones. The tomb of one who had been dead a long, long time. This place had the same feel to it—of things long dead and better left to sleep out the rest of eternity undisturbed. Breath drifted from his mouth and nose, and he realised that he had been holding it this few seconds past. For no reason other than his own imaginings. Or, maybe not.

He could hear Bruda's voice in the background, but saying little of interest—only the conventional courtesies of rank to absent rank by way of a very junior non-com. 'I convey by you respectful greeting to the noble commander, and desire that he permit us . . .' And so on. It certainly wasn't enough to account for the low-intensity warnings sounding intermittently at the back of Aldric's mind. But neither would they stop.

There was heat in his left hand and he knew that if he chanced to roll back the cuff of his glove, this whole place would be flooded by the blue-white glare of the Echainon stone. It was fully active now—through no desire on his part—with waves of heat that rose and fell with his pulsebeat and a sensation of contained force that he was certain the others could feel as well. Yet there was no sign of any such reaction. Either they couldn't feel it—or they were hiding the fact that they could. Either way, what was going on?

The *eldheisart* presently commanding the Red Tower's garrison was scarcely an imposing figure when at last he appeared, for all the neatness of his indoor-duty tunic. He looked more like a uniformed innkeeper than a soldier—fleshy around the waist and jowls, a man who enjoyed good food and drink—and Aldric wondered how much that might be due to the very special guest housed here.

Certainly there had been nothing in the least soft about the other troopers and officers whom he had seen; for all the relaxed and casual way in which they carried out their guard duties, they had struck him as a capable and dangerous group of men. More dangerous, indeed, *because* they were on duty here, rather than in spite of it. 'A reward for good conduct' was how Bruda had described a posting to this garrison— which suggested that all the hard-eyed men inside and outside Egisburg's Red Tower were here because they were better than their comrades. Better at the soldier's trade of killing; for their look was not that of men whose superlatives lay in the gentler arts.

Then Aldric overheard something which made his heart start to race, but which at the same time had him forcing a sardonic smile off his face before it became too obvious. He had been standing a little off to one side while Bruda and the garrison commander made polite small talk over little glasses of some locally distilled spirit. It was as colourless as water, cold, heavy as oil and reeking of juniper; and most unusually where any alcohol was concerned, Aldric had found it vile. Mixed with something—anything!—yes, perhaps, but not neat. Unfortunately the others were swallowing both their small measures and the refills at a most affable rate and with every indication of enjoyment. That obvious disparity was making him look different and had most likely prompted the plump *eldheisart*'s remark; that, or the fact that by the look of him these hospitality-cups were far from being his first drink of the night. No matter.

What did matter was that Aldric heard him sniff through a red nose and then say quite plainly, 'He seems a little, well, young for a *hanalth*. Don't you think, Commander?'

That had made him nervous, but it was Voord's equally

audible reply which almost made him laugh out loud, for all the sincerity of its insulting tone. 'That little bastard—your pardon, sir—doesn't wear the thunderbolts right now, but he's with *Kagh' Ernvakh* all the same. And he's here about Princess Marevna.' It was a spur-of-the-moment improvisation which was almost worthy of applause, because when it was recalled later in the light of events that Voord still thought were yet to come, the few words of that remark and the poorly hidden detestation in it would point yet another finger at the 'murderer' of the Princess.

Right now, however, it served the more immediate purpose of diverting the *eldheisart* from any continued interest in a guest who might have just turned into a venomous snake, if the portly officer's reaction was anything to go by. And so far as Aldric was concerned, that was entirely to his liking.

The stairways inside the Red Tower were all wrong, for a fortress. They were far wider than they should have been and they didn't spiral to inconvenience an attacker's shield-arm. Surely even in the Drusalan Empire the basic practicalities of defensive architecture hadn't been overlooked? Of course, all those years ago the purpose of the building had been changed; it had ceased to be a fortress and had become a residence for the Overlords of a notably wealthy city-state. Lords who would wish to flaunt that wealth with the construction and the decoration of broad, high halls, lofty windows and—*yes, all right,* Aldric conceded to himself—stairways that were both straight and five times wider than was proper.

At least there was no need to climb right to the top of the Tower, as he had first feared that they might. But it was still five levels up, an ascent made in armour maybe twice as heavy as his own, and Aldric was only glad to see he wasn't the only person out of breath when at last they stopped. 'How—how many levels—are there?' he gasped.

The trooper sent along to guide them—in tunic rather than armour, *he* was in full possession of his breath—gestured upwards. 'Fourteen more and then the roof-top, sir,' he replied. Politely, for he had been primed or maybe simply warned about the young man with the *hanalth* insignia. 'If you're interested, then in daylight and better weather . . .'

'And no armour.' The words all came out in a rush as Aldric waved a hand, dismissing the offer. 'No, soldier. I'll forego'—and his next hesitance wasn't so much a pause for breath as a meaningful stare at Voord—'the chance for sight-seeing. Now, at least.'

Any hotter and the spellstone would be raising blisters on his skin! Oh for a moment to himself, a moment's privacy to tug away the glove and look, only to see even if not to understand what the crystal talisman was doing. Apart from hurting him. There was more power contained now in the Echainon stone than at any other time he could remember; it thrummed with it, vibrating down the innermost core of his arm's three bones so that he felt as though the limb itself trembled uncontrollably. Yet a surreptitious look revealed nothing of the sort—nothing whatsoever.

Then the guide trooper paused and tilted his head back as if listening to something. After a moment he shrugged, dismissing it as unheard or at least as unimportant. Nobody else noticed. Except Aldric, for just at that instant he had been leaning against the wall, his hand flat, and he alone knew that what had been heard was less a sound than a vibration in the stone, set aside by the trooper as perhaps snow-slip from a ledge or the slamming of a distant door. It would take more than snow, or a bigger door than any he had so far seen, to create such resonance in the ponderous blocks of which the Red Tower was built. But something settling on the roof, something with sufficient mass to well-nigh drown the fore-deck turrets of a Fleet battleram? That was another matter.

'Fourteen levels to the roof-top, soldier,' said Voord in a voice that was brisk and to Aldric all too businesslike, 'but surely Princess Marevna isn't being hel—has her quarters somewhere more convenient? Where, exactly?' It was a genuine enough question, just the sort of thing that a man fed up with climbing stairs would ask, and the trooper read nothing more from it than that. He pointed along the corridor.

'Fifth on the left, sirs. Will I make your introductions?'

Voord's smile inside his helmet was more pleasant than the thought which had prompted it. 'No need. I know the lady, so we'll surprise her.'

You should be on the stage, thought Aldric sourly. *Or on the scaffold.* There was a few minutes of scuffling as they tugged and neatened their clothing and armour—brushing away real or imagined dirt, water-beads and snow-melt smudges, straightening rank-robes, setting helmets just so.

Bruda and Tagen each slid their broad nasal-bars up through
the helmet-peaks and clear of their faces; but Aldric found it
significant that Voord made no move to follow suit. Indeed,
he seemed to have settled his harness more securely, rather
than just making it neat. Aldric nodded imperceptibly; he
knew now, for certain. Voord's actions had confirmed the
suspicion born when Voord—again—had dismissed their honour
guard before they climbed the stairs. So. Aldric too kept peak
and cheek-plates and nasal locked down in battle position. He
didn't trust *Hautheisart* Voord at all—except where this need
for ready armour was concerned.

Then Bruda swore, very softly. Aldric's head jerked round
with a rustle and a click of metal, but saw only a man
emerging from a doorway much further down the corridor.
He turned, stooped and fumbled with keys until he had
locked the door behind him. There was a cup in his hand—a
dainty thing far removed from the beakers Aldric had seen
used by the other members of the garrison when they were
sitting off-duty in the lower levels, watching him go by—and
there seemed nothing dangerous about him. Yet Bruda's face
was stamped with a flare of recognition that faded even as
Aldric watched to a wary, guarded apprehension.

The man walked towards them, but stared past them, deliberately ignoring them completely . . . until he came close
enough to see the glitter of rank badges in the lamplight.
Only then did his pace slacken and a certain interest come
into his face. It was a thin face, with thin hair and set on a
thin body; his only noteworthy feature was the pair of promi-
nent ears which Aldric fancied would never fit inside an army
regulation-pattern helmet.

Bruda was less inclined to humour, because he knew this
man by brief acquaintance—and more particularly by his
reputation. He was well known—or rather, notorious—among
several branches of service for what he called 'attention to
detail' and they more bluntly described as 'bloody nit-picking'.
His gods were the Books of Regulation and Instruction, and
one story behind his room-locking custom held that there was
a shrine to those gods hidden inside, in a cupboard.

Not even the best-laid plans were proof against such a
man, whose life revolved around minutiae and pettiness. He
could probably spot some overlooked error from where he
stood. All that Bruda could hope was that this encounter was

a coincidence and not something far, far worse; and that Aldric Talvalin would keep his mouth tight shut around that obviously non-Imperial accent.

'Bruda? Yes, Prokrator Bruda!' The newcomer laughed as he recognised a more or less familiar face. It was an unmistakable laugh, but it was also unreadable, because Bruda knew already that it would sound exactly the same whether sincerely meant or as a screen for something more sinister.

'Yes, indeed!' Bruda was being as jovial as he could manage, given the circumstances, and was relieved to see that Tagen, Voord and Aldric had all backed away, conscious of the 'wrongness' of this situation and—certainly in two out of the three—ready to respond with total violence should such be required. The young trooper who had been their guide looked from one to another, saw the gathering clouds of a senior-level disagreement and, with a very sketchy salute indeed, made himself scarce.

Aldric watched him go. It was just as well; there was trouble brewing here, even though this new officer hadn't yet seen it and Aldric for his part couldn't guess the reason behind it all. But he was staying well clear of what was only an internal wrangle and nothing to do with him at all. Until the thin man turned to him in all innocence and like the *eldheisart* downstairs asked: 'What did you do to earn gold diamonds so young, *hanalth? Hanalth . . . ?*'

Before he could begin to flounder or look otherwise obviously trapped, Aldric caught Bruda's swift nod over the stranger's shoulder. *Go on—tell him*, that nod said. Aldric didn't shrug, or sigh resignedly, although it was a time for doing both; instead he drew himself a little straighter and as he had replied once already tonight, said, 'Dirac, sir. *Hanalth Kagh' Ernvakh* Dirac.'

Those few words were enough; Imperial officers of such seniority spoke only with the accent of the central provinces— and Imperial officers of any rank at all did not speak with the unmistakable Elthanek burr of northern Alba. The man stepped back sharply, a frown creasing his face; then he swung on Bruda. 'What is this?' he snapped.

'Not this—*he*,' Bruda returned simply. '*He* is an Alban.'

Shock at the blunt, impossible answer left the man—whatever his name was—speechless for an instant (for a wonder), and those who could see his eyes watched a dozen speculations

flicker through them in the brief silence. 'And what's he
doing here?' No laughter now; no curiosity. Just an angry,
tending-to-shrill immediate demand for information.

Bruda glanced at Aldric and allowed himself to smile,
because the Alban was ready for anything short of outright
murder. It was enough. 'Right now? He's going to hit you
just as hard as he can manage. *Do it!*'

Aldric's hand had already flattened into a chopping blade
and the muscles of his entire body were still tingling with the
energies leaking from the overcharged spellstone. So he didn't
do as Bruda said and strike as hard as he was able, because
feeling as he did now it would likely have knocked the thin
man's head clean off. But he hacked down on the close-
clipped neck with feeling, right below one of those ludicrous
ears, and he certainly seemed to have hit with quite enough
force to do what was required. The thin man jolted forward
half a step without moving his legs and while still in the
process of being utterly astonished, and would have measured
his length along the corridor had Bruda not caught him in
time. His pretty cup exploded into fragments on the floor.

'I have wanted to have that done,' Bruda said, 'or do it
myself, from the first moment that I met this . . . Well
struck, Alban.'

'My pleasure.' Aldric massaged the edge of his hand thoughtfully and flicked a speculative glance at Voord. 'I know what
you mean, I've met one or two like that.'

'See to the Princess, *Hlensyarl*,' snarled Voord, nettled
despite himself. 'We'll attend to this and then I'll be right
behind you.'

I'm sure you will, thought Aldric. *And alone—but for a
telek.* He said nothing aloud, but turned his back and walked
quickly down the corridor to the fifth door on the left. Behind
him he could hear Tagen being instructed to carry the unconscious man downstairs and have his 'accidental' injury at-
tended to. *That leaves you, and Bruda—and me. Well, well.*
Aldric unbolted the door, tried the handle, found it unlocked—
and went inside.

'Dear God!' gasped Dewan. They had both seen it this time,
beyond denial even by the driest of dry humour; seen it as
clearly as the swirling snow allowed. A monstrous shape
made more monstrous yet by the darkness which surrounded

it, vast wings, lean body and a brief bright lick of flame—all
landing with audacious ease atop the Red Tower. By now
Gemmel and Dewan were close enough to see how a length
of parapet broke away under the dragon's weight and went
tumbling down and out of sight. Neither of them saw or heard
it striking ground.

'How many men in the garrison?' Gemmel had the
Dragonwand braced now in both his hands, held like a weapon
rather than a walking-staff; that pretence was over, for the
energies which it contained and focused were overflowing
now, illuminating the snowshot darkness with a fluttering
actinic glare like summer lightning behind clouds, the lightning's brilliance muted by great distance—or by the will of
he who held that lightning's power in check.

Dewan could hear the sound which emanated from the
spellstave; for Ykraith sang to herself with a thin atonal
screaming that spoke of nothing less than utter power. The
ebb and flow of that high, sweet wail, a song without words,
matched every nuance of the arabesques of force dancing
along her dragon-patterned length. And both matched the
beating of someone's heart. Not Dewan's, for his heart was
racing again, pounding the blood through his veins in a
percussive arhythmic counterpoint to the spellstave's music;
and most likely not Gemmel's either—even if what he was,
man-shaped though it might be, had a heart that Dewan ar
Korentin might recognise as such.

'I said, "How many men?" ' There was an impatience in
the sorcerer's voice, an urgency which spoke of more important things than merely calculating odds.

'Forty, most likely. Maybe more, given the circumstances.
But Gemmel, that still makes it twenty-to-one at the very
least!'

'Count again,' Gemmel reproved. 'You're forgetting Aldric—
and you're forgetting . . .' He gestured just once towards the
top of the tower, invisible now behind a curtain of snow. 'I'd
say that evens things a little.'

'But what are you planning?' Tactical and strategic studies
had never included a scenario quite like this one! 'What are
you going to do?'

'Diversion. Remember what the Vixen told us? When the
alarms go off, the guards should only think of running in one
direction. I'm'—his gaze shifted briefly, apologetically, to

where Ymareth crouched unseen high above them both—'no.
We're going to force them to a choice—confuse them with
decisions just a little. Let's get closer. I want to hear just
when the shouting starts.'

They began edging forward, eyes narrowed and squinting
against a snowfall that was winding up towards blizzard
proportions, until after a few steps Gemmel straightened himself and strode as best he could along the middle of the street,
as if he had every right in the world to do so. Dewan stared at
him, saw the wizard's outline waver towards invisibility as
the white-swirled distance between them increased, and realised
what had made him bold. There was no need to hide in *this*.

'I've never seen it fall like this before,' Dewan said as he
drew level again, 'at least not so early in the season. Oh, of
course! I'm not seeing it again, am I?'

Gemmel turned to look at him and grinned a grin made
vague because white teeth and white beard and white snow
were all running into one another. 'Snow's easy, if it's
already there,' he said. 'Fog's much more difficult.'

Neither saw the cloaked and muffled figure standing with a
little group of horses in the wind-lee of the buildings nearest
to the wall-gate of the Tower. If they had—and Dewan in
particular—then memory and recognition might have stirred a
chord. But as the snow fell and danced and whirled across the
thick, cold air, not even Gemmel knew that there was someone there.

The room beyond the door was snug and warm, illuminated
by scented lamps and by the flickering of a large log fire.
Applewood, by the smell. There was a sense of ease and
comfort rather than real luxury, but certainly nothing to suggest that this might be a prison cell . . . except for those thick
bars across the outside of the door.

But it would have taken far less than that to make Aldric's
suspicions gather momentum again. Already there had been
too much trickery, too much deception; too many things
which had not been as they first appeared. What if the
Princess was here willingly? Or if he had been unknowingly
involved in some internal political power-play? Or if the
assassination itself was just another trick?

What if there was no one here at all?

But a book lay on the floor where it had slipped off the arm of a chair, its pages ticking slowly over one by one by one, and there was a tray of honeyed fruit on a nearby table, sweet glaze glistening stickily in the firelight. Beside the tray was a crystal wine flagon and two partly filled—or partly emptied—goblets. *Two?* Aldric's mind yelled in alarm.

Two.

A woman rose from the concealing embrace of one of the deep, padded chairs which faced the fire and rounded on him, dropping a needlework tambour as she did so. There was a sleepiness in her face, as if she had been dozing until awakened by the clatter of his arrival; but that sleepiness did not conceal the expectant look which he had caught in her dark eyes as their gaze first met. It was a look which faded almost at once as she realised he was not the one for whom such expressions were intended, but it worried him. It was wrong. Surely princesses did not carry on liaisons with their jailors—no matter how handsome, or how boring the imprisonment? Although, knowing the Drusalan Empire, such snap judgments were as well avoided.

But even the way she looked, dressed, *stood*, was unprincesslike—to Alban eyes at least. Taller then Aldric, almost as broad in the shoulders—which contrasted dramatically with a neat waist—and plentifully endowed both with curves in all the proper places and aquiline darkly glamorous good looks, this woman was scarcely Imperial. But imperious? There was no doubt about that at all.

'Have you not heard of knocking on a door, soldier?' she demanded. 'Or of waiting to be invited into a noble lady's presence? Answer me—then get out!'

'To your questions, lady: yes and yes. To your order: no.' Aldric glanced backwards over one shoulder, saw nobody behind him and stepped quickly further into the room. 'Where's the Princess Marevna? Not you, I think.'

'What are you talking about?'

'I'm here to take her out of this, lady; where is she?'

'And where's your written authority for the move?'

'Listen to me: there aren't any authorities—written, spoken or bloody well sung! This isn't a move—it's supposed to be a *rescue!* If you'd be good enough to let it!' He back-heeled the door shut and looked in vain for bars and catches, finally leaning his weight against it for want of anything better, then glared at the tall woman whom he had now categorised as one

of those over-protective waiting-women. Though why she had
to look the way she did, he couldn't understand. 'And if *you*
don't start to move, it'll turn into attempted murder!'

A knife appeared from somewhere in the woman's elaborate clothing, and with that length of bright steel jutting
thumb-braced above her fist, she suddenly looked capable of
such a crime herself.

Aldric coughed a mirthless laugh. 'Not by me, lady—I
wouldn't have announced my intentions otherwise; but there's
one outside who— Never mind that; quick—boots and gloves
and cloaks. Foul-weather travelling gear. And the Princess!
Move!'

'Why so excited?'

Aldric's helmeted head snapped a few degrees right to
pinpoint the source of this new voice as the depths of the
second chair and whoever was sitting in it—and he saw her:
the Princess. The one for whom, or against whom, or because
of whom, time and money and blood had been expended as if
they had as little worth as leaves in autumn. She looked like a
princess indeed, the way he had imagined the sister of an
Emperor should look: small and slight, dressed simply in a
pure white robe with silvery patterns embroidered on its back
and shoulders, with enormous brown eyes that regarded him
gravely from a pale, heart-shaped face. As she stood up and
flicked long, long dark hair away from that high-cheekboned
face, he could sense the dignity that she wore about her like a
garment, a measured control which refused to let all she had
overheard disturb the way in which she paced forward to look
up at him.

Up—because the top of her head came only to the junction
of his collarbones. Even Aldric's desperate urgency had to be
leashed in the face of such awe-inspiring serenity, for although a failure to comprehend the situation lay behind it,
Marya Marevna an-Sherban's vast calm was indeed an awesome thing in one so small. Trained tranquillity; and something which, regretfully, he would have to shatter.

'Chirel,' she said across his chest to the other woman,
'who is this person? And why is he here?'

'Princess, you were sitting there and you heard me well
enough. I came to take you from the Tower. By command of
General Goth—and I presume your brother.'

'For how long has the Lord General used Albans over and above our own excellent soldiers?'

So she recognised the accent. And wouldn't therefore move without an explanation unless he knocked her out and carried her. But her companion had heard the word *Aalban'r* and moved instantly to shield Marevna with her own body and poised knife. Against a fully armoured man it was a useless gesture, but very fine for all that.

'Lady, ladies, it's a matter of politics.' Despite the helmet he could hear movement just outside and an instant later the stealthy pressure as someone tested the door. Aldric braced his feet flat and wide apart against the floor and held firm. 'Because my king wants to show support—'

He would have kept on talking as persuasively as he knew how had he not heard a sudden, familiar thrumming in the air, felt a tremor in the wood at his back, tasted an acrid flavour both in his mouth and in his mind. All of it too familiar by far.

'Get *down!*' He screamed it, hurling himself forward and sideways, clear of the door and the doorway and the straight line from them to the corridor beyond, but he hadn't even hit the floor before thick timbers and iron hinges and steel bolts all jolted out of their frame in a single mass which was twice the weight of a man and went scything across the room as if flung from a catapult, leaving a swathe of destruction in its wake. Something ponderous plucked at Aldric's shoulder and no more, but all of a sudden a hand's span of the cloak and the rank-robe—and the splint-mail under all—were ripped away and his whole arm struck numb by the impact.

High Accelerator! Aldric almost retched with the shock and with the pain of returning sensation in his arm, but most of all with his own stupidity which had almost lost him the game before he had begun to play. *Voord!* he thought frantically, his mind log-jammed and overloaded with conflicting signals. *And Bruda even* told *me of his talent!* He glanced sideways even while he still sprawled on the floor, his face gnat-stung by the cloud of sparks exploded from the fireplace when the door's wreckage struck it. The Princess was safe; the Princess's feet weren't even on the ground for Chirel, the big woman with the knife, had actually plucked up her small and slender charge in the crook of one arm. Marevna dangled there now like a doll, all white robe and long dark hair, all dignity gone. But alive . . . for the moment.

Voices outside, coming closer. Fragmented shouts. Bruda's voice: 'Voord, what in hell happened?'

Voord's voice right outside the door: 'Don't know! Magic! The Princess . . . Treason? Can't be treason—not with a foreigner. Murder?'

Oh, clever, clever Lord Commander, to sow that seed so quickly!

A figure appeared in the doorway, ill-defined through the dust and shadowy because so many lanterns had been snuffed out. One hand a crooked claw, almost useless—but not quite. Aldric could see the hazy shimmering of power around it. How did he gain so much? What bargains did he strike, what promises were made? And in the other hand, half-raised, poised and ready: a *telek*.

'Princess, are you safe?' Voord's voice was loud, full of concern—for other ears to hear. The *telek* spoke silent truth of his intentions. 'My lady, where are you?'

'Don't move! You, Chirel—both of you keep out of sight!' Aldric's yell broke into a fit of coughing as he choked on the dust and the stinking smoke from dead lamps and smouldering fabrics and the charred, scattered, still-glowing logs.

Voord snapped sideways out of the back-light at the door, and as he moved Aldric saw the *telek* drop forward to a ready position. The Vlechan said nothing. Yet. Did nothing. Yet. But he waited for a target, any target, to show itself. Alban, Drusalan, male, female. Anything or anyone that he could kill.

Another silhouette filled the space where the door had been, more clearly seen now that the dust was settling. Too tall for Tagen and not broad enough. Anyway, Tagen had been dismissed. Bruda. The Prokrator had a drawn sword in his hand. 'Voord?' He spoke cautiously, still shaken by the suddenness of events.

'Look out, sir!' Voord's voice had all the right notes of horror in it. 'He's trying to kill the Princess!'

'Impossible! Where are you, Alban?'

'Get out of sight, sir! He's got a *telek!*' And as he named the weapon, Voord used it to shoot his own commander at close range.

Aldric heard the slap of discharge and saw Bruda's tall

figure stagger back three steps, then fall to the floor. He didn't know where the man had been hit, but even point-blank no *telek* dart could punch through proof armour like this officers' issue they all wore. That left the vulnerable places: face and throat. And both of those were fatal.

But if a soldier of the Drusalan Empire could use a *telek* and sorcery, then how much better might an Alban *kailin-eir* who was also a wizard's fosterling? Aldric tugged free his own *telek* from beneath the layering of garments which had concealed its presence, cocked the weapon quietly, released its safety-slide—then laid it down beside him on the floor. More quietly still he stripped away the glove from his left hand and looked at the spellstone of Echainon, the Eye of the Dragon, as it seemed to look at him. There was still no flare of azure energy; just that cat's-eye pupil at its centre, twisting, turning, pulsing to the rhythm of his heart. Pulsing fast; very fast indeed. Aldric slipped it around his wrist so that the stone was snugly cradled in the hollow of his palm, then closed his fist around it as if trying to absorb something of the crystal's power into himself.

'Abath arhan,' he said. Light that was as blue and brilliant as a summer sky began to stream between the interstitial spaces of those clenched fingers, painting vivid dapples all across the walls and floor and ceiling, cutting through the smoky air in rods and fans of luminescence that seemed almost solid. The stone was primed now. Ready. Waiting.

And the Red Tower shook to its foundations. Aldric felt the floor beneath him lurch like a battleram's deck and saw more wreckage tumble from the shattered door-frame. He heard glass beyond the window-shutters fragment to shards, and by the half-light of the crushed and dying fire he saw a fresco-decorated wall abruptly crack from side to side and top to bottom. Great chunks of the painted plaster fell away, clogging the air with dust once more. But most of all, there was that sound from outside and above.

Piercing shriek and sub-bass bellow all melded together into a single huge atonal roar and the window-shutters blew in, spraying the room with broken wood and with a whirl of snow made phosphorescent by the flood of light behind it.

Ymareth!

A female voice screamed something, even though the sense of the words—if words there had been—was lost. But the mere sound was enough for Voord. Locating on it, he sent another dart whipping through the air towards the source of that cry. It hit hard, stone or metal amid a shower of sparks, then ricocheted further and drew a shrill yelp of pain from someone. Chirel—or the Princess?

'Bastard!' Aldric sent four spaced shots across the most likely target zone in as many seconds; there were more sparks, the clack and clatter of metal missiles hitting stone and the chiming diminuendo of their rebound—then the rewarding soggy thump as a dart hit home, and Voord's voice raised in agony.

But how hard had he been hit? There been none of the thrashing of limbs which normally accompanied a *telek*-strike—nor even the slack, felled-tree thud of a body knocked dead off its feet. Only that single cry. Aldric thought *ruse*, thought *decoy* and cuddled the rubble-strewn floor until he was sure.

It happened sooner than he thought. That hazy, translucent globe of contained force which he had seen perched like a falcon on Voord's ruined hand came surging from the shadows, almost unseen, crossing the room in a flicker of refraction where verticals and horizontals kicked nauseously out of line. It hit the wall over the fireplace, striking square and hard as a siege-ram, and splashed a coruscation of rainbow fire all through the room. The wall slumped downwards, shearing near the ceiling as it folded noisily into the space where thirty square feet of its substance had been ripped into a sparkle of disrupted matter.

Where in hell did he learn that? Even as the thought coagulated in his brain—an organ right now as capable of coherent thought as a bowl of beaten eggs—Aldric knew, knew, *knew* that Voord hadn't been taught that spell or any of the others he might use. They were a gift. Not a gift like the ability to play music, or shoot straight, but the sick, sardonic gift of shoes to a legless man or a beautiful painting to one struck blind. Voord was a channel, a pipeline to this world from somewhere else. Aldric had said it himself: 'Where in hell?'

'Fool! Thee has power to match this petty casting—power and more! Why lie ye thus in the dirt, O Dragon-lord? Rise up! Rise up and smite!' The voice which burst into Aldric's skull was Ymareth's; but now its background of heard sound was not the metallic rustling hiss which he had—just about—

grown used to. Oh, no. This was the draconian equivalent of a
yell half urgent and half enraged by stupidity, and it had all
the delicacy and subtle nuance of a full-great chord on a pipe
organ. It was devastating. What little was left of the window-
shutters fell apart with the sheer volume of sound, and the
remnants of the fresco wall first crazed with a network of fine
cracks then went to powder.

And Aldric stood up; uncertainly, unsteadily, because the
floor still quivered beneath the soles of his boots, and because
the blast of noise which had been Ymareth's irritation had
stunned and almost bled his inner ears so that his balance was
none of the best. But he stood, crimson and black in the
Imperial Grand Warlord's livery which he had come to hate,
with the blue-white fire of the Echainon stone crawling along
his arm like some eerie embroidery set into the red-enamelled
metal. Yet it was the human weapon, the *telek*, that he
extended towards where his enemy must be; a *telek* cocked
and ready, loaded with clean steel that was shod with lead for
penetration's sake. And at the very back of his mind Aldric
wished that he had loaded with pure silver.

'Voord? Voord, you traitor, you mocker of honour, come
out!' It was stilted, formal, unreal—but it worked, for Voord
emerged from the shadows and stood quite still with both
hands by his sides. The other *telek* was still gripped in one of
them, but it pointed at the floor and was harmless; Aldric's
own ready-levelled weapon could shoot unerringly true before
Voord's could rise through enough of an arc to make it
threatening. 'You failed, Voord—your own worst crime, I've
been told. So . . . why Bruda, then?'

'How little you understand, Alban, He's dead. So I'm
promoted.'

'Why? You killed him.'

'Quite. I live—he doesn't. Promotion.'

Aldric stared at him, lit by the fires of burning wood and
leashed-in power. The words wouldn't take shape in his
mouth, wouldn't take their places on his tongue or in his
throat. Not in Drusalan, anyway. It was a foul language at the
best of times. Alban was better by far and much more appropriate for the formal, age-old declaration. 'Then I bring you
your most necessary death.'

He squeezed the *telek*'s trigger and with a noise like a
chisel into grained timber, a dart sprouted just above Voord's

right eye. Just clear of the helmet's nasal and just below its peak. At that range—fifteen feet, maybe less—the Vlechan's head was snapped back; right back, so that his skull struck between his own shoulderblades. Even without the dart, that jolt would have broken his neck. The ridge of his helmet-crest grated against the wall behind him . . .

Then grated again as he drew himself straight once more and with a heave which needed both hands on its stubby shaft, wrenched the dart out of his head.

The frontal skull-bone might not have knitted straight away, but with his own eyes Aldric saw the bloodflow stop and the torn flesh run together like wax smoothed with a hot iron. *Like cu Ruruc!*

'You see, *hlensyarl?*' There was a vile phlegmy thickness in Voord's voice when he spoke now. 'You see? You can't hurt me. I'm deathless! Marevna, can you hear me? I'm undying—and I'll come for you again. Enjoy sweet dreams till then, my lady!' He twisted out of the doorway and was gone—and still the power of the spellstone whorled around Aldric's arm, contained, unused. Useless now.

'Does use of this touch over-closely on thy honour, man?' Ymareth's voice was cold, sarcastic, disapproving. 'Then hear me this last time and believe, for I shall never speak it more. Honour is mine to judge and thou art not yet wanting; but these ladies are now thine to guard and to keep in safety. How wilt thou, when thou knowest not the place wherein thy foe now hides?'

'Get out of my head!' Aldric wrenched at the straps of the Imperial helmet and pulled it free. He stared at the golden insignia, inverted triangle over diamond over double bars, none of it rightfully his—all of it a lie, all lies lies lies—and flung the helmet away from him in a clatter of metal and leather. It bounced from half-a-dozen things, broken furniture and smouldering logs and sideslipped heaps of crumbling stone, then rolled and came to rest and see-sawed to and fro a moment on the brightmetal comb of its cavalry cresting. Afterwards was very quiet in the room. As quiet as the grave. *Was all this useless?* Aldric thought, fearing for the worst. All the sneaking and the lying and the killing, all wasted by a stray dart of a fallen piece of masonry. 'My lady?' He no longer troubled to hide that Elthanek accent of his. 'My lady, answer—if you can.'

'I can,' said Marevna an-Sherban and coughed. She lifted her head and upper body on braced hands and fragments of what had once been a comfortable, pretty room tumbled from her back. 'Neither of us is hurt. Much. Thanks to you!'

When both women were on their feet, Aldric was better able to see the extent of that 'much'. There was a ragged hole through Chirel's upper arm; from the state of her sleeve it had bled heavily until staunched by a torn-off strip of material, and in its triangular *telek*-dart shape it exactly matched the shallow puncture on Princess Marevna's face. Had Chirel's far-from-feminine bicep not been around Marevna's head, cuddling it as she must have done when the Princess was a frightened child—or had she been one of those willowy ladies rather than the muscular, capable person she was, then . . . The *then* was obvious.

For the rest there were scratches, bruises, blisters from the sparks and embers flung out of the fire; but nothing worse. Aldric sucked in a deep breath, heedless of the plaster-dust and smoke suspended in it, and felt reborn even as he bent double in an eye-streaming coughing fit. He had known it all along, and had refused to even think about: the possibility that something might go wrong. For if Marevna had come to lasting harm, then everything—all the fear, and the pain, and the lies, and the death—would have been for nothing. Wasted.

'It feels like an hour ago that I last said this, lady, ladies— but I *am* here to rescue you. Dress warmly and follow quickly, please!' Events of the past few minutes had convinced even Chirel far more than his most plausible speech could ever have done, and neither took very long over wrapping themselves in furred garments which were the first sign of real riches Aldric had so far seen. He handed them courteously across the threshold of the room, no longer quite a threshold or even a definite boundary between outside and in; but more particularly, he placed himself and his supporting hand between their eyes and Bruda, for though dying fast the Prokrator was not yet dead. Not quite. He was hanging on to life not to save himself but to do, or say, or pass on something of very great importance. So great that he had held himself away from oblivion for a time which must have seemed far longer than all the years of his life.

His fingers were bleeding, their cracked and broken nails flexing convulsively in and out of his shredded palms as if that little pain could distract fast-ebbing life from its departure through the inch-long rip beneath his ear which had nicked both jugular and carotid, opening them to the pungent air. But not enough for quick release. He still lived—each minute, second, breath marked by the crisp spurt of blood against the floor.

'Talvalin,' he gasped as Alric stepped over him, and in his voice was the sudden fear that this *hlensyarl* with no reason to love either the Drusalan Empire or its Secret Police would walk on, walk away and leave him alone to listen to his last drop of blood as it dribbled out into the Red Tower's dust. But Aldric was already dropping to one knee, heedless of or disregarding the moist dark warmth which soaked through his breeches.

'*Tlei-ai, Bruda'ka; mn'aii ch'aschh.*' 'Lie easy, friend, here I am.' It was the form of Drusalan which lay easiest on an Alban tongue; amiable and warm, without the strata of rank and separation he always had cause to use before. There was neither time nor place for that now. Not here. A dying Chief of Secret Police on his back in the dust was a dying man first and last. Nationality didn't matter; if there was a way of recognising accent in a wordless sound of agony, Aldric had no wish to learn it.

'. . . should have trusted you,' Bruda mumbled. 'First. Foremost. Last. Honour, you see.' The man's hands were already cold as they reached out, and sticky with blood. Aldric caught them; let himself be caught. Like marble: no feeling, no pulse, no colour. Nothing. '. . . both betrayed. Me. You. Trust ice in summer first. Voord wanted, wants . . . *has* my place now. My rank. My power . . . '

Bruda was surely rambling, passing into delirium as shadows gathered about him, talking only because the sound of speech was the sound of living and hearing his own voice was proof that he was not yet lost. But for all that there was an uncomfortable reality behind the slurring, broken sentences. Too much so. 'You were given to us. For fear—no, in case they got to you first. And I sent Voord!' He laughed, a horrible bubbling sound which brought red froth welling from the corners of his mouth. 'But it wasn't right. Wasn't decent. Your King . . . to give an honourable vassal like a slave. Not right to betray . . . '

Bruda's cold hand tightened on Aldric's warm fingers,

closing so convulsively that in another circumstance the Alban might have sworn and wrenched away. But not now.
Never now. The Prokrator's head and shoulders lifted from
the planks which pillowed them, and that strain sent a long
spray of darkness splattering across the floor. It seemed
wrong that the blood of so educated, so intelligent, so politi-
cally aware a man should soak into the hungry dust like an
unthinking wave on a beach. 'All the honour is yours alone.
She is safe. Free. Living.' Bruda's eyes opened very wide,
blue and ingenuous as the eyes of a child; deceptive to the
last. 'Go to Durforen, Al'Dirac-*an*. To the monastery. They
were expecting us. Hah! You and Marevna should get quite a
welcome. Bid Ioen the Emperor live for ever. From me. Who
cannot live . . . a . . . moment mor—'

Aldric knew the slack weight of death, cradled in his two
hands. He laid Bruda's head back to the floor, very gently,
for whatever the man had done and planned to do, he had still
died well and it was not for Aldric Talvalin to treat his corpse
with disrespect. He closed the fixed and staring eyes and
respectfully arranged Bruda's hands crosswise on his chest so
that—if tradition spoke truly—he would go with dignity into
the Void. Did Drusalans believe in Void, and Circle, and the
hope to go from sure melancholy to rebirth and the chance of
gladness? He didn't know the answer. But just in case, he did
all that was proper by his own beliefs, as he had done once
before to a corpse pulped out of recognition. Because fire was
clean . . .

Urgency was set aside just for this brief moment, as a
respect for that which was an Ending in every faith. Aldric
crossed his hands—palms outwards and the stone of Echainon,
the Eye of the Dragon, outermost of all. Its fires still rolled
upwards, over and around and through his fingers, cool,
warm, barely and yet always present. '*Alh'noen ecchaur i
aiyya,*' he said, and let those fires wash from the crystal,
across all that remained of Bruda, Prokrator, *hauthanalth,*
man.

Then he rose, and turned from the low mound of dry grey
ash, and walked away.

'Diversion, the man said!' crowed Dewan delightedly, all but
clapping his hands. 'If that's a diversion, then I wouldn't

want to be in the same city as a real attack! Mercy of Heaven, will you just look at that!'

Ymareth was skyborne once more, circling the Red Tower in a tight, steep constant bank, black and gigantic against the falling snow and the firelit crimson of the Tower. Flame plumed constantly from its jaws in great hot billows that blasted the snow to steam. Around the Red Tower, it was raining.

All of Egisburg must be awake now, thought Dewan; no matter how sodden they might be, nobody could sleep through *this!* That first roar was fit to wake the dead, never mind the drunken; he had heard windows shattering all across Tower Square after that brief flicker of blue light from one very particular window a quarter up the Tower's grim height. It was then that Ymareth had roared, and launched with heavy grace into a dive from the ramparts which had become full flight within a hundred feet. He had seen that as the wavering curtain of snow had thinned for just a moment, and then as the fires began he could see even despite the storm's renewed fury. Still the dragon circled, flaming, and yet, through all the flames and the roaring, Dewan couldn't put aside the thought that Ymareth was laughing.

There were no soldiers to be seen. Oh, there had been plenty and enough to spare a few minutes past, when they had poured from the Red Tower's doorway like ants from a kicked nest, but they had kept on running—through the slush and the deluge of dragon-melted sleet, out of the perimeter gates, into the white whirl of the blizzard and out of Dewan's concern. He had seen soldiers run like that before, twice; they wouldn't be back tonight. Except for Aldric and Princess Marevna, the Tower was surely empty now.

Gemmel was plainly thinking the same thing. He scraped snow from his beard and brows, knowing the gesture to be a useless one, and hefted the no-longer needed Dragonwand. 'Move in,' he said.

Directly they stepped forward, the hoofbeats came up behind them both. Several horses, at the trot. Dewan drew blade and swung around, dropping to a fighting crouch—and then relaxed, his moment made perfect by Gemmel's splutter of astonishment as the wizard saw Tehal Kyrin approaching them through the snow. She was leading six horses at a sort of jog-trot: Aldric's black Lyard and his packpony, her own grey gelding K'schei and three more riding-horses with empty saddles.

'Expecting someone, my dear?' purred Dewan as he bowed low.

' I keep telling you not to call me that,' said Kyrin, but her feigned exasperation was half-hearted and lacked spirit; all her concentration was elsewhere, on what was happening around the Red Tower, and Gemmel had to address her twice before she heard him.

'Lady? Lady! Are you also a part of this—or are you acting independently?'

'I . . . You'd be Gemmel. Yes. Who else?' She was still uncertain of how one spoke to sorcerers—cautiously, of course, that went without saying—and twitched him a little bow whose effect was rather lost when K'schei threw up his head and yanked her not only upright but momentarily off tip-toe. 'Tehal Kyrin,' she introduced herself when she had a little breath back. 'And no: I'm not concerned with politics Alba's, the Empire's or yours. Sir,' she added, thinking it prudent.

'That's a relief,' said Gemmel, meaning it. He glanced at the sky: Ymareth had swept away from the Tower and was for the moment invisible through the snow, but the old wizard was quite aware of what was going on. The dragon was lining up for a landing run, and in this filthy flying weather was taking plenty of airspace for it. 'Now, since we have a moment, Dewan. Explain this young woman.'

Dewan did, editing where he thought it wise, but even then wasn't entirely sure what Gemmel thought of it all. The wizard's jewel-green eyes were fixed on him, and if they blinked once during the telling of the tale, Dewan ar Korentin didn't see it. Still there was no reaction—favourable, disapproving or even dismissive—and to break the uncomfortable stillness he looked up and asked, 'Where's the dragon?' even though he had noticed it gone before he began to speak.

Gemmel regarded him disdainfully, but forbore to sniff. 'Out there'—he pointed downwind—'and coming back.' Then with just the merest touch of vitriol, 'Any more questions? Or can we actually do something constructive?'

Same old wizard, thought Dewan. He still hadn't really come to terms with what he had learned about Gemmel Errekren, but there were occasional flashes of expression or phrase which were comforting in their familiarity. He shrugged, the movement accentuated both by his furs and by the snow which had collected on them. 'Whatever you like. Lead on.'

But not even Gemmel was willing to go inside the Red Tower itself. Caution, superstition, a desire not to tempt providence in its present shape of those poised and ominous spiked gates. Or, for Dewan's and Kyrin's part at least, the obvious if unadmitted wide-eyed wonder they both showed as Ymareth the dragon came gliding into view through the very teeth of the snowbearing wind, its flight-path cleared in brief, bright swathes of fire. Heat and the smell of steam washed across them as it settled onto the snowbound earth in a rolling cloud of vapour, and its head swung to regard them as it grinned that long fox's grin, all fangs and tongue and—this time—flames and smoke.

'Many others watched,' Ymareth reported, 'from doorways and from windows. But I doubt thee will be troubled by their interest.' Just to add weight to the pronouncement, its great wedge head turned away a moment and unleashed another blast towards the city proper. Somewhere in the distance, beyond the rushing bellow of the flame, a chorus of doors slammed shut.

'Any s-sign of him yet?' Kyrin managed. Her voice was as steady as she could make it—which meant that it could still be understood. Just about. But then, she wasn't quite so used to the company of dragons as Dewan had become.

'Nothing yet.' Less inclined to worries than the other two, Gemmel had wandered a good deal nearer to the Tower, and now he returned with a motley collection of things bundled in his arms or draped across the Dragonwand. 'Just these.' He was mystified by the discovery; a helmet, a cloak and an overrobe with rank-tabs on it. 'The rest of the armour's back there as well. Looks like somebody wasn't wearing much when they left.'

'Looks like they didn't stop to put these on, you mean. And I can't say I'm surprised.' Dewan reached out for the helmet, smiling thinly. A diamond over twin bars, all silver. *Hautheisart*. He grunted and dropped it into the snow, then nudged it carelessly with a boot. 'I didn't reach so exalted a rank.' There was a touch of bitterness in his voice. 'Because I was born on the wrong side of the border. No other reason, even though they always had several— Aldric!'

The helmet, kicked, rolled sluggishly aside and was forgotten as all three—all four, because Ymareth lowered its head to see inside the Tower as well—looked through the gateway to where Dewan had first heard the patter of approaching footsteps and Aldric's voice, trying to make some explanation in two directions at once.

'Another thing,' he was saying, 'is that one of my companions is, well, different. Don't be frightened; you won't be harmed.

'But how different can he be, if we're—*Father of Fires!*'

'True enough, I suppose; but I didn't say "he" at all.'

It was big, strong Chirel who was most upset by her first sight of Ymareth, reclining in the melting snow and gazing at her through those awesome phosphorescent eyes. She screamed and would have fainted on the spot had not someone—Aldric suspected Kyrin—been ready with a generous handful of snow unsympathetically applied. Even afterwards she seemed seldom far from hysterics.

While Marevna was . . . Marevna. As serene as he had seen her at their first meeting. It was only when he watched closely that he saw how rapidly the white puffs of exhaled breath were pumping from her slack, slightly smiling lips. The calmness, the control, even the smile were all shields to hide behind, just as much as Bruda's mask had ever been. Something with which to fend off reality. But the reality of the dragon for Princess Marevna was a wild, wavering blend of terror and delight; discovering that at least some of the old stories were true was enough to overwhelm anyone.

'My ladies, my gentlemen,' Aldric courteously pitched his voice loud enough to include Ymareth in the situation, 'I would as soon not wait a moment longer here; we've already outstayed any welcome Egisburg might offer. Mount up, all; let's go.' Then more privately to Kyrin, after an embrace that was of necessity both brief and restrained: 'I already knew you were beautiful, love; but this goes beyond mere cleverness.' He waved a hand towards the horses. 'How did you know to bring exactly the right number?'

Kyrin laughed and laid her head sideways on his shoulder— the nearly-bared one that the chamber door had clipped. 'Easy enough: your horse, my horse, the pack-pony—and everything else in the stable.' That would have been Bruda's, Tagen's and Voord's mounts, of course. 'Although somebody's going to be riding a pack-saddle. I suggest the pretty Princess.'

'Jealous already?'

'God, no! She's lightest, that's all, and I don't want the horse overloaded,' Kyrin walked away, a little distance beyond Dewan, then thought a moment and turned back. 'But I did see that piece you had in Tuenafen. Don't do it again . . .'

Ar Korentin, between them, looked with amusement from one to the other. And froze.

'All *stop!*' said Lord Commander Voord.

He stood just at the corner of the Red Tower's gate-house, his face pinched and bluing with cold, and the *telek* in his outstretched hand wavered with the shivering that racked his body. 'I've been waiting for you; listening to you congratulate each other, listening to you feeling so pleased with yourselves! I've been waiting a long time.'

Not even the dragon would have seen him, for he was no longer wearing armour, or rank-robe, or cloak. Instead he was dressed in what he must have been wearing under the armour: close-fitting garments of some white material which blended with the snow and made him all but invisible. Too late now, Dewan glanced with all the bright vision of hindsight at the rank-marked *seisac* helmet he had thrown aside. Yet how should he have known?

Other than the white tunic and trews, Voord wore one other thing—itself white now with the sleet and snow which had fallen on it while he crouched in the freezing shadows and waited for his opportunity with that dreadful hatred-fuelled patience, but a thing more usually black as night. A sleeveless vest. A *coyac* made of wolfskin.

Aldric was the only one to realise what was meant by his wearing of that garment, but the instant he opened his mouth Voord's *telek* lined up on his face. It still trembled, but not so much that he might miss. 'Say it,' the *hautheisart* invited. 'Say anything at all and see how far it gets before this rams it back down your throat.'

Nobody spoke. Aloud. But inside his head Aldric heard the dragon's voice, carried on a whisper of metallic sound that Voord would never recognise as speech. 'Thou, Dragonlord, and all of thy companions block my way—else I would roast him to ash and cinders. Move aside.' Encharmed with understanding, Gemmel and Dewan heard the words as well and where line of sight permitted, knowing eyes met in swift agreement. Then the sorcerer took a step to one side and Dewan to the other.

Voord glanced at both and smiled like a shark. 'Back to where you were,' he snarled, 'or this one dies!' The *telek* levelled at Kyrin. 'Don't think that I'm here and you're there and that thing'—a chin-jerk at Ymareth—'is where it is just by accident. Oh, no. Credit me with that much wit at least.'

'W-what do you want?' Marevna an-Sherban was no longer quite so calm as she appeared—unless it was a chillborn shiver that ran the tremor through her voice—but there was still all the dignity of the Imperial line in the way she faced Voord now.

'Want? You, of course, and alive—for the present. And they'll let me take you with me, because then they'll think you have a chance. And because they know what I'll do right now if anybody tries to play the hero!'

'Then do it right now,' Marevna snapped, 'and at least spare me the delights of your company!'

Voord almost did; his lean face twisted with rage and had he been just a little closer he would have taken pleasure from knocking her to the ground. But discretion returned to him just in time, and with it the realisation that any change of position whatsoever might leave him open to a devastating reprisal. 'No, lady,' he said, and now it was undiluted fury rather than cold which was making him shiver, 'not until you ask again. Beg. Without that pride of yours. You'll lose that first, I promise—because I'm due a reward for all my trouble. And then I'll make a gift of you to—' He stopped short, leaving the uncompleted sentence hanging in the cold air, but his smile remained and that was quite enough.

Kyrin, Dewan and Gemmel had all seen Kathur the Vixen and all knew exactly what he meant. So did Aldric—not because of what he had seen, but because of what he had been told by Voord himself. Those threats. That 'persuasion'. He could guess well enough what the future might hold for Princess Marevna, and as slowly as the pouring of chilled honey his hand began an imperceptible climb up and across to where his own *telek* was pushed through his belt.

'If I think rightly, *hlensyarl*,' Voord continued, staring malevolently at Aldric now, 'if I remember things that I've been told, you've been a thorn in my flesh for a long time. If I'm due a reward, then so are you. Something suitable.' His *telek* steadied as he braced it over the crook of his left arm and squinted down the weapon's polished, moisture-spotted cylinder. 'Enjoy it!'

He squeezed the trigger.

In that instant which joined word to action, Dewan ar Korentin spasmed sideways from where he stood between Aldric and Kyrin. It wasn't a leap—nothing so dignified—but a convulsion of muscles, moving his fur-bulky body from where it had been—

—To where Kyrin was. Because he knew the way a mind like Voord's would work. And he was right.

Aldric saw it all: saw, and could do nothing. He saw Voord's finger flex and the *telek* jolt as a dart sped from it; saw the missile's metal glint as it flew; and saw Dewan wrenched out of line in midair the way a running rabbit jerks and tumbles when the arrow hits it square, saw him flop against Kyrin and bring her down into the snow. And saw the brilliant spattering of blood that stained it.

'*No . . . !*'

His hand blurred the last few inches to the waiting maple-wood stock and tugged his own *telek* free, jabbing the safety-slide with one thumb while the weapon was still rising, and snap-shot in the flicker that it came on line. The dart, his dart, hit Voord underneath the chin and hammered deep into the soft pale flesh.

And then fell free again, unstained. The Vlechan's outline blurred, altered, contracted in a shape-shift far, far faster than Aldric had expected would be possible—and fast or slow, none of the others had expected it at all.

Between one eye-blink and the next, man became Beast. A huge wolf stood in Voord's place now, its pelt pure white save for the black saddle-mark across its shoulders—as if it wore a jacket. A wolf which, as it turned to flee, ran slightly lame on a twisted, crippled left front paw.

Ravening energies splashed across the ground where it had been as Aldric and Gemmel both unleashed the power contained in Dragonwand and spellstone—but the wolf was already gone. Behind them, Ymareth went for the sky in a single bound and a thunderous clap of wings, passing low above their heads with a huge hot rush from a fanged mouth already agape and flaring. Fire scoured the ground—and snow became superheated steam, the grass and shrubs it shrouded turned to ash and the very topsoil baked to sterile dust from the Red Tower's base to its perimeter wall. But in all that open space, there was no wolf either alive or dead.

'Don't die, Dewan. Oh please, don't die!' On her knees in the snow, Kyrin held one slack-fingered hand in both of hers as if the grip might somehow help; but she had already seen the look in Gemmel's eyes as the old man straightened and she knew her words were worthless. Just air.

Marevna and Chirel stood off to one side, knowing that this was none of their affair right now. Their arms were about one another, for comfort more than warmth, and Chirel did not stir even when Ymareth landed and stalked forward with that grave, pacing grace to spread the vast canopy of its wings above them all.

Dewan's eyes opened and gazed at the three around him. He looked at Gemmel, found a sort of smile somewhere and offered it wanly to the sorcerer. 'I thought my heart might let me down,' he said quite clearly. 'So did you. But not like this.' His eyes closed again briefly, a little fluttering movement like a drawing-down of blinds, and could not open quite so wide next time. 'You didn't tell them how I died, that time on the beach. He brought me back, then. Now?'

Gemmel said nothing. Could say nothing. He only shook his head.

'Oh . . .' Again that smile, but fraying fast. 'Just as well. Man in—in my position could get careless without the fear of . . . It. But . . . hurts, old wizard, old friend. *Hurts!*' This time his eyes were squeezed shut and the lips half-hidden by his snow-caked moustache compressed to a thin line. 'I-I wish it wouldn't do that,' he said again, shakily. 'Kyrin, lady?' He forced the hand she cradled to close a little, enough to squeeze her own fingers with a gentle, reassuring pressure. 'Just for me: tell L-Lyseun I did love her. Really. But tell her, b-because I never did. I'm cold. I hurt. I . . .

'Aldric? Aldric, where are you? I can't see you any more. . . !'

'I'm here, Dewan. I'm listening.' Aldric's calm voice belied the tears on his scarred face; cold tears, flayed by the icy winter wind.

'Nothing of the Empire for me, Aldric. Not now.'

'I understand. I know.'

'Let me be Alban at the last. Not in the earth. No. Give me to the flames. Fire is clean . . . and I'm so cold. So . . . very . . . cold—'

'*An-diu k'noeth-ei, Dewan-mr'ain.*' Aldric said the words and made the sign quickly, perhaps more quickly than was proper, and then shook his head violently to clear his face of tears and his mind of a thought, a possibility that was beyond bearing. That the words of a curse might just have been fulfilled.

He neither asked for, expected nor would have wanted any help as he gathered Dewan in his arms, a big body like a bear in all its furs and leather. But a bear whose hunting days were done. Staggering a little under the limp deadweight until he found his balance, Aldric walked slowly and carefully into the Red Tower. When he emerged a few minutes later, his hands were empty and hanging by his sides but he was still weighed down with grief. 'He was my friend,' he said. 'Whatever he did, he was my friend. And now there isn't enough wood.' Aldric turned and stared up and up at the slick red stones which were the colour of the blood on his gloved hands. 'I wish that I could burn it all.'

The voice inside his head was very quiet. 'All things burn,' said Ymareth. 'Just let the fire be hot enough.'

Aldric half-turned; looked at Gemmel, who nodded, then at the dragon. 'True?' he said. Ymareth's majestic head dipped once, in what could only be another nod.

'True. Only give the word.'

'He was my friend,' Aldric said again. 'He deserves a worthy monument: one that Egisburg and the Empire will remember.' He did as he had done once before, and looked straight into the dragon's glowing eyes. 'The word is given. Let us get clear—then torch it.'

There was no one on the streets of the city as they rode out, and none of those who watched from behind closed shutters made the slightest move to obstruct their passage. It was just as well. Neither Aldric nor Kyrin nor Gemmel were in any mood for mannerly dispute. Two drawn swords were enough to discourage all but the city militia; but the crackling nimbus of force which hung about the riders and trailed tendrils of energy in their wake would have given pause even to the Bodyguard Cavalry at Drakkesborg. *Dewan's old regiment* thought Aldric on the heels of his first notion. He nudged Lyard to a canter and led their way to the gates.

Egisburg seemed content to watch them leave its precincts; but even after they had gone, the city held its breath. Waiting.

'I don't care about the snow,' said Aldric as he dismounted, 'we're all lying flat. You too.' Most of this was to the Imperial women, and particularly Chirel who did not care for his high-handed treatment of the Emperor's sister. 'And make your horses lie down as well—like *this!*' He twisted Lyard's bridle in the proper fashion until the big Andarran stallion sank down and rolled onto his side, very black against the snow. 'Do it; I'll help.'

Gemmel was looking at him strangely. 'You seem to know exactly what you're doing,' he said.

Aldric glanced towards him, smiled thinly and shrugged. 'If that was the case, Dewan would still be alive,' he said bitterly. 'I know how to be careful; that's all.' Then he lay full-length in the snow, his upper body across Lyard's neck and one hand over the animal's exposed eye. His other hand reached out, met Kyrin's and gripped it tight.

'Aldric, do you really think that even Ymareth—' She saw Aldric's face in the dimness and stopped, for though his eyes were still huge and shining with the last remnant of weeping for a dead friend, they also shone with anticipation of what another—yes, another friend—might do as a memorial.

'I don't think,' he said softly. 'I believe.'

Silence. Snow drifting down from the iron-grey clouds. Cold and darkness.

And then—

Light! It scored the sky, a column of fire so hot that its core was tinged with violet, so brilliant that the shadows which it threw were edged like knives, and through the black and purple-glowing flecks crowding his vision Aldric saw the Red Tower. It was more than a mile distant, a tiny pin-sharp image that was as red as blood, as red as murder. And it was shimmering. The crimson that was its true colour began to change, shading up through scarlet and incandescent orange to a flaring citrine yellow—and at the last it reached a silvery pink-white which forced him to flinch away.

The air temperature began to climb, slowly at first; then it

abandoned so gradual an increase and soared. Falling snow
became rain, warm drizzle, and after that stopped altogether
as the clouds which carried it were ripped to tatters, seared
out of existence by the blast of heat rising from the heart of
Egisburg. In the sky above the city, stars appeared again.

And in front of Aldric's eyes two feet and more of snow
began to melt, rivulets of water pouring out of it with the
chuckling sound of a brimming stream in springtime. He
raised his head a fraction, and through a dancing haze could
see the Tower—a structure that he knew was two hundred
feet of stone and iron and massive timbers—slowly squirming
from base to ramparts like a tallow candle in a furnace. Even
that brief glimpse felt like staring at the noon sun on mid-
summer's day, and it was blazing brighter yet.

The earth bucked beneath his prone body in a sudden
convulsion beside which Lyard's terrified thrashing was like a
lover's caress, and Chirel began to scream—but it was a
scream that nobody heard completed. Just as she reached her
highest pitch a noise from the direction of Egisburg rolled
over them, breaking like a great dark wave of thunder peaked
and crested with chain lightning. The very air howled in their
ears with the appalling reverberance of that long rumble of
destruction, and in its tingling aftermath they heard, high
overhead, Ymareth the dragon's awesome roar of triumph as
its dark wings scythed across the starlit sky.

'Oh sweet and loving—!' whimpered someone's voice.
'Look there . . . Dear God, *look!*'

They looked. A dome-topped unstable pillar of smoke and
dust lifted into the sky above Egisburg, criss-crossed with
filaments where yet-burning debris was still falling from the
main mass of the cloud. It looked monstrous; evil and obscene, like some gigantic fungus rearing up to spread its
rotting cap over the ruins of the Red Tower.

Except that the Red Tower was gone . . .

Gemmel stared at the cloud, at its shape, and then turned to
Aldric with all the depths of infinity in his green eyes. He
said nothing, but the Alban thought his face was that of a
man confronted by the reality of an ancient, long-forgotten
nightmare.

'You believed,' said Kyrin, still holding Aldric's hand.

He nodded. 'But I'm still learning. There are things I'm
coming to believe in that you and I have never heard of. And

I sometimes wonder if I really want to hear of them at all.'
He shivered a little, then turned to help as the horses scrambled upright, snorting and stamping. 'Princess, I'm taking you to Durforen, it seems. That was the arrangement with . . . with your brother. We're expected at the monastery.'

Marevna an-Sherban gazed levelly up at him with those enormous eyes whose expression he could never read. Framed in the dense dark fur of her hooded cloak, she looked like a little mouse and not like a princess at all. But there was that stillness about her again, that calm which had all the weight of Empire behind it. 'Then best go there at once, my lord Talvalin,' she said in clipped, accented Alban. 'For though your company is stimulating, neither I nor the Empire can take much more of it. We have only a limited number of cities, after all.'

TEN

Coda

They reached Durforen at noon on the fourth day out from Egisburg. *Hethra-hamath, de Marhar.* The eighth day of the tenth month. The eighth day of winter and the Hour of the Hawk. All was silent beneath the silver sunlight, without even a trace of wind to move air that was edged like a razor. There was only that chill, glittering stillness; and, three miles up in the icy sky, what might have been a thread of smoke unravelling white against the bleached blue vault of Heaven.

Black on black against the snow, Aldric reined Lyard to a standstill and pushed the hood of a black military rank-robe. Black on black on black, for beneath the robe he was once more wearing his own sable battle armour and the horse he rode had a coat like polished jet. Three days from Egisburg, and half-way through a fourth. Light of Heaven, it seemed so short a time since . . . everything. And yet perhaps it was only right and proper that such a journey should be short, so that he could more swiftly give Princess Marevna into the safe-keeping of whoever, in dead Bruda's words, might be expecting her. And thus more swiftly call a finish to this quest, this exercise in duty to Rynert the King.

It was the discharge of an obligation which had befouled his honour, for all that there were those and one in most particular—he glanced upward with the thought—who still said otherwise; and none could question that it had claimed the life of a man he had called *friend*. Before God, there were few enough with that title; so small a group that he could ill afford to lose a single one. Aldric could still see, and would always see, the light going out in Dewan's eyes.

He swallowed down a throat suddenly narrower than it had been—that memory was still too recent and too painful—and swept a long stare across the flawless field of white which sparkled back at him as though dusted with crushed diamonds; then his gaze went out and away and up and beyond. And he shivered slightly.

Aldric would as soon have left the Drusalan Empire far behind him; as the old tale said, shaken its dust from off his feet. But he had not, and he would not. Not yet. There were matters—matters of consequence but no affair of Alba's king—which required his attention. Personal attention.

As personal as anything confided by a father to a son.

For in the evenings past, after they had found lodgings at farms and steadings so isolated that gossip regarding their presence would travel slowly if at all in this foul weather, Gemmel had spoken to him. Confided in him. Told him such truths that, though often half-way guessed at already, hearing them confirmed and detailed had shaken him to the soul. There had been times when only the gentle anchorage of Tehal Kyrin—Aldric had refused to send her out of earshot—had kept his mind secured to sense and sanity. And there had been times when her nails had sunk deep into his arm while she too tried to come to terms with what was said.

Those words had changed the way that Aldric looked at his world. *His* world, no longer *the* world; for there were other worlds that were not his. Gemmel had said so. One of those was Gemmel's own. They were words which had fathered, mothered, brought to term and borne those thoughts of enormity, of time and distance beyond understanding, which now made him shiver as he stared at the vastness of the sky. Yet it was not a shiver of fear, not quite. There was awareness in it too; the awareness that comes to eyes newly opened, appreciating for the first time the infinity of light and shape and colour which had always lain beyond the limits of their closed darkness. Eyes that now saw a world far smaller than it had been, but a Heaven far, far larger than a man could ever hope to simply dream of . . .

Below the ridge where he sat, thinking vast thoughts and waiting for the others, was Durforen monastery. It was no longer a religious house, but unquestionably a ruin. Not even an especially picturesque one, although the contour-softening coat of snow on its old grey stones had given it a certain charm. But that charm was offset by its present occupants and

incarnation, for the monastery was vivid with the scarlet
banners and red armour of the host of soldiers encamped
there.

Imperial Household troops, thought Aldric. Even at this
distance of half a mile, and squinting through a glare of sun
on snow that made his eyes smart and his head ache, he could
see—if not read—the gold writing on the banners. Those
were never seen outside Kalitzim except in one very special
circumstance: when the Emperor himself was in attendance.

'Quite a reception, eh?' Aldric said aloud to Lyard and
whistled piercingly between his teeth. The horse flicked both
ears disapprovingly; he didn't care for such whistles overmuch, for they were too shrill by half and more suited to the
summoning of dogs. The Emperor's dogs, this time.

Aldric could see a sudden flurry of agitation in the monastery camp and knew that either his whistle had been heard—
not so unlikely in this still air as might appear—or his silhouette
had been spotted on the skyline. As other figures joined his
own—Kyrin, then Marevna and Chirel close together, and
Gemmel as a self-appointed rearguard—the agitation increased
and within a few seconds coalesced into a light cavalry patrol
heading for them at the gallop amid a haze of churned fine
snow.

As the riders boiled over the crest of the ridge in open
skirmish order, their line swung through a crescent to a
closed circle with the intruders trapped at its centre. And then
everything stopped, for the 'prisoners' hadn't moved at all
but merely sat on their own horses and watched the cavalry
manoeuvre with . . . interest and enjoyment? Nor was their
reaction the only thing wrong. What the patrol had found was
not what the patrol had expected: certainly not two girls, a
woman, an old man—and a young man who wore the insignia and the arrogance if not the armour of a cavalry *hanalth*.
The soldiers looked nervously from one to another, then at
their own officer in hope of guidance; none of them troubled
to hide their own confusion.

It was Gemmel who broke the muttering, indecisive stale-
mate. Perhaps the old sorcerer was lacking patience, or maybe
he was just feeling the cold. Nudging his horse forward a step
or two, he snapped a very creditable salute towards the patrol
kortagor—creditable enough for the man to return it—and

for some reason he was smiling at some private joke in his own words, even before he spoke. 'Take me,' said Gemmel, 'to your leader.'

Goth was here. Of course Goth was here. Aldric might have—and at the back of his mind probably had—expected it; certainly he betrayed not even a flicker of adverse emotion at first sight of the jutting, pugnacious spade beard. Instead he offered beard and general alike a lazy, deep, utterly false bow of respect. And even now, an hour and much talking later, he hadn't yet decided whether or not Goth was glad to see him alive. Or even if he had been troubled by Bruda's murder. It was, as always, impossible to tell what might please or annoy such a man.

Ioen the Emperor, younger, with a freckled milk-pale skin and flaming red hair, was somewhat easier to read. The very presence of this armoured storm-column so relatively close to the borders of *Woydach* Etzel's territory was an indication of how he felt about—what? That was the real question. His sister—or the policies which her capture had affected? But either was sufficient reason to make him pleased to see her free and unhurt; and enough to make him wax generous.

'My lords, my lady,' he said in stilted Alban—a compliment which, following Aldric's lead, both Gemmel and Kyrin acknowledged with courteous nods—'for this gift of my dear sister, her liberty, gift I in turn gold, land, riches.'

Maybe it wasn't just because of those policies after all, Aldric thought; then he saw Goth lean over in his saddle and whisper something which, although he couldn't hear it, was probably an exhortation to restraint. He grinned slightly and made quite sure that Goth saw him do it. 'I'm not a poor man, General. Nor particularly greedy. So there's no need to fear for the Exchequer. Not this time.'

Goth straightened with a jerk, clearing his throat and pretending that he hadn't said a word. He even had the decency to colour slightly—if it was a blush born of decency and not the flush of rage.

'But there are two matters I'd like settled, Majesty,' Aldric continued. 'One concerns the Jevaiden holding of Seghar.'

That name provoked a deal of muttering between Ioen and Goth, so much so that Aldric wondered what he might have started. He was privately relieved to see the beginnings of a

smile on the Emperor's freckled face. An absolute monarch
with freckles and a schoolboy's face, he thought irrelevantly.
Lord God!

'Your concern is for Gueynor-Overlord, rather than the
holding itself, yes?' There was an archness in the light,
youthful voice that had no place there and could easily become an irritation, but in the circumstances Aldric thought
best to let it go.

'Uh. Yes. Put like that, Majesty, yes.'

'Concerned with regard to her safety, yes?'

Feeling certain that this was a speech prepared in advance
and learned by rote, Aldric nodded silently. He had left
Gueynor abruptly, with only a middle-aged demon-queller as
protector—he, and the keys to hidden money-chests which
gave her power over the long-unpaid garrison. But second
thoughts had been suggesting that it might not have been
enough. He had to know.

'Then have no fear; she was confirmed as Overlord, with
all due rights of rank and privilege within the Empire, two
months ago. It pleases me that your wish has been so quickly
answered, yes?'

'Yes.' Aldric bit the word off short; it pleased Goth as
well, apparently, for the width of his grin was such as to put
the general's ears in jeopardy. So quickly answered, thought
Aldric maliciously—and so cheaply. He coughed in a significant fashion and saw the grin snuffed out. 'You forget,
General,' he reminded delicately, 'I said *two* matters. The
second involves passes for three to any part of the Empire.
Any—regardless of current political allegiance. I'm sure that
you can think of some clause to ensure that, dear Goth. Yes?'

'No!' Goth was shocked beyond measure. 'Never! Of course
not . . . !'

Aldric wasn't amused to see how, after his first vehement
refusal, the general had to pause and think of reasons *why*
not. To cover the workings of that tricky brain, Goth began to
bluster about foreigners and lack of rights, and—more dangerously than he knew—duty and obligation. Aldric didn't
trouble to hide his grimace of distaste.

But then his attention shifted beyond both General and
Emperor, to where Princess Marevna sat side-saddle on a
palfrey—red-roan like all the Imperial mounts—and watched

and listened. Her simple white clothing had been changed in this past hour to the rich crimson and burnished gold more fitting to an Emperor's sister, but save for that quarter-hour she had heard the whole exchange between the scarlet and the black. Always herself quite silent, not even coughing in the icy air; saying and doing nothing.

Until now.

Now she leaned down to where Chirel stood by her horse's head, tapped the woman on the arm with a slim, scarlet-lacquered scroll cylinder plucked from the long cuff of one glove, and directed that it be taken straight to Aldric.

Aldric himself had seen their little by-play—he was ostentatiously ignoring Goth—and there was already a laugh simmering within his rib-cage as Chirel reached up past his stirruped leg to hand the scrollcase over.

'That should prove sufficient.' Marevna's voice, not particularly loud, still cut across all the others sounds—of Goth, of the horses, of the military camp two hundred yards away. But the General and the Emperor jerked round in their saddles, not expecting to hear this little quiet mouse of a sister speak at all. Then they exchanged glances and turned slowly back to Aldric . . .

Who sat, cylinder in one hand, tapping it indolently on the gloved palm of the other as he met Goth's stare with a bland, cool smile. Then, holding the General's eyes with his own, he held out the little container to Gemmel.

'I only speak it, *altrou-ain*. Could you do the honours here?'

Gemmel did so, scanning the high-quality parchment with its neatly brushed characters and the red-and-black cluster of seal impressions both at top and bottom. He didn't read the message aloud, but his indrawn whistle of amazement—an unfamiliar reaction from him, and one which made Aldric look round with raised eyebrows—said more than enough. The sorcerer looked at his fosterling, and at that fosterling's lady, and tapped the scroll with one long finger. 'Citizenship,' he said, 'while we're within the Empire's borders. Scholarly passes. Confirming that we are without any political bias. Commanding aid and protection. Senatorial seals: High, Low and Priestly.' He let the scroll snap shut and returned it almost reverently to its case. 'Go anywhere, do anything, where the law permits. Lady . . .' he bowed very low towards Marevna, 'you have my thanks.'

'What point,' said the Princess, 'in having high-placed friends, if they aren't sometimes of use?'

'You listened,' Aldric said, faintly accusing. But pleased for all that.

'One learns that way.'

'Uh . . . true. My lady, Majesty, oh yes, and Goth. Thanks to you all. For a great many things. Education, mostly. And now we really must be going.'

They went.

Aldric stood up in his stirrups again, scanning a non-existent horizon for non-existent signs of life, then settled back into Lyard's saddle and exhaled a smoky sigh of relief. It was now four in the afternoon—the Hour of the Serpent—and they had ridden constantly since half-past one, pushing their horses as much as they dared. Seven horses now; the three additional pack-ponies loaded with provisions were a token of Imperial generosity and also, Aldric had suspected at first, a means to slow them up. He distrusted Lord General Goth, who was the sort of man to overhaul them and take away their Imperial travel passes, not for any really malevolent reason but simply in order to regain face by having the power to withhold or return them.

But perhaps he was wronging the General by such a thought, because there had been no sign of pursuit all afternoon—and now at last the day was darkening into twilight once more. Or maybe, Aldric thought with a quick grin, someone else had suspected how Goth's mind might work and had forbidden any move which might resemble an attempt to follow them.

No matter now. All that truly mattered was that there had been nothing to see and nothing to fear. Only Kyrin and Gemmel, a little way away, sitting with the horses in a thin fog of exhaled breath which clung about them all like the skeins of spider-silk that night glimmer on a meadow in the first light of dawn. Only Ymareth, high above where the first cold jewelled stars began to show.

Only snow, and more snow, its once-blinding whiteness shading down now to a silver and smoke-blue in the shadowed dusk as it flowed out like a waveless sea towards the cloudless evening sky. Aldric touched heels to Lyard's flanks and rode forward, eastward, to be with his companions; the lady lost and regained, and the father more than any parent. At his back, the pale blue of Heaven was washed with rose and saffron as the sun set into a distant fringe of haze which was all that showed where a horizon might have been. Ahead was that same haze, velvety, darkening to a star-fired night where the world reached up to touch, to meld with, to become the very sky itself.

A sky that went on for ever.

DAW

A Writer of Epic Fantasy in the Grand Tradition

Peter Morwood

THE BOOK OF YEARS

☐ **THE HORSE LORD: Book 1**   (UE2178—$3.50)

Centuries ago, the Horse Lords had ridden into Alba to defeat an evil sorcerer and banish magic from the land. Now an ambitious lord has meddled with dark forces, and the ancient evil is unleashed again. Rescued by an aging wizard, young Aldric seeks revenge on the sorcerous foe who has slain his clan and stolen his birthright.

☐ **THE DEMON LORD: Book 2**   (UE2204—$3.50)

Aldric must undertake a secret mission that will lead him to the troubled border provinces. There he finds unexpected allies: a mysterious, not-quite-trustworthy Demon Queller, and the beautiful young heir to a demon-possessed citadel. Together, they journey to the fortress of Seghar to challenge the demon spirit that holds it in its wrathful grasp.

☐ **THE DRAGON LORD: Book 3**   (UE2252—$3.50)

As a warrior's honor leads Aldric into the heart of the Drusalan Empire on the king's orders, unbeknownst to him, the king has betrayed him into enemy hands. Slowly the trap closes about him, while powerful allies are riding to his aid: the wizard Gemmel and the mighty warrior Dewan. But can even they help Aldric against dark and deadly sorcery and a monstrous dragon?

NEW AMERICAN LIBRARY
P.O. Box 999, Bergenfield, New Jersey 07621

Please send me the books I have checked above. I am enclosing $_____
(please add $1.00 to this order to cover postage and handling). Send check or money order—no cash or C.O.D.'s. Prices and numbers are subject to change without notice.

Name_____

Address_____

City _____ State _____ Zip Code _____
Allow 4-6 weeks for delivery.